The Greatest Heroes
of the Realms!

After battling orcs and ogres to save the people of Pengallen, Drizzt Do'Urden finds himself wondering who the real monsters are. . . .

The halfling lord of Lowhill braves the Palace of Skulls in search of a gift for Tristan and Robyn, rulers of the magical Moonshaes. . . .

Elminster bests all challengers at the magefair, only to come face to face with an enemy he thought slain long ago. . . .

As patriarch of the Church of Mysteries, Adon fights to lift a curse from the village of Tegea, but an old wound comes back to haunt him in ways he never suspected. . . .

In the days before he became king of Cormyr, Prince Azoun finds himself facing a trio of weird assassins, with only a young boy named Artus Cimber to help him fight.

Arilyn Moonblade and Danilo Thann, Koja of Khazari, Jander Sunstar—these and many more of the heroes from the best-selling FORGOTTEN REALMS® novels come together for the first time in this collection of eleven magic⸱ ⸱⸱⸱⸱

FANTASY ADVENTURE

FANTASY ADVENTURE

Realms of Valor

Edited by James Lowder

Interior Art by Ned Dameron

REALMS OF VALOR

Copyright ©1993 TSR, Inc.
All Rights Reserved.

First Printing: February 1993
Printed in the United States of America.
Library of Congress Catalog Card Number: 92-61077

9 8 7 6 5 4 3 2 1

ISBN: 1-56076-557-7

TSR, Inc.
P.O. Box 756
Lake Geneva, WI 53147
United States of America

TSR Ltd.
120 Church End, Cherry Hinton
Cambridge CB1 3LB
United Kingdom

To the loyal readers of Realms novels. You've made this anthology possible and worthwhile

Acknowledgments

Thanks to all the authors for finding time to contribute to the collection; to Clyde Caldwell and Ned Dameron for the excellent cover and interior illustrations; to former book department guru Mary Kirchoff for helping to shepherd the anthology onto the schedule, and to current head honcho Brian Thomsen for seeing it through to the somewhat grisly end. Thanks especially to Rob King for his deft editorial work on "The Family Business" and for smiling patiently through a coordination nightmare.

CONTENTS

THE LORD OF LOWHILL

Douglas Niles

Pawldo emerged from his burrow to bask in the air of a rare summer morn: not too hot, neither windy nor cloudy, with just a kiss of warm breeze to carry the scent of ripening grapes and lush, well-watered pastures. A mile away, the waters of Corwell Firth gleamed in the sunlight, the barely rippled surface casting a million diamond-spots of reflection between encircling arms of verdant land.

The stout halfling stood before his sturdy, whitewashed wooden dwelling. In typical halfling fashion, it was buried halfway into a grassy hillside, but the burrow was unquestionably the largest house in Lowhill. The air of affluence extended to the occupant of the burrow as well.

Pawldo's long hair, slightly gray, curled below his ears and just touched the edge of his elegant silken collar. Even this early in the day he wore well-tailored, expensive clothing. Any observer would know immediately that he was a halfling who knew the finer things in life.

Below and beyond a stretch of lush pastureland, nestled against its sheltered harbor, Corwell Town awakened to the businesslike bustle of the Ffolk going about their human activities. The curraghs of fishers already bobbed beyond the breakwater, while the clanging of hammer and tongs told of an early-rising blacksmith tending his forge. Carts of fresh produce and milk, some drawn by small ponies and others by long-legged, shaggy hounds, rumbled into Corwell through its open gates.

High on the knoll overlooking the town, Pawldo saw the squat form of Caer Corwell, the wooden-walled fort that served as home to Earl Randolph and, for those weeks when Tristan and Robyn visited, as the summer quarters of the high king and queen themselves. He thought of his good friends with a flash of pleasant anticipation, remembering that in a little less than a fortnight the royal family would return to Corwell for their summer holiday.

Finally the stocky halfling's eyes drifted closer to home, to the cozy warren of cottages and burrows built around this small, rounded hill. Barely a mile removed from Corwell Town, Lowhill provided a pastoral setting for the little halfling community of which Pawldo served as honorary lord mayor.

Nearby bloomed the lush vineyards, and to these fertile hedges Pawldo now sauntered, inspecting with pleasure the clumps of unripened grapes growing plump and sweet in the sun. To his bare feet, covered on the tops with a coat of silky hair, the grass felt softly cool and inviting. Pleasantly reminded of the many good wines he'd sampled from these very vines, he settled himself to a comfortable seat on a patch of shady grass.

I'll have to cart a load of last year's vintage over to Kingsbay, Pawldo reflected. The prospect of that trip interested him, in a lackadaisical sort of way. He wouldn't go today or tomorrow, and probably not the day after that either, but it was something to think about. In fact, he remembered a cute little barmaid there, a cherubic-faced halfling wench with whom he could certainly strike a profitable deal.

Indeed, if she remained as friendly as he remembered, he would be strongly tempted to wile away a few days in that pleasant fishing town.

Not too long, he reminded himself, since the king and queen will arrive in Corwell for the Midsummer holiday, and I'll have to be home by then. After all, this was not just any summer holiday—this marked the tenth year of Tristan's reign and the tenth year of his marriage to Robyn. All in all, the occasion called for some kind of appropriate acknowledgment.

At this thought, the halfling's round-cheeked face darkened in a momentary scowl. He wanted to give them a wondrous gift, something appropriate to the grand occasion. Yet, whatever his gift to the royal couple would be, Pawldo doubted that he could find something sufficiently unique or fabulous in either Corwell or Kingsbay. What to do? This question had nagged at him, off and on, for the last several weeks, yet the stout halfling had not let his lack of solutions cause him undue distress. Sooner or later something would come up.

Of course, he could have sailed for the Sword Coast when he first faced the problem. He would be on his way back by now with some fabulous and rare token of his friendship and respect. Yet such decisive action was not the halfling way, and now, of course, he didn't have enough time to make the trip and still return for the festival. Mildly irritated—with the calendar, not himself—Pawldo shook away the concern and continued his inspection of his eyelids.

"Lord Mayor! Mayor Pawldo!"

The high voice came to his ears from beyond the hedges—a young halfling, male by the sound of it.

"Over here!" Pawldo replied, sitting up with a grunt of annoyance. He climbed to his feet slowly, aware that he no longer moved as nimbly as he had a decade or so before. Peering over the nearby hedge, he looked to see who had disturbed his meditations.

A red-haired halfling skidded to a stop before Pawldo and hastily doffed his cap. Cheeks glowing from exertion, shoulders bouncing as he struggled to regain his breath, the stranger could only pant for a moment as the lord mayor looked him over. The young halfling was a Hairfoot, not quite an adult, dressed in plain country garb and carrying a satchel over his shoulder. The newcomer smiled in a hopeful sort of way, wiping the sweat from his brow with his free hand. True to the Hairfoot tradition, he wore no shoes.

"What is it?" Pawldo inquired, suspecting that his quiet morning would remain so no longer. In spite of himself Pawldo felt a measure of curiosity.

"Cafwort the barrelmaker . . . told me that . . . I'd find you here," said the younger halfling, still panting.

"As you did. And who might you be?"

"Oh. I'm terribly sorry!" The youth looked chagrined. "I'm Stefanik of Llyrath Downs," he explained hastily. Pawldo knew that community of Hairfeet, which was located several days travel to the east, in the fringes of Llyrath Forest. "And, well, I found this—and I didn't know where else to take it. I mean, every halfling on Gwynneth knows about you and your adventures! Why, if it wasn't for you, the Darkwalker would have—"

"Enough!" cried Pawldo, raising both his hands in mock surrender. "Tales have a way of being exaggerated—though I *did* play a small role in the defeat of that menace. In fact, there's a certain element of truth . . ." He shook his head, forcing away the pleasant wave of nostalgia. "But enough of that. You have something to show me, it would seem?"

"Oh, yes." The halfling thrust the satchel, still unopened, toward Pawldo. "Here! What is it? Where did it come from? How did it get to be in the forest?"

"Right now you've got about ten questions for each of my answers," the mayor chuckled, taking the leather sack. It proved to be surprisingly heavy, containing a large object made of metal—and a lot of it. "Let's see what you've got."

Pawldo casually stretched the mouth of the satchel wide, but when he looked inside, he could not suppress a gasp of astonishment. Shiny metal gleamed even in the shadowy confines of the leather pouch, too pure for silver—it must be platinum! He reached for the item's blunt, rounded end, allowing the satchel to fall to the ground and reveal a long-bladed dagger.

The lord mayor held the weapon by the hilt, thinking that it was much too heavy to be an effective weapon, yet that hardly mattered. Sunlight reflected in dazzling patterns from the gleaming surface, twinkling in brilliant colors where it struck the facets of a multitude of gems. A straight blade, sharpened on both sides, extended nearly a foot from the impractical, jewel-encrusted hilt.

"I know you've traded all sorts of things—rare weapons and treasures!" Stefanik continued breathlessly. "You've been to Waterdeep, and Baldur's Gate, and *lots* of places. I bet more than any other halfling in the Moonshaes! Why, even in Llyrath Downs we've heard how you rescued the king from the firbolg giant-kin! When I tried to think of who could answer my questions, well, there was just no one else who even came close!"

"Aye," whispered Pawldo, too overcome by the object's splendor to even acknowledge the praise.

"It's some kind of knife," Stefanik noted unnecessarily. "But how did it get there? Whose is it?"

"Some kind of thief's dagger," Pawldo observed with a silent whistle. "It's a blade of little utility, but truly exceptional worth. Quickly, lad, where did you find this?"

"In the forest! Llyrath Forest!" stammered Stefanik. "I was hunting well into the woods. I found the dagger at a place I camped, where two streams flow together. It was lying there beside the stream, just like this, so shiny I couldn't possibly have missed it!" He noticed Pawldo's scowl of concentration. "Did I do something wrong?"

"No, not that I can see." Pawldo couldn't take his eyes from the silvery surface. He identified the gems—here was a plump ruby on each handguard, there an array of emeralds around the base of the hilt, in the middle of the handgrip a huge diamond! With difficulty, he kept his hands from trembling. Never had he held an object of such worth, such splendor! "So it looked like it hadn't been there long?" he asked, trying to keep his voice level.

"No. But that's the funny thing, since no one had been there before me—at least, not for a long time. I'm a pretty fair tracker," Stefanik added with bucolic honesty. "I'd have known."

The lord mayor turned the dagger over in his hands, examining the blade. Platinum there, too, polished and honed to the sharpness of a razor. Then a small imperfection caught his eye, near where the blade met the hilt. Raising the knife so that full sunlight fell on the blemish, he looked closely—and felt a sudden chill of apprehension.

The image was no flaw in the polished surface. It was a tiny etching of a leering, fleshless skull.

"What is it?" asked the youngster, following Pawldo's gaze. He gulped audibly when he got a close look. "I never noticed that before! What does it mean—a skull?"

"You say you found this in the depths of Llyrath Forest?" Pawldo inquired meaningfully.

"Yes! But I don't—"

Stefanik stopped abruptly, his face blanching, his eyes growing to saucers in sudden suspicion. "The Palace of Skulls?" he whispered.

"It's one explanation . . . the *only* one," Pawldo concluded grimly. "It's supposed to appear in Llyrath Forest only once a generation . . . and then, only for the waxing of the summer solstice moon!"

"The new moon was but four days past," Stefanik said, his tone full of wonder.

"And the knife—when did you find it?" Pawldo pressed.

"Three days ago!" the younger halfling exclaimed with a shudder. Then he squinted, a surprisingly mature skepticism appearing in his expression. "But I thought the tales of the skull fortress were just legends! Sure, my grandmother used to frighten us with stories of evil Prince Ketheryll and his curse—but now that I'm a grown-up I can't take them *seriously!*"

"Can't you?" inquired the mayor of Lowhill archly. "Don't

you think there might be some basis to the tales?"

Again Stefanik suppressed a shudder. "I know the stories—that Ketheryll still dwells there, but he's no longer a man. Just some kind of shadow that can suck the soul and the life right out of you!"

"What about the *other* stories?" Pawldo grew increasingly excited as he considered the possibilities. "Tales of treasure beyond your wildest dreams, mountains of wealth, glories such as you've never seen, all there for the taking—but only until the rising of the full moon. . . ."

"You mean treasures like this?" Stefanik asked, his eyes dropping to the dagger. "You think the dagger comes from the Palace of Skulls?"

"Ouch!" Pawldo declared, abruptly dropping the weapon and blowing on his palm. "It got *hot!*"

"Look!" hissed Stefanik, pointing to the dagger as it twisted on the ground.

The blade had fallen on its tip, and for a second it wavered back and forth, as if it might stick into the ground. Then it bounced into the air, flopped onto its side, and flipped around so that the blade pointed just a little south of due east. The platinum surface glowed with a brightness greater than the sun's reflection.

"It's . . . it's like it *heard* me," Stefanik said softly. "As soon as I said the name of the place, it heated up."

"And look at the way it's pointing," Pawldo said. The glow subsided, and he reached out to touch the weapon's already cooling hilt. "Straight into Llyrath Forest."

"Can it be from that place?"

"Like I said, it's the *only* explanation!" Pawldo's mind worked furiously. The fortress meant treasure beyond belief. And that might mean a suitable present for the king and queen! "Can you find your campsite again?"

"Of course!" Stefanik proclaimed. "I'm a good scout, too! I know that woods like the inside of my own burrow!"

"Splendid! Let's see, we'll need some supplies and a couple of ponies. It'll take me a few hours to get ready. You can rest up at my house, and we can leave in the afternoon."

His estimate proved conservative. In actuality the two halflings rode down the King's Road sometime before lunch, a fact that the road-weary Stefanik regretted but was too timid to mention. They spent the night at a comfortable inn in Cantrev Koart and made such good time the next day that by early evening Stefanik led them southward from the road until they reached the very fringe of the forest. There, amid a sparse scattering of dry-needled fir trees, they found a grassy meadow for their camp.

During their journey, Pawldo found himself developing an avuncular affection for the young halfling. Stefanik's blatant hero worship did nothing to impair the relationship, and the lord mayor's restrained silence only served to inflate the youngster's somewhat exaggerated assessment of his skills and exploits.

As twilight fell on their little camp, they passed some time in more serious conversation, comparing the tales they'd heard about the Palace of Skulls. Among the Ffolk of the Moonshaes and their halfling neighbors the place was a common setting for tales of heroism, though few believed that it really existed. Pawldo found that the version of the legend told in the village of Llyrath Downs differed somewhat from the stories he'd heard elsewhere in the Moonshaes. Yet, since that little village of halflings was nearer to the ancient structure's reputed location, he placed strong credence in that folklore.

"Llyrath Downs," Pawldo remarked as he settled down near the crackling embers of their fire. "There aren't many who live there, true?"

Stefanik shrugged. "Until I saw a great city like Lowhill, I would have disagreed with you. But, truth be told, we are but a dozen families, scattered over a wide hilltop."

Pawldo suppressed a smile—the "great city" of Lowhill, indeed! "You live in the forest proper?" he asked.

"Only the fringe. No one lives in the middle of that dark wood. We won't pass through my village, though—Llyrath Downs is another day's journey east of here. It's not on the way to the place where I found the dagger."

"And the legends you've heard, they hold the Palace of Skulls to be in this part of Llyrath?"

"Yes. It's said that mad Prince Ketheryll built the great fortress in Llyrath with the heads of his enemies. That was at the time when Gwynneth and the rest of the Moonshaes were only a lot of small principalities. Ketheryll made war on all of his neighbors. They say his cruelty was surpassed only by his might." The youth shrugged. "He must have been pretty tough, since he eventually drove all the other humans from southern Gwynneth."

"All the tales claim that he was a ruthless master," Pawldo agreed. "His conquests are matters of history, though I'd always presumed his reputation for bloodshed to be exaggerated. Still, no one seems to doubt the tales of his Doomed Legion." At Stefanik's puzzled look, Pawldo added, "At least no one outside of Llyrath. The legion was made up of his lieutenants, each magically branded with the skull that was their master's symbol."

"I'd heard that each of the prince's men had sworn to give his life to protect him," Stefanik admitted, "but never anything about them being branded. It's not surprising, though, since the prince was always so interested in magic."

Pawldo laughed. "It's so ironic that the wizard Flamsterd and his spellcasting finally proved Ketheryll's undoing, since he was so taken with sorcery himself."

"Aye—the wizard and the Earthmother. The humans say the goddess exacted revenge against Ketheryll because he distressed the Balance." Stefanik nodded seriously.

"The tales I've heard all over the Moonshaes include the Earthmother," the older halfling said. "Had you heard that Ketheryll dedicated his gruesome fortress to the new moon of the summer solstice? He held a great celebration with his most loyal followers. They killed hundreds of captives in a grim arena—called the Circus Bizarre, I seem to remember—simply for the amusement of the prince and his evil band. It's said that he captured the young king and queen of a human realm and put them to death along with the rest."

"They were the first human monarchs to fly the banner of the Great Bear," Stefanik chimed in. "Imagine—they were put to death by Ketheryll, but their symbol has lived on to become the talisman of the high kings of the Ffolk. I used to believe that the king must have been taken by treachery, but now I think maybe he was captured by the Legion of the Damned."

"The Doomed Legion," Pawldo corrected.

"And it was on the moonless night of the slaughter that the curse took effect," Stefanik whispered, then glanced at the night sky.

"Yes—the spell of the wizard, coupled with the vengeful might of the Earthmother. A black fog rolled from the forest," Pawldo said, his voice a hoarse whisper, his eyes wide as he looked into the shadows around their fire. "It cloaked the gathering for a full fortnight, and for all that time Ketheryll and his legion huddled in their palace, fearing to go forth into the world. Then, on the night of the solstice, under the light of that full moon, the fog dissipated. And the Palace of Skulls was gone—Ketheryll and all his men with it," the lord mayor concluded.

"All but one!" Stefanik interjected. When Pawldo looked at him in surprised confusion, the young halfling continued. "That's the tale in Llyrath, at least. A thief named Garius, a rogue who'd traveled all across the world, was among Ketheryll's men. Garius had grown to despise his evil master—the thief appreciated wrongdoing for profit's sake, but had no taste for wanton cruelty. It's said that under the cover of the fog, he fled his master and his gruesome palace!"

"Did he escape?" inquired Pawldo, intrigued by this new version of the legend.

"No one knows for certain," Stefanik said, his voice hushed. "Everyone thinks he got away before the curse took Ketheryll, but no one saw him again. Some say he escaped the castle, but not the prince's terrible magic." He shrugged. "Most of the old folks in Llyrath Downs say Garius was transformed into something horrible as punishment for his treachery."

"Maybe that's true," Pawldo noted with a yawn. "But we won't ever find out if any of these legends are true unless we get some rest."

"Then we can talk about it more tomorrow, I guess," Stefanik said cheerily. "We'll have time, since it'll take us most of the day to get to the place where I found the dagger. But it won't be hard to find. Like I told you, it's at the fork of two streams."

"Splendid, splendid," replied Pawldo. His voice trailed off, and, despite a few persistent questions from his young companion, the lord mayor of Lowhill would make no more speculations—aloud, at any rate.

The next day they began to move through the shadowy reaches of the forest. Dark, thick trunks rose around them, leafy branches crowding the air, forming a dense canopy overhead. The verdant ceiling blocked any ray of sunlight from reaching the ground, and the two halflings rode through a dim twilight. A soft bed of moss, leaves, and pine needles covered the ground, allowing for easy travel.

Pawldo felt a confining, almost claustrophobic sense of oppression as they rode between the pillars of rough bark. He soon missed the open stretches of the moors, where even the mist seemed distant and friendly compared to these looming sentinels. The air was moist and cloying, with humidity that dampened his forehead and an overpowering scent of dirt and pine. He longed for a breath of wind—an eternal companion on the moor—and yet not a breeze stirred the trees.

Toward the middle of the day they reached the bank of a deep, cold creek. "The Birchbrook," Stefanik announced. "If we follow it upstream, we'll come to the place where I found the dagger."

Even the waterway lay within the shroud of Llyrath's canopy, for the trees on either bank were so huge and soaring that the width of the streambed could not keep their branches from mingling. Gray boulders jutted from the murky waters, the river washing around them in eerie silence.

For the rest of the afternoon the halflings made their way along the banks of the Birchbrook. The stream surged with relentless force, but it seemed unusually quiet to Pawldo. The water was deep, often collecting in dark pools after a tumbling spill down a chute or over a short drop. Yet even in these rapids the Birchbrook did not splash and froth as he would have expected. The veteran traveler found something in the stealthy stream even more unsettling than the cloaking forest.

"There!" cried Stefanik, urging his pony forward. "See where the two creeks come together?"

"Yes. Good guiding, lad," Pawldo replied, pleased.

Two smaller streams formed a **Y** as they merged to create the deeper, wider Birchbrook. The right branch frolicked down a stairwaylike progression of stone shelves. In some places, the branches overhead actually gapped slightly, allowing thin beams of sunlight to reflect brilliantly from the surface. The river's left branch seemed to Pawldo more like the Birchbrook proper—it meandered through a channel that was not as steep as the other. Though the current moved quickly, the water didn't splash with the same vitality as its neighboring stream.

"In the middle—that's where I camped. I found the dagger there," Stefanik explained.

As they approached the spot, Pawldo saw that the place between the two channels indeed seemed like a perfect camping site. The ground was flat, free of trunks and roots. Several large rocks had been gathered in a protective circle, providing a windbreak for a fire and screening any blaze from casual observation.

"We can cross the right branch," continued the young halfling. "There's a good ford there."

The two ponies waded into the stream, which splashed only to their knees, then emerged onto the flat clearing. The charred embers of an old fire huddled between several of the boulders Pawldo had seen earlier.

"Is that the remnants of your blaze?" he asked Stefanik as they both dismounted.

"Yes. Here's the old birch root I pulled out before I went to sleep," replied the younger traveler, kneeling beside the gritty fire scar. "No one's been here since me."

"I'm not surprised," muttered Pawldo. The murkiness of the forest was now unnervingly oppressive, but he shrugged off the feeling as best he could. "Where did you find the knife?"

"Over here." Stefanik crossed to the left fork of the converging streams, indicating a shallow depression near the bank. "It was lying right here. This hole is where I pulled it out."

Pawldo knelt beside the shallow excavation. Freshly turned dirt lined the hole, although tufts of moss already tinged the exposed earth. The depression matched the dagger's length. The object had rested just above the water level of the stream, between a pair of rocks.

Looking up the channel, Pawldo saw gloomy outcroppings of granite looming through the trees. The creek emerged from a deep cut between these high walls. Though tree trunks blocked much of the view, he saw the passage nestled between these bluffs—a narrow canyon, source of this left branch of the Birchbrook. He studied the steeply sloping streambed, dropping from that narrow gap to the small backwater at his feet.

Confidently Pawldo took the dagger out of his pouch and held it before him. "Show me the Palace of Skulls," he commanded, waiting for the telltale flush of heat to infuse the handle. Nothing happened.

"Maybe you have to drop it on the ground," Stefanik suggested.

Pawldo threw the blade to his feet, but it lay lifelessly in the dirt.

"What did you do before—to make it glow, I mean, and point toward Ketheryll's palace?" Stefanik wondered.

"I don't know," Pawldo snapped, but then bit his mouth shut. "Look!" he hissed.

As it had in Lowhill, the dagger began to glow. The halflings could feel its warmth as they stood over it. Then, very slowly, the weapon wiggled across the ground. In a few moments it lay still, pointing directly at the narrow, rocky gap up the stream.

"Up there," Pawldo said. "That's where it came from."

"It—it looks pretty dark," Stefanik observed hesitantly.

"Morning will brighten it up," Pawldo announced, his voice heartier than his thoughts. In truth, the forest-shrouded chasm seemed like a foreboding place. It didn't take him more than a moment to decide to postpone its exploration until the morrow.

Stefanik unsaddled the ponies while Pawldo gathered some dry branches he found scattered conveniently around the camp. He set them beside the fire scar and looked to Stefanik—only to see the younger halfling freeze taut, his eyes bulging at a sight behind Pawldo's shoulder.

The lord mayor whirled to confront a pair of unblinking yellow eyes, less than six feet away. A canine face stared impassively. A narrow snout gaped, while a pink tongue lolled between long, white fangs.

"Wolf!" Stefanik hissed.

Pawldo had already recognized the powerful body of the predator. The creature squatted upon a rock, ready to pounce.

Yelping in astonishment, Pawldo fumbled for his sword, but all he managed to do was stumble backward to collapse into an ungainly heap. All the time the wolf stared at him with those penetrating yellow eyes. By the time he had his sword half-drawn, the halfling realized that the creature presented no immediate menace.

"He looks hungry," observed Stefanik. The wolf's flanks showed the clear outline of his rib cage, screened only slightly by scattered patches of mangy fur. One of its ears flopped sideways, scarred by an ugly red wound. At the sound of the voice, the wolf shifted its gaze to the younger halfling's face, the good ear cocked forward attentively.

"Give him something to eat!" hissed Pawldo, more than a little embarrassed by his clumsiness—and still not certain of the wolf's intentions.

"Here, fellow," said Stefanik, pulling an entire slab of bacon from the saddlebags. He threw it onto the ground near the animal.

The wolf's eyes followed the meat but then came back to Pawldo. Finally, hunger won out. The creature sniffed tentatively, then hopped down from the rocky perch. With another look at Pawldo, who still had not climbed to his feet, the wolf settled to its haunches, tearing at the tough meal with teeth still white, long, and sharp.

In short order the wolf put a dent in their stockpile of cheese as well. Keeping a wary eye on the beast, Pawldo built the fire while Stefanik stretched out the bedrolls. They cooked some bacon for themselves, throwing another morsel to the wolf, as full darkness descended. Finally the animal dropped its head onto its outstretched forelegs with a contented sigh.

"I think we've found a friend," Stefanik said as the wolf closed its eyes.

"I suppose we could have a worse companion in these woods," Pawldo observed warily. The thought of sleeping here, with this huge carnivore just a few feet away, bothered him more than a little. "Maybe we should give him some more bacon."

"I think we should let him rest. He looks all worn out."

In fact, the animal appeared to have reached the end of a long and grueling trail. The shaggy flanks, now noticeably bulging, rose and fell with deliberate breathing. Pawldo noticed that the animal's muzzle and forelegs were also scarred, though not so badly as the ear. Many wounds, however, showed raw and moist—they had not yet had time to heal.

"Don't wolves usually travel in packs?" asked the younger halfling. "It seems odd to see one by himself."

"Do you see lots of wolves in Llyrath Forest?" demanded Pawldo.

Stefanik shook his head. "They're rare. Once or twice in the fall and winter we've seen them running past the village—like gray ghosts in the forest. They don't bother us.

In fact, they haven't even gone after the sheep kept by Whitebeard Karywether. But even then, when we see them there's *always* a pack—at least a dozen, sometimes twenty or more."

"From the look of this one, he's had to fight for his life. I wonder if he's the last survivor of his pack," Pawldo mused.

"I don't know what could slaughter so many wolves," Stefanik said. "There are bears out here, but a wolf could outrun one of them without a problem. What about firbolgs?"

Pawldo shook his head. "Even if the giant-kin came this far south, they wouldn't do this to wolves. Sometimes they capture them for pets, but they wouldn't torture and maim them."

Soon the unsettled pair of halflings curled into their bedrolls and went to sleep. Neither slumbered soundly, and Pawldo stirred as soon as the gray dawn filtered through the mist of the streambed.

The wolf, he saw, was still there—though the animal no longer slept. Indeed, the yellow eyes followed Pawldo's every move as the halfling rose and crossed to Stefanik, nudging the youngster to wakefulness. They packed up their camp, half-hoping the wolf would be on its way. But when they started into the narrow canyon, the wolf bounded ahead, picking a way around gnarled roots and over massive rocks. He led them straight into the canyon.

The chasm walls, great shoulders of granite, glowered overhead. Streaks of moss and lichen ran across their weathered faces, and the rocky walls projected a chill that sapped every vestige of warmth from the air. The stream narrowed to a channel choked with debris. Nevertheless, Pawldo had no lingering doubts that the source of the splendid dagger would be found near the headwaters of this creek.

"We won't be able to take the ponies through," Pawldo announced, gesturing into the steep and narrow canyon. "Let's picket them here and try to get back by nightfall."

Stefanik, too, realized the futility of taking the steeds through the maze of rocks and deadfalls. The wolf watched them from its vantage of a high boulder as they dismounted, loosely tied the mounts, and selected a few important items—weapons, flasks of oil, and the platinum dagger—to carry as they progressed on foot. Surprisingly, the wolf seemed more interested in them than in their horses.

The ragged animal again sprang forward, disappearing behind the large rock. It popped up a dozen paces ahead, its face turned alertly back to see if the halflings still followed.

"Yeah, yeah. Wait a minute!" muttered Pawldo, irritated at the ease with which the animal negotiated the rough terrain.

"If he's coming with us, we ought to give him a name," Stefanik suggested, struggling over a fallen trunk that bristled with prickly branches.

"Be my guest," grunted the older halfling as he, too, worked his way over the obstacle.

"How about 'Half-Ear'?" suggested Stefanik, taking Pawldo's frustrated mumbling for acquiescence. "Hey, wolf! Half-Ear—how about finding a better path?"

But Half-Ear only regarded them impassively. For several minutes they scrambled silently along the streambank to the wolf's latest vantage. By then, of course, the animal had bounded forward another two dozen paces.

Pawldo and Stefanik grunted and cursed their way up the narrow canyon. There was no path—indeed, deadfalls, rockslides, and thorny thickets all choked the base of the narrow chasm, making every step a struggle. Always Half-Ear remained before them, crawling under logs that blocked the halflings, scrambling up a steep surface of tumbled rock in a few bounds. Following slowly, the two-footed explorers climbed with painstaking care, hoisting their packs by rope only after they had made these perilous ascents.

The stream continued to flow beside them, rushing with silent power along a deep channel, for the most part free of the rocks that so typically obstructed the streambed lower down. Finally the walls to either side began to lean away from them, and soon they reached the top of the tangled chute. Struggling up a pile of boulders that spilled along the shore of the stream, Pawldo paused to catch his breath. Half-Ear waited patiently in a forest glade a short distance ahead.

"Open space," grunted the lord mayor as his young companion joined him. "Looks like the same kind of forest we saw below."

"Thank the Earthmother for that!" moaned Stefanik, collapsing on the rock pile in exhaustion. Then he looked around. "Where's Half-Ear?"

"Wait a minute, you mangy cur!" barked Pawldo as the wolf started through the glade toward the shadowed forest on the other side. "Give us a—" His shock swallowed the rest of his complaint.

"What is it?" asked Stefanik, following his companion's gaze. Then his voice, too, faded into stunned silence.

The structure in the woods before them was at first barely visible, so dense was the screen of tree trunks. Yet as the halflings squinted, a blocky outline came into view— a rectangular shape, like a long, high wall, pale gray or even white in color. Pawldo's first thought was that the outline was far too regular to be a clump of rocks or a hill.

"It—it's some kind of building," Stefanik said, unconsciously lowering his voice to a whisper. "And Half-Ear's going toward it!"

"Well, best not let him go alone," muttered Pawldo, surprised at his lack of enthusiasm. Something about the appearance of this bizarre structure—they had yet to get a good look at it—unsettled him in a way he found difficult to ignore.

"Uh, is it me, or do you think it's starting to get dark?" asked Stefanik. He glanced nervously at the dim forest surrounding them.

Pawldo didn't answer, but the growing twilight made him realize that they had spent the bulk of the day climbing through the tangled canyon. The usually shaded wood had already begun to sink into heavier shadow. Cautiously, as if he expected attack at any moment, he crept toward the edifice, darting from tree trunk to tree trunk, examining his goal from each vantage before moving forward again.

Half-Ear, in contrast, trotted right up to the thing and sat down expectantly, as if impatient for his companions to join the bold expedition.

Soon the halflings were close enough to see the details of the building, looming behind a screen of huge pines. As they emerged from the trees the whole structure opened up to view, and they stared in wonder. The white surface they had first spotted was the front wall, and it was not as smooth as Pawldo had originally thought. A multitude of turrets and parapets extended along the top, and a single doorway—large and yawning open—stood in the exact center. The wolf sat directly before this entrance.

And though they thought they had taken full stock of the castle from their vantage, only as the halflings approached the entrance did the true nature of the structure become apparent.

"The whole place is made of bones!" whispered Stefanik. "Look—skulls—*human* skulls! The legends are true!"

Pawldo felt a deep chill shudder through him as he stared at the wall of eyeless sockets. Most of the castle's surface, he saw, consisted of these grisly remnants stacked neatly together, as if placed by a master bricklayer. The frame of the doorway was formed by only three bones, like thighbones, only each was at least ten feet long.

"Even firbolgs don't have legs that big!" Pawldo murmured, awestruck.

"Do you think that's where the knife came from?" Stefanik asked reluctantly. "Maybe we were, uh, wrong about the mark."

"I'm sure it came from here," Pawldo replied and stepped boldly forward. Though the garish structure awakened feelings of abiding terror within him, it also drew him forward with the thrill of discovery, adventure . . . and treasure. He had, after all, earned his reputation as a hero by facing supernatural threats even more threatening than this phantom castle.

"Say, what about the ponies?" Stefanik looked back at their path, his face wistful. "We can't leave them alone all night."

"They'll be all right. There's plenty of grass around there."

"What about wolves?" Stefanik wondered.

"I'm sure Half-Ear's the only one, and he's with us. You might even say he's showing us the way. Come on." Pawldo started once more toward the looming entrance. His mind whirled with images—mounds of coins, gleaming gemstones, fabulous artifacts. Half-Ear bounced to his feet and paced ahead of them through the doorway.

One boldly, the other reluctantly, the halflings followed the wolf under the bone arch.

Enough light filtered through gaps in the crude stonework—*bonework*, Pawldo reminded himself—to light the interior just a little. Before the halflings had advanced two dozen paces, however, the darkness grew heavier and they paused to remove lanterns from their packs. Filling them with oil, touching spark to wick, they soon resumed their exploration under brighter illumination.

The entryway was a wide corridor, smoothly paved below their feet—apparently with actual stone, Pawldo saw with a measure of relief. The walls to either side, however, formed an array of eyeless sockets and grinning teeth, for they were built exclusively of skulls.

"There are *thousands* of them," gasped Stefanik as they came to an intersection and saw three other corridors, each lined with leering skeletal faces. The air was dry and odorless, but each breath seemed to parch the halflings' tongues and throats of moisture. They each gulped a swallow from the waterskin, as much to calm their nerves as quench their thirst.

"Which way should we go?" asked Stefanik. A longing glance back to the entrance registered the youngster's vote on that question.

"The dagger!" Pawldo hissed. He took the platinum weapon from his belt pouch and held it before each of the three passages. "The Palace of Skulls," the lord mayor intoned, picturing vast piles of treasure in his mind. He waited for several moments, remembering that the effect had been delayed before. Yet now, perhaps because they were in the palace, it gave them no clue. "We'll have to guess. Let's go this way," Pawldo announced without pause.

Pawldo had taken only a half-dozen steps down the hall straight ahead when his lamplight reflected with a telltale gleam from a scattering of metal along the base of one wall.

"*Gold!*" exclaimed the lord mayor, forgetting even to keep his voice down. Eagerly he knelt to investigate, holding the lamp over several dozen gilded coins shining up at him from the floor.

"Shouldn't they be dusty?" wondered Stefanik aloud.

"No!" Pawldo's voice hissed with delight. "This place is only here for a fortnight, then it disappears! When is there time for dust to collect?"

"But. . . ." Stefanik's voice trailed away.

The older halfling scooped up the coins and dropped them quickly into his satchel. Their bulk created a satisfying weight in the bottom of the bag.

"Come on!" Pawldo urged, picking up the pace. Half-Ear trotted readily beside him, while Stefanik hurried to stay close behind.

They passed into a huge, vaulted chamber, where the light from their lanterns created little pools of illumination in a great waste of darkness. Stefanik started across the flat floor, but Pawldo called him back.

"Look—niches along the wall. Let's have a look as we go." He held the lantern up between a pair of arches, lighting an empty space, small and square with a high ceiling supported by arching bones.

"Alcoves . . . maybe this is where Ketheryll's Doomed Legion had their quarters!" whispered Stefanik, awestruck and terrified.

"Maybe," Pawldo said, then added triumphantly, "but they're empty now! There's no haunted guards here, waiting to suck out your soul. So much for the old legends!"

"No treasure, either," the younger halfling countered.

"Patience, Sprout. We've barely begun to search."

Pawldo moved on, following the row of nearly identical compartments. He checked the next, and the one after—and in a few moments he was rewarded.

"What do you know?" he announced smugly, kneeling down to lift a small statuette, a figure of a crouching lion, from the floor. Like the gold coins, it gleamed as if it had been freshly polished. "Pure silver, with rubies for eyes!"

Quickly he popped the object into his satchel, continuing his explorations. Before he had completed his investigation of the room, which took the better part of an hour, a pair of golden earrings, an emerald-studded brooch, and a jeweled headband had joined the objects in his bag. The shaggy wolf followed him through the entire circuit, yellow eyes sparkling in the torchlight as if he, too, understood the worth of their finds.

"If these were the chambers of Ketheryll's loyal followers," Stefanik observed, "they must have lived in pretty cramped quarters!"

"Look here!" Pawldo stooped to lift another gleaming treasure from the floor. "It's another figurine," he added softly, turning over the hand-sized image of a human warrior. He examined it carefully, then drew in his breath. There, at the base of the figurine's back, he saw the faint outline of a skull.

"Shouldn't we get going?" asked Stefanik as Pawldo cinched up the bag.

"There's *lots* more of this place to explore," Pawldo replied with a firm shake of his head.

He led the other halfling on a winding, circuitous exploration of the Palace of Skulls. Half-Ear preceded them along some corridors, while Pawldo's curiosity and intuition took them down others. They found high galleries and a great ballroom, and even a deep pit that Pawldo guessed had been the Circus Bizarre. It was surrounded by rings of benches, all made from various pieces of bone.

Here Pawldo almost overlooked a pair of rings. Unlike

the other treasures, these lay under a thin film of dust and dirt. Each was inscribed with a stamp in the image of the Great Bear. After a quick appraisal—the gold was pure, Pawldo decided—he dropped the items into his satchel with the rest.

"The bears prove it!" Stefanik said. "The story is *true*—he *did* kill the king and queen who bore that symbol as their own!"

Several more treasures yielded themselves to the intrepid explorers—or to Pawldo, actually, for Stefanik spent most of the time staring wide-eyed into the shadows, urging the older halfling to hurry. Yet the lord mayor of Lowhill would not be rushed. He found a gem-studded necklace and bracelets that, he felt certain, were fully equal to the worth of a large house. A few steps later a tiny crystal image of a knight on horseback caught his eye with its glittering diamond facets and slender lance of platinum. Half-Ear paced along ahead of him, nosing the shadows, looking back with apparent impatience at the halfling.

They pressed around a corner and found a stairway leading up. Pawldo didn't hesitate to start climbing, with Stefanik following reluctantly, his eyes wide, flicking this way and that at the grotesque death's-heads lining the walls to both sides.

"Wait! I think I saw something!" hissed the youth.

"What? Where? More gold?" asked Pawldo, whirling around on the stairs.

"No—something *moved*!" wailed Stefanik. "Down there—something *dark*!"

Pawldo followed his companion's trembling gesture, but he could make out nothing beyond the shadows cloaking the foot of the stairs. The light from their lanterns seemed suddenly a very feeble counter to the oppressive darkness. As Pawldo held the sputtering flame, the halfling felt acutely conscious that its illumination made him perfectly visible to someone—or some*thing*—lurking within the gloom.

Quickly he shuttered the vessel, ordering Stefanik to do

the same. In the fullness of the dark, they waited sound-lessly. Slowly their eyes adjusted to the murk. Though they could see nothing in the way of detail, the vague contours of the walls and stairway gradually took form around them.

"Stay here!" commanded Pawldo, setting down his oil lamp. He drew his short sword, little relishing the familiar weight in his hand. Then, as an additional precaution, he reached into the satchel and took out the platinum dagger. Holding the smaller blade with his left hand, he raised his sword and started down the stairs. He felt the reassuring presence of Half-Ear's shaggy flank beside him.

Step by careful step he descended, brandishing the sword with more menace than he felt. He reached the bottom step, then felt the smooth floor of the corridor under his feet. Staring to the left and right, he could barely make out the obscure outlines of the passageway. Beside him, Half-Ear's rapid breathing created a taut cadence for his fear.

"There's nothing down here," he whispered. Stefanik made no sound on the stairs, so Pawldo repeated the observation more loudly.

The silence up the stairs was more frightening than anything he'd imagined in the shadows.

"Stefanik!" he barked.

But still there came no answer.

Pawldo and the wolf bounded up the stairway, stumbling into the soft mound of his satchel. Sheathing his sword, he fumbled for the lantern and opened the shutter.

Stefanik was gone, though the youngster's lantern rested on the step above the satchel. Desperately the lord mayor looked up the rest of the stairway—the young halfling could not have gone down the stairs without being seen, and Pawldo had noticed no doors. Cold terror seized Pawldo, along with a profound sense that disaster had over-taken them with stunning speed.

Shrugging the pack over one shoulder, the halfling took the lantern, albeit awkwardly, in his left hand. Again draw-ing his sword, he started up the remaining steps, ten or twelve in number, until he came to a landing, where wide corridors extended in three directions.

"Stefanik!" he called again.

Pawldo felt a wave of awful loneliness sweep over him. Suddenly the treasures in his satchel, the lure of wealth that had compelled him farther and farther through this dolorous palace, paled to insignificance against the weight of his young companion's life.

Half-Ear growled softly. Then the wolf started down the middle passageway, pausing after a few steps to look back at the halfling.

Grimly clutching his short sword in one hand, the dagger and the lantern in the other, Pawldo followed the pacing animal down the central corridor, through a room of tall columns and under a narrow archway beyond. Several places along the way gold winked seductively from niches in the walls, or the telltale glitter of gemstones tried to coax him from his course, but the halfling moved on resolutely.

He entered another large chamber, a domed ceiling standing high above his head. Crossing carefully, he held his lantern up and tried to look into the shadows. Half-Ear paced beside him, head up and eyes alert. Suddenly the wolf froze, growling deep within his chest. Pawldo saw a dim form standing utterly still in the darkness—an erect figure, no more than three feet tall.

"Stefanik!" Pawldo yelped, running toward the young halfling.

But as abruptly as Pawldo started forward, he stopped. Stefanik had not turned, had not reacted in any way to his shout. Something's definitely wrong, he decided.

Then the shadows beyond the young halfling moved, and Pawldo felt a chill creep to the very marrow of his bones. A shape loomed there—a *huge* shape—and the halfling could not prevent a dull moan of horror escaping his lips. The murk parted, but only to reveal a thing of even more profound darkness, a hulking figure, larger than a man, with shoulders and head rising in the inky chamber.

Pawldo saw upraised arms, black and menacing—yet

somehow tenuous, like thick, oily smoke. Cold swirled around him, threatening to suck the heat and life from his body. He saw long, wickedly curving claws at the ends of the reaching limbs. Then a hideous visage materialized—snarling jaws, spread wide to reveal a crimson tongue and blackened, hideous teeth. Most horrifying, however, were the thing's eyes, hellishly gleaming embers of hatred and doom that stared unwaveringly at the trembling halfling.

"Who are the thieves seeking to pilfer the treasures of Ketheryll?"

The voice rumbled through the cavernous room, and Pawldo felt as though a bolt of lightning had welded him to the floor. The hair at the back of his neck stood on end, and he sensed the unmistakable aura of magic crackle in the air.

Then he realized another terrifying fact: the wraith's voice had come from all around him! Spinning through a frantic circle, he saw a dozen shapes, all menacing, all rather indistinct. Yet the same hellish eyes gleamed from each, and taloned limbs reached out from them all, eager to tear Pawldo to pieces.

"Who *are* you?" the halfling gasped, finally summoning the strength to speak.

"I am Prince Ketheryll." Again the voice, a storm ravaging a distant valley.

Beside Pawldo, Half-Ear growled and crouched, eyes gleaming in the lamplight, flickering from first one to another of the circling horrors.

"Stefanik!" shouted Pawldo.

The tousled head twisted, as if the youngster tried to turn but failed. It was as if Stefanik were trying to look at his companion, but could not muster the strength. Again Half-Ear growled, fear tingeing his snarl.

"Do not waste your breath!" hissed Ketheryll. "Like you, he is my prisoner."

"What did you do to him?" Pawldo asked, slowly circling to face all the looming figures. What did *I* do to him? his conscience added harshly. He well remembered Stefanik's pleas to depart from this place and his own insistence on pursuing the elusive treasure.

"I've done nothing, but I plan to make him one of my treasures . . . my trinkets," said Ketheryll. "I understand you have spent much of the night collecting the others."

"What do you mean?"

"They were all shiftless and deceitful—even my fearless legion—all like that traitor Garius." Ketheryll smiled horribly. "He fled my home at my hour of greatest need, but that couldn't protect him from my wrath."

The voice deepened, gurgling with a hellish boil. "Like all those lured here by the promise of riches, drawn deeper into my web by their own greed, you and your thieving friend shall forever linger among these walls. Like all those who've tried to rob me or lie to me, you'll become things of imaginary value—all glitter, but no substance."

"I've seen plenty of substance in here," challenged the halfling, though he instantly regretted the foolish outburst.

"Do you think so? Perhaps you should look again."

Suddenly sick to his stomach, Pawldo realized that the platinum dagger felt surprisingly light in his hand. Glancing down, he saw the thing as it really was: a piece of cheap tin set with glass baubles. He knew immediately that the rest of the treasures in his satchel would prove no more valuable.

Pawldo tried to still the trembling in his limbs. Desperately his mind sought a plan. He looked around frantically, seeking some inspiration.

Half-Ear stood beside the halfling, his yellow eyes darting around the circle of figures. The hackles on the wolf's back bristled. His nose twitched as canine lips curled into a teeth-baring snarl.

Pawldo raised his lantern, acutely conscious of the sputtering flame, the small reservoir of oil still feeding the wick. The clay jar was heavy in his hand; more than half the fuel remained.

"Stefanik!" he called again. Once more the young halfling struggled, caught in a battle of wills—but still he could not turn, could not speak.

"Fool!" spat Ketheryll. Again, the sound came from all over the chamber.

The flickering light of Pawldo's lantern trembled as he tried in vain to still the shaking of his hand. He saw one chance—a slim, desperate gamble, but that gamble was the only thing that offered even a faint hope of escape. *If* he'd guessed correctly.

He cast the dagger onto the floor and shouted a word—not the name of this nightmarish place, for he had realized that the Palace of Skulls was not the dagger's true point of orientation. Instead, he shouted a name. And with the speaking of the word the dagger flared like the sun.

"Ketheryll!" Pawldo cried.

The blade whirled on the floor and abruptly came to a stop. It pointed toward one of the encircling images, farther from Pawldo than the rest, almost lost in the shadows. The instant its true identity was revealed, the wraith lunged forward, extending icy claws toward its foe. With shocking speed those deadly talons neared Pawldo's face.

Half-Ear growled, the sound low and rumbling in the cavernous room. The animal crouched momentarily, nostrils twitching, then leaped. His growl building into a savage snarl, Half-Ear clamped his jaws on one of Ketheryll's writhing limbs. The cursed prince lashed out, sending the wolf flying, but the valiant attack gave Pawldo the instant he needed to raise his arm, hoisting the flaring lantern high over his head.

Grunting, he hurled the makeshift missile. The clay jar struck the floor at the prince's feet, smashing to pieces and splashing oil across the hissing creature. As the wick touched the slick stonework, orange flame leaped to engulf the body of Ketheryll.

"*No!*"

The sound was a shrieking wail, like a hurricane of wind swirling through a wide canyon, tearing at trees and rocks and even the earth itself. The trembling became real then, more than the gale of an unnatural wind. Pawldo staggered as the floor moved beneath his feet. The prince surged toward him, trailing fire.

Pawldo grabbed the gaudy dagger that had lured him to the palace. He knew now that it was only a trinket, but one with a difference. The dagger was the only one to be found *outside* the Palace of Skulls. The Doomed Legion and the other treasure seekers had been converted to cheap baubles, but always within the walls of the palace. That meant the dagger could be the ensorceled remains of only one person.

"Here, Garius," Pawldo whispered, cradling the knife before him. "Now's the chance to return to your master."

He hurled the blade toward the prince, and he saw—or imagined he saw—Ketheryll's eyes widen in horror. The blade sank deep into the creature's chest, and the monster stumbled backward in a cloud of hissing steam.

Pawldo didn't wait to see what happened next. He leaped forward, seizing Stefanik's collar and yanking the young halfling around. The red-haired youth gaped at the spectacle of Ketheryll's agony, blinking in astonishment.

"Come on!" shouted Pawldo.

"You are *mine!*" shrieked the cursed prince, creeping forward, extending flaming limbs toward the two halflings. Half-Ear roared forward in a raging attack, ignoring the flames to sink his teeth into the black figure's torso.

The thing that had been Ketheryll lashed out with its long talons, but the wolf ducked underneath the swiping blow. In the flashing light Pawldo saw the wounds on Half-Ear's flank and he knew: *this* was the creature that could destroy an entire pack, could nearly kill this brave wolf who had all but led the two halflings here on a quest for his own vengeance. The black shape and the snarling canine whirled around on the floor, the two intruders forgotten for the moment.

Stefanik stumbled to his knees as the floor pitched beneath him, but then scrambled back to his feet. His will had returned with the breaking of the monster's concentration. Pawldo propelled him toward the door, and the youth sprinted from the room, followed by the lord mayor and then the bounding wolf.

In blind terror they ran through the halls of the Palace of Skulls, fleeing the menace that they felt, rather than saw. They raced along corridors, hurled themselves down long stairways, gasping for breath but not daring to slow the frantic pace of their flight. Objects bounced from the satchel as Pawldo ran. Glass baubles and cheap metal figurines clinked and shattered along the floor behind him, and he took no note of the lost treasures.

Finally the door, with its overhanging arch of bone, yawned before them. Lungs straining and eyes tearing, the two halflings tumbled out of the bone-walled structure, collapsing onto the forest floor amid the gray mists of advancing dawn. The wolf followed them through the portal but then spun and crouched, glowering into the palace.

They saw no sign of movement or pursuit as they hugged their aching sides. Their breathing slowed and their rubbery legs gradually regained their strength. Staggering against a tree for support, Pawldo dropped the satchel in frustrated anger.

"Were they *all* worthless?" asked Stefanik as he looked through the junk in the satchel.

"Illusions," Pawldo said in disgust. "Stuff to draw intruders farther into the palace—until finally they faced Ketheryll."

"Look! Here's something that didn't turn into junk!" Stefanik exclaimed. He pulled out the pair of golden rings, set with the Great Bear—the only objects that had been dirty when Pawldo found them.

"The rings," mused the lord mayor. "These were real—a treasure of slain victims, not the transformed minions of Ketheryll."

"Here," said Stefanik, handing the two bands of metal to Pawldo. "You should have these."

"Nay, lad. Too much trouble has come of this."

Yet, when Stefanik insisted, Pawldo remembered his original intention in seeking the source of the platinum dagger—to find a present for the king's and queen's anniversary. The rings bore the symbol of the Moonshae's royal family, a symbol that now could be traced back to the human rulers slain long, long ago by the mad prince.

Pawldo slipped the rings into his pocket. At least, he reflected, he had found a suitable present for Tristan and Robyn.

ELMINSTER AT THE MAGEFAIR

Ed Greenwood

What's more dangerous than a mage out to rule the entire world? Why, a mage at play, of course. . . .

The Simbul, Witch-Queen of Aglarond
Warnings
Year of the Dark Dragon (1336 DR)

The rosy light of early morning had scarcely brightened into the full radiance of day, but the bard and her gaunt companion had already been in the saddle for some time.

Storm Silverhand, the Bard of Shadowdale, was an adventurer of wide experience and fame. She was also a senior and respected member of the Harpers, that mysterious band always working for the good of the world. A veteran of many perilous forays, always alert, she watched her surroundings constantly as the she traveled, hand never far from the hilt of her sword. Its blade had run with blood more than once already on this journey. As she rode, Storm sang softly to herself. She was happy to be in the saddle again—even on a ride into known danger.

For two tendays she had ridden beside a white-haired man as tall as herself, but thinner. The man was aged and a clumsy rider. He wore simple, much-patched robes covered with old food stains, and trailed sweet-smelling pipesmoke wherever he went.

Though he didn't look it, the old man was an adventurer even more famous than Storm: the Old Mage, Elminster of Shadowdale. More than five hundred winters had painted his long beard white. His twinkling blue eyes had seen empires rise and fall, and spied worlds beyond Toril, vast and strange. He knew more secrets than most wizards— and simpler, more honest men, too—might ever suspect to exist. The years had sharpened Elminster's temper and his tongue, and built his magic to a height that most mages could only dream of.

This great wizard wore old, floppy leather boots, and, most of the time, an irritated expression. At night, on the far side of the fire, he snored like a crawhorn in torment— but he knew it and used magic to mute the noise for sake of his friend and trail mate. Storm loved him dearly, snores and all, even if he tended to treat her like a little girl.

Despite their friendship, it was unusual for Storm to be riding at the Old Mage's side. When Elminster left Shadowdale on prolonged trips, it was his habit to trust the defense of the dale to the bard. This time, just before the mage's departure, a Harper agent had brought a request from one of Storm's sisters: would she please guard Elminster when he went to the magefair?

In all her years of adventuring, Storm had never heard of a magefair, but the very name sounded ominous. She had been surprised at the easy good humor with which the Old Mage had accepted her announcement that this time, when he left home, she'd be riding with him. In fact, she suspected he'd used horses for the trek, rather than whisking himself across Faerun in a trice by magic, just to prolong their time together.

Every night Elminster settled himself and his pipe down beside their fire to listen to her pluck a harp and sing old ballads. In return, when she lay down under the watching, glittering stars, he'd softly tell tales of old Faerun until sleep claimed her. After years of riding the wastes with hearty, hardened warriors, Storm was astonished at how much she'd enjoyed this trip with the odd mage.

But now, it seemed, they had reached their destination, though it was nothing at all like the bard had imagined.

"Why here?" Storm Silverhand asked with tolerant good humor as she reined in beside Elminster on a ridge far from Shadowdale. The bright morning sun cast long shadows from the stunted trees and brush around them. As far as the eye could see, rolling wilderness stretched out, untouched by the hands of man. "We must be halfway to Kara-Tur by now."

The Old Mage scratched his nose. "Farther," he replied with seeming innocence, "and 'here' because one we seek is close-at-hand."

As he spoke, a man appeared out of thin air and floated in front of them. The horses snorted and shifted in surprise. Elminster frowned.

The man stood on nothing, booted feet far above the ground. Midnight eyes glowered down out of a thin, cruel white face. He towered impressively over them, clad in a dark and splendid tabard adorned with glowing mystic signs and topped with an upthrust high collar. A carved, gem-adorned staff winked and pulsed in one of his many-ringed hands.

"Challenge!" He addressed them with cold, formal dignity, raising his empty hand in a gesture that barred the way. "Speak, or pass not!"

"Elminster of Shadowdale," the Old Mage replied mildly, "and guest."

The man's eyes narrowed, and he said even more coldly, "Prove yourself."

"Ye doubt me?," Elminster asked slowly. "Why, Dhaerivus, I recall thy first magefair!" He nodded in reflection and added dryly, "Ye made a most fetching toad."

Dhaerivus flushed. "You know the rule," he said harshly, waving the staff. Lights began to race along its length, brightening the crystal sphere that topped it. With slow menace, the floating man brought that glowing end down to point at the Old Mage.

"Aye," Elminster replied. Then he wagged a finger back and forth and announced lightly, "Nice-*ly!*"

The staff that menaced them snapped back upright, forced away by the power of Elminster's sorcery. The sentinel who held it gaped at them in astonishment and fear before the muscles of his face rippled and lost their struggle against another dose of the Old Mage's spellcasting.

The magic made Dhaerivus giggle involuntarily for a few moments, then released him. His grin turned rapidly into a scowl of dark anger.

Elminster took no notice. "There ye go," he said jovially to the shaken sentinel as he urged his mount onward. "Happy magic!"

Storm looked back at the furious man as they topped the next ridge. The staff was flashing and flickering like a lightning storm at sea, and the sentinel was snarling and stamping angrily on the empty air. Storm glanced at Elminster and asked wonderingly, "You cast a *cantrip*? Making him giggle is 'proving yourself'?"

Elminster nodded. "A wizard must prove to a magefair sentinel only that he can work magic. Er, to keep the rabble out."

He rolled his eyes to show what he thought of that attitude and calmly urged his horse down through a tumble of boulders and long grass. "Guests like thee are exempt from the testing, but each mage is limited to only one such compatriot. No mage can avoid the test and be allowed into the fair. Generally, young bucks cast powerful explosions and the like, or exquisite and—ahem—voluptuous illusions, but in this case I, ah, well, ah . . . meant it as an insult."

Storm wrinkled her brow. "I see," she observed carefully. "I'm going to have to be very careful at this fair."

Elminster waved a hand. "Ah, nay, nay," he replied. "I must merely get a certain magical key from someone who isn't expected to be insane enough to bring it here—or to have anything at all to do with it—and then have a bit of fun. Certain Harpers asked me to come here to protect this friend I must meet. No doubt ye were asked to come along too—to keep a certain Old Mage out of trouble." He favored her with a level look. Storm smiled and nodded ruefully.

The Old Mage chuckled. "These magefairs are private little gatherings. I haven't been to one in years, and we're far enough from home that my face won't be well known. Certain rules govern those who attend, rules meant to keep things from sinking into a general spell-brawl, but ye'd do well to keep in mind that most everyone here can wield magic—quite well. Walk softly. Drink things that are offered to ye only if I am present and deem it wise. Draw thy magical blade only if ye must. Some come here to gain new spells, but most come to show off what they can do, like children at play. Cruel, overpowerful children, a lot of them."

He scratched at his beard and looked thoughtful. "As to those who work against us, the names and faces of their servants at the magefair are unknown to me." He grinned suddenly. "Suspect everyone, as usual, and ye should do all right."

"What is this key we seek?," Storm asked, "and why is it so valuable?"

Elminster shrugged. "It's precious only because of what it opens. Its form and purpose ye'll learn soon enough—which is another way of saying I scarce remember what it looks like and haven't the faintest idea why, after so many years, its importance has risen so suddenly and sharply." He cast a dry look at her and added, "Mysterious enough for ye?"

Storm replied with a look that had, over the years, plunged more than one man into icy fear.

Unperturbed, the Old Mage smiled at her as they rode up the heather-clad slope of another ridge. "Sorry, my dear, but I got quite a lecture last time—from thee, as I recall—on speaking freely about all sorts of little details that should be kept secret in matters like this, so I'm flapping my jaws as little as I can this time around and acting as if only I know the great secret upon which the safety of the entire world rests—oh, there I go. Ye see, I just can't help myself. 'Tis so hard to do all this intrigue and world-saving with grim and solemn seriousness when ye've done it so often down the centuries. Now, where was I? Ah, yes. . . ."

There were worse fates, Storm reminded herself with an inward smile, than traveling across half of Faerun with Elminster. To buoy her spirits, she spent some time trying to remember what some of them were.

That dark reverie took them across several scrub-covered ridges, to the lip of a deep, bowl-shaped valley. A narrow trail wound down into it from somewhere on their right, crossing in front of them to enter a grove of trees. The trees hid the rest of the valley from the two riders.

It was then that a man in rich purple robes sailed into view. Floated would be a more accurate term, since he perched serenely on a carpet that undulated through the air like an eager snake, following the narrow trail far below. And as the bard and wizard watched, the man on the flying carpet sailed into the trees. Their leaves promptly changed color from their former green to a bright coppery hue, and several voices could be heard, raised in cries of praise of the new arrival.

They had obviously reached the magefair.

Far off, on the heights that rose on the other side of the still-unseen valley, Storm saw balls of fire bursting in the air. Elminster followed the direction of her stare and said, "Ah, yes—the fireball-throwing contest, d'ye see? Magelings get all excited about it . . . something about impressing their peers. No doubt we'll end up there all too soon. They're allowed to challenge us older dweomercrafters, ye see, to prove their manly mettles by beating feeble dodderers. Er, womanly mettles too, mark ye, though many maids have sense enough to avoid such vulgar displays of power."

Storm raised an eyebrow. "How does one fireball impress more than another? As the saying goes, aren't all that hit you the same?"

The Old Mage shook his head patiently. "If a few words of the incantation are changed, the spell becomes more difficult to cast and the size and force of its blast mirrors the power and experience of the one throwing it. One wizard can boast that his is bigger than that of the next wizard, y'see. An archmage's firesphere can be quite impressive."

He paused meaningfully, then added, "I mean to get in and get out of the fair, mind ye, with a minimum of dallying. Tossing fire about is more a sport for the green and foolish. Try not to seek out trouble by challenging anyone. Stay close and speak not. It's safer."

And with these melodramatic words the Old Mage kicked his heels and sent his horse galloping down the steep track in reckless haste, raising dust. At the bottom, Elminster plunged his mount into a crowd of laughing, chatting mages. Storm, close on his heels, had time for one stare before she entered the assembled mages.

The gorge was full of folk standing shoulder to shoulder. Their robes formed a moving sea of wild colors, and the chatter was nearly deafening. There were men and women of all shapes, ages, and sizes—and a few whose gender the bard wasn't sure of. Traditional dark, flowing, wide-sleeved robes were amply in evidence, but most of the mages wore stranger, more colorful garments. Storm, who had seen much in the way of garb over many years of wandering, stared in wonder. It is widely held in Faerun—among non-mages, at least—that those who work Art are all, in varying degrees, crazy. In eccentricity of dress, Storm saw, this was certainly correct.

All manner of strange headpieces and body adornments bristled and sprouted around her, shimmering and sparkling and in some cases shifting shape in fluid movements. One lady mage wore nothing but a gigantic, many-feathered snake, which moved its slow coils continuously around her lithe body. A man nearby seemed clad only in dancing flames. The wizard he was speaking to wore a shifting, phosphorescent fungus, out of which grew small leafy ferns and thistles. Next to them stood a half-elven maiden clad in a flowing gown of gleaming, soft-polished gems strung upon many silken threads. She was arguing with a long-haired dwarf wearing furs and leather upon which a pair of insect-eating lizards crawled ceaselessly, long tongues darting. A snatch of their conversation came to Storm's ears:

"Well, what did the Thayan do then?"

"Blew up the entire castle, of course. What else?"

Other voices crowded in, drowning out the previous speakers. "What was that? *Purple* zombies? Why purple?"

"She was bored, I guess. You should have seen the prince's face the next morning. She made a dozen tiny red hands appear out of thin air and pinch him in all the places he had pinched her . . . in front of all the court, too!"

Elminster was riding steadily through the throng. He seemed to know where he was going. Storm followed, past a man who was balancing a full bottle of something dark and red on his large nose and protesting in muffled tones to those watching that he wasn't using any magic to help him. She looked away just before the bottle toppled and spilled all over him, but could not resist looking back at the damp result. She was careful not to smile.

"How many times must I tell thee? *First* you kiss, *then* cast the spell—or it stays a frog forever!"

Storm shook her head, trying to concentrate on Elminster and ignore such talk. A terrific din of conversation, strange music, humming, and weird little popping noises raged over the crowd. Wizards gestured to impress those they were speaking with, and varicolored smokes and many-hued globes of radiance obediently bobbed or writhed in the air over their heads. Enspelled birds sang complicated melodies, and some flew graceful aerial ballets. Storm peered this way and that, trying to see everything, watching for danger.

Everywhere folk stood talking, arguing, laughing, or dickering, with goblets and flagons of varying sizes and contents in their hands, or floating handily in midair at their elbows. Some sort of rule, Storm guessed, kept the mages themselves from flying, floating, or teleporting about. Mostly they just stood in groups, talking. Storm threaded her mount carefully among them. Three olive-hued tentacles slid out from under a mage's hood as she passed. Small, glittering eyes opened at their ends, surveyed her, and winked. She tried not to show her involuntary shudder as she rode on, past a man with bright green hair and beard who was juggling a ring of hand-sized balls of fire in the air. The lady mage he was trying to impress was in the act of stifling a yawn.

The next group was made up of old and wrinkled crones with cold dark eyes and sinister-looking black robes. They were chuckling and swigging beer from clear glass tankards that didn't seem to empty. "First babe I ever saw that was born with wings," one was saying delightedly. "Flew around the nursery, *giggling*, the little scamp. Well, the king nearly swallowed his crown, I tell thee!"

Storm left the women behind, riding across a little open space where rising smoke and ashes suggested someone had experienced a warm and possibly fatal accident very recently. Beyond it, she plunged into the chatter once again.

"You must understand, old friend, that taking the shape of a dragon is an experience that changes one forever—forever, I tell you!" A mage in florid pink and purple, lace at his wrists and throat, was underscoring this point by flicking a long, forked tongue at the mage he was speaking to—a wizardess with white, furry hair running down her arms and the backs of her hands. Her skin was a deeper purple than the garb of the wizard speaking to her. Her reply to his claims about dragonshaping was an eloquent snort.

Then Storm was threading her way past six enchantingly beautiful half-elven sorceresses, whose heads were bent together in low-voiced intrigue. One looked up alertly, only to relax and give the bard a relieved smile. The others, intent on deal-making, never saw her.

"Well, just change the name and the way you cast it, and he'll never know. I mean, anyone could have come up with a spell like that. Teach it to me, and I'll not tell where I got it. In return, I'll show you that trick of Tlaerune's, the one that makes men swoon and—"

Shaking her head, Storm hurried on through the magical bedlam, trying to catch up with the Old Mage. Where had he gone? She looked up and down the crowded gorge— there were hundreds of mages here! Yet, thanks to her keen eyes, she managed to find Elminster again. The Old Mage continued to cut through the gathered wizards without slowing or dismounting—until he came to a tree-shaded corner on the far, rocky wall of the gorge. There, in the dappled gloom, a short, stunningly beautiful lady mage was talking with five or six obviously smitten men of the Art.

Storm saw laughing black eyes, flowing black hair, and a gown whose scanty front seemed to be made of glowing, always-shifting flowers. Then the Old Mage vaulted, or rather fell, straight from his horse into the arms of the lady, with the words, "Duara! My *dear*! Years have passed! Simply *years!*"

Dark eyes sparkled up into his, and the Old Mage's effusive greetings were temporarily stilled by a deep kiss. Slim hands went around his neck, stroked his tangle of white hair, and then moved downward, in a tight, passionate embrace.

After Elminster's glad greetings and the long kiss, Storm heard a low, purring voice replying enthusiastically. On the faces of the men around she saw astonishment, then anger, resignation, or disgust, and finally resigned disinterest. Storm also noticed Duara's fingers at the mage's belt, moving nimbly.

Other eyes had seen it, too—particularly those of a tall, hook-nosed man in a dark green velvet doublet with slashed and puffed sleeves. He'd been watching the Old Mage's affectionate greeting closely, his expression hidden by the smoke from his long, slim clay pipe.

When Elminster finally bid the smiling beauty a noisy adieu, the hook-nosed wizard let his pipe float by itself as he strode forward, gesturing wordlessly. In response, Elminster's pouch levitated upward and opened in midair. Silence fell among the mages standing near. It was obvious by their expressions that the green-clad wizard's spellwork was a serious breach of etiquette.

Storm half-drew her sword, but Elminster's bony hand stayed her firmly. In merry tones, he asked, "Lost thy magic, colleague? Want to borrow a cup of this or that?"

The wizard in green looked narrowly at him and at the lone item the pouch held: a twig. "Where is it, old man?"

"The powerful magic ye seek? Why, in here," replied Elminster, tapping his own head with one finger. Unsettled, Storm peered at him; his voice seemed thicker than usual, but his eyes were as bright as ever. "But ye can't get it with a simple snatching spell cast in a moment, ye know. Years of study, it took me, to master even—"

The green wizard gestured curtly. The twig flew toward his open, waiting hand. Before it got there, Elminster snapped his fingers and wiggled his eyebrows. As a result, the twig shot upward, curved in a smooth arc, and darted back toward the Old Mage.

The wizard in green frowned and gestured again. The twig slowed abruptly, but continued to drift toward the smiling face of Elminster. The wizard's hands moved again, almost frantically, but the twig's flight—and Elminster's gentle smile—held steady as the wood settled into the Old Mage's hand.

Elminster bowed to the white-faced, shaking wizard. Pleasantly he said, "But if it's this magical staff ye want—" the twig instantly became a grand-looking, ten-foot-long, smooth black staff with brass ends wrought in coiling-snake designs "—by all means have it." And the staff flew gently across empty air to the astonished man's hands.

"But . . . your staff?" Storm asked in wonder as she watched the sweating, dumbfounded wizard in green catch the staff not four paces away. "How will you replace it?"

"Cut myself another one," the Old Mage replied serenely. "They grow on trees."

Clutching the staff and eyeing Elminster anxiously, the velvet-clad wizard reclaimed his pipe, muttered something, and rapidly gestured. Abruptly, he was gone, staff and all, as though he had never been there at all.

Elminster shook his head disapprovingly. "Bad manners," he said severely. "Very. Teleporting at the magefair! It just wasn't done in my day, let me tell ye—"

"When was that, old man? Before the founding of Waterdeep, I'll warrant," sneered a darkly handsome young man who stood nearby. Storm turned in her saddle.

This mage was richly dressed in fur-trimmed silks. His black-browed, pinched face was always sneering, it seemed. Storm recognized him as one of the wizards who'd been speaking with Duara when Elminster arrived. His voice and manner radiated cold, scornful power as he curled back his lip a little farther and said, "By the way, graybeard, you may call me 'Master.'"

Gripping his own staff—one made of shining red metal, twelve feet long and adorned with ornaments of gold—the dark-browed mage reached for the reins of the Old Mage's riderless horse.

Storm kicked out at his hand from her saddle. The toe of her boot stung his fingers and smashed them away from Elminster's mount. The handsome mage turned on her angrily—to find a gleaming swordtip inches from his nose.

"Heh, heh," chuckled Elminster in thick, rich tones. "Not learned to leave the ladies alone yet, Young Master?"

The mage flushed red to the roots of his hair and whirled away from Storm's blade to face the old man again. "Why, no, grandsire," he said sarcastically. "Although it's obvious you've been without one for many a year!"

The loud insult brought a few snickers from the younger mages standing near, mingled with gasps and whistles of shocked amazement from older wizards who evidently knew Elminster. The murmuring intensified as some mages shoved closer to watch the coming confrontation, while others suddenly recalled pressing business elsewhere and slipped away to a safe distance.

Elminster yawned. "Put away thy blade," he said softly to Storm. Then he said more loudly and almost merrily, "It appears boastful striplings still come to magefairs for no greater purpose than to insult their betters."

The Old Mage sighed theatrically, and went on. "I suppose, cockerel, that now ye've picked a quarrel and will challenge me, eh? Nay, nay, that's not fair. After all, I've the wisdom of ages with which to make the right choices, whereas ye have only the hot vigor of youth . . . um, pretty phrase, that . . . so I'll even thy odds a trifle: *I'll* challenge *thee*! Fireball-throwing, hey? What say ye?"

A cheer arose. The red-faced mage waited for it to die, then said scornfully, "A sport for children and, I suppose, old lackwits."

Elminster smiled, very like a cat gloating over cornered prey, and said, "Perhaps. On the other hand, perhaps ye are frightened of losing?"

The mage's face grew redder still. He cast a look around at the interested, watching faces, and snapped "I accept." Then he struck an ostentatious pose and vanished.

An instant later, amid a puff of scarlet smoke, he reappeared on the edge of the gorge and made an insulting gesture at the Old Mage from afar. Elminster chuckled, waved a lazy hand in reply, and climbed clumsily back up onto his long-suffering horse. Storm saw him salute Duara with a wink. Then Duara's eyes met her own, and Storm could read the silent plea in them as clearly as if the young sorceress had shouted it in her ear: *Look after him, lady—please*.

By the time they had ridden up out of the valley to the meadows beyond, many wizards had gathered to watch. Haughty young sorcerers had been hurling fire about all day, but the expectant silence hanging over the scene seemed to indicate that the mage with the red staff had won a reputation at the fair, or many elders remembered Elminster, or perhaps even both.

With more haste than grace, Elminster fell from his saddle. He hit the ground at a stumbling run, staggered to a halt, and dusted himself off. Then he saw his waiting opponent and, with obvious pleasant surprise, said, "Well . . . lead off, boy!"

"One side, old man," said the young mage darkly, waving his staff. "Or have you no fear of dying in a ball of flame?"

Elminster stroked his beard. "Yes, yes," he said eagerly, his mind seemingly far away. "Well do I remember! Oho, those were the days . . . great bursts of fire in the sky. . . ."

The young mage pushed past him.

"Now, how did that one go, eh? Oh, my, yes, I think I recall. . . ." Elminster burbled on, voice thick and eyes far away.

Contemptuously the young mage set his staff in the crook of his arm, muttered his incantation in low tones so the Old Mage could not hear, and moved his hands in the deftly gliding gestures of the spell. An instant later, above the grassy meadow, fire grew from nothingness into a great red-violet sphere. It seethed and roiled, rolled over once, and burst in orange ruin over the meadow, raining down small teardrops of flame onto the grass. Heat smote the watchers' faces, and the ground rocked briefly.

As the roaring died away, the quavering voice of the Old Mage could still be heard, murmuring about the triumphs of yesteryear. He broke off his chatter for a moment to say mildly, "Dear me, that's a gentle one. Can't ye do better than that?"

The young mage sneered. "I suppose you can?"

Elminster nodded calmly. "Oh, yes."

"Would it be possible to see thee perform this awesome feat?" the mage inquired with acidic courtliness, his voice a mocking, over-pompous parody of Elminster's own thickened tones.

The Old Mage blinked. "Young man," he said disapprovingly, "the great mastery of magic lies in knowing when *not* to use the power, else all these lands would long ago have become a smoking ruin."

The young mage sneered again. "So you won't perform such a trifling spell for us, O mightiest of mages? Is that the way of it?"

"No, no," Elminster said with a sigh. "We did agree, and ye have done thy little bit, so I—" he sighed again "—shall do mine." He gestured vaguely, then paused and har-rumphed.

"Ah, now," he said, "how does the rhyme go?" There were a few titters from the watching crowd as he scratched his beard and looked around with a puzzled air. The young mage sneered at his back, and then turned to favor Storm with the same disdain. The bard, who stood close by, hand on the hilt of her sword, met his gaze with a wintry look of her own.

Elminster suddenly drew himself up and shouted:

> "By tongue of bat and sulphur's reek,
> And mystic words I now do speak,
> There, where I wish to play my game,
> Let empty air burst into *flame*!"

In answer, the very air seemed to shatter with an ear-splitting shriek. A gigantic ball of flame suddenly towered over the meadow, its heat blistering the watchers' faces.

It was like the sun had fallen.

As mages cried out and shaded their eyes, the fireball rolled away from the awed crowd for a trembling instant, then burst in a blinding white flash, hurling out its mighty energies in a long jet of flame that roared away to the horizon. The earth shook and seemed to leap upward, throwing all but the Old Mage to their knees.

When the shaking had died away, Storm found herself lying beside the horses on the turf. By the time she had struggled to her feet and shook her head clear, the roiling smoke had died away and everyone could see what Elmin-ster's magic had wrought in the meadow. Or rather, what had been the meadow. Where a broad expanse of flame-scorched grass had stretched a moment before, a smoking crater now yawned, large and deep and very impressive.

"Umm . . . nice, isn't it?" Elminster said rather vaguely.

"I'd forgotten how much fun hurling fire is! How does the spell go again?"

This time, the Old Mage merely waved a finger.

His young opponent, clinging to a red metal staff now battered and bent in six places, was just getting to his knees when another ball of flames as big as the first roared over the meadow. That was enough to send him tumbling again, and the young mage soon found himself atop a dazed and rotund Calishite sorcerer. When he could see clearly again, the mage saw a second crater smoking in the distance. Awed murmuring could be heard from the watching wizards all around.

"Now," Elminster said mildly, drawing the stunned young mage to his feet with a firm hand, "was there aught else ye wanted to speak of? Sendings and such, or prismatic spheres—pretty, aren't they? I've always enjoyed them. Or crafting artifacts, say? No? Ah, well then . . . fare thee well in thy Art, Young Master of the Cutting Tongue, and learn a trifle more wisdom, too, if ye've the wits to do so. Until next we meet."

Elminster patted the young mage's arm cheerily, snapped his fingers, and vanished. A moment later he reappeared beside an anxious Storm. "Mount up," he said cheerily. "We've realms to cross tonight."

"Realms?" asked Storm. As they rode up the ridge and left the magefair behind, she did not look back. "I thought you had to get a key—or was it the twig? Did that mage take the key from you?"

"Oh, no," replied Elminster merrily. He rode close and touched her forearm.

Abruptly the landscape was gone, replaced momentarily by shifting, shadowy grayness. The travelers seemed to be standing on nothing, but the horses trotted as if it were solid ground. Even before Storm could gasp a breath, there was another jolt, and they were somewhere else again—a place of darkness where rocks of all sizes crashed together endlessly, tumbling and rebounding as they hurtled through the emptiness. There was a constant thunder of stone smashing into stone, the scene lit by flashes of phosphorescence from each violent impact.

Storm took one look at the scene and tore her weathercloak from behind her saddle, flinging it over the head of her mount to prevent its rearing and plunging forward off the rather small area of rock they'd appeared on. The Old Mage's mount stood calm, controlled by his magic, no doubt.

Storm stared around at the endless destruction and found herself ducking low as a large, jagged boulder thundered toward them. It was easily as large as four horses and tumbled end over end as it came at them.

Elminster gestured unconcernedly, and the boulder veered off to strike another, larger rock nearby. A deafening crash filled the air, and a shower of stone chips rained down upon the bard. Storm shook her head. Whatever this place was, they were no longer in Faerun.

"The green-clad dolt thought he had taken our prize," the Old Mage continued casually. "He suspected Duara might pass me the key, but he's found by now that his mighty staff is indeed just a twig. Now he'll have to go on watching her for the rest of the magefair, trying to see if she passes the key on to someone else. And for all he knows, anyone might be me, just wearing another shape. Duara'll lead him a merry dance. She likes hugging young men, and all that." He chuckled. "Shining schemes oft come to naught, ye know."

Boulders rolled and crashed right in front of them. Storm bit her lip to quell an involuntary shriek, shielded her eyes against flying stone shards, and asked, "Duara? You got the key from her, didn't you? I saw her hands at your belt."

Elminster nodded. "Aye, she gave it to me. All three of our foes at the fair saw it, too: the two who challenged me, and one who did not dare come forward."

He fended off six small stones hurtling toward them. "The third mage was there only to watch what transpired, no doubt, and report where we went. I used magic to blind him—and the Young Master of fire-hurling, too—under cover of my firesphere blast. They're both fortunate mage-fair rules prohibit spells that enfeeble the wits, or they'd be staring at nothing for a long time, indeed. The blindness will wear off soon enough, but they'll find us safely gone, and the key with us."

"What—and where—is this key?" Storm asked patiently, reaching into a saddlebag for some cheese. "Why did they not know where you'd hidden it?"

"They saw, but they did not see," the Old Mage replied, using magic to float the cheese she held out deftly to his mouth. "They knew not that Duara and I were old friends—or how quick her wits are."

He reached into his mouth and drew out a small spindle of metal set with a large emerald. "The key," he said grandly, his voice suddenly its usual clear-edged, fussy self again. "It's been in there since Duara first kissed me." He licked his lips consideringly and added, "She still likes almonds." The waiting cheese slid into his mouth. He chewed, made an approving face, and took Storm's hand. Around them, at his will, the world shifted again.

In the blink of an eye, the darkness and crashing rocks were gone. Now their horses stood on a crumbling stone bridge in the midst of a fetid swamp, ringed by vine-hung trees. Slimy stone statues protruded from the still, black waters on all sides. Storm could see they perched on a raised avenue, part of an ancient city that lay drowned in the mire around them.

As Storm glanced behind her, several glistening black tentacles rose lazily from the inky waters and rolled in languid curls across the stone span. After these questing limbs bobbed and swayed—almost as if they sniffed the air—they slid slowly into the water again.

The bard pointed to a trail of ripples, which seemed to mark the path of something large moving toward them just under the water's surface. Elminster nodded, smiled, and waved a hand casually—and they were somewhere else again. This time, the horses were on an old, sunken road in the heart of a dark forest.

Storm sighed. "The Harpers wanted me to protect you?" she began to ask. But when she spied the dull glint of many eyes watching them from dim, shadowed places under the trees, Storm reached for her sword.

Elminster grunted and pitched himself heavily from his saddle. Then he reached up and laid gentle fingers on the wrist of her sword-arm. "Nay," he said softly, "'Tis more likely, far, they wanted ye to protect others from me."

Storm rolled her eyes. Smoothly she swung herself down from her saddle. "I shouldn't be here," she said. "Key or no key. This hopping from place to place, world to world, is neither safe nor wise."

Elminster grinned. "And coming to the magefair with me was? I've taken us this way home, jumping so often, to give the slip to any mages who might have followed us. Few have the breadth of mind to shift from one world to another as often as we have." The Old Mage patted her arm. "Thanks for thy patience, lass. 'Tis not long now before we'll be at ease, and ye can chat with a good friend."

As Elminster led the way on foot down an uneven path through the trees, bright morning dawned upon the old, unfamiliar forest. The rosy light seemed to make the Old Mage recall something. He turned and gestured behind them. Storm looked back in time to see their horses vanish. She looked at Elminster. He answered her wordless question only with a merry grin and headed back down the path again.

Holding her tongue, Storm followed. And she drew her sword, despite the Old Mage's words; knowing Elminster, this 'friend' could be a blue dragon—or worse.

The path led between two old, moss-covered stones. As they drew near, Elminster reached back and took Storm's hand. They stepped between the stones together, and the bard felt an an odd, tingling chill.

They were somewhere else again. Somewhere familiar. Storm knew almost at once that she was in Shadowdale.

Elminster let go of her hand and strode away, reaching into his robes for his pipe. Storm stood staring after him for a moment. Then, in two quick strides, she caught up to him. Setting a firm hand on his shoulder, the bard spun Elminster around.

"Not a step farther," she warned. "Not until you tell me just what's going on. Where are our horses? Why'd we have to ride across half of Faerun for the key, anyway? Can't this Duara teleport? And wh—"

Elminster laid a finger over her mouth and said, "The need for haste is past. I doubt anyone could have followed us through all the places I took us—not yet. Our mounts have preceded us to the Twisted Tower's stables. Come to my home. There ye'll meet a friend to us both: Lhaeo."

The Old Mage lit his pipe and said not a word more until they were strolling up the flagstone path to the door of his ramshackle stone tower. It opened at his approach, and he turned and said, "Put away thy blade, Storm, and be welcome."

As they went in, his scribe Lhaeo called from the kitchen, "Tea shortly, Old One!"

"For Storm, too," Elminster said softly. By some trick of magic, Lhaeo heard his master and called out, "Welcome, Lady Bard!"

"Hello, Lhaeo," Storm replied, looking at the Old Mage with amusement. Elminster was calmly shoving piles of papers onto the floor, emptying a chair for her to sit in. Dust curled up in thick tendrils. Muttering, he gestured, and it was gone.

"A mite dark in here for me to see beautiful lady guests," the Old Mage murmured, then reached out to touch a brass brazier. He made a popping sound, and flames flared up, casting a warm, dancing glow on the chair.

Elminster gestured with courtly grace, indicating that Storm should sit down. The bard stared at the brazier in puzzlement. "How does it burn, without any fuel?"

"Magic. Of course." Elminster turned away, raising yet another dust cloud on his foray through more piles of parchment.

"Of course." Storm reached out and tapped his shoulder.

"Elminster," she said coldly, "talk." Her tone held the sudden ring of steel.

The Old Mage seated himself calmly on thin air, puffed on his pipe, and grinned at her through the rising smoke. "Ye deserve to know, lass. Right, then: Duara was briefly an apprentice of mine. She dwells in Telflamm, these days, and joined the Harpers a summer back." He puffed his pipe, and a blue-green smoke ring rose slowly up into the low-ceilinged gloom overhead. "She can't use a teleport spell because she hasn't the power yet. Like all young, overeager mages, she took to adventuring to gain magic quickly—and unlike most magelings, came across a dragon hoard."

Another smoke ring rose up from the pipe. The Old Mage watched its drifting journey, nodded approvingly, and went on. "Er, the hoard had a dragon attached to it, of course, but that's another tale. Among the baubles, she found my key, so she sent word to me by caravan-letter that she had it and would bring it to the magefair if I was interested."

"Who are your mysterious foes, then? How did you lose the key?" Storm asked. "And why was Duara so dim as to send open word to you?"

Elminster shrugged. "She'd no idea anyone save me would be interested in the key—or even know what her letter was about. When I got her note, I used magic to farspeak with her, telling her I'd be coming to the fair. She told me that since sending the letter, she'd been attacked several times, twice found her tower ransacked, and even been threatened one night in her bedchamber by a mysterious whispering voice demanding the key."

Storm rolled her eyes. "So what is this key?"

"The key to this closet, of course," Elminster said calmly, reaching out a long arm into the dusty gloom behind him. The key gleamed in his hand as it slipped through a slyly smiling dragon head carved into the wall. Lines appeared in the stone around the small carving, outlining a door. It began to swing open by itself.

Elminster pulled the key out and waved it at her. "This

was stolen from me by an unscrupulous man, long ago, who was—very briefly, mind ye—my apprentice. He was an ambitious Calishite, I recall, named Raerlin. I suppose he ended up in the jaws of Duara's dragon."

"Well, what do you keep in there, that mages chase after the key?" Storm asked, looking at the closet's dusty door.

"Old spellbooks, picked up over the years while wandering the world," Elminster replied as the door swung wide. Storm saw an untidy pile of thick, moldering tomes.

Eerie green and white light flashed suddenly from behind her. As it lit up the Old Mage's face, Storm saw his look of surprise and whirled around, upsetting her chair.

The eerie light came from a flickering oval of flame. It hung upright in the air, in the middle of the tiny, cramped room. Its presence defied the mighty magics that guarded Elminster's tower, magics, Storm knew, that kept the place safe from the archmages of the evil Zhentarim, the Red Wizards of Thay, and worse. No one should have been able to open a gate into the tower.

But the oval of flame was, Storm decided, most certainly a gate. When the bard looked through the flickering magical doorway, she saw a long, stone-lined hall, stretching away into darkness. And something was moving in the gloomy passageway . . .

Elminster strode forward, frowning, hands weaving spells out of the air. "Impossible," he murmured.

A shadowy figure was walking slowly toward them, out of the darkness of that phantom hallway. The creature was tall and very thin. Its eyes were two cold, glittering points of light set in dark pits. As it came nearer, Storm could see that the robes it wore hung in tatters, eaten away by rot.

The bard's heart sank. This must be a lich, a wizard whose magic was so powerful that he lived on, beyond death. Few could fight a lich and hope to survive, few even among the ranks of the great archmages of Faerun.

The lich came still nearer, and Storm met its fell gaze, staring into the cold, flickering lights of its eyes. They danced in the empty sockets of its skeletal face, measuring her, and then turned from her contemptuously to Elminster.

"Death has come for you at last, Old Mage," the lich whispered, its hissing voice surprisingly loud. It was still far down the hallway.

"D'ye know how often I've heard those words? Every murderous fool in Faerun tries them on me at least once." Elminster raised an eyebrow. "Or in thy case, Raerlin, twice." With one hand he traced a glowing sign in the air.

The lich gave him a ghastly, gap-toothed smile and kept coming. Elminster's other eyebrow went up. His hands moved swiftly in several intricate gestures.

A barrier of shimmering radiance sprang into being across the mouth of the portal. Raerlin's hands moved in response, and the barrier burst into tiny motes of light that scattered like dancing sparks from a campfire, then winked out.

The lich's fleshless skull managed, somehow, to sneer. "You thought yourself very clever, duping my two servants at the magefair, Elminster," came that hissing whisper again, "but I am not so easily fooled or defeated."

The skull seemed to smile. "I was at the fair, too. Your blindness spell failed against me, of course, and you did not even see through my spell-disguise. Are such simple sorceries beyond your understanding now?"

From the kitchen, muted by its stout, closed door, came the sudden rising, incongruous shriek of Lhaeo's kettle coming to a boil.

Elminster's hands were moving again. Storm saw lines of crackling power form between his fingers before he cast forth a bolt at the lich. As the energy flashed away from his hands, it lit up his face in tints of growing worry.

The lich laughed hollowly as Elminster's bolt crackled around its desiccated form. Tiny lightnings spat and leaped around its body, but seemed unable to do any harm. The lich raised a bony hand and cast a spell of its own.

Storm looked back at Elminster in alarm—and saw one of the books in the open closet behind the Old Mage glow suddenly with the same green and white radiance as the flames of the lich's gate. And when she glared at the lich, its eyes glinted at her in triumph. Ghostly gray tendrils of force were moving from the undead mage, toward them both. Raerlin was very close now, only paces away from entering the room.

"Flee, Storm!" Elminster snapped. "I cannot protect thee in what will follow!" His hands were moving in another spell.

Storm shook her head, but stepped back out of the way. Shimmering light burst from the Old Mage's fingers, lancing out to encircle and destroy each reaching tendril in crackling fury. Yet the lich merely shrugged, and its bony fingertips wove another silent spell. The book in the open closet glowed again.

Storm saw a sheen of sweat on Elminster's forehead as his hand darted to his robes and drew forth some small talisman. Then the talisman was gone, vanished right from the Old Mage's hand. As if in reply, a red-glowing band of energy shot out from the lich's shoulders as it stepped over a toppled chair into Elminster's study. The ghostly magical arm reached menacingly forward.

A shield of shimmering, silver-blue force suddenly hung in the air in front of the Old Mage, guarding him. The red arm swung easily, almost lazily around it, reaching for, not Elminster, but the closet behind him.

The lich was reaching for the book, Storm realized, then lashed out at it. There was a sudden hissing shriek of horror from the portal, and the red glow rose around her.

The lich's spell-arm clawed at her, trying to hold her back. Leather was torn away, and Storm felt sudden, searing pain across her breast. Thin, dark ribbons of her own blood curled past her eyes, borne upon the energy of the lich's sorcerous arm as it enveloped her.

The Bard of Shadowdale set her teeth and struck backhanded with her magical blade, trying to free herself from the crimson band of force. There was a sudden flash and a roar. Sparks snapped and flew. The riven shards of her blade glinted brightly before Storm's eyes as she was flung back into a stack of dusty tomes. Blood ran into her eyes, and her breast felt like it was on fire.

Dimly Storm heard Elminster groan. Blinking furiously to clear her sight, she struggled to her feet. The Old Mage was crumpled to the floor, a thin beam of light from one out-flung hand reaching toward her. Behind him, the lich stood triumphant, outlined in a flaming crimson aura. Hands on hips, it laughed hollowly.

The light of Elminster's spell touched Storm, and she felt warm, fresh strength flowing into her. Her fingertips tingled, and the blood was suddenly gone from her eyes and brow.

The lich gestured sharply, and the red cloud around it became a forest of tendrils, overwhelming the darkening spell-shield over the Old Mage. As Storm watched, the shield crumbled and was gone—and the crimson force swirled around Elminster. He gestured weakly, then fell onto his face and lay still.

The blue-white energy of the Old Mage's last enchantment was drawn up into the red cloud. The mystic aura blazed brighter as the lich stepped over the Old Mage's body and strode toward the bard. Raerlin was draining Elminster's magic to power his own dark spells!

Another crimson arm lashed out from that cloud, smashing the bard aside with casual, brutal force. Storm was flung into another pile of books. She saw the red arm reaching in a leisurely manner for the tome inside the hidden room.

Storm got up from the tumbled heap of books as quickly as she could, panting, the smell of her own singed hair strong in her nostrils. Blood still trickle down her chest, and she still held a blackened, twisted sword-hilt in her hand. Taking a deep, shuddering breath, she flung the ruined blade at the lich and dove for the tome for which the creature had risked so much. Redness swirled around her, but the book was clenched tightly in her fingers.

Raerlin's voice rose into a hollow, fearful shriek as Storm clutched the book to her bloody chest. "Myrkul take you, wench!" the lich cried. "You'll ruin it!"

And at last Storm was sure of her course.

She tore at the pages with trembling fingers and thrust the crumpled scraps into the flames of Elminster's magical brazier. The fire flared, and the bard held the parchment in the rising flames, heedless of the searing pain in her hand.

Raerlin's magic struck. Red claws tugged and tore at her. Storm snarled and fought to hold her position, one arm crooked around the brazier. Flames licked greedily at the crumpled pages she held.

Storm felt hair being hauled out of her scalp, yanking her head back. Tears blinded her, and something—her own hair!—tightened around her throat, driven by the lich's magic. The Bard of Shadowdale set her teeth to hold back a scream as she hauled the book up, wrestling against the lich's dark sorcery with all the strength in her arms. And she thrust the tome into the brazier.

There was a hungry roar, and Storm was hurled away. She had a confused glimpse of flying bones and the brass brazier tumbling end over end, away from a rolling, motionless ball of bright flame. Then she crashed again into Elminster's chair with bruising force. Hair blinded her for a moment. Impatiently Storm raked it aside and stared at the ball of fire.

It hung a few feet above the floor of the study, roiling and crackling. At its heart, the blackening, still-glowing book was wreathed in many-colored flames. As she watched, the tome crumbled to ashes and was gone. Off to Storm's left, there was a hissing sound.

She turned time to see the lich's skull crumble to pieces. The red glow of Raerlin's magic flickered and faded away to nothing. In a moment, the lich was only so much eddying dust.

In the sudden silence, Storm closed weary eyes, wondering when her burned hands would stop trembling.

From somewhere to her right came a loud cough. The bard blinked her eyes open and tried to rise. Elminster was shaking his head as he got slowly up off the floor, patting at smoldering patches on his robes.

"I must not forget, lass," Elminster said with dignity, "to thank ye properly, at some future time, for once again saving my life."

Storm sputtered in sudden mirth, despite her pain. A moment later, they were laughing in each other's arms, eyes shining. As they shook together in a tight embrace, a door opened, spilling kitchen sounds into the devastated study. The sudden clatter of crockery was followed by Lhaeo's cheerful voice saying, "Tea's ready! You were making quite a racket in—" He sobered suddenly and blinked at the two singed and wounded friends. "Wh-what happened?"

Elminster pushed Storm away and waved his hands with incredible agility for one so old. An instant later, Storm found herself on her chair again, wearing a splendid gown. The raw pain in her chest and hands was gone. Across a round table set for tea, Elminster sat facing her, clad in splendid silken robes embroidered with dragons. He was smiling gently, his lit pipe ready in his hand.

"Nothing," the Old Mage said airily, "more than a visit between old friends."

As the tea-tray descended, Elminster winked at the bard. Storm shook her head, smiling helplessly.

ONE LAST DRINK

Christie Golden

First Lieutenant Rhynn Oriandis sat astride her white mount, guarding the main entrance gate to the town of Mistledale. As always, tonight the gate stood cheerfully open. The stone wall that encircled the two dozen or so buildings was breachable if a trespasser was determined, but sleepy Mistledale would hardly be worth the effort. There was only one major street, which wound haphazardly through the town.

It was the middle of Marpenoth. The wind that ruffled Rhynn's indigo hair had the bite of the winter to come. The breeze chilled the moon elf's white cheeks as well, but she was warm enough in her black leather armor and cloak. She felt the horse beneath her shiver. Moonmaid had no such protection, and as Rhynn was on a stationary patrol tonight the elderly mare didn't even have movement to warm her. Apologetically, Rhynn murmured comforting nonsense noises to the animal that had been her friend for the past fifteen years, then stroked the white neck with a gloved hand. Moonmaid whickered softly, craning her neck to glance back at her rider. Her eyes glistened in the moonlight, sparkling with what seemed like, to Rhynn at least, rueful humor.

"Don't look at me that way," the elf reprimanded in a teasing voice. "I don't like it out here either."

Moonmaid snorted as if in derision. Rhynn laughed, then grew somber as the mare, wearied by even that much effort, drooped her head almost to the cobblestones. Why did horses have to age so much faster than elves?

Rhynn had been one of the esteemed Riders of Mistledale for several decades. The bond these expertly trained soldiers shared with their white mounts was close; each Rider raised the horse from a foal, and no one else was permitted to ride the beast, save in emergencies, for the rest of the horse's life. When the animal was too old for further service, the beast received a final, bittersweet gift from its master. Tomorrow or next week—at any rate far too soon for Rhynn—it would be time for her to put an end to her mare's life, to kill with kindness and spare the beast the pains of old age. Then there would be a new foal, milky white, to train and love and eventually slay. Rhynn had been paired with many mounts in her time as a Rider. But that did not make the final ritual any easier.

Without warning, Moonmaid started violently, yanking on the bit and prancing. "Whoa, girl. Calm down," Rhynn soothed, her gentle hands comforting the mare somewhat. Moonmaid still trembled, and Rhynn glanced about to see what had so spooked the animal.

From a short distance away, a familiar figure gazed at her. "I'm sorry, Rhynn," came a honey-sweet, soft voice. "I didn't mean to startle Moonmaid."

"Don't worry, Jander. She's getting old and easy to surprise. And you have a knack for sneaking up on people." The latter was full of mock accusation, but Rhynn smiled warmly at Jander Sunstar, revealing her true feelings for her friend.

The gold elf was tall as the People went, and his bronze skin was complemented by shoulder-length, wheat-gold hair. He wore a cape carelessly fastened about his throat. It billowed open in the icy breeze, offering little protection from the chill night. His face was a white oval in the moonlight, but Rhynn could still distinguish his sweet smile. He seemed more than usually pleased to see her.

"I thought for certain you were going to be at the bardic competition tonight," Jander said.

Rhynn shrugged, making her leather armor creak. "So did I," she confessed. "But this one," she added, patting Moonmaid, "took a tumble a couple of days ago and isn't fit for anything other than a stationary patrol. Besides, Captain Theorn's volunteered for this duty for the past five years so that I could enjoy the music. It's time someone else took a turn."

Jander glanced around, his smile turning wry. "Oh, yes," he agreed mockingly, surveying the peaceful little cottages and farmsteads that comprised Mistledale. "One must protect the innocent in so criminal an environment."

Rhynn, however, didn't laugh. "Normally this patrol is nothing more than a gesture, but this year . . ." Her voice grew hard, and she unconsciously sat up straighter in the saddle. "You're a warrior by trade, Jander, so I suppose I can tell you. We found bodies this afternoon—two farmers and their child, hardly more than an infant. Their throats had been ripped out."

Jander's expression was difficult to read in the moonlight, and he turned his face away quickly. "Knifed?"

"No. It looked like they'd been savaged."

"Perhaps a wolf?"

Rhynn frowned, and her voice sharpened. "You're an elf. You ought to know better than that. Wolves are generally shy creatures, hunting to feed and protect their young. They don't even attack the livestock around here unless the winter is unusually harsh. It's not winter, not yet, and that girl wasn't slain for her flesh."

Jander laid a gentle hand on her arm. "That must have

been a terrible thing to discover. I'm so sorry."

Rhynn shook her head slowly. "We deal with drunken brawls, lost children, and stray sheep around here, Jander, not murderers. I'm just not used to it, that's all."

There was an awkward silence for a moment, then Jander cleared his throat. "Changing the subject a bit, I am glad I ran into you. I . . . I won't be seeing you after tonight. I'm leaving Mistledale."

Rhynn's beautiful face fell. "Oh, Jander, why?" Her eyes brightened with sudden hope. "Are you going back to Evermeet?"

Before she had met Jander, Rhynn had known of Evermeet, the land of the fair forests, the realm of magic, the true, paradisiacal home of all elves. It lay far to the west, a secluded island where only the People were welcomed. The evil dark elves—known as the drow—and elves of mixed blood were not permitted to tread those blessed shores. When Rhynn had learned that her friend had been born there, she was a little in awe of him. Jander had intimated that he was unable to return to the island for some reason. Now she hoped that, somehow, whatever ban that had been imposed upon him had been lifted.

But apparently such was not the case. Jander shook his head sadly. "No, not there. I would have liked to have had one last drink with you, First Lieutenant Rhynn Oriandis. I must content myself with a farewell here." His hand gripped her arm tightly. "I thank you for your friendship. I will never forget you. Sweet water and light laughter."

Without another word, he turned and strode off toward the Black Boar Inn, his cloak billowing about him. Rhynn opened her mouth to call after him, then closed it. Jander was obviously distressed about leaving, and she had no desire to embarrass him by prolonging the farewell. She herself was grieved to hear of his departure. She would miss the gold elf, with his wonderful tales, gentle humor, and sweet smile. Rhynn sighed, shifted in the saddle, and resumed her patrol.

The time passed with little to break the monotony. Many

dalesmen passed through the gates, calling out greetings. Rhynn stopped those she didn't recognize, searched them, and politely confiscated all weapons. No one protested; they knew their arms would be returned to them when they left the little village.

An hour or so after Jander's visit, Rhynn caught sight of a familiar figure clad in black leather armor walking toward her. Again, Moonmaid started, stepping about nervously, and again Rhynn gently calmed the mare. "There, there, girl," she said softly, her attention focused on the approaching man.

"Lieutenant Rhynn, I relieve you of your duty. From this moment, your orders are to enjoy yourself at the bardic competition." Captain Theorn planted his big hands on his hips and grinned up at her, teeth gleaming whitely in the dim light.

"But, Theorn . . . why? And where's your mount?"

His smile faltered. "Either Moonmaid's lameness is catching, or else they need to replace some cobbles on the streets. Snow Lady sprained a leg." As Rhynn opened her mouth to voice further concern, Theorn added reassuringly, "She'll be fine in the morning. I thought since this was a stationary patrol I'd do it on foot. Now, you go on ahead to the Black Boar."

Rhynn's delicate blue brows drew together in a puzzled frown. "Theorn, we went over all this three days ago."

"Are you telling me you don't want to go?"

"Certainly I want to go, but fair's fair, and—"

"That's an order, Lieutenant." Theorn's booming voice, normally so jovial, had gone suddenly cold.

Rhynn whipped her hand up into a salute. "Aye, Captain," she replied in a coolly efficient tone. Theorn's words stung her, but she obeyed. Rhynn "the Fair" was nothing if not an obedient soldier.

* * * * *

Jander sat at the bar with an untouched ale in front of him. His thoughts went back to Rhynn's grisly discoveries. Wolves, he had suggested. The elf snorted derisively to himself. Would to all the gods he was something as clean, as simple, as a wolf. Turning his attention to the crowded room, he surveyed the merry scene before him with sad silver eyes.

The Black Boar was lit dimly enough to be cozy, but not so dark as to be threatening. Smoky oil lamps hung from the rafters, and the fire at the end of the large taproom burned cheerfully. This was the stage area, such as it was. At the moment a slender wild elf was performing there on a hammered dulcimer. Delicate fingers flew as the musician used a small wooden spoon to coax melodies from the instrument's metal strings.

A black cat also watched the performer from his perch on the mantlepiece above the fire. This was Indigo, so named because his pelt was so black as to be almost blue; he was the tavern's mascot. He had, as always, hissed angrily at Jander when the gold elf had entered; now Jander reached out and calmed the animal's mind with a mental touch.

Beaming patrons, seated at ten tables and at the bar, listened attentively and applauded with gusto as the bard finished and took his bow. It was time for a break, and the wild elf and some of the other performers took the opportunity to wet their throats before the competition resumed. Jander continued to peruse the crowd.

Few of the patrons would pose a threat. There were a couple of possible brawlers, but they were weaponless save for their eating knives. Most of the crowd consisted of local farmers and musicians. Jander regarded the old man seated to his right at the bar. Too frail to be a warrior. The man had an air of quiet assurance about him, though. He could be a wizard, the elf decided.

"Uncle Pogg!" came a shrill youthful voice as a boy burst into the inn. Some heads turned, and a few people regarded the interloper curiously.

"Trevys!" cried the heavyset barkeep, his thick brown

eyebrows drawn together in a puzzled frown. "What in the name of—come here, lad!"

Breathlessly the shaggy-haired boy hastened to his uncle's side.

"Uncle, we found a Rider's horse, and Papa said I was to come here and tell you. He thinks we'd better get her back to her master, and—"

"Yes, yes. We can do that in the morning. Didn't your father remember that the competition was tonight?" Pogg sighed heavily, rolling his eyes. "No, Shomar wouldn't remember such things."

"But the Rider—"

"In the morning, Trevys. It's dark outside now, and I'm very, very busy."

The elderly man sitting next to Jander had watched the scene with amusement. Now he broke in. "Your uncle is right, Trevys. Here's something to take your mind off your troubles." He waved the slim, soft fingers of his right hand, and three glowing balls appeared over the boy's head. Trevys gasped, reaching hesitantly for the radiant orbs.

"Toss them up gently, and they'll float like snowflakes," the mage said, smiling. Enchanted by the lovely magical conjurations, Trevys obediently wandered into an unoccupied corner, bouncing the balls in front of him.

"Ah, to be so young and so easily amused," sighed Jander. The mage turned toward him, and the gold elf gazed deeply into the old man's pale blue eyes. "What is your name, good wizard?"

The man blinked, trying to tear his eyes away from Jander's intense gaze. "Pakar," he murmured at last, surrendering to the silent command the elf was issuing.

Jander took silent assessment of the man's powers. He's a strong magician, he noted to himself, but not quite strong enough to resist me. Aloud the elf said, "And I am Jander Sunstar. Should I need your skills someday, learned Pakar, I hope I may be able to call upon them."

Pakar stared, captivated. "Certainly."

The gold elf smiled. "Aluise, another drink for my

friend," he told the barmaid as she approached the bar to refill several mugs. The girl wasn't beautiful, but she had a full, shapely figure and impish, laughing eyes. A pert, tilted-up nose added to the impression of mischief. She winked amiably at Jander as he placed the coins on the bar and turned his attention back toward the stage.

The present performer was well worth his attention. His voice was sweet and pure, and the intricately carved harp cradled against his shoulder marked him as a bard of consequence. One, thought Jander, who had obviously traveled a long way. The bright yellow tunic, echoing the pale blond of his hair, and the rose hue of his breeches clearly marked the young man as an outsider. Folk in Mistledale dressed more soberly, especially at this time of year.

Jander's eyes narrowed. The singer wore something draped around his neck on a leather thong. It hung down into his tunic, out of sight, but the garment's top buttons were undone. The bard reached for a lower note on the harp, moving forward slightly to pluck the strings, and an object fastened on the end of the leather thong swung into view. Jander saw the object for only an instant before it disappeared back into the folds of the singer's clothing, but that was long enough.

It was a wooden disc, with no decorations marring its simple beauty, painted a rosy shade of pink. Jander knew the symbol well. That would explain the singer's clothes, too, hues of yellow and rose—

A painful, ironic joy rose in Jander's heart. The bard was a priest of Lathander Morninglord, the god that Jander had once followed. He wished desperately that the young priest had chosen someplace, anyplace, else to pass the evening. His presence at the inn would definitely cause a problem.

"For once I managed to sneak up on you," came Rhynn's teasing voice. Jander whipped around, startled, as she slipped into the empty seat on his left. Still clad in her black leather armor, sword at her side, she presented an odd picture as she laughed brightly at the gold elf's obvious surprise.

"Rhynn! What are you doing here? You're guarding the gate tonight!"

"Well, that's a wonderful way to greet a friend," she snapped, genuinely hurt. "I thought you'd be—"

"You can't stay here."

Rhynn crossed her arms over her chest. "Damned if I'll take orders from a civilian! This is a public house, and the only one who can order me out of here is Pogg. Besides, you owe me a drink, remember?"

"Will ye be takin' him up on the offer, Lieutenant?" Aluise queried, ever ready to pick up on a cue.

"Aye, Aluise, I'll have a glass of wine," the Rider decided, then added archly, "It's so nice to *linger* over a good wine, don't you agree?"

"Oh, aye. And what'll ye be drinkin', Master Jander?"

"Nothing, thank you," the gold elf replied. Aluise nodded and, armed with refilled mugs, turned to deliver them to their proper destinations.

Rhynn frowned, and Jander's heart began to sink. Did she suspect?

"That's right. You never do drink with me, do you? Something's going on," she said slowly, her indigo eyes searching Jander's face. "You're sorry to say good-bye when I'm on patrol, but when Theorn relieves me of duty and I show up here, you don't want to see me. What's happening, Jander? I'm not a fool."

He had to get her out of here, and swiftly, too. "Rhynn, please, trust me when I say leave here right now."

"One last drink, and I'll be on my way," Rhynn agreed. She smiled impishly. "I'll have it out of you by the time I'm done."

" 'Scuse me," came a small voice at her elbow. Rhynn glanced down to see Trevys peering up at her. The three glowing balls trailed languidly behind him in the air. "My Uncle Pogg said you was a Rider." Rhynn nodded. "We found a white horse. Papa says it's a Rider's mount. Might you be able to take her to her owner?"

"You must be mistaken," Rhynn replied. "All the Riders

would have been notified if one of ours had gone missing."

The boy looked distressed. "Please, miss. She's pure white, with a black leather saddle on, and—"

"A black leather saddle? Take me to her," said Rhynn, rising at once.

As she passed Jander, the gold elf hissed in her ear. "Please, just take the boy and go!"

Rhynn spun around, an angry retort on her lips, but Jander was gone. Thoroughly baffled, she grasped Trevys's small hand firmly and wound her way through the press of people.

She had almost reached the door when, abruptly, it banged open. Indigo yowled, his fur standing up, and dove for the shadows. Reacting instinctively, Rhynn pushed Trevys behind her and reached for the sword buckled on her hip. Trevys needed no further urging and fled like a young hare for the bar and Uncle Pogg.

From behind, a hand closed on Rhynn's upper arm with a cold, steely grip. "Stay quiet and pray they don't notice you." She didn't need to see the man holding her to know it was Jander. He pulled her backward toward a shadowy corner of the taproom.

A young man entered. He was a beautiful youth, with a full, thick head of copper-colored hair and a high, pale brow. Sensuous lips curved in a grin that housed a world of malice. The cut of his clothing bespoke wealth, although his shirt and breeches had seen better days and appeared rather antiquated in style.

Following him were two young women, a blond and a brunette, both human. They were as beautiful as he was handsome, but, as with the youth, an air of malevolence hung about them like a poisonous perfume. The two entered without the stranger's flamboyance and purposefully moved toward the back of the room. Keeping his eyes fixed on the crowd, which had grown silent and tense, the stranger shrugged out of his cloak, tossing the garment carelessly toward one of the wooden pegs in the wall. It caught, held, and swung slowly like a hanged man for a few seconds.

There were rust-colored patches on the fine linen shirt, and a few spots that were still freshly scarlet with newer blood. Again the Rider reached reflexively for her blade, and again, the gold elf prevented the movement with a painful pressure.

Gasps arose. Jander heard the grating sounds of benches being hastily kicked back and the frustrated yelps of those who, too late, remembered they had handed their weapons over to the Riders upon entering Mistledale. The elf glanced toward the bard and the mage.

The cleric of Lathander, fear and determination mingled on his face, had placed his harp down and was slowly starting to his feet. Pakar had flung his cloak aside and now rose to defend himself against one of the brutally beautiful women.

Jander narrowed his eyes and concentrated on sending the mage a mental command. If he could control him, prevent him from attacking, he might save his life. *All right, Pakar,* Jander thought, *it's time for you to—*

Jander's concentration shattered as Rhynn tried to squirm out of his grasp. He was distracted only for an instant, but it sufficed. Ignoring the unformed command from the gold elf, Pakar stuck his hands out, thumbs together. Flame erupted from his fingertips to singe his assailant, filling the inn with the scent of charred flesh. The fair-haired intruder yowled in pain, but she did not slow her attack. Delicate hands with inhumanly sharp nails ripped bloody furrows across Pakar's face and throat. The mage cried out and toppled to the floor, sending two of the chairs crashing down beside him.

The woman cried out, and her form shimmered, becoming nearly transparent, then reshaped itself into the likeness of a deep-chested gray wolf. She leaped onto the still-thrashing body of the mage and stopped his screaming with her sharp teeth. A pool of liquid crimson welled beneath the dying man's body, and the wolf-thing lapped thirstily, tail wagging slowly back and forth.

Jander was about to call the dark-haired woman's attention to the priest when he noticed that the young bard had resumed his seat. His right hand crept up to gingerly pat his breast, to reassure himself that the holy symbol of Lathander was safely hidden. Coward, thought Jander at first, then revised his opinion when he saw the determination in the bard's blue eyes. Not cowardice—wisdom. The priest was waiting until he had a better chance.

Jander allowed himself a thin smile. He should have expected no less from a priest of Lathander Morninglord.

In the time it had taken her colleague to slay the wizard, the other woman had already dispatched two of the biggest men in the Black Boar. As she sucked at the blood that pumped from the severed head of one of them, Jander realized that the room had fallen silent. Shock and terror had momentarily paralyzed the horrified crowd. That didn't last long, though.

One young man panicked and bolted for the door. The youth with the blood-spattered shirt caught him with unnatural ease, snapping the man's neck effortlessly. The body fell to the floor with a thud.

"Oh, you don't want to leave just yet." The newcomer smiled. "The party's just beginning."

At that moment, Theorn appeared in the doorway. Cries of relief rippled through the crowd, and Jander felt Rhynn twitch with a sudden spurt of hope. Swiftly, the gold elf clapped a hand over her mouth to prevent her crying out to her ally. The big captain of the Riders strode up to the stranger, who was watching the slaughter with amusement, and bowed. "What next, my lord Cassiar?"

"Can you smell them?" was the youth's response. Theorn swallowed hard, nodding eagerly. "A sweet, sweet scent," Cassiar continued. He reached up a hand and patted Theorn's bearded cheek in an oddly affectionate, yet utterly patronizing gesture. "Smile for me. There's a good fellow."

The captain's lips drew back in a horrible grin. Theorn's incisors had lengthened to almost three times their natural length.

Whimpers and cries arose from members of the crowd,

who cringed back. Jander felt a wave of pity. These were farmers and musicians, not wandering sorcerers or sellswords. He, Cassiar, Erith, and Marys were like wolves in a rabbit hutch.

"You must be famished," Cassiar continued. Again Theorn nodded. "Well, for your very first meal as one of us, you may take your pick." He waved a thin, pale hand expansively, brown eyes twinkling with malicious humor. Theorn's undead gaze, blazing now with an unnatural fire, settled on Rhynn.

Fear leaped in Jander's unbeating heart. "No, Cassiar. She's mine."

The master vampire pouted. "But Theorn wants her, and he's been *very* helpful."

"And I haven't? You and I have been together for over a century now. I've scouted out every town for you, found the best time and place for feeding, and covered your tracks when the slaughter was over." He paused, holding Cassiar's gaze. "Have I ever asked for a particular victim before?"

The petulant frown deepened. "No," Cassiar admitted.

"Give me this one, then."

Brown eyes narrowing, Cassiar asked, "Why her? Why now?"

Hoping he sounded convincing, Jander replied, "Because she's my kind. An elf." He brushed his chin across her dark hair. Rhynn cringed, fear rolling off her in a rank scent that the vampire could smell. "I find her attractive."

Cassiar continued to stare speculatively for a moment, then nodded once, curtly. "Very well. Enjoy her. In the meantime," Cassiar announced, raising his voice, "I understand there was a bardic competition taking place. By all means, let us continue with the festivities."

But the people were too terrified to comply. Members of the formerly happy gathering now stared stupidly, silently, while the blood of their dead soaked into the floorboards of the Black Boar. Cassiar frowned, annoyed at their lack of obedience, and gestured to Theorn.

The Rider tangled his gloved hands in the long, flowing

hair of the unfortunate woman nearest him—one of Pogg's barmaids—and yanked her head back. Jander felt Rhynn twist in his arms, but he kept his hold on her. With a guttural moan, Theorn bit clumsily at the exposed white throat, his teeth ripping, not piercing. Blood exploded, covering his face and the dying woman's chest and bodice. Theorn gulped hungrily, and Erith, the vampiress who had retained her human form, applauded.

Jander licked dry lips. He could smell the hot scent, and it pierced him painfully, reminding him that he hadn't feasted in a long time.

"Unless I get some music very soon," Cassiar warned, "everyone here will end up like her." He strode to the front of the room. The patrons moved back, frightened, clearing a place for him to sit. He did so. "You," Cassiar said to a half-elf who clutched her flute like a staff. "I think I'd like to hear *you*."

Trembling, the woman rose and made her way to the front. The priest made way for her. Jander opened his mouth to warn Cassiar about the young man's profession, but something made him hold his tongue. An idea, so daring it would have made him catch his breath had he still breathed, was beginning to form in the gold elf's brain.

The flutist's slim fingers shook badly, and her breathing was too shallow for performing. The sweet notes of the flute were fragile, hesitant, and Jander knew with a sick certainty what would happen next.

Cassiar frowned. "No! Boo! That won't do at all!" He leaped up to seize the hapless woman. A quick bite opened her wrist, and the vampire sucked at the spurting blood. Laughing, he turned his crimson mouth to Erith. "A fine red, with a delicate bouquet but a full, robust flavor!" Cassiar let the woman drop, not draining her, content with his sampling. Whimpering and clutching her ragged arm, she scuttled away.

Rhynn began to twitch again, but her movements were different this time. Speaking in Elvish, Jander hissed in her pointed ear, "Don't get sick. He'll notice you and make me rip your throat out. I don't want to do it, but I must obey him. If you'll be quiet, I'll take my hand away. Can I trust you?"

She nodded, and Jander, hoping desperately that she would keep her word, removed his hand. Rhynn gasped and shuddered, gulping in air. The elven vampire longed to hold her, to soothe her, but he knew she didn't desire such gestures from him now.

When Rhynn regained her composure, she hissed, "You're a traitor to your kind, Jander, and I hate you for it!"

Despite himself, Jander flinched from the insult. "No more than I hate myself," he whispered back softly, still speaking in his native tongue.

She glanced up at him, and he could see emotions warring on her delicate, lovely face. The priest was performing now. His voice was astoundingly steady, and his fingers caressed the strings of his instrument with assurance despite the fact that Death was a yard away, staring him in the face. Cassiar was pleased and made no move to interrupt the song.

"That bard's a priest," Jander whispered to Rhynn.

"Then why didn't he—"

"He's not a fool. He's biding his time."

"Are you going to kill him?"

Jander's look was angry now. "I am not what you think me to be, Rhynn the Fair. Wait until all the facts are in before you pass judgment upon me!" He paused, aware that his voice had risen slightly, and brought it back to a soft murmur. "I had not wanted you to be here, but perhaps it is best this way. I have an idea that could save at least some of the villagers."

"Why should I trust you?"

Why, indeed? He released his hold on her. "Go for your weapon if you wish. Or else trust me."

He half expected her to draw her sword. One hand moved toward the weapon, but at the last instant Rhynn clenched her fingers into a fist. Then, with a deliberate effort, she brought her hand down to her side. Jander permitted himself a slight smile.

The bard finished his song, and Cassiar applauded. When the rest of the room stayed silent, he craned his neck to look back at the silent crowd. Merciless brown eyes took in the scene: Pogg and Trevys huddled behind the bar; four corpses sprawled on the floor; the half-elf clutching her mangled hand and looking paler by the moment; the sated, smug vampiresses; the overturned tables; the slack-jawed men and women at the seven remaining tables, staring in terror.

"Come now," Cassiar chided. "Wasn't he wonderful? Don't you think you should clap for him?" The vampire threw back his head and laughed as the terrified crowd burst into frenzied applause. The bard bowed politely and returned to his seat.

Jander watched, knowing the next step of this grisly dance. Cassiar rose and began to peruse the crowd until he found a woman who struck his fancy. Jander's heart sank as he saw that it was Aluise.

"Well, aren't you the pretty thing," Cassiar said. He reached down and pulled her to her feet. "I like your eyes," he stated, heading toward the stairs. Aluise began to whimper, then suddenly shrieked and tried to pull free. The vampire lord paused halfway up the stairs, turned, and leveled his gaze at her. Aluise stared back. Her sobs turned to sniffles, then ceased. Cassiar glanced around, his eyes finding Theorn. He pointed a finger at the Rider.

"You've fed and won't be hungry for a while. You can guard the door." He grimaced a bit at the Rider's blood-matted beard. "You are a messy eater, aren't you? Well, put your helm on and no one'll notice. You're one of the militia. Remember that, and you'll be able to allay suspicions if anyone should come." He caught and held the new vampire's gaze. "No one enters. No one leaves."

"No one enters. No one leaves," Theorn repeated dutifully.

Cassiar turned to Erith and Marys. "Keep an eye on Jander, my dears. His heart's a little too soft for the sort of sport we enjoy."

"Aye, master," said Erith obediently, smiling a little. The wolf, Marys, whuffed. Cassiar continued up the stairs. Jander watched him go, hatred twisting his face.

Rhynn's voice interrupted his dark thoughts. "You won't get away with this. If any of the Riders notice that no one's on guard duty—"

"Theorn will send them off on some fruitless search," Jander interrupted harshly. "Your Riders won't know you're here until they stumble across your body tomorrow."

She flinched at the brutality in his voice, but Jander didn't soften his words. She had to see the true horror of the thing and join him if he was to accomplish what he wanted tonight.

"He'll take Aluise—in every way possible—and when he's done he'll throw her away. It won't be that long. Then he'll come down and everyone will be systematically killed and the place set aflame. We'll flee like the gods-cursed night things we are, and wait until the talk dies down. And then we'll go to another town, and we'll do it again. And *again*."

"Stop it."

"Only if you help me stop it."

"Excuse me," came a tentative voice. Jander glanced toward the speaker, startled to see that it was the young priest. *He's braver—or stupider—than I thought*, Jander noted to himself.

"May we tend to our wounded?" the priest asked.

Jander's face flooded with compassion. "By all means, care for your injured," he said, raising his voice slightly. Erith overheard him and lifted a ruby lip in a snarl.

"Cassiar's right. You are soft, elf," she hissed.

Jander growled. His eyes locked with hers, and she retreated a few steps, glancing over at her compatriot for support. Marys shrugged her massive wolf shoulders, unconcerned. Erith frowned, but ceased to protest. She kept her eyes on Jander, however, and snapped acidly, "Have it your way. Do your bit of good and busy yourself with the cattle. Cassiar will be down soon enough, and don't think I won't tell him."

Jander ignored her. "And clean up the floor," he told the priest. "The scent—" He broke off and turned away.

Confused, Rhynn queried, "Don't vampires like the smell?"

"Gods, Rider, are you blind?" he cried in Elvish. "I haven't tasted human blood since we met! Starve yourself for a month, then have someone lock *you* in a bakery. Perhaps you'll have some faint idea of what it's like! I haven't had so much as a rat in almost a week." The anger faded, and he made a halfhearted joke. "Pogg runs far too clean an inn."

"You do not feed," said the priest in perfect Elvish. Both Rhynn and Jander turned to stare at him. Few humans in Mistledale spoke Elvish. "You let us care for the wounded and even seem distressed by what is happening. You are not like the others. Why?"

Jander answered with a smile, also speaking in Elvish. "Of course a morninglord would know my tongue. Now you answer me, why have you not attacked us, priest?"

The young man's green eyes widened. At last he said, "I did not think I was so obvious. My name is Frajen. I have been a bard longer than I have been a priest, and the odds were hardly in my favor. I was waiting, watching you. Tell me, what keeps you from doing as your friends do?"

"My name is Jander Sunstar of Evermeet. I—"

A sharp hiss interrupted him. "Don't say things that I can't understand, elf," Erith snapped.

"Cassiar commands my movements, not my tongue. I'll speak my native language if I wish. Unless you want to force me to stop."

Erith knew the better part of valor and quieted. Jander returned his attention to Frajen, his voice gentling. "I followed your god, priest, and as long as I can remember the beauty of the morning, I will not willingly embrace evil. If you and Rhynn will trust me, we may be able to save lives here tonight."

Frajen nodded without hesitation. Slowly, Rhynn did likewise. Jander let himself relax. "Give me time to think. Frajen, be careful—keep your symbol well hidden and do not use any magic. Our kind can sense it. And tell Pogg to clean up the blood. It's becoming hard to resist."

The priest nodded and went to the innkeeper. Jander watched as Pogg brought in a bucket of water and three towels. He and Trevys wordlessly began to wipe at the puddles of red soaking into the floorboards while Frajen and Rhynn moved among the wounded. They recruited the rest of the patrons, more to keep the frightened people occupied than for the feeble assistance they could offer.

Jander glared at Marys and Erith, aware that they were still watching him. At first they were intent on watching the gold elf's every move, but the women were young and inexperienced, so he paid them little mind. Jander returned his attention to Frajen, and his eyes widened at what the priest was doing.

Frajen had gone to kneel beside Pogg and Trevys, ostensibly to help them clean the floor. To a casual observer, he did indeed seem to be doing that, holding onto the wooden pail with one hand and wiping at the bloody floor with a wet rag held in the other. Jander saw, however, that the morninglord's eyes were half closed and his lips moved slightly.

He was consecrating the water.

Why can I not sense the magic? Jander wondered fleetingly, then realized that creating holy water was nothing so arcane as magic, merely a holy blessing. Very clever, Frajen! he admitted silently.

The elf's gaze flickered to Erith and Marys. Erith was looking about for new amusement, and Marys, still in wolf form, lay curled up near the dead mage, though her eyes remained open and watchful. Soon, the two would notice what the priest was up to. Jander needed a distraction.

The odds would never be better—Jander had a trained soldier and a cleric on his side, and all three vampires nearby were newly undead. Cassiar would be dangerous, and deadly. Jander knew that he was not up to that confrontation, not in his present voracious and weakened state. But he had to try.

"No more," he said softly to himself. "No more. Aluise is the last."

He strode to the wall lined with wooden pegs and tore down the cloaks. The movement drew the attention of mortal and vampire alike. He felt their eyes on him, their tension, as they wondered what the strange gold-skinned vampire was going to do next. The cloak pegs were about nine inches long—just long enough for Jander's purposes. Grimly the elf splintered off several of them, glancing back over his shoulder to gauge the reactions of the vampiresses.

Marys had risen to all fours, and the hair on her neck was standing up. She began to growl softly. Erith's eyes narrowed. "Beware, elf," she began menacingly.

Jander glanced surreptitiously at Frajen. Imperceptibly, the priest inclined his blond head. The elven vampire glanced over at Rhynn, and he saw her expression harden into a mask of cold comprehension.

In one swift movement, Jander tossed a stake apiece to Rhynn and Frajen, keeping a third for himself. Erith rose as swiftly, the severed head tumbling from her lap and landing with a dull thump on the floor. Jander was no longer a fellow predator. He had crossed the line, and now, he was prey.

"Do it, Trevys!" Frajen cried.

The farm boy got to his feet and hurled the bucketful of bloody, blessed water directly into Erith's face. The sacred liquid acted like acid upon the vampiress's profane flesh. Her face melted, dripping like candle wax from a flame. Erith's wail was keen and sharp, and she clawed at her horribly disfigured, smoking face. She fell to the floor, no longer a thing of horrible beauty, merely a thing of horror.

Frajen cried Lathander's name as he lunged at Erith. He stabbed the writhing undead again and again in the chest. Her hands clutched and scratched at him, scoring his cheek, but the priest didn't falter. At last, he pressed the deadly point of wood deep into the vampiress's heart.

Marys, meanwhile, had leaped in deadly silence at

Rhynn. Not even Jander had fully appreciated how swiftly the beast could move, and as he watched her attack, he knew he would be unable to reach the Rider in time to shield her. Desperately he hurled the wooden dagger toward Marys's gray shape. The sharpened peg bit into the vampiress's hindquarters.

Marys arched in mid-leap, yelping from the sting of the wooden weapon, and landed heavily atop the Rider. Rhynn went down under the wolf's weight. Hot breath fanned her face, but before Marys could secure a deadly grip on the elfmaid's throat Jander was there. He twined his gold fingers into the thick ruff about the wolf's neck and yanked Marys's head back. Rhynn rallied, thrusting upward with the sharpened peg, plunging the wood deep into the wolf-thing's broad chest.

The vampiress's howl of outrage suddenly changed to a choked whimper. Blood flowed around the wood. Rhynn kept her hold, shoving ever deeper, grimacing only a little as Marys's blood dripped into her eye, stinging horribly. The Rider blinked it away. At last Marys ceased to struggle, and her weight pressed heavily down upon the slender elf woman.

Jander heaved the corpse aside. "Are you all right?" the vampire demanded.

Taking a shaky breath, Rhynn nodded and let Jander help her to her feet. Frajen stumbled over to them, covered with blood and breathing heavily.

"Jander," gasped the morninglord, "Pogg says there's a way out the back, through the cellar. May we go?"

"Of course. But you'd best hurry." Jander glanced up at the ceiling, toward the room where Cassiar was having his sport. "I'll get the third. See them to safety. The boy should go first. Be careful, Frajen."

Frajen smiled ever so slightly. "The blessing of Lathander be upon you, Jander Sunstar," he said softly, then turned to help Pogg and young Trevys with the trap door in the kitchen.

"I must go too," said Rhynn brusquely. She was every

inch the professional soldier now, and her face was hard and implacable. "I'm a Rider, and the villagers need me."

Jander smiled, but his silver eyes were sorrowful. "Of course, Rhynn. Hurry."

She nodded once, her blue eyes revealing no trace of softer emotions, and ran lithely to join Frajen.

The gold elf strode to the door, stooping to pick up one of the coat pegs, then heaved the oaken door open with a swift movement.

Instantly Theorn turned to him, indignant fury in his voice. "No one enters—"

"No one leaves," Jander finished smoothly, driving the makeshift stake home through the thick leather armor. "I'm not leaving."

Theorn made a small choking sound. Then, his chest heaving, he managed to bellow a single name. "Cassiar!"

His dying cry mingled with a sonorous chiming, and Jander realized that someone was ringing Mistledale's warning bell. The other Riders would be alerted. Jander only hoped there was enough time to complete the bloody task he had set for himself before they arrived. The elf whirled as Theorn's body fell against the door frame with a heavy thump.

A movement by the bar caught Jander's eye. He jumped, teeth bared, hissing. "It's me," came Frajen's reassuring voice as he climbed out of the trap door and closed it after himself. "Rhynn's taking care of the locals. I'm staying. You might need some help."

"No!" Jander cried. "You don't know what he is. You don't know what he'll—"

"What in the Nine Hells is going on!" shrieked a shrill, nervous voice. Elf and priest looked up to see a very angry Cassiar hastening down the stairs. He had removed his vest, and his open shirt fluttered as he ran. His copper hair was tousled. Except for the blood that had splashed on his bared chest, Cassiar looked more like an interrupted libertine than a vampire. "Who called for me? Jander, what's— Bane's black heart! Where is everyone?"

"They're gone, Cassiar," Jander said, suddenly laughing. "You'll not torture them, or anyone else, ever again. You die tonight, you bastard. And these—" he held up his golden hands "—are the instruments of your death."

Cassiar frowned. "Jander, stop it. You were wrong to let them go, and you'll be pun—What have you done to them?" he cried, catching sight of the bodies of the vampiresses.

Jander continued to grin savagely, exposing his fangs. Raw excitement was coursing through him, fueled by his anger and his driving hunger. "They are at peace."

Cassiar, full of wrath, turned upon the elven vampire. "On your knees!"

It was a ritual they had performed often before. Each time Jander had tried to thwart Cassiar, urge him to mercy or pity or outright defied him, the vampire lord would command the gold elf's obedience. And Jander, weeping tears of blood at his impotence, could not help but comply. He would kneel and bare his throat. Cassiar would then drink of his blood until he was satisfied his wayward slave had been sufficiently punished. For a vampire to be drained by another was excruciatingly painful, and Jander would be pathetically weak for several days.

Jander winced as he felt the force of Cassiar's will, but stood firm. Gritting his teeth, he growled, "You were a spoiled, arrogant little aristocrat when you breathed, and you're a spoiled, arrogant little aristocrat now. I'll obey you no longer."

Cassiar's face was flushed with fury. His elegant brows drew together over commanding, irresistible brown eyes. "Kneel!"

Jander could not hold out. Gasping in pain, he dropped to the wooden floor. But he still held out hope. Cassiar was angry now, and when he grew angry, he was careless.

"I have indulged you because you were a novelty," the vampire lord continued, moving to stand in front of the kneeling Jander. "But the novelty's gone."

Against his will, Jander reached a hand toward one of the makeshift stakes. He gritted his teeth, fighting to disobey the mental command, but his slim golden fingers curled around the piece of wood. Slowly Jander's hand moved closer to his breast, the tip of the wooden stake pointed toward his heart.

"Your hands are the instruments of *your* death, not mine," Cassiar gloated.

"No!" came a choked cry. Frajen shoved the holy symbol toward Cassiar's face. "In the name of Lathander Morning—"

Cassiar was an old vampire, far too powerful to be undone by the desperate actions of a young, inexperienced priest. He rolled his eyes and muttered, "Oh, please." With one pale hand, he reached out to pull the priest toward him. With the other he tore open Frajen's neck with a single swipe.

Jander cried aloud. Frajen's sweet voice would never again fill a room with music. The priest had allied with him. Now he was dead for the choice. In his mind's eye, the elf again saw the look of loathing upon Rhynn's face— she who had once called him friend—and the torn body of the little girl who had fallen victim to Cassiar at the farmhouse outside of town. He remembered Aluise's girlish laugh, choked now by her own blood. He saw the frightened, helpless townsfolk and musicians. And he had doomed them, and dozens like them, by aiding Cassiar on his rampages.

Cassiar had relaxed his will for an instant, his attention diverted from the gold elf to Frajen. Jander had a second or two where his will was his own, but he did not squander that precious blink of time in fighting.

Instead, he called for help; he summoned Indigo. From the shadows leaped the black cat, a silent shadow himself, launching his lithe frame with deadly intent toward Cassiar. Claws reached for the vampire lord's brown eyes and raked.

Cassiar shrieked as blood spewed from his damaged eyes. He groped frantically for the cat. Indigo continued to scratch and claw until Cassiar's own nails pierced the creature's sides. With a last frantic meow, the cat spasmed and died.

Blinded, Cassiar could no longer focus his compelling gaze upon Jander, and his power over his minion was suddenly diminished. Jander sprang for his master. The two vampires crashed into a table, sending goblets flying. Despite his blindness, Cassiar recovered swiftly. As Jander's mouth yawned open and descended to the vampire lord's throat, Cassiar heaved. He rolled over, pinning the slighter elf beneath him.

The elven vampire managed to get one arm up to protect his throat—and cried out as Cassiar's fangs sank deeply into his flesh. Teeth met in Jander's forearm, and Cassiar ripped away a chunk of meat. The elf dropped the wooden stake.

"You ungrateful wretch," the master vampire growled through blood-stained teeth. "One day of rest and I'll heal. Then I'll get another elf—maybe that little wench you're so fond of."

Not Rhynn. Never Rhynn. Jander would never permit another one of the People to be corrupted by Cassiar. His rage channeled the strength for one last attack, but Cassiar outweighed him. Laughing, the vampire lord opened his mouth, and his fangs drew nearer.

Abruptly Cassiar jerked upward, snarling. He spun around, clawing blindly at his shoulder. Jander could see that someone had fired an arrow at the vampire lord, but he didn't bother to seek out his would-be savior. Instead, he grabbed a stake and shoved it into Cassiar's breast.

Driven by Jander's hatred and his vampiric strength, the wooden weapon all but disappeared in the sudden redness that was the vampire lord's chest. Cassiar clawed ineffectually at Jander's face, then collapsed on top of the elf. Jander scrambled free, then looked up to see who his unexpected ally might be.

He wasn't really surprised to find a beautiful young woman wearing night-black leather armor leaning against the closed front door. Rhynn clutched her spent bow, but did not meet his eyes. She was staring over Jander's shoulder, her lip curled in a grimace of disgust. The elf followed her gaze.

Cassiar's body was beginning to decay with astonishing speed. The two elves watched in horrified fascination. The corpse rotted, then dried, then even the bones crumbled into fine dust.

Jander looked up at Rhynn. "The Riders?"

"Outside. With Theorn dead, I'm in charge." She hesitated, then continued. "I told them to wait."

Jander was puzzled, but did not press the point. Weakly he pointed toward the one remaining makeshift stake. He'd made five stakes; five stakes for five vampires.

"Finish it."

Rhynn shook her head slowly, her eyes never leaving his pale face. "You saved lives tonight. You've earned another chance."

He laughed harshly. "At what? What's left for me?"

"Evermeet."

"Don't mock me, Rhynn, not now."

"I'm not. You're free from him, Jander. You can travel anywhere you want now," she said, speaking with increasing urgency. She moved closer to him, hesitated, then stroked his cheek. "Maybe you can find someone who can cure you."

He smiled weakly, without humor. "Cure a vampire?"

"You haven't looked, so you don't know. Anyway, you don't deserve to die like they did." After a pause, she said, "You're hungry, so you'll need this." Rhynn rose, went unsteadily toward the door, and returned carrying a pail half full of deep wine-red fluid.

Jander shook his head. "I won't drink human blood."

"It's not. It's from—" her voice caught a little "—from my mare."

The elf's eyes widened. Now he saw her reddened eyes, the tracks of tears down her flushed cheeks. "You're a Rider and you—"

"When a mount grows old, it's the Rider's duty to kill it.

Moonmaid's time was here. One more day, maybe two, and I'd have had to . . ." She fixed Jander's silver eyes with her own. "Take it. Heal. Travel through the world and then back home to Evermeet. Fair's fair, Jander. You saved my life. Let me return the favor." She held out the pail and smiled weakly. "This time, the drink's on me."

The elven vampire hesitated. Only an elf could have understood how precious a place Evermeet was. Rhynn had seen past the monster to the elven part of him, had slain her beloved Moonmaid to help him return to what he had been. Was there really a chance for one as bloodied as he? Might there truly be, somewhere in the world, a wise man or woman who knew how to cure vampirism?

Slowly Jander sat up. Rhynn's strong arms reached to steady him as he carefully stretched out a hand for a discarded goblet.

"What is the year?" he asked suddenly. When Rhynn frowned at the curious question, he explained with a smile, "I forget, you know. It's been so long. . . ."

"As we reckon the year here in the Dales, eight hundred and ninety-two," Rhynn replied gently.

"Eight hundred and ninety-two," Jander repeated. "The year of my freedom." He nodded slightly. "One last drink." Then the cursed elf dipped the goblet into the bucket, saluted his friend, and raised the liquid to his lips.

THE BARGAIN

Elaine Cunningham

The one thing Arilyn Moonblade hated above all else was being followed.

"But how do you know someone's trailing you?" demanded Arilyn's companion, a nattily attired nobleman who picked his way delicately along the littered docks of Port Kir. "If you haven't actually seen or heard anything suspicious, how can you be so sure?"

With a frustrated sigh, Arilyn tucked a handful of her dark curls behind one pointed ear. How could she explain to Danilo Thann something that, to her, was both art and instinct? She just *knew*. There was a silent rhythm to stalking, a rhythm known only to the best hunters and rangers—and assassins.

"A wizard can sniff out magic," she said slowly, absently waving away an overeager merchant attempting to spray her with jasmine perfume. "And I believe a paladin can often sense when evil is near."

"Ah." Danilo's gray eyes warmed with understanding as he studied the distracted half-elf at his side. "I take it that patience, for lack of a better word, has an aura of its own."

Arilyn smiled without humor. "Something like that."

"Has this been going on long?"

She shrugged. "Since Imnescar."

"Since—" The nobleman broke off abruptly, then let out a long hiss of exasperation. "Arilyn, my dear, someone's been stalking us through two kingdoms, and you don't see fit to mention it? Never came up in conversation, is that it?"

"This is the first time we've been alone," Arilyn said, a trifle defensively.

Danilo glanced pointedly around the teeming marketplace. Beyond the docks the Sea of Swords gleamed silver in the waning light, the horizon touched with the last faint pink of sunset. Most of the merchants were busily folding their bright silk tents and rolling up the mats that had displayed pottery, crafts, and exotic produce. The crowds had not diminished, but evening shoppers generally had goods of a different nature in mind.

"We're alone, you say? How odd," Danilo mused. "I've often been alone with beautiful women, and things were never quite so hectic and noisy. Not initially, at any rate."

"You know what I mean," the half-elf said curtly. For many days, she'd had little opportunity to speak to Danilo in private. They'd arranged to travel with a merchant caravan en route from the northern trade city of Waterdeep to Calimport, its counterpart in the South. Merchants were the only northerners welcome in parts of Tethyr, and, swept along on the tide of commerce, Arilyn and Danilo had moved unquestioned through the southern lands. Today they were to begin their true mission.

Arilyn and Danilo had been sent by the Harpers—the self-appointed guardians of freedom and justice in Faerun— to bring a warning to Tethyr's ruling pasha. This was not an easy task, for Pasha Balik wanted nothing to do with "meddling northern barbarians." Repeatedly he'd refused Harper messengers or missives, and attempts to gain the ear of someone in his inner circle had also proved futile. Danilo had been charged with finding or creating a back door into the pasha's court; Arilyn's task was to keep the young nobleman alive during the process. Knowing Danilo as she did, Arilyn felt that her mission was sufficiently challenging without the added aggravation of an extra shadow.

Despite the new problems he or she presented, the half-elf had developed a certain grudging respect for her pursuer. Granted, tracking a merchant caravan along the major north-south trade road was no test of skill. Avoiding detection for so long was another matter. No other member of the company had realized they were being stalked, not even the powerful Harper mage at her side.

Arilyn cast a sidelong glance at Danilo, who was idly whistling the melody of an off-color ballad. Few who knew the young man might guess that he was either Harper or wizard. Danilo Thann was known as a dandy, an amateur mage whose spells comically misfired, a foppish dilettante with amusing pretensions toward bardhood. His self-satisfied smirk and extravagant attire bespoke wealth, ease, and privilege. In truth, Danilo cultivated that image. Prominently displayed on the amethyst silk of his jacket was the crest of a noble merchant family of the Northlands. His billowing trousers were tucked into impractical suede boots, and the voluminous sleeves of his silk shirt were embroidered with tiny runes in gold and violet threads. The nobleman's garments were loose and flowing, cut to mask his lean, powerful build, just as the sparkle of jewels on his sword's hilt distracted the eye from its keen and well-used edge. Danilo's facade made him an effective Harper agent, but it annoyed the Nine Hells out of Arilyn.

"It's getting late," she said abruptly. "Let's find a quiet place to plan our next move. Some food wouldn't hurt, either."

The nobleman's face lit up at the suggestion. "I know the very spot. Local color, and all that." He took Arilyn's arm and led her down a maze of alleys to a low wooden building that possessed all the charm of an abandoned warehouse.

"Local color, just as promised," Danilo said with enthusiasm as he swung open the door. He removed his plumed hat and tucked it under one arm, then patted his blond hair carefully into place as he beamed down at her. "Isn't this splendid?"

"This" was a tavern of sorts, a vast sprawling taproom that was anything but splendid. If the room were thoroughly swept and aired, it might qualify as squalid, Arilyn noted with distaste. The taproom was crowded with tables and booths, most of them filled. It was a local haunt, judging from the swarthy faces and the distinctive blue-purple robes of Tethyr's natives. The crowd comprised men of all ages and social classes. *Only* men, Arilyn noted, though a row of doors lining the north wall of the taproom suggested that women were not entirely absent from the establishment.

Danilo ushered Arilyn into the room. The patrons nearest the door studied the new arrivals, their faces betraying a mixture of interest and hostility. At one table, however, three well-dressed locals eyed Arilyn with speculation and began to argue.

"Ah, Lord Thann!" proclaimed a nasal voice. Arilyn turned to see a squat, dark-robed man waddling toward them, his pudgy hands outstretched in welcome.

Danilo greeted the innkeeper by name, inquired after the health of his wives and children, and requested his customary table. The man ushered them to a corner table—which was already occupied—and dismissed the lesser patrons with a few curt words in the local dialect. Beaming widely, the innkeeper wiped the table with the sleeve of his robe, promised them a wine fit for Pasha Balik himself, and hurried off.

"Is there one tavern in the world where you're a stranger?" Arilyn asked with a touch of asperity.

Danilo pursed his lips and considered the matter. Before he could speak, a blue-robed man approached their table.

"I am the servant of Akim Nadir," the man told Danilo, and he gestured toward one of the three men Arilyn had noted earlier. "My master wishes to purchase your woman."

Danilo placed a restraining hand on Arilyn's arm. "Let me handle this," he said. Turning to the servant, he asked, "How much does your master offer?"

"Twenty gold."

"Danilo, this is no time for foolishness—"

"I quite agree," Danilo broke in. He reached across the table and patted her sword hand as if consoling her. "You're worth several times that amount, I should say."

"Let go of my wrist and get rid of this man," she said through clenched teeth.

"And miss a chance to hone my bargaining skills?"

"Twenty-five?" the servant suggested.

Danilo shook his head, his face alight with mischief. "Eyes that shame the desert sky," he noted in a wheedling tone.

"Thirty gold. No more."

"Look at her," Danilo persisted, deftly swiveling in his chair to move his shins beyond the reach of the half-elf's booted feet. "Have you even seen such skin? Moonlight upon pearls! A hundred gold would be a bargain."

"Perhaps fifty," the servant allowed. "Has she any special talents?"

"Well, she's rather good with that sword of hers," Danilo said thoughtfully, "though I doubt that's what you had in mind."

"That's it." Arilyn jerked her hand free of Danilo's grasp. Rising to her feet, she glared down at the servant. "Take your business elsewhere."

The man blinked, not comprehending. A woman unveiled in such a place was surely for sale. "To whom should I make an offer?" he asked, his eyes darting about the room.

Arilyn drew her sword. "To this."

Light glinted off the ancient moonblade, pooling in the elven runes carved down its length. The man's black eyes widened and he stepped backward so abruptly that he stumbled over the hem of his robe. The matter settled to her satisfaction, Arilyn sheathed her sword and resumed her seat.

Danilo shook his head. "Your bartering technique could use a little work."

"Didn't it occur to you that he was serious?" Arilyn demanded, stabbing a finger in the direction of the retreating servant. "The saying here is 'Barter met is bargain sealed.' What would you have done if he'd met your price?"

"I'd've asked him to throw a couple of camels into the deal."

"Cam—" Arilyn broke off, dropping her head forward. "All right, I'll play: why camels?"

"For my mother, of course. The redoubtable Lady Cassandra bid me acquire something interesting for her stables," Danilo replied mildly.

Arilyn fought against laughter, but the mental image of the elegant Waterdhavian noblewoman astride a camel was too much for her.

"You really ought to laugh more often. It becomes you. Ah, thank you," Danilo said as the innkeeper appeared at their table with two large goblets. The nobleman sipped at his wine and praised it extravagantly.

"The grapes are grown on my own lands," the innkeeper said modestly. "I'm honored that you are pleased."

"More than pleased," Danilo said. "My family deals in fine wines, you know. Perhaps if I were to join your guild, I could carry your wine—and your fame—to the North."

The innkeeper's smile faded abruptly. "I would like that very much, Lord Thann, but I doubt it will be possible. You will excuse me." He bowed quickly and scurried away.

"What was all that about?" Arilyn asked warily.

Danilo picked a bit of cork out of his wine. "You may have noticed that this establishment is not the sort of place I usually frequent. It is, however, a meeting place for guildmasters. Didn't you see the sign outside? The Guilded Dagger? Terrible pun, but there you have it."

"Yes? So?"

"The guilds control every aspect of trade in Tethyr, which makes them rather influential. If Pasha Balik refuses to give the Harpers an audience, perhaps he'd listen to a representative from one of the local guilds." Danilo took another sip of wine. "Namely, me."

Arilyn choked on her wine and set down her goblet with a thunk. "Danilo, the guilds are plotting to overthrow Pasha Balik. We're here to *warn* him, not join the other side."

"Guild membership would give me access to the pasha's court," Danilo argued. "Moreover, as a guild insider, I could find evidence that would force Balik to listen to us."

It wasn't a bad plan, but Arilyn was in no mood to be generous. "Which guild would you join? The procurers?" she asked in an acid tone.

"Now, there's a thought," Danilo said with a grin. "Come now, Arilyn. Don't tell me you're upset over a little harmless bartering. My asking price was too low—is that it?"

"It's not easy to get into the guilds here," the half-elf said, ignoring his teasing. "Membership is passed down from father to son, or earned through apprenticeship. You could buy your way in, I suppose, but these people are more likely to be impressed by a clever bargain than by a pile of gold and jewels. Do you have a plan?"

"Not yet," Danilo admitted ruefully. "I'll think of something, though."

"Another thing." Arilyn leaned in closer and spoke with quiet urgency. "If the guilds learn you're a Harper, they'll assume you're here to meddle—"

"A reasonable assumption," he broke in.

"And you'll be as good as dead. I say keep away from them."

"Guild rule was attempted once in Waterdeep," Danilo reminded her, his voice suddenly serious. "It was, to put it mildly, a disaster. Pasha Balik might have his faults, but he's the strongest leader in Tethyr and the best hedge against political chaos in the area. If I have to go through the guilds to get the pasha's ear, I'll do it."

As Arilyn nodded reluctant agreement to Danilo's plan, a grim possibility occurred to her. Perhaps guilds allied against Balik—which would include the powerful Assassins Guild—had already discovered their Harper identity. That would explain the mysterious pursuer and his skill at stalking; southern assassins were peerless killers trained at a secret college known as the School of Stealth. It also meant that the Guilded Dagger was the most dangerous spot in Port Kir for them to be lingering over a glass of wine.

"Let's get out of here," she murmured, and quickly explained her fears. The nobleman was silent for a moment, then reached across the table and covered one of her hands with his.

"Arilyn, we're not known as Harpers. If someone is indeed watching you, it's undoubtedly due to your unfortunate reputation as—"

"Point taken," interrupted the half-elf quietly. Although she had worked for the Harpers for years, she had just recently joined their ranks and few who knew of her would suspect her affiliation. She was known as an incomparable sword-for-hire, an adventurer, and an assassin. Given the political unrest in the area, the sudden appearance of a known assassin would be cause for concern. Any number of beleaguered rulers might want her watched.

Danilo gave her hand a quick, sympathetic squeeze and then nodded toward the entrance. "Who do you suppose that man is?"

Grateful for the change of subject, Arilyn glanced at the front door in time to see the innkeeper fold himself into a deep bow. The recipient of this courtesy was a lone man whose dark purple robes were drawn close against the sudden chill of the night. Light glinted off a golden ring on his outstretched hand. "I wouldn't know. Does it matter?" she asked.

"It might. Look where he's being seated."

The half-elf watched as the newcomer was escorted to the taproom's finest curtained booth. Just before the innkeeper drew the gaudy drapes, Arilyn caught sight of the newcomer's face. He was a beardless lad, probably no more than fourteen or fifteen, and he returned Arilyn's scrutiny with an intensity remarkable for a boy his age.

"Here we go again," Danilo observed calmly. Arilyn followed the line of his gaze and immediately forgot about the youth. An enormous bearded man approached their table, his black mustache twisted with a sneer of challenge.

"You wish to barter with your sword, eh?" taunted the man. He drew a scimitar, its broad, curved blade serrated along the inner edge, and leered down at Arilyn. "Let us make a bargain, elfwoman."

"You know the ordinances, Farig!" the innkeeper scolded, rushing up to the table. He flapped his hands at the brute as if he were shooing chickens. "Outside, outside."

As Arilyn rose from the table, she murmured to Danilo, "You're the one who likes to barter. Do you want to take this one?"

Danilo brightened. "In a manner of speaking, yes. You handle the sword end of the deal, though." The nobleman removed a large gold-and-amethyst ring from his finger and held it aloft. "I'll wager this that the elfwoman wins," he said loudly. There was a rumble of laughter, and soon a small crowd circled Danilo's table, arguing odds and laying bets.

The half-elf suppressed a smile as she followed the tavern bully out into the street. She knew what Danilo would bet against his ring and her skill: full guild membership.

The Guilded Dagger emptied as its patron followed the combatants outside. Arilyn noted that the strange, intense lad was among the crowd. To her eyes, he looked troubled and oddly disappointed.

But other, more pressing matters demanded her attention, so Arilyn turned back to her opponent. Drawing her sword, she held it before her in a defensive stance. If at all possible, she wouldn't harm more than the man's pride.

The big man shrugged off his outer robe, baring massive arms and a thick torso gone soft around the middle. "What price does your sword require?" he asked, clearly enjoying himself. "Do I let it draw first blood?" The crowd laughed at his jest.

"Offer the sword a new scabbard and get on with it, Farig!" one man called. "Why tire the elfwoman in battle?"

The answering chorus of bawdy laughter abruptly faded

when the fighters crossed swords. For several moments Arilyn simply parried the blows, giving Danilo the chance to raise the stakes on his wager. It proved to be good strategy; before long a sheen of perspiration glistened on the man's dark skin, and his breathing grew labored. When his confident sneer wavered and disappeared, a murmur began to ripple through the crowd.

The game forgotten, Farig put his full strength behind each slash of the scimitar. The bloodlust in his eyes proclaimed that Arilyn was no longer a prize to be won, but an enemy who must die. With a fierce yell, the southerner delivered a backhanded blow, striking Arilyn's forearm with the dull edge of the scimitar. The force of the blow jarred her to the bone and knocked her sword from her numbed hand. Farig shouted again, this time in triumph, as he raised the scimitar aloft for a final strike.

The nimble half-elf ducked and rolled clear of the descending blade. Drawing a dagger from her boot, she threw herself upward. Her knife drove hard under her opponent's ribs and found his heart. Arilyn felt more than heard the faint metallic click as her steel met another blade. With a puzzled frown, she yanked her knife free. The huge man fell face forward into the street.

From the corner of her eye, Arilyn noted that Danilo had become the center of an arguing, gesticulating crowd. Unnoticed by the tavern patrons, Arilyn stooped over Farig's body. As she had suspected, a knife protruded from between his third and fourth ribs. She pulled it out, and her eyes widened. Carved on the handle was a curving Calishite rune. Arilyn had seen the symbol before. It was a badge of pride, carved into each weapon owned by an assassin trained at the School of Stealth. And as she turned the knife over, she found many smaller markings scored into the handle, one for each person the knife's owner had killed.

Arilyn tucked the weapon away in her boot, and her eyes scanned the dark streets. Although there was no sign of her mysterious "rescuer," she could sense that he was near,

Determined to catch him, Arilyn hurried to Danilo's side and grabbed his arm.

"Let's go."

"Soon," he said in a smug tone. "I'm bartering for guild membership. Given time, I might even get them to throw in those camels for Lady Cassandra."

"Now," she insisted, giving him a sharp tug.

His lazy smile never faltered as he shook his head and peeled her fingers from his arm. Holding her hand in both of his own, he kissed her palm then briefly rested it against his heart. The courtly gesture was a pointed one; through the fabric of the dandy's jacket, Arilyn felt the outline of his concealed Harper pin. "Remember why we're here," he murmured.

By the time Danilo had been sworn into the Wine Merchants Guild of Tethyr and had brought several rounds of drinks for his fellow businessmen, a frustrated Arilyn had discarded any thought of pursuing the mysterious man who had stalked her, then tried to save her. Not until the Guilded Dagger's last patron staggered out into the night did she have the chance to tell her story. Danilo agreed that they should try to catch her pursuer with as much discretion as possible, to avoid compromising their larger task. The best way to do that, assuming the skilled tracker would still be on Arilyn's trail, would be to draw him away from the crowds of Port Kir.

The Harpers quickly retraced their steps to the camp their caravan had made on the city's outskirts. They made their excuses to the caravan leader, claimed their horses, and set off south through the Forest of Tethir.

The night was dark, and the pale sliver of moon did little to dispel the deep gloom of the forest trail. Even though the road was wide enough to allow merchant wagons to pass, ancient trees met overhead in a thick canopy. On either side of the trail grew a tangle of vines and underbrush. Merchant caravans usually braved the Forest of Tethir only by day, to avoid the bandits and wild beasts that prowled the forest after nightfall. Knowing this, the Harpers rode without speaking and kept alert for the smallest signs of danger.

Daybreak was near when the half-elf finally caught sight of her pursuer. Feeling secure behind his leafy screen, the assassin had ventured close enough for Arilyn to get a look at him.

More precisely, the half-elf's night vision detected the pursuer's body heat. By the complex pattern of colored light cast by the horse and rider, Arilyn could tell that the assassin was lithe and slender, with a proud bearing. His stallion—Amnian, by the looks of him—seemed to share his rider's haughtiness as he moved on cloth-wrapped hooves through the shadowy forest. The night vision revealed other details, too—the thickness of the man's clothes, the length of his hair. Even the small knife clenched in the assassin's hand glowed with his borrowed warmth, cooling to bluish tones near its sharp tip.

The knife puzzled Arilyn. Why would this man try to save her at the tavern, only to attack her now? Determined to snare the elusive stranger and get some answers, she reached into a saddlebag and withdrew a small throwing knife attached to a coil of unbreakable spider-silk thread. At one end of the thin rope was a small noose; this she slipped over the pommel of her saddle. A quick tug secured the rope.

The tethered knife at the ready, Arilyn unpacked a small, round iron disk no bigger than the palm of her hand. After adjusting the tiny shield's strap over her left hand, she hefted the small throwing knife to remind her muscles of its weight and balance. Her movements were so small and unobtrusive that even Danilo did not note her preparations.

From the corner of her eye, Arilyn saw her pursuer slip down from his horse. Bent low, he crept silently toward her through the thick, night-shrouded underbrush. When only a thin strip of foliage separated him from the path, he straightened to his full height and readied his own blade for the attack. Arilyn, too, tensed in readiness.

The assassin's throw went wide, spinning toward the

flank of Danilo's horse. Arilyn flung out her left hand, and the knife glanced harmlessly off the tiny shield in her palm. In the same instant, she hurled her own blade. It whizzed toward its target, the thin cord streaming after it. The half-elf's keen ears heard the silken whisper of the uncoiling thread, the rustle of leaves parted by the missile, and then nothing.

"I say! What's going—"

Danilo's startled outburst was cut short by the fierce expression on his companion's face. Arilyn motioned for the nobleman to stay put, then swung down from her horse.

The half-elf was certain her knife had hit its target, yet her victim had not cried out. Considering the weapon she'd used, that was strange indeed. The knife was cunningly designed so that the tip would spread upon impact into four barbed prongs. The resulting wound was shallow, but it was painful and exceedingly messy. Nearly impossible to withdraw, the knife was an effective way to stop and snare someone at close range.

Arilyn silently parted the curtain of vines and took a look at her attacker. He stood in a small clearing, his back toward her. His head was turned in profile as he tugged at the weapon embedded in his hip. From the wound's location, Arilyn could guess why his throw had gone wide; he must have spun around too far on his follow-through. He'd have to learn not to do that, if he intended to hit anything.

As Arilyn watched, the assassin abandoned his attempt to withdraw the pronged blade. Drawing a small hunting knife, he began sawing frantically at the spider-silk cord. Her gaze shifted upward to his face, and she recoiled in surprise. Her captive was the lad she'd seen back at the tavern.

The boy had the deep black eyes, prominent hooked nose, and swarthy skin common to natives of neighboring Calimshan. Since leaving the Gilded Dagger, he'd discarded his robes. Now he was clad in loose-fitting silk garments of a dull, indeterminate color, clothes that struck Arilyn as being a uniform of sorts. If the young assassin was a student at the School of Stealth, his skillful stalking and his stoic acceptance of pain would be a credit to his masters. His aim could use work, though.

Arilyn slipped silently into the small clearing. Moving directly behind the boy, she tapped him on the shoulder. Startled, he whirled toward her, dropping the knife in his surprise. A flick of Arilyn's booted foot sent the weapon flying into the underbrush. Shock claimed the boy's face for only an instant, then his young features firmed into a grim mask.

"Do you have a name?" Arilyn asked in a calm tone.

Her question took the boy by surprise. "Hasheth," he answered, before he could think the better of it. He glared at her with a mixture of youthful bravado and fierce pride. It would seem, Arilyn noted wryly, that I've snared a small hawk.

"That blade has to come out," she said. Even in the faint moonlight, she could see Hasheth blanch. A sympathetic smile curved her lips. "It's not as bad as you'd think. A hidden device on the handle releases the barbs, and they fold up as the knife withdraws. There is no more pain than any other shallow wound would cause." She paused and raised one eyebrow. "They do teach you to withstand pain at the School of Stealth?"

"Of course," he responded indignantly.

So she was right about the boy, Arilyn mused. He was a student assassin. She stood and took a step forward. "You'll have to turn around," she suggested. The boy drew back from her.

"No man turns his back on an enemy," Hasheth proclaimed.

"Really." Arilyn folded her arms. "In that case you'd better prepare to walk back to the School of Stealth. You'll never sit on a horse with a knife in your—"

"Enough!" The lad silenced her with an imperious gesture. Pride and pain fought for dominance of his dark face. Finally he turned, averting his eyes. "Quickly," he muttered from between gritted teeth. "I have not all night to waste."

"Have a few other assassinations lined up, do you?"

Danilo asked cheerfully as he strode into the clearing.

"Didn't I tell you to wait?" Arilyn asked.

"Sorry," Danilo responded without a touch of repentance. "I would have died of curiosity. Let's have a look at your would-be assassin, shall we?" The nobleman drew a bit of flint from the bag that hung at his waist and muttered an arcane phrase. His spell was rewarded with a flash of light, and a small campfire appeared in the clearing's center.

"I say, that must have stung," Danilo said as he eyed the boy's messy wound.

Hasheth's black eyes swept over the nobleman's silken attire and expression of prissy dismay. The lad sniffed and he turned aside, dismissing Danilo as one unworthy of notice or comment. "The knife?" Hasheth reminded Arilyn.

The half-elf selected a slender pick from the small tool pouch at her belt. She slid it into a hidden opening on the knife's elaborate handle. When her keen ears heard the tiny click, she pulled the blade free. The boy's only response was a quick intake of breath.

Danilo made an exaggerated show of sympathy, then took a vial from his leather bag and handed it to the boy. "A healing potion," the nobleman explained in response to Hasheth's suspicious glare.

"I have no use for your barbarian sorcery," the would-be assassin said with contempt.

"Ordinarily I'd consider that a mark in your favor," Arilyn told the boy. She eyed him sternly and ordered him to drink up. After one final suspicious glance at Danilo, the young assassin complied. The bleeding slowed, and color began to return to his face.

Arilyn folded her arms across her chest. "You've been following me since Imnescar. Why?"

"I do not know what you're talking about," he said flatly.

She drew the assassin's blade from her boot and held it out. "Maybe you'd like to explain why you killed that thug at the tavern."

"You speak nonsense," Hasheth said with scorn. "That is the knife I threw at you just now."

"No, it isn't," Danilo said, producing an identical knife from the bag at his waist. "I picked up your knife before I strolled over. By the way, have you any idea how close you came to skewering my horse?"

Arilyn took the knife from the mage and studied the blades. Both were carved with the School of Stealth's mark, but the weapons differed subtly in weight and balance. She flipped the knives over. The one that had killed the tavern fighter was scored with dozens of small carvings, while Hasheth's was smooth and unblemished. If the unmarked knife told a true story, the young assassin had not killed before.

The half-elf looked up at Danilo. "There are two assassins," she said quietly.

"Oh, marvelous," the nobleman replied wryly. "I'm traveling with the most popular woman in Tethyr."

She ignored him and turned to Hasheth. "Where's your partner?"

"I have none," he said. "If you met another assassin this night, what of it? Assassins are common enough around taverns."

"But knives like this are not," Arilyn persisted. "Someone from the School of Stealth wanted to keep me alive back at the tavern. Why?"

"That I cannot tell you, but I owe him a debt," Hasheth said bluntly. "If you had died at the hands of that drunken oaf, I would have been cheated of my sand-hue sash."

Arilyn and Danilo exchanged a puzzled look. "You're talking nonsense," the half-elf observed derisively, hoping to draw more information from the boy.

Hasheth's eyes flashed as he took Arilyn's bait. "Ignorant barbarian! I don't know how northern assassins assess merit, but here each level of skill is marked by a different color sash. To advance, one must stalk and slay an assassin of the next level. His rank then becomes yours. You were my assignment, of course."

Only Danilo saw the stricken look that flashed briefly into Arilyn's eyes. The half-elf had long ago earned the reputation of an assassin, a reputation that had proved as dangerous as it was undeserved. Arilyn had worked long and hard to rise above her dark past, only to be confronted with it time and time again.

"No offense, Hasheth," Danilo drawled, "but did it ever occur to you that you might have skipped over a few levels here?"

"That is absurd," Hasheth said haughtily. "The school's masters would not dare mock me in that manner."

"They wouldn't dare, eh?" A reflective look crossed Arilyn's face. "Where do you hail from, Hasheth?"

"My home is in Zazesspur, if that is what you mean."

"But you have the look of a Calishite," she noted. "Perhaps your mother was from Calimport?"

"Is this a state dinner, that we make polite conversation?" Hasheth asked sharply. "I am your prisoner. Kill me if you will, but don't trouble me with your woman's chatter."

"Charming kid," Danilo murmured. "Nice of him to suggest such an attractive option. Can we take him up on it?"

Arilyn shook her head. "Hasheth will ride with us to Zazesspur." It was hard to miss the relief in the boy's black eyes. "Sorry, Hasheth, but you'll have to find some other way to earn your sash."

"A wise man knows when the battle is lost," the boy agreed.

Danilo regarded their captive warily, noting the sly twist to his lips and the smooth insincerity of his tone. His gaze shifted back to Arilyn. Her lovely face was inscrutable, but she was obviously up to something. Since Danilo had no idea what her plan might be, he had little choice but to play along. He did not have to be happy about it, though.

"Marvelous," he muttered, just loud enough for Arilyn's elven ears to pick up. "We've adopted a pet adder."

"If you are determined to reach Zazesspur," Hasheth said to Arilyn, "it would be wise to keep riding. The Forest of Tethir soon gives way to the Starspire Mountains. The road itself follows a pass between these mountains, a wasteland as hot and barren as any desert. In the heat of day your northern skin would peel like that of a molting snake," he said with relish.

"Charming kid," Danilo repeated.

"Still, he's got a point," Arilyn commented. "The sun will rise within the hour. If we press on we should get through the pass before highsun."

The dandy sighed deeply. "Can't we at least stop here long enough for some breakfast? I'll cook. We've already got a campfire."

Arilyn agreed reluctantly, and the trio settled down around Danilo's fire. The nobleman began to rummage in his bag, drawing forth a small cookpot, a tightly covered dish of salted fish, a package of dried mushrooms, a package of herbs, a large silver flask of water, and another containing a dry cooking wine. Hasheth watched agape as each item appeared from the small sack.

"It's magic," Danilo explained as he deftly combined the ingredients. "The bag holds much more than appearances would indicate."

The young assassin quickly masked his astonishment. "No porcelain? No linens, no candelabra? You have adapted well to the rigors of travel, I see," he noted with keen sarcasm.

"I try to keep a civilized touch," Danilo said mildly. "Under the circumstances, that might not be easy."

Arilyn caught the underlying warning in her companion's voice. "Do you still have any of that coffee, Dan?" she asked quickly.

Hasheth brightened at the mention of the ubiquitous southern beverage. "I would be happy to prepare it. No northerner has the ability to brew a decent cup."

"Such a gracious offer," Danilo said dryly. He rummaged in his bag again, found an oddly shaped covered pot and a package of ground coffee beans, then tossed them to the boy. Hasheth took up the water flask and busied himself with the task.

When the coffee was ready, Hasheth filled Arilyn's mug and handed it to her with a courtly bow. Then, almost as an afterthought, he poured another cup for Danilo. Coffee was not widely known in the northern lands, but Arilyn had grown quite fond of it during their travels southward. Hasheth's offering was thick, black, and syrupy, identical to the coffee she had tasted in a dozen Amnian bazaars. She inhaled deeply, and her sharp elven senses picked up a foreign note in the fragrant steam. She caught Danilo's eye, glanced down at his mug, and gave a subtle shake of her head. The mage raised his eyebrows and painted an "I told you so" smirk on his countenance.

"Would you be offended if I didn't drink first?" she asked Hasheth.

"Of course not. Only the prudent live to old age," the lad replied graciously. He reached for her cup, offering, "I myself shall taste it for you."

The half-elf had anticipated that response, and the faint gleam in Hasheth's eyes confirmed her suspicions. Without doubt, he had an immunity to whatever poison he'd slipped into the coffee. It was one of the less common and more subtle tricks of a skilled assassin's repertoire.

"I would not dishonor you with such a task," Arilyn said with grave formality. "Actually, I'd thought of feeding the coffee to your horse."

Hasheth's smug expression melted into the slack frustration of defeat, and he pounded the ground with balled fists. "Why?" he blurted out. "Why have the gods sent you to torment me!"

The half-elf waited until the boy's rage was spent. "Why would your masters want you dead, Hasheth?"

"Apart from the obvious reasons, of course," Danilo added.

Hasheth turned furious eyes on his captors. "Can you not hear? My masters decreed that *you* must die, elfwoman. Then I can advance to the next sash level."

"Let's step into reality for a moment, shall we?" Danilo drawled. "Our home is many days to the north. Didn't it occur to you that an assassin whose reputation had traveled so far might prove a bit of a handful to someone your age?

Besides, the lady doesn't wear a sash." The dandy's eyes swept over Arilyn's plain traveling clothes: trousers, shirt, and a long, dark cloak. "Or any other ornament, for that matter," he added in an aggrieved tone.

Before the young man could respond, Arilyn broke in. "How old do you think I am?"

Hasheth blinked, clearly puzzled by her question. His eyes traveled over her delicate features, curly raven hair, and slender form. "Three-and-twenty rains," he guessed.

Arilyn shook her head. "Try three-and-forty."

"It is not possible," Hasheth protested, his brow furrowed in disbelief. "You are young and most beautiful."

She brushed back her thick curls to display pointed ears, faintly tinged with blue at the tips. "I'm a half-*elf*, remember? I'll probably outlive your grandchildren. When I started sword training, your mother was no doubt an infant. How old was she when she came to your father's harem?"

"Fourteen," he answered absently.

"For as many years as you *and* your mother have lived, I've been a hired warrior. I fought for the Alliance in the war against the Tuigan barbarians. I've earned a place of honor among the Harpers. Knowing all this, do you still think you were sent to fight an equal?"

Arilyn softened her harsh words with a smile. "In a few years, this may change. You have much talent, Hasheth, and one day we may well meet on an even field. But that day has not yet come." She paused, and her expression hardened. "No one uses me or my sword against my will. I don't intend to be the instrument of your death, despite your masters' best-laid plans."

"You lie," Hasheth said, but his face betrayed a touch of uncertainty.

"Someone wants you dead," Arilyn repeated softly. "That's easy enough to prove. Since *I* won't take the job, it will go to another."

Hasheth stared at her for a long moment. "I will think about your words."

The three travelers turned their attention to Danilo's fragrant stew. Hasheth scorned the offer of a spoon, instead using pieces of flat, hard travel bread to scoop up bits of fish and mushrooms. The lad ate hungrily, but with a nimble delicacy that struck Danilo as oddly familiar. He resolved to mention his suspicious to Arilyn as soon they could speak privately.

After their meal, at Danilo's insistence, Arilyn tied a length of rope around Hasheth's ankle and secured the end to her own saddle. The boy submitted to the indignity calmly, and not until they left the forest behind them did he speak to her again.

"I have heard of the Harpers," Hasheth stated casually, but his tone clearly implied that he had heard nothing good. He wheeled his horse aside and placed as much distance between himself and his captors as the tether rope allowed.

Danilo reined his horse close to the half-elf's mare. "For his next act, His Majesty will no doubt stick out his tongue."

Arilyn grinned. "Ease off, Dan. He's just a boy."

"Is he?" Danilo asked pointedly. "He appears to be a good deal more than your average sophomore assassin."

"Oh? How so?"

"Noblemen in Tethyr seldom use forks or spoons. It's supposed to be uncouth. Another of the pasha's notions about northern barbarities, I believe. Then there's the matter of that horse," Danilo pointed out. "I'm a excellent judge of horseflesh, and I can assure that only the very wealthy could afford such a mount. And have you noticed the boy's ring?"

"I was wondering when you'd get around to that ring," Arilyn murmured. "So Hasheth has money."

"And another thing. He's clearly both noble and wealthy, but he disdains such things in others. He positively despises what he sees in me—"

"For that he needs a reason?"

Danilo reached over and took Arilyn's chin between his fingers, turning her face to his. "You're enjoying this far too much," he said dryly.

"Get used to Hasheth, Dan," she said as she eased her horse away. "He's our contact at Pasha Balik's court."

Danilo squinted at the sun, which had crested the top of the Starspire Mountains. Already it glared at them like an angry red eye. "My dear, I'm afraid this desert heat is addling you."

"Why? You've concluded that Hasheth is noble. He names Zazesspur as his home, but his face is that of a Calishite. Pasha Balik's palace is in Zazesspur. The pasha is a native of Tethyr, but he's known to stock his harem with the women of the South. Hasheth admitted to being born in a harem. Does his dislike of northerners remind you of someone?"

"All right, it's possible that he's the pasha's son," Danilo conceded. "*Possible*. We can't be sure."

"We could *ask* him."

"I like it," Danilo mused. "Simple, direct. The youngster likes to talk, so it just might work." He cupped his hands to his mouth and called out, "Tell me, Hasheth, how does Pasha Balik feel about having an assassin in the family?"

"Your father would disown *you* sooner than mine would me," the boy responded curtly. "Better an assassin than a fool."

Arilyn chuckled. "That answer your question?"

"It'll do," Dan said flatly. "You win. But what makes you think that Hasheth will work with us?"

"He will if we can convince him his life is in danger."

The nobleman's face suffused with unholy glee. "I can think of several ways to accomplish that feat."

"Don't bother. The second assassin will strike soon. He has to, if they plan to blame Hasheth's death on a northern barbarian."

"Ah." Danilo drew in a long breath. "I think I've got it. Hasheth's masters send him after you, fully expecting you to kill him. It was a chance to be rid of him and remain guiltless. And knowing how Pasha Balik feels about 'northern barbarians,' they're probably expecting Hasheth's death to put the old boy right over the edge."

"That's my guess," Arilyn agreed. "His son's death might prompt Balik to limit trade with the North—making the people of Tethyr turn against him. The way would be clear for the guild alliance to make its move."

"Devious," the nobleman muttered. "And the other assassin—the one who's been following us since Imnescar—was supposed to make certain you and Hasheth met up, I suppose."

"Probably. If I don't kill Hasheth, *he* will. You can bet I'll still be blamed, though."

Danilo was silent for a long moment. "So what do we do now?"

"We keep Hasheth alive," Arilyn said in a grim voice.

As the three travelers rode deeper into the pass, the day grew oppressively hot and the landscape more barren and forbidding. Heat rose in wavering lines from the sand and from the scattered clusters of rock. The only signs of life were the colonies of lizards sunning themselves on rocky ledges. The creatures seemed to be everywhere, and Danilo marveled that anything could enjoy the punishing heat.

"Look at that large rock formation," the half-elf said quietly. The pass narrowed up ahead, with a flat ledge to the left side of the trail and a huge, jagged pile of boulders blocking escape to the right.

"Is our assassin lying in wait there?" the nobleman asked.

"Could you choose a better place?" Arilyn asked. "Once I move, you keep an eye on Hasheth."

They rode until they were almost level with the rock. Suddenly Arilyn threw herself from her horse, tugging violently at the line that bound their young captive. Caught unaware, Hasheth fell heavily to the rocky ground.

Arilyn was back up in a heartbeat, moonblade in hand, rushing toward something Danilo had yet to see. A tall, dark-bearded man sprang up from behind the rocks, a pair of scimitars flashing in the sunlight. Danilo noted that the attacker's dark, close-fitting attire was identical to the garments worn by Hasheth.

For his part, the pasha's son staggered painfully to his feet. As he watched the battle raging before him, fierce joy filled his heart. The accursed woman would die, and at the hands of a brother assassin! Hasheth's eyes narrowed at that thought, and he stooped to pick up a shard of stone, wedge-shaped and sharp. Perhaps this was a gods-granted chance to fulfill the duty assigned him. . . .

"I wouldn't recommend it," said a voice edged with steel. An equally sharp blade bit into the base of Hasheth's neck. "Turn around slowly."

Hasheth did as he was bid, silently cursing himself for being bested by the barbarian peacock. He'd forgotten about Danilo, so accustomed had he become to ignoring the fool.

"Look over at the rock ledge," the northerner ordered, lowering his blade until it was level with the young man's heart. "It could change your outlook considerably."

Puzzled, Hasheth looked—and recoiled from the sight before him. All but one of the sun-loving lizards had fled in fright. The lone remaining creature writhed and twisted, impaled by a slender, familiar knife. The blade flashed in the bright sunlight as the lizard flopped about. As the young man gaped, the creature was seized by a final, convulsive shudder. Only moments before, Hasheth had been directly between the dead reptile and the former hiding place of his "brother assassin."

"Arilyn cut that a bit close, wouldn't you say?" Danilo observed in his irritating drawl.

"The elfwoman spoke the truth," Hasheth said softly. He turned and met Danilo Thann's eyes squarely. "Return my knife," he commanded. "She saved my life. Now I would come to her aid."

The nobleman chuckled and lowered his sword. "Not if you value your skin, you won't." He motioned toward the ledge. "Have a seat. This shouldn't take long."

"But—"

"If she gets into trouble, we'll help. Agreed?"

Absorbed in the battle before him, Hasheth could only

nod. He clambered onto the rock, barely registering the dead lizard beside him, or the northerner's comic grimaces as he fastidiously removed the creature.

Arilyn Moonblade fought like no other Hasheth had seen. She held her ancient sword with both hands, yet her strike was as quick as a desert snake. Easily she engaged both of the Calishite's flashing scimitars. Within moments the man fell backward, clutching at his slashed throat.

The half-elf stooped and cleaned her sword in the sand. Like one asleep, Hasheth slid from the rocky ledge and drifted forward, his eyes fixed in horrified fascination on the dead man.

Danilo came to stand beside Arilyn. "If ever I had doubts about your assessment of Hasheth, one look at his face now would dispel them. I'd wager my entire gem collection that the boy had never seen death close at hand—until now, that is."

"He's lived a sheltered life," Arilyn responded softly. "Few men die in a harem."

"And those who do, die happy," the young mage murmured.

Oblivious to the Harpers' conversation, Hasheth dropped to his knees beside the body. His hands reached toward the man's outer shirt, hesitated, then parted the dark folds. A quilted sash of pale silver silk girded the dead man's undertunic. Hasheth looked up at Arilyn.

"This man wore a shadow sash," he whispered, "and you killed him with ease."

The half-elf pushed a handful of black curls off her damp forehead and shrugged. "He was better at stealth than at honest combat."

"Even so, the gray sash marks its wearer as an assassin of the highest rank and skill," the lad said quietly, never taking his eyes from the corpse.

"Oh-oh," Danilo murmured, suddenly realizing what was coming.

Hasheth drew in a steadying breath and quickly unknotted the sash, tugging it free of the dead man's body. He rose and presented it to Arilyn with grave formality. "This belt and rank are now yours."

Arilyn eyed the proffered sash and swallowed hard. "What am I supposed to do with it?"

"Wear it with pride," Hasheth responded earnestly. "The sash will bring you much respect in these lands, and many offers from men of wealth and power. The shadow sash also grants you entrance into the Assassins Guild, and even a position in the ruling body of the School of Stealth, should you desire it."

Arilyn's shoulders sagged. For much of her life, the half-elf had struggled to be known as something other than an assassin. Ironically, she had just earned a badge that proclaimed her false identity anew.

"Two guilds," Danilo said softly. "Between the Assassins Guild and the Wine Merchants Guild, we could surely get the information we need."

Arilyn cast a rueful glance into Danilo's sympathetic face and gave a curt nod of agreement. She gingerly plucked the sash from Hasheth's outstretched hands and tied it quickly around her waist.

"I was not ready to listen to your words," Hasheth said, an apology in his tones. "Will you now tell me what brings the Harpers to our lands?"

"We would like Pasha Balik to remain in power," Danilo began.

The young man smiled. "Already you have my interest. That is my wish as well."

Hasheth listened politely as Danilo spoke, but the boy's face darkened with shock and outrage as the mage related the guilds' plot against the pasha. He sat in silence for many moments after the story had ended.

"What's wrong, Hasheth?" Arilyn prodded.

The young man shifted uneasily. "Clearly I must withdraw from the School of Stealth if I wish to stay alive, but doing so would be regarded as a failure. The guild would not hesitate to spread false tales of my cowardice, which would bring great dishonor to me and to my father. This is more than a matter of pride," Hasheth added quietly. "I wish to aid my father, but will he regard the words of a man without honor?"

"You might be able to leave the School of Stealth without dishonor," Danilo said thoughtfully.

"I do not see how," the boy replied, his face glum.

The nobleman grinned. "Barter much, Hasheth?"

"That is generally a task for merchants and servants, but I am familiar with its principles. One begins by suggesting an impossibly high price, which is countered by a equally absurd low figure. Eventually both parties settle somewhere in the middle."

"Precisely," Danilo said. "This is what you do: You and a servant will take this man's body to the assassins' guildhall. If I understand the rules, his death earns not only the sash rank, but guild membership and a position at the School of Stealth. Demand all three. That's the high bid."

"But I did not kill him," Hasheth protested.

"This is barter, remember? What place does honesty have in making a bargain?"

A touch of humor lit the boy's eyes. "Go on."

"The guildmasters will counter with a low bid, perhaps offer to pay you this man's bloodprice. You merely sneer and toy with that priceless scarab of yours," Danilo suggested, casting a covetous glance at the boy's ring. "Then, after a suitable pause, you suggest that you might be willing to give up the position at the School of Stealth."

"The guildmasters won't be satisfied with that," Hasheth protested. "It is true that they will not willingly make a man of my years a master assassin, but if they indeed plot against my father, they cannot allow me into the guild."

"Exactly," Danilo said patiently. "Guild membership is the main issue, and most of their attention will be focused on it. When they release you from your commitment to the School of Stealth, they'll be thinking of you in terms of a potential master assassin, not a failed student."

"Go on," urged Hasheth, a crafty smile lifting the corners of his mouth.

"They'll release you from the school and make a counter-offer. Since they can't have you poking around in guild business, all they can offer is the shadow sash itself. You pretend to think it over, then casually observe that an assassin of such high rank *must* be allowed into the guild, so that her activities can be monitored and her fees properly tithed. Emphasize 'her' subtly."

"Ahhh." A slow, admiring smile crept across Hasheth's face. "That will befuddle them."

Danilo grinned. "That's right. You'll change the direction of negotiations abruptly, gaining an advantage through surprise. Introduce your 'servant'—that's you, Arilyn—as the woman who overcame the shadow sash. Repeat your demand for rank and guild membership for her—and imply you were speaking for Arilyn all along. Chances are they'll be so relieved to be rid of you that they'll embrace Arilyn. Figuratively speaking, my dear," Danilo hastily assured the half-elf.

"But what of my assignment? I can hardly champion a woman I was ordered to kill," the boy pointed out.

The nobleman raised one eyebrow. "If the guildmasters bring that up, remind them that you were released from the school. Barter met is bargain sealed, as they say hereabouts. You'll have gotten the better of them, and they'll probably admire you for it."

Hasheth threw back his head and let out a peal of delighted laughter. "You think like a southerner: devious and subtle. It would seem that I have misjudged you."

"Everyone does," Arilyn said dryly. "That's why he's such an effective agent."

"Lord Thann is a Harper, as well?" The young man's brow furrowed as he thought this over. "A nobleman can join such a group?"

"Even a pasha's son," Arilyn said with a smile. "In time."

Hasheth nodded thoughtfully. "I might like that."

Danilo folded his arms and smiled broadly. "Then perhaps it is time for you and me to barter. Tell your father all that has happened. Tell him that Arilyn and I will seek proof that the guilds threaten his power. Ask him to hear what we say and judge for himself."

"That is your high bid?" scoffed Hasheth.

"You interrupted me too soon," the nobleman said plaintively. "I was going to ask for that ring of yours, as well."

The boy's dark eyes flashed. "That is absurd! This ring is a mark of royalty. Here is my offer: as you ask, I will deliver your warning to my father. You may not have the ring, but I will be your ears and eyes in Tethyr. From this day, I will pass to the Harpers whatever information reaches the pasha's court."

"Throw in a couple of camels, and you have a deal," Danilo offered.

"Done."

The young man concluded the bargain in such solemn fashion that neither Harper had the heart to explain that Danilo had been joking.

"Congratulations, Danilo," Arilyn murmured, struggling to keep the laughter from her voice. "We've done our duty to the Harpers and you finally got your two camels."

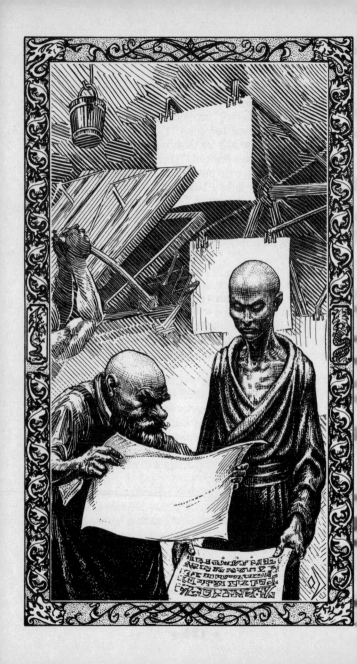

PATRONAGE

David Cook

"Master Koja, have you forgotten? Tonight is Duke Piniago's dinner. You are going, aren't you?"

The pricking scratch of my quill ends as my secretary's
shadow falls across the parchment sheet on which I am toil-
ing. Light is precious in this dim tower closet the priests
have granted me, and now my aide, granted by those self-
same clerics of Denier, has managed to position his broad
self in front of the only window.

Looking up, I blink as his girth is swathed in the glow of
daylight beyond. I am annoyed by his presence, since it is
an interruption of my solitude, but I cannot ignore his question. Besides, my secretary is a good priest, so I curb my
temper, pushing back the stack of parchment before me,
and considering.

"I am undecided, Firstborn Foxe." I cannot manage the
accents of his honest family name, foreign to me though
common enough in this city, so I call him Firstborn in

honor of his birth. "I have heard your gossip about his table, all the magnificent dishes he serves—the finest in Procampur. What if it were to overtax my humble stomach? Besides, I am not learned in the ways of your western courts and might offend him. After all, I am only a simple lama."

Foxe will not relent as he gathers up the sheets and fusses in a bass voice that matches his size. "Simple lama, indeed," he mutters, once again assuming because of my weatherbeaten and shaved looks that I am old and therefore hard of hearing. "You are a famous historian. You were a guest of the king of Cormyr and wrote a history of the Tuigan wars for him." From one of the book-crowded shelves, he takes a bundle of blotting paper and cuts the twine.

"It was not a history, Firstborn Foxe, only a few incomplete notes on the customs of the Tuigan—nothing at all compared to Goodman Reaverson's complete account of the wars." I recall the bard Reaverson's patient translation and guidance with those notes. For the time he put in, my work had been as much his as mine.

"The duke has money and he likes the arts," Foxe reminds me with an irritated glare. He thrusts my manuscript into the hands of waiting scribe. The boy nods and slowly backs down the stairs, apparently reluctant to miss any of our words. I wave him away. It is clear I will write no more today.

"The duke has all the manners of a foreigner." My insult, the worst to any born in the East as I have been, is lost on Foxe. "He is less than pleasant," I explain. "I am a poor ambassador, Foxe. I will say something foolish to anger him. There must be some other way to raise the money to pay the scriveners and binders or some cheaper way to have a book copied. Perhaps a wizard could conjure duplicates." I barely glance at my secretary. Perhaps he will disappear if I do not look at him, the way the epistemological Brother Ulin claims everything should—what we do not observe does not exist.

"Hah! That kind of work's beneath most mages. Too much like a trade." Foxe snorts; he has seen through my deceit. "You know there is no need for this. You can stay with us here at the temple while you write. I'll make sure the high scrivener sends copies of your Tuigan history to every temple of Denier throughout the Heartlands."

I shake my head. We have discussed this before and he knows some of my feelings, but both Foxe and I are too stubborn to relent. Part of the problem is my pride, for I have been too long a guest at this temple of the Lord of Glyphs, ever since leaving King Azoun's court in Suzail. More importantly, and the point I have not told Foxe, is that in all those temples, the priests will tuck my history of the Tuigan into their great vaults and no one will ever see it again. I do not feel heroic enough to make such a futile gesture.

Tired of arguing, I look out the tower's small window, signaling Foxe I wish him to go. My high chamber gives me an ample view of Procampur, looking across the walled wards to the sea at the far end of the city. Smoke drifts lazily above the colorful roofs, whole districts tiled in blue for seamen, yellow for taverns and other services, and the sea green that denotes merchants. All are dotted with patches of late winter snow, dull white and sooty gray. It is this peculiarity of Procampur's people, reflected in their roofs, that I like, far more comforting to me than Suzail, where I spent my first years in the West.

In the capital of King Azoun, victor of the crusade over the Tuigan, there was always the feeling that I was a spoil of war—a scholar oddity from the conquered court of Yamun Khahan—no matter how kindly I was treated, no matter how fascinating the city was. When Denier's priests offered me the chance to travel, I accepted eagerly. Looking over the city now, I welcome my decision. Procampur, with its walled wards carefully dividing the city into merchant, noble, and priest, reminds me of a proper Khazari city—of home. There is a sense of order and place here that Suzail lacked.

Perhaps, I realize with a start, I stay here because I want to go home.

Foxe's deep voice rumbles up from the stone stairwell as he undoubtedly accosts the boy still lurking near the top steps. "Lay out the master's orange monk robes for tonight. After that, get to work on today's pages. Have them transcribed before morning."

"More pages," whines the reedy-voiced lad with resignation. "Master Koja doesn't make Azoun's crusade heroic enough. It's got no dragons or anything."

"Maybe you should leave now," comes Foxe's suddenly gruff reply. "Go do your copying."

The youth is oblivious to Foxe's reproach. I am glad Foxe cannot see my smile. "If it were like, you know, like the *Lay of the Purple Dragons*—the one that bard—uh, Talamic—sings at the Griffin's Claw. That's a good story of a crusade, full of knights and magic. I really like the part the part where the gods appear to King Azoun and bless the crusade. Master Koja should write about that."

"Go!" Foxe snarls as fiercely as a priest can manage. There is a scuffling of feet as the acolyte complies.

The stairs silent, I return to my writing for another try, shifting the table slightly to make better use of the sunlight. The legs scrape over the hard stone floor, the sound quickly swallowed up by the walls of sea-mildewed tomes. I take up the quill again.

During the summer season, a popular sport among the Tuigan men was to hunt the snow beasts of the mountains—

There is an ink blot on my parchment, caused by my inattention, so I must set aside the quill and carefully clean the stain. I am thankful for the coarse parchment's poor absorbency as I daub it up with a scrap of leftover paper—a sample of real paper that Foxe has brought for me to examine. It is a cheap handbill, covered with large blockish script:

Announcing the services of Forgemaster Inkstain and his wondrous printing device!

More writing is obscured by absorbed ink. In trying to read the rest, it stains my fingers smudgy black.

"Firstborn Foxe!"

Hurried footsteps come up the stairs in response to my excited cry. "What is it, Master Koja?" my flushed secretary wheezes as lumbers up the stone steps of the tower.

"Who is this Forgemaster Inkstain?" Unable to restrain my curiosity, I leave my desk and come face-to-face with Foxe as he plods, face red and puffy, through the arched doorway. The foolscap flutters eagerly in my fingers under his nose. I have never before seen letters so black and methodically drawn. Foxe looks surprised as he takes the sheet and holds it close to his face, squinting to read it in the dim light.

"He's one of the new-fangled printers, sir."

"A printer—some type of scribe?"

Foxe puckers his fat cheeks as he seeks a way to explain it to me. "Like a scrivener, master, except he uses some sort of contraption to copy the pages."

"Like Sister Deara's enchanted copyist?" The sister had been working in one of the vaults to form a perfect scribe from sculpted clays, a creature called a golem. In the one test I witnessed, her hulking brute smashed a writing desk by driving a quill through the wooden top. The thing now stands mute guard over the main hall, porter to occasional guests.

"Not like that, sir," Foxe allows with a smile. "It stamps out the pages, making lots of copies at one time."

"I would very much like to see this. Can you find the place?"

Foxe squints at the sheet again. "It says he's on Scribes' Alley, I think. That's easy enough."

"Then, Foxe, I ask you to take me to Forgemaster Inkstain. If we are quick, your dinner will not go to waste. We must inquire about printing—and its costs."

DAVID COOK

Foxe stands flustered as I slip past him and pad down the steps. "Printing costs? What for?" Foxe cries as he hurries after me, his paunch jiggling. "The church already has one copy of your work, bound with Goodman Reaverson's history, and we will happily copy your next book. Master Koja, why waste your money to make more?"

I stop at the bottom of the steps, and out of unbreakable habit give the man a polite bow. "Call it this one's wretched vanity, but it would be good for more people to know the truth of the war. Do you not agree?"

"Master Koja, not that many souls can read anyway."

"Perhaps my humble work will inspire them to learn." I hurry on, determined not to be delayed. "Besides, I might be able to avoid Duke Piniago's dinner."

Foxe hurries after because he knows me too well. "At least wait until I get my get my coat," he says with resignation.

*　*　*　*　*

The walk to Forgemaster Inkstain's is cold, not the dry cold of my mountainous homeland, but a damp wintry breeze from the harbor, a cold that I have grown accustomed to here. The road that we follow, known here as the Great Way, is quiet, but that only stirs unease in me. The growing shadows from the sun as it sinks toward the swelling waters of the Inner Sea only add to the barrenness. I have never been comfortable with solitude, despite —or perhaps because of—the bleakness of my native Khazari.

I am relieved when we leave the main avenue and Foxe guides me through the gate of the Merchants District, where the narrow streets are close-pressed by the green-roofed workshops and apartments. The air is rich with smells that only cities have, whether from Khazari to Cormyr. Procampur reeks of wood smoke and sewage, overripe fish and buttered pastries. By curious connections it calls to mind the days spent sipping buttered tea around dung fires in my lord Yamun's tent on the open steppe.

"Hurry up, master. This air will make us ill." Foxe has wrapped his face with a thick scarf until I can barely see his small eyes. "It is bitter cold out today."

I almost laugh, since I am walking beside him bare-headed with only my spring robes on, but that would be impolite. "Firstborn Foxe, were I home in Khazari—then I would be cold. By now the trails to the Red Mountain—where I was a lama—might be barely passable. This is only a little wind, like the spring breeze on the steppe."

"Do you ever miss your home?"

"What?"

"You told me you've been away ten years, first with the Tuigan and then here in the West. Don't you ever get homesick?"

I think about Khazari—soaring mountains crusted with glaciers, isolated monasteries for those seeking enlightenment. I watched Yamun Khahan conquer my homeland; I rode at his side when he did it. Now my lord Yamun is dead and his empire gone. Furo, the Mighty One, forgive me, but I miss the khahan more than I miss Khazari.

"It is my shame to admit I miss proper food, Firstborn Foxe. I may never get used to your Procampan cooking—too many rich meats and raw vegetables. I would dearly like a little kumiss, rice, and tea."

"Ugh—kumiss—soured horse milk. Your stomach is stronger than you say."

"Ah, Firstborn Foxe, in the *Yanitsava*, it is said all things have their balance. Kumiss fires the blood and purges cooling humors from the body. Those roasts such as you eat unbalance the weak and strong animus within you." I look with meaning at Foxe's broad waist.

Foxe returns my look evenly. "I am balanced just fine, Master Koja. After all, I carry your books up and down those stairs every day. Mind the mud there."

We avoid the puddles in Procampur's unflagged streets, the water fresh from yesterday's winter rain. And as the sodden way clears before us, we hear the bellow of machin-

ery. It comes from a rickety shop through the next alley's
archway.

"Oi, watch that bucket, you ink-sloppin' runt o' an apprentice! I'll take every drop out o' yer miserable wage. How'd
you like that, eh?"

Forgemaster Inkstain is in.

The shop is nothing more than a lean-to slapped onto the
side of a teamster's stable. A paper sign, tattered and water-
stained, is tacked near the door. The black ink is streaked
from the lettering till it runs into the grain of the pine
boards. This is not encouraging, but through the gapped
boards comes the squeaking rumble of grinding metal that
ends in a thickly padded thump. It is as if a host of rusty
knights is stumbling about the room. Foxe's puzzled look
tells me he, too, is mystified.

Inside, the clanking bedlam maintains its thunderous
tempo. The source is a squat mass of metal and wood
crammed into the center of the shed, surrounded by buckets and bales of rag paper in all colors. Nearby, the dwarven
master berates his ogre apprentice from atop a crate. The
din has concealed our entrance. The thick, hairy back of
the apprentice bends and strains in time with the contraption as his thick, warty arms pull on a long lever that
wrenches the grinding gears into the motions. Iron arms
rise and fall, metallic claws snatching sheets of foolscap
from a stack and pushing them into a mechanical maw.

"Don't push her so hard, you lout! Here, ease off an'
grease her up. I'll—" Forgemaster Inkstain catches sight of
us from the corner of his eye. His demeanor instantly
changes. "Gentlemen, I'm favored to have you visit my
humble shop," the dwarf shouts as he clambers down from
his perch. "I be Forgemaster Inkstain, master printer.
Aguul, shut her down, so these gentlemen can hear."

I am afraid I am rudely gawking, having never dealt
much with the dwarves—creatures of the West as they are.
The master printer is nothing like the fierce ironlord who
commanded the dwarves of King Azoun's army. Truly the
name does him justice, for Inkstain seems to be a single

blot of ink, all four-and-a-half feet of him. His leather apron and starched linen shirt are a smudgy black. I think his beard is white, though now it is a gray mass tucked into his belt for safety. Only the top of his bald head is undaubed.

"I had her shipped up from the Deep itself," the dwarf proudly says, the machine's racket finally stilled. Aguul lumbers off, barely squeezing his way through the door to the stable.

"The deep?"

"The *Deep*—Dwarves' Deep, home to me kin an' all that. Now, what can I do fer you gentlemen?"

Foxe intercedes on my behalf, slipping his portly body between us. "Forgemaster Inkstain, my master is Koja of Khazari, lama of the Red Mountain, emissary of the Tuigan, and grand historian of Yamun Khahan, former emperor of the steppes. He has come to discuss terms for a printing."

I do not like these titles, but Foxe has already explained the need to impress the dwarf. I thought this would not work, and I am proved correct. Forgemaster Inkstain remains stolidly unimpressed. "Printin' what?"

I let Foxe negotiate. "My master is just completing his *Observations of the Tuigan Historian, Recording the Life of Yamun Khahan from his Rise to his Death in the Lands of the West, from Notes made for King Azoun of Cormyr.*"

"Title's kind o' long."

"We can call it *A History of the Tuigan.*" Foxe concedes too willingly, I think.

Forgemaster Inkstain gnaws at a nail before finally clearing off a corner of the half-buried desk that is his office. "Well then, how many copies? What kind o' paper? Any illuminations? Illustrations? Ordinary bindin' or would you be wantin' somethin' odd, like dragonscale or wyvern hide? You be holy men—ain't no magical verse, would there be?" Forgemaster Inkstain asks the last with a slow suspicion in his voice.

"There will be a sutra at the beginning—to invoke Furo's favor," I offer.

"Magical?" The dwarf's face is a wrinkled scowl.

"No. Just a verse of the *Yanitsava*."

"Oh, that's all right then," the dwarf says, smiling once again. "Ain't able to print magic on a page, you see. Just won't take."

The rest of the details are beyond me, so I sit in the corner, letting Foxe negotiate. Each point seems to take an interminable amount of time; there is nothing for me to do but meditate, but I cannot blank my mind. Memories intrude on the emptiness—snow melting from the grassy steppe, the sharp taste of kumiss in Yamun's tent, the wind blowing across the granite spires of Khazari. Even the failure to meditate brings forth memories of my teachers at the Red Mountain. Of late, I have been thinking more and more of places past, as if the present is an empty shell that must be filled.

Finally Foxe concludes the negotiations. His face is dour, and I can see it has not gone well. Forgemaster Inkstain steps forward, no longer beaming but serious. "Well, honored sir, your servant has concluded a price o' no more than ten thousand gold lions or—let's see—eight if it all be Procampan coin—fer the necessary plates an' supplies fer one book. After that, let's say five hundred lions fer extra copies. Is those acceptable terms to you, honored sir?"

Ten thousand gold is more than I have, more than the value of all Yamun's gifts I still possess. Foxe's helpless look tells me the price will be no lower. I look at the walls, hung with flimsy sheets covered with rows of splotchy black printing. The paper is coarse and ragged, the illustrations crude. The sheets I see cannot compare to the careful illuminations prepared at the temple or the vermillion scrolls I have collected from Shou Lung. The cost is too much for such poor quality. "Forgemaster Inkstain," I answer with a bow, hoping to save face, "I will consider your terms. Come, Firstborn Foxe, we must go."

I hurry out the door before the dwarf can protest. I am embarrassed by this adventure, that Forgemaster Inkstain knows what I cannot pay, even that I considered the plan at all. Foxe runs after me. "I told you this was unnecessary," my secretary chides. "The dwarf's device is only a toy good for nothing but handbills. Besides, Inkstain would not come down a copper bit in his price. Please understand, I tried very hard for you, Master Koja."

"You have done what you could, I am certain," I answer to placate Foxe. "I have wasted your time with a foolish idea. I have no choice. . . ."

"You'll go to Duke Piniago's tonight? Everything will be prepared. Don't worry, master."

I feel a repugnance about begging from the duke, but I am ashamed to rely any longer on the generosity of the clerics. Am I acting out of pride, though? When this dinner is over, I must increase my meditation and regain the center of my being. But for now, there is inescapable duty. Since leaving the monastery, I have lived through war and treachery at Yamun's side. Now, it seems, I am reduced to peddling my knowledge to aristocrats. In a previous life I must have strayed far from the Path of Enlightenment for things to be such as they are now.

"Very well. I will go. Let us hope your acolyte has laid things out as you instructed." Watching Foxe, I see his jowls relax with relief at my decision.

* * * * *

Reluctance delays my footsteps, punctuality urges me onward, until at last I arrive at Duke Piniago's palace—neither late nor early. The manse is well back in the Nobles District, where the silvered roofs of that quarter gleam in the unflickering light of the magical street lamps. As I wend through the well-cobbled avenues, the fog trumpets gloomily warn of the impending encroachment of mists over the city, a final encouragement to hurry before that wet chill arrives.

The duke's palace is encompassed by walls, high and carved with grotesque creatures that leer fiercely in the shadowy night. Between the statues jut iron spikes, clearly meant to deter the outside world, including me.

Palanquin bearers brusquely order me aside as I near the courtyard gate. From the passing windows of the closeted boxes, perfumed and powdered faces stare at me in disbelief. No one of importance walks through the streets of Procampur, especially alone. I do not find the walk arduous—even on this damp night. The city air is bracing. Besides, a palanquin would be an ill-befitting indulgence, and I must be more diligent with myself.

Like the guests, the guards at the courtyard gate stare at me. Foxe was right about my choice of clothing. With my orange lama's robes and shaved head I hardly look like one of the duke's customary guests. Nonetheless, I wear the faded cotton as a connection to my past.

Inside the palace, a powdered servant in showy livery guides me through the carpeted outer chambers where enchanted music wafts ethereally through the halls, theme and tempo changing to suit each room. Already the guests have taken their places in the banquet hall, crowded at a table burdened with glowing tapers and platters heaped with viands. My seat, two down from the duke, is the only empty one of the twenty-two chairs I count at the long table. Habit makes me count—the need to know numbers, reasons, and causes.

"Greetings to our distinguished foreign guest," hails Duke Piniago from the head of the overfull board. He heaves to his feet, massively tall and broad, his thick black beard stained with wine. Waving a goblet around so it splashes wine on the shoulder of the plump courtesan next to him, he proclaims, "This is a rare occasion everyone, for I have lured the eminent anchorite from his lair!" He bangs the goblet on the table, showering wine across the white tablecloth. The elaborately coifed heads at the table turn to him, then to me. The other guests do not disguise their opinions of my humble appearance.

The duke continues, but I cannot say if he is in his cups or naturally so coarse. "Fellow lords, esteemed gentlemen and ladies, I introduce to you a truly unique dinner guest, the—um . . ."

"Lama, your lordship."

"Lama Koja. I am sure he has many interesting and curious stories about the Tuigan—those savages who believed they could conquer all the West. Lama Koja, you see, was a scribe of the barbarian leader, Yamun."

So, I am to be tonight's entertainment. "Indeed, it is true that I was grand historian to the court of Yamun Khahan." I gently try to correct his description of my post. It is a vain attempt.

"Sit at our table, lama, and enjoy. Tonight, let no man say you are poorly fed." The duke settles back heavily into his thronelike seat.

Barely have I taken my place before the meal is served. The roasts, sauces, and pies presented certainly uphold the duke's reputation as a gourmand, but I only gingerly sample them, more accustomed to simple bread and vegetables. Next to me, a thin venerable, his wispy beard floating like white yak hair, piles the rich offerings high. Noticing my gaze, he nods an over-solicitous smile and plops a quivering, rare slice of beef on my platter.

"Is it the custom of your people not to eat or drink?" the duke rumbles, noticing my reticence. "Perhaps you are one of those races said to subsist on air."

"He's certainly thin enough, Jozul," giggles the consort seated next to him.

"My greatest apologies, Your Lordship. I assure you I require sustenance like all mortals. It is just that since arriving in Procampur, I have tried to adhere to the sutras— that is, the teachings of the mighty Furo."

"So?"

"By Furo's law, strong drink and flesh are to be avoided—"

"Stuff and nonsense," the duke interrupts while waving a servant for more wine. His black brows are knit, his face a scowl. "People say the barbarians ate insects."

"Perhaps in times of great hunger, honored sir. I never knew of such habits among the Tuigan. Nonetheless, it is true that among the Tuigan vegetables were unknown and so I was compelled to violate the teachings of Furo and the dictates of the Red Mountain. However," I add quickly while accepting a dish of boiled root vegetables, "your table is civilized, so that I need not starve while retaining my vows." The duke seems placated by my answer.

"I can't imagine living among such savages," remarks the ancient next to me, who I guess to be a priest from the temple of Tymora. Duke Piniago nods in agreement as he tears a wing from a roast goose.

"It is held by some sages of my homeland that the gods choose every man's life at birth. It is our duty to discover what life is intended for us. I do not think many of Yamun's warriors could imagine sitting here either."

"But we westerners beat those horse thieves, didn't we?" It is Duke Piniago who speaks to the murmured approval of his guests. I know, because Foxe told me, that Duke Piniago took little part in the war, profiteering on the supplies the crusading army needed. These pampered and groomed peers are nothing like the hard-minded and stoic warriors who met the Tuigan horde. I remember the plain of Thesk where King Azoun met my lord Yamun and slew him, although I think my memories are quite different from the men whose glory to duke seeks to inflate.

I phrase my reply carefully. "Indeed. As the great sage Chih said, 'Truly a kingdom's victory is shared by all her people from the noble to the peasant.'"

"Precisely—every man in Procampur feels proud," the duke blithely agrees, raising his glass for a toast.

"It is sad the people think you only fought a tribe of bandits, Your Lordship. Would it not be wise to print a history of the Tuigan, so that others would know their true might?"

"A history such as yours, priest?"

"I have expanded the notes I made for King Azoun into a small volume. I hesitate to offer it."

Duke Piniago leans over his plate. "You're being coy with me, priest. What'll it cost?" he demands in a fierce whisper so only those near us hear.

There is no point trying to be polite with this blunt-headed man. "Ten thousand golden lions, Your Lordship."

"Ten thousand! For one book?" The duke hurls a gnawed bone to his dogs. His voice is no longer quiet.

"That is the necessary cost to prepare the impressions for the printer—so I understand, Your Lordship. Additional books would be five hundred lions." It seems that everyone at our end of the table has fallen silent, waiting for the duke's response.

"Additional copies?" the duke queries. He turns to the old priest beside me. "Since when do scribes deal in multiple copies at cut-rate prices, Hierarch?"

"Never, Your Lordship."

I wet my dry throat on some fruit nectar brought for me. "I was going to have the books made by a printing machine, not a copyist, honorable sir."

The hierarch snorts in disgust. "Printing machines—hah! Only good for cheap broadbills. Can't even make a proper prayerbook with one—won't print the magic, you see."

"The book is not magical," I protest.

"It doesn't matter. A scribe can do the job just as well," the duke interjects. "What do I need with multiple books? I only need one for my library."

I am stunned, unable to think of any reasoned reply. "Surely others might want to read my book—"

"Of course they will, you silly man," the duke's gaudy consort sneers, batting her eyes as she does so. "Do you think Jozul would spend all that money so everyone might own a copy? He keeps the only book in his library so anybody who wants to read it has to ask his permission."

I look to the duke, hoping he will correct her, but his face is set in an smug smile. She has described it all too well.

I am at complete loss for words. All these years I have worked as a historian, carefully checking the letters I managed to save from Yamun's downfall, interviewing the occasional Tuigan prisoner who passed through Procampur on a slave galley, even poring over the maps of caravan masters who have traveled to the East. All this work and the duke wants to hoard it for himself. It is impossible.

Stiffly I rise from my chair, unable to think of any polite wording to express my refusal. I bow to the assembled company, two rows of aristocrats and their sycophants, glittering among the candelabras and chandeliers. They are all silent, watching me like spirits in an evil-omened dream where sinister faces observe from every turn.

"I have imposed upon your table. Please forgive me, Duke Piniago. I will leave you now," I say stiffly. Without inviting any further discussion, I take my leave, backing politely toward the exit.

The duke makes no effort to stop me. Even as I leave the banquet hall, the trickles of unsubdued laughter follow. I have not failed, at least, as entertainment. The footman guides me out of the palace. At the gate the startled guards watch me pass. No one, I imagine, has ever walked out early on one of the duke's parties.

Cold winter mists are roiling in from the port, soaking my thin robes as I leave the Nobles District to cross the Great Way for home. The vapors diffuse the lamplight, making the walled compounds and flagged streets shine greasy black. The silver roofs glow as if of their own accord. Dogs bark at my passing and guards eye me suspiciously, a solitary stranger in foreign robes prowling the night.

By the time I depart the Nobles District, my distaste for the duke has grown, feeding on the wet night and the day's frustrations. The pangs of homesickness return, and more than ever my heart longs for the ice-flecked mountain air of Khazari. The desire is strengthened by the memories of things from my youth—tsampo porridge, buttered tea, playing on the fresh snowfields, even the rattling drone of the prayer wheels as they endlessly turn.

My abrupt appearance before the gate startles the guards of the Temple District, just as their sudden emergence from the fog wakens me from my reverie. They greet me with familiarity as they unbolt the closed gate. I make no answer; I have no mood for talk.

Inside, the stone temples, their black roofs invisible in the night, ascend into the mists. It is quiet, the business of saving souls done for the day. Back in Khazari, the monastery would echo with the chanted sutras and cymbals of the lamas who maintained the vigil through the night, keeping order in the universe.

Is there no place for me among these outlanders? Only a few care for learning, but they know nothing of inner harmony. Foxe is among the few who have shown any desire to understand. He would make a good lama if he were not so hasty in his judgments. Yet haste is valued here, in this city of dukes and dwarven printers. . . .

It is then I decide that I have been away from the center of my being too long. It is time to go home.

Entering the shrine of Denier by a side door, I pad barefooted across the main chamber, guided by the light of a thousand votive candles arranged on the altar. I feel guilty as I take one to light my way up the stairs to my cell, not far from the study where I write. There I begin arranging my belongings, trying not to wake Foxe, who sleeps in the cell across from mine. I must leave a gift to the temple for their kindness—the copy of my manuscript and perhaps, as I heft it, Yamun's golden *paitza*. I doubt this warrant of safe passage from the khahan will afford me much aid recrossing the steppe now that he is dead.

The rustling of my papers wakes Foxe. His cell door creaks as it opens, and he ambles into the room, nightshirt flapping around his bare legs. Sleep clings to him as he sees me, his eyes blinking in their puffy sockets. "Master, you're back! What did the duke say?"

"The honorable duke requested only a single book." I continue sorting my papers.

"Oh, no." Foxe notices my packing. "You didn't—" There is a look of reproach in his brightening eyes, like a teacher disappointed in his pupil.

"One gains no merit in harsh words, Foxe, but the learned duke will not print my history. He would have made a single copy and kept it all for himself. This history is not written for just him, but for all who think songs like *Lay of the Purple Dragons* and the tales told by old warriors around the fire are the truth of your 'crusade.' Yamun Khahan never called it a crusade; he never tried to make it more than it was—a war. Neither does King Azoun. He knows what the war cost."

I stop packing. I am tired and do not want to do anything more this night. Closing my eyes, I chant a prayer to Furo for strength. "I have written what I know, and no one wants to read it."

"As a priest of Denier I'll read it, master. You know that." Perhaps thinking he can change my mind, Foxe begins unpacking what I have prepared.

"To put it away in your secret vaults with all the other volumes your faith has collected."

"Our libraries are open to all." Foxe does not fail to defend his church, but his scowl softens. He is more concerned for me, I believe, and that is why I will miss him. "There are always others besides the duke."

"Foxe, I am tired of begging from city to city. There is no more reason for me to be here. I am going back to my homeland." I rub wearily at the stubble of my shaved head.

Foxe's hands stop in midair, holding a ream of ink-traced parchment. "You're leaving?"

I nod.

Foxe sets the paper down and carefully smoothes his nightshirt. He speaks with great sorrow. "There's no need for you to go. Everyone at the temple will agree. Even the high scrivener praises your knowledge and wisdom."

"No, Firstborn Foxe, there is nothing for me here."

He sees that I am resolute and gives up. For a time he stands just watching me, until at last, with great reluctance, he passes over those things he has unpacked. We work in silence, feeling the bond that can sometimes be built between a scholar and his secretary. I thought him rude and rash when we first met, but it was only his way of trying to help me. I have learned more about the West from him—less about kings and more about common people—than I ever learned in Suzail. In exchange, I have tried to teach him proper manners, but Foxe can only become whatever he is fated to be by his karma—my influence is pre-ordained within it. I, too, must accept the fate I have earned from previous lifetimes.

We have done little more than organize the sheaves of yellowed parchment and tied a few in corded bundles when the stairwell rumbles with the distant clap of the temple's door knocker. A twinge of irrational dread chills me. Have I offended Duke Piniago more than I know—enough that he might send thugs against me? The thought passes as quickly as it came; assassins would never pound on the main doors.

"Quickly, let us see who it is before the entire temple is roused." I look to Foxe; even through the sleepy gape that gives him a double chin his curiosity shows clearly.

"Nothing but trouble and surprises all night," my companion moans as he looks at his bare toes, barely visible from beneath the curve of his nightshirt, and hurries to his cell to clothe himself in more proper attire.

Hastily dressed, Foxe follows me down the coiling stairs, belting his robe as he goes. The knock resounds again as I hustle across the main hall, still lit by the votives on the altar. A tall figure stands by the door. At first I mistake it for our caller, then I note it is nothing more than Sister Deara's failed copyist. At Foxe's command, the clanking golem draws back the ponderous door to admit our caller.

Without a word, a man steps in and bows deeply to Foxe and me. In the luster of candlelight his clothes are silken, dyed deep blue, but cut like the robes I wear—Khazari in design. His hair is black and braided. No mark of office or heraldry does he wear, yet from his poise there is no mistaking the dress as servant's livery.

"Lama Koja of the Red Mountain," the servant says politely. His voice has the familiar accents of home. "My mistress has heard of your travails this night. She hopes you will honor her by attending a late dinner."

How could anyone have heard what happened and act so quickly? Sorcery possibly, but who would bother to waste such magic on me? "Dinner? Mistress? Explain yourself," I demand out of caution.

The servant smiles. "There is no cause to fear, Lama Koja. My mistress is a friend to scholars. You must come quickly, for we stay in this city only for a little while."

"I wouldn't do it, master," Foxe indiscreetly advises. "This could be a thief's trick."

Foxe may be right; I shouldn't go, but I am too intrigued to refuse. Besides, I am perfectly capable of protecting myself. I did more than just watch during my years with Yamun's armies, and the lamas of the Red Mountain monastery taught me well how to deal with spirits. With a few charms I was packing I will be safe. "My simple robes would dishonor my hostess. Wait while I change, then lead me to her."

The servant smiles once more. There is a catlike gleam in his eyes and a sharpness to his teeth that startles me. Upstairs I find the protective fetishes I seek. On the way back down I review my prayers and charms to ward off evil.

Once outside the temple, fog closes about us until I can barely see my guide. He sets a brisk pace, but always stays just within sight. We pass through the gate of the Temple District, so cloaked in the mist that the guards do not even challenge us—and never have I known the guards to be so lax. I quickly recite the Pure Thought sutra to fortify myself against evil. There is no wisdom in foolish bravery.

On the Great Way, I turn automatically toward the Nobles District, assuming that is where my hostess resides. "Not that way, good lama," the servant calls from the fog as he turns toward the waterfront. "As I said, my mistress is only passing through this city."

We pass more gates along the Great Way—the Merchant District, the red-roofed Adventurers' District, and then the ill-warded district of the poor. At the end of the Great Way the path takes us closer to the heart of the sea fog, passing under the massive towers that mark the waterfront. Unchallenged, though we should have been, we enter the port. The roofs here are of all colors, as if to show what little influence the thultyrl of Procampur holds over the unregulated waterfront.

We venture quickly off the main streets and plunge into a maze of alleys I have never explored. Our route goes past tawdry wineshops and apartments of questionable purpose. A sailor, slurring out a war song I heard soldiers sing in Thesk, staggers by. He is shadowed by a lean pair of half-elves who eye me with far too much interest. A single look from my guide discourages them, and they disappear into the night. I hurry to keep pace, for the streets here are more active than I might wish.

After more twists and turns than I can remember, the servant stops at a gate. Pushing the creaking iron open, he steps aside and motions me to enter. "My mistress awaits you in the garden."

I have not been throughout Procampur, but I do know the waterfront is a crowded and dank place where one would never find gardens. Certainly I have never seen anywhere in the city a garden of the sort that now unfolds before me. The mist that washes the port is here riven to unveil a carefully tended landscape. Unwavering torches light a garden path that wanders past blooming bushes and green grass. A spring breeze warms my aching bones.

I rub my charms, half-expecting to feel the tingle that will alert me to the presence of evil. When nothing happens, I follow the lit path until it comes to a circle of carpets spread under of full-leafed willow.

The rugs are Tuigan, a weave I cannot mistake, and there are dishes and trays arranged neatly at their center. From the wooden pots and silver bowls I smell the barley-porridge odors of tsampo and the smoothness of rich yak-butter tea. There are leather bags I know are filled with kumiss, and steaming plates of greens and roots I have not seen since I was a child. It is wondrous, but because of its very strangeness I do not eat. I have heard the outlanders' stories of ensorcelled food—the snares laid by the treacherous denizens of their Realm of the Dead. Seeing no one else around, I recite a protective sutra to cleanse and purify the food. Satisfied, I gingerly dip my finger in the nearest bowl.

"Wise Koja, I mean you no harm. Please sit and eat, if you would honor my table."

I cannot help a guilty start at the words, moist finger at my lips. I feel like a novitiate caught dozing during meditation. The voice carries musical tones, light as a gong sounding the dawn prayer over high mountain slopes. The willow switches rustle, and a woman dressed in the draped robes of a Khazari noblewoman steps out of the darkness. The silks of her brilliant gown swirl gently as she moves, rippling the embroidered flowers and clouds of gold and red thread on her sleeve. Necklaces of strung silver coins hang layered around her neck, yet she carries her displayed wealth with ease.

For all her dress, she is not a dark-haired and small Khazari woman, but tall and strong. Her thin, pale face is framed with hair so long and golden that it spills down into the silver chains. Small mouth, wide eyes, and nose a trifle too long all combine in a way that transcends these little flaws until she is beautiful beyond the mere physical. Without waiting for me, she sits cross-legged on the mats and begins the meal.

While she samples the dishes, I, marveling at her arrival, test her with the Hundred Lotus sutra, one that would surely cause an evil spirit pain. When I softly chant the words, she shows no sign of having noticed. Perhaps she is not a spirit, as I first suspected. My hostess might be a powerful sorceress—though one is no less dangerous than the other.

I take a seat opposite her, not wishing to be rude but not eager to sit close. I ladle a small bowl of porridge and eat with her. The flavor is more than I held in my memories, full of fall mornings when I sat by the hearth and watched my mother stir the simmering kettle. I savor the taste, knowing the food has been purified by my sutra. Hunger, both immediate and for the things of my past, yearns to be satisfied as I eagerly pick from the other plates set before me. There are types of sweet melons I have not seen since I came among the outlanders and cabbages that only grow in the high valleys outside Manass. My hostess watches, never speaking.

"Dear lady, I must know. How did you obtain such delicacies? Such food could grace the table of a Khazari prince."

She bows slightly to acknowledge my compliment. "I have traveled many distant lands. Once you know of such foods, they are not hard to obtain."

I know this is not true, for I have tried and failed. Considerable magic is needed to gather these ingredients, still fresh, from the East. I carefully press my questions. "I am unworthy to ask, but I must know. Who are you that you are so kind to me?"

She smiles, and by it I know her answer will not be the truth. "I am a simple benefactor of scholars. I have heard of you, even in distant lands."

"By what name shall I call you?"

"None, for you will never see me after tonight."

"What is it you seek of me?" Her soft tones make me shiver, not with cold or fear, but excitement tinged with awe.

My mysterious hostess rises calmly, as if not to alarm me. "You have worked for many years on a history of the eastern raiders—the Tuigan—and now you have finished it."

My throat goes dry, and I cannot swallow. "It is almost completed."

"Now you seek a patron to print your history. Tonight you visited Duke Piniago."

My replies grow softer as my caution returns. "I made a bad judgment in doing so. The duke was not interested in my work."

She laughs like water over stones. "I understand he was all too interested, that it was you who said no. Some say you were rude to the duke, but from what I know of that boor, there must have been some cause."

"You have quick and accurate sources." I answer, wetting my mouth with a swallow of tea. "It is true I refused the duke, but only because he wished to hide the work from others. My pride is my failing, great lady. I could not accept his terms, when others might gain some small knowledge from my work."

She cocks an eyebrow at my claim. "You care so strongly to spread learning, yet you are ready to quit and go back to your homeland."

"How do you know this?" I carefully sidle away from her. The woolen carpet pulls at my robes as I move.

"My man heard you speak with your servant when I sent him to fetch you."

I do not believe her, especially while I sit in this spring garden, green like none other in Procampur. The fact that she knows this, though, only suggests further the extent of her power. Prudently, I do not challenge her lie.

"Koja of Khazari, there are some who think the world needs learning, but there are far too few who will seek it. If you give up, the world has one less seeker. Soon there would be no true scholars left, just men like Duke Piniago."

The memory of a charm slips into a corner of my mind, a way to see things as they truly are. I remember the verses and the ritual, but I need something to activate the sutra.

"I have come," my hostess continues, "to make you an offer. I am willing to be your patron, see your book printed—for a service. I, too, have an interest in knowledge." Her lips part to show the hint of white teeth as she waits for my reaction.

Kumiss, I note silently. I could trigger it with a sprinkle of kumiss. "What service would you require of me, great sorceress?" I try the title to gauge her reaction.

She laughs again, icicles breaking into a frozen brook. "You honor me with your titles, lama. I am just a lady." She slides effortlessly across the carpets to sit by me once more. "An oath, binding and unbreakable. Will you do that?" Her eyes are fired with eagerness.

"An oath?" I dally with the kumiss bowl before me, surreptitiously dipping my finger in the white fluid. "There is no sin in this oath?"

"Sworn of itself, it causes no ill to you or any other.

Beyond that, your fate is your own."

I am ready. Almost fearful at what I will see, I flick a few drops of kumiss toward the woman and utter the Sunlight After Storm sutra, the words which clear the mind from illusion. My hostess recoils slightly in surprise. Then, as I watch too startled to move, her golden hair grows dark black, banded by a golden circlet. Her body ripples and her face changes as the mask of femininity falls away. A white glare, like a furnace that gives no heat, blinds me temporarily. When my eyes adjust, a man stands at the heart of the light, stocky and straight, in a tunic and cloak of purest white.

"By the great and mighty Furo!" I gasp, quickly looking away. This is no sorceress or even a spirit, but a power greater than any mortal, living or dead.

"Koja of Khazari, you have seen what I am." The voice is symphonic, strong chords resound within the words. "Know that I will not harm you. I am Denier, Lord of Glyphs and servant of Oghma, the patron god of bards. I am Denier, in whose temple you have toiled. Now, lama, will you swear my oath?"

The voice from the fire is powerful yet soothing, so that even in the god's mighty presence I feel no fear. Shielding my eyes from the corona that encases him, I am able to look on the spirit once more. "Immortal radiance, what do you demand of me, an unworthy scholar?"

Denier, demipower of words, waves his hands toward the still-dark walls of Procampur. "Write for the outlanders so that they will be encouraged to learn. Stay in the West and become a muse for them. Do this and you need never despair."

I stop at the scope of this oath. "Then I could not go home."

"Not until you are ready to die, lama. I have given you the taste of home you longed for. Would your homecoming now be as sweet as you imagined?"

I look at the food before me, spilled over the carpets and awash in his radiance. With Yamun dead, the Tuigan have

DAVID COOK

no reason to welcome me back into their lands. And what kind of return could I expect in Khazari, a land Yamun conquered while I rode at his side? Sadly I admit what I have always known—my memories have become illusions, ephemeral dreams of places I can no longer call home.

"I accept."

"Then it is done." There is a flare of light, and I am blinded. I stumble forward, my senses fleeing into the dark and cold. My eyes burn, my skull throbs with pain. The soft cushion of the carpet vanishes beneath me, and suddenly I fall to the stone, cold and wet.

Finally the brilliant sparkles fade from my vision, giving way to fog-clad night. The garden and soft carpets are transformed to leafless branches and chill stonework. On the gray cobblestone before me is a small bag. Taking it, I unwork the strings and pour a small stream of dazzling gems into my hand, worth no less than ten thousand golden lions, I would guess.

"Master!" It is Foxe's voice. I turn as the fog swirls away to reveal the portico to Denier's temple before me. Foxe is hurrying down the steps, still hastily dressed, just as I had left him an hour or more before. I suddenly feel foolish, sitting in the darkness in my limp, damp robes. "Master, what happened? I warned you not to go. Are you safe?"

What can I tell him of this night? Surely he would believe me possessed or charmed. Were it not for these gems, I myself would doubt the tale, and yet I have to give him some answer. "I've been home and back again."

"What?"

"Later, Firstborn Foxe. I am tired. Help me back to the temple. Tomorrow we can pack." I look around, just to make sure I am where I think I am.

"You're still leaving us?" His voice is sad as he slips a strong, thick hand under my elbow to help me up. I stand a little unsteadily, still disoriented by my sudden appearance in front of the temple.

"Yes and no, Foxe. I think—" I roll a few gems in my hand, trying to guess how many books they might purchase. "I think there is business to attend to here before I do anything. And after that. . . . Have I ever told you how much I should like to visit Waterdeep?" We slowly climb the temple steps. "I could use a good secretary, if I make such a trek. You don't know where I might find one, do you?"

A VIRTUE BY REFLECTION

Scott Ciencin

Penn Othmann couldn't explain why he felt so nervous as he closed up his small, exclusive shop. The day had been uneventful, and, following his usual routine, he had worked well into the evening cataloguing antiques. Yet as Othmann was about to pull the door shut behind him, lock it, and speak the word that would have engaged the shop's magical wards, a terrible fit of anxiety overtook him. He wanted to go back inside and hide. That would be childish, he told himself. There's nothing to fear from the night in a civilized city like Arabel. Nothing at all.

Then the figure leaped out of the shadows. Othmann felt an explosion of pain in his upper arm, and he cried out. He had been stabbed. Futilely he wished he had trusted his instincts, but it was too late to chide himself. Survival was all that mattered now.

Before Penn Othmann could make another sound, his mouth was covered by his assailant's hand. Othmann was forced back with incredible ferocity, his head slamming into the wall. A burst of pure white light filled his vision.

His attacker gripped his arm and spoke into Othmann's ear in a low voice. "Run. If you scream, I'll gut you."

The merchant desperately wanted to tell the dark, misshapen figure that he was a wealthy man, that he could pay any price for his life, but the tone of that threat told him such pleading would gain him nothing.

Instead, Penn Othmann ran, just as he had been told. He raced through the darkened streets of the city, darted into alleyways, leaped over gates, and plunged down deserted avenues. The flaxen-haired merchant prayed his heart wouldn't give out. He wanted to stop, to catch his breath and rest, but his pursuer was never less than a few paces behind. The physical regimen he had endured as training for the city's weekly footraces had kept his body hard and lean, but the cold night air bit deeply into the bloody wound in his arm. Othmann's proud, handsome features were screwed up in pain and exertion. His sky-blue eyes were fixed on the continuous maze before him.

He wasn't aware that he was being driven along a chosen path, toward a particular destination, until he turned a corner and saw a dark green wall of foliage ahead. A nightmare-black gap was carved into the shrub wall, a dark archway that served as entrance to the beautiful gardens of the Citadel. Two guards lay on their chests. They might have been dead, but Othmann couldn't tell for sure.

Suddenly he knew exactly why he had been brought here. He stopped, and the footsteps behind him ceased. The cold realization that escape had never truly been possible flooded into him, accompanied by a fear unlike any he had ever known. Trembling, Penn Othmann turned and looked into the face of his executioner.

The dark figure grinned in delight and advanced.

* * * * *

A delicate whisper moved through the fabric of Myrmeen Lhal's dreams, causing the lithe, sensuous brunette to stir gently awake. "Myrmeen," the voice said in rich, melodic tones, "it's time to begin your day, my dearest."

Her dark blue eyes, tinged with slivers of gold, fluttered open. It was morning. The voice repeated its message, and Myrmeen reached over to the ornate nightstand beside her bed and allowed her hand to drift to a beautiful crystal phoenix.

"Myrmeen, it's time to—"

The voice was abruptly silenced as her fingers grazed the small statue. The phoenix was a gift from an admirer, a magical construct that had the ability to capture sounds then release them once again at a time of her choosing. The voice that had woken her had been her own.

Myrmeen sat up in bed and turned to appraise the quality of the light streaming through the large window to her left. The radiance was delicate and soft, filtered through pale blue curtains that fluttered ever so gently, though the windows were closed and there was no breeze. Myrmeen smiled at this. The curtains had been charged with several spells of protection—as had many of the objects in the vast, opulent bedchamber—and the energy moving through them caused them to sway. If an intruder were to somehow break through the glass, the curtains would rap themselves around the unfortunate fellow and slice him to pieces. Brutal, yes, but such protective measures were not uncommon or unnecessary for the ruler of any large city in Cormyr.

And the traps and wards might be hidden anywhere in the room. The wall behind the bed was decorated with a bronze mural of barrel-chested fighting men grappling in various death-duels. The metal reverberated with a low, rhythmic thump, not unlike the beating of a human heart. A sunken bath with rapidly churning scented waters lay a few steps away. On the walls, between paintings of startling elegance, weapons of arcane origins were mounted. Any of these might prove to be far more than the trappings of wealth.

Myrmeen frowned, fell back upon the bed, and tried to go back to sleep. She had been burdened by nightmares that were already beginning to fade, and she worried that the effects of the restless night she had endured would plague her the entire day. If she could get an hour or two of proper rest, she might be able to face the day without yawning in some dignitary's face.

The dreams were of her troubled childhood, her disastrous first marriage, and the death of her second, beloved husband, Haverstrom Lhal. She knew that she should be used to the nightmares, but they disturbed her with renewed power each day. She was no longer certain they would ever leave her alone.

A warm, comforting wave eased through her body as she settled upon the bed, her bare back exposed to reveal the network of scars she had gained in her days as an adventurer. Suddenly she felt a hand gripping her shoulder, as hard and cold as bronze. She snapped instantly awake and turned to look at the mural behind her. The warriors were locked in their familiar poses.

Shaking her head, Myrmeen untangled herself from the twisted mass of sheets and swung her legs over the side of the bed. As she faced the sunlight, the shards of gold within her dark blue eyes sparkled.

The phoenix sculpture by her bed trembled and delivered another message: "It is time, milady. The delegation has arrived. I, for one, do not envy you. On the other hand, all I have to worry about is getting a good night's sleep. Fare thee well, and enjoy the delegation."

"Another delegation," Myrmeen muttered. "Kill me now." A knock came at the door. "One moment!"

Myrmeen reached to a spot in midair, as if she were pulling apart an invisible set of curtains. A shining rift appeared in the air, and, from that opening, a sparkling black gown leaped over her shoulders, slimming itself about her thin waist, generous breasts, and perfectly proportioned hips. Her headdress followed, along with her gloves, jewelry, and shoes. Another mage had given her this gift—a beautiful dresser that existed half in this plane of existence, half in another. She could also use the dimensional rift to make a hasty retreat from her quarters if the Citadel were overrun by attackers. The amorous sorcerer had assured her that only she could open or close the gate.

"Enter!" she called.

The door opened, and Myrmeen turned to face Evon Stralana, Arabel's minister of defense. The tall, wiry, dark-haired man seemed quite troubled. His already pale skin had gone pure white.

"The delegation," Myrmeen said, smiling. "I'm late."

"It's not that," he said gravely.

Her stance changed suddenly. This was no trivial matter, she sensed. Something was terribly wrong, something that had broken through Stralana's cool, reserved shell.

"Tell me," Myrmeen snapped.

"There's been a murder."

"Who was killed?"

"A merchant. Penn Othmann. I don't believe I've ever seen his name on your appointment schedule."

"No, the name doesn't sound familiar." She waited. There had to be more. Stralana wouldn't have been this concerned over a murder. Arabel was a large city and violent death was not uncommon. "What else?"

"The body was found in the gardens."

Her hands curled into fists, her nails biting into her palms with enough force to draw blood. "Was the man killed there, or was the body dropped there?"

"He died in the gardens."

Myrmeen felt her skin grow cold. "What about the guards?"

"They were found this morning, ensorcelled but unharmed. They have no memory of what occurred."

"The spells protecting the gardens?"

"Stripped away."

"I want to see."

"Yes," Stralana said. "I thought you might."

*   *   *   *   *

The fiery tongue of sunlight darted between the leaves high above the central gardens near the Citadel. Gazebos, rose-entangled archways, and topiary renditions of various gods and demigods surrounded the two figures who stood at the center of the gardens, where Othmann's head had been discovered. Soldiers had been posted to keep out the curious.

"By all the denizens of Hades," Myrmeen whispered as she turned to Stralana. "There are pieces of this man strewn from one end of the garden to the other. Whoever—or whatever—did this obviously hated him with a passion."

"Yes," Stralana said flatly.

As she studied the carnage, Myrmeen began to shake; the gardens had once been a private retreat for her and her husband. "I want to know who did this."

"I understand. Procedures have been followed, but the body resists all forms of divination and spirit magic. His soul has taken flight and cannot be reached."

"Then other means must be applied. Have our hunters gone over the tracks?"

"Of course. They claim the murderer—or murderers—covered any traces they may have left behind. It's impossible to tell how many were here, if they were men or women, if they were even human."

Myrmeen frowned. "He was a merchant you say?"

"Yes. He sold artifacts. Some magical, some not. His shop was near Elhazir's Exotica."

"I've heard several of the cleaning staff talk of Elhazir's. They display the fake jewelry they find there proudly, as if it were the real thing. Elhazir sells copies of my best dresses. She peddles trinkets she claims were blessed by the gods with fearsome power." Myrmeen paused. "Was Othmann in competition with Elhazir? Could this have been a case of professional rivalry?"

Stralana shook his head. "I sincerely doubt it. As with everything else, the magic items Elhazir sells are cheap fakes. Othmann sold genuine objects of power." The minster cleared his throat and added, "On a related matter, several youths came upon the open door to Othmann's shop during the night. They went in, unaware that a series of magical wards had been set in place. Two of the boys were burned, but not fatally. Another was reduced to the mental level of infancy, and still another was transformed into a pale, brittle creature for whom the slightest movement could result in shattered bones and ruptured organs.

"That's how we came to know Othmann was missing. We had been trying to locate him to ascertain the nature of the shop's wards, so that the mages hired by the parents of the children could have the spells countermanded. We also wanted to know why he had left the door open in such an enticing fashion. The boys had been wrong to go inside, but they had practically been invited.

"One of the guardsmen who had been given Othmann's description was also one of the first men to arrive at the gardens this morning. That's how the victim was identified so quickly." Stralana gestured to a guard standing apart from the others. "I've asked the lad to wait until you're done here, in case you wish to speak with him." When Myrmeen shook her head, he shrugged and continued.

"I sent two of our finest sorcerers around to Othmann's shop the moment we had the body identified, along with several of our investigators. Elhazir was upon them very quickly. She was filled with questions, and when she learned that Othmann was dead, she seemed genuinely grieved. The woman told our agents much of what we needed to know—that Othmann specialized in high-priced artifacts, magical and otherwise. His shop was open by appointment only. Elhazir gave him referrals whenever it became obvious that her clients knew what they wanted and would not be tricked by her fast tongue. In return for sending him clients, Othmann gave her a healthy commission."

"Was Othmann a sorcerer?" Myrmeen asked quietly.

"No one seems to know."

"But he trafficked in items of power. I would wager that if he was not well-versed in the Art, he was closely affiliated with someone who was. That person may have been the one who subdued our guards, defeated the spells protecting the gardens, and killed Othmann."

Stralana nodded. "That would make sense, but Elhazir made no mention of a partner. Othmann seemed to run his trade completely alone."

"She's lying or ill informed. What did she tell your men of Othmann's personal affairs?"

"Only that he kept them extremely private. They enjoyed a professional relationship and nothing more."

Myrmeen paused to consider this. "I don't want anyone going into Othmann's shop until I'm through with the blasted delegation this morning. Then I'll join the men there. Oh, and I'll want to talk with Elhazir myself."

The pale-skinned man waited patiently for her next command.

"Evon, I need to visit the gazebo. It would be best if I did it alone."

"Of course. But . . ."

Myrmeen leveled a cold gaze on her minister. "But what?"

"Nothing, milady," he murmured. Lowering his eyes in respect, Stralana left her and returned to his men.

Alone, Myrmeen walked through the gardens until an elegantly adorned gazebo loomed before her. Carved into the far wall was a representation of a phoenix, her late husband's symbol. She thought of his funeral pyre and the vain, ridiculous hope she had nurtured that somehow he would rise from his own ashes. He had risen only in her heart, where a part of him would remain forever.

But those mournful thoughts were quickly replaced in Myrmeen's mind by shock. Blood spattered the gazebo's walls, marring Haverstrom's phoenix. Whoever had murdered Othmann had left his body in the gardens as a message to her. There could be no other reason for this senseless vandalism.

Anger flooded into her with renewed vitality. Since her husband's death, there had been many times when the pressures of ruling Arabel were too much to bear. She needed a place to which she could retreat, a place where she would always feel safe. The gardens—and this spot in particular—had been that sanctuary. Standing in this gazebo, Myrmeen had always been able to recall the joy, love, and comfort she had found in her husband's arms.

Images raced into her mind. She thought of one morning after invaders had attempted to take the city. Haverstrom had been stabbed, and his healers called it a miracle that he had survived. She could almost hear his voice as he raised his armored fist in the air and railed against his enemies, promising that they would experience the dark miracle of his vengeance. And now she, too, would seek out that dark miracle.

Myrmeen cried out in rage, the shout of a warrior thirsting for revenge. When she had regained control of herself, she placed her hand on the wall for support. Her husband had proposed to her in this gazebo. They'd kissed for the first time in its cool shade. . . .

The sight of what had been done made Myrmeen want to draw blood of her own. Quelling those dark thoughts as best she could, she walked from the gazebo until she came upon a collection of her men, then commanded three of them to strip off their breastplates and give her their padded doublets. They did not hesitate to obey.

On the way back to the gazebo, Myrmeen tore the shirts into strips and paused at a small fountain where she soaked the rags she had made. She returned to the small building and stared at the crimson spatters. Stralana had been over this place; his hesitation earlier told her that much. And since he did not say otherwise, it was safe to assume they gained no clues from it.

Myrmeen began to wipe away the blood staining the white walls. Soon she was covered in sweat and her clothes were ruined. She made several trips to the fountain, but all the water in the Inner Sea wouldn't restore the gazebo to its former pristine condition. And even if she could wash away the blood, the place wouldn't be the same, for she could never wipe away the memory.

"I miss you, Haverstrom," she said, running her fingers lightly over the walls. "But know wherever you are that I will avenge this."

She turned and silently stalked out of the gardens.

*   *   *   *   *

An hour later, Myrmeen stood in her throne room, flanked by guards. Evon Stralana and several of his soldiers observed the scene stoically from the back of the room. Two men, a woman, and a collection of almost a dozen cats, both domestic and wild, milled before the throne. The delegation had identified itself as representing a race that rarely revealed itself to mortals—the cat lords.

Myrmeen stiffened, worried that her fear of the jaguar they had brought might become apparent to the animal. She was surrounded by guards and magical wards, but she was quite familiar with the speed and ferocity of such animals.

The female cat lord smiled, apparently sensing Myrmeen's discomfort. She wriggled her gloved fingers, and the jaguar lay at her feet. Myrmeen watched the creature nervously, thinking of Penn Othmann's shredded corpse.

"My name is Siobhan," the woman said. "With me is Niccolo and Sauveur."

Myrmeen nodded as she looked at each of the cat lords. Siobhan's age was impossible to discern. She seemed quite young, but there was a stiffness to her movements quite unusual for one of her race. Perhaps it was the high leather boots she wore; they looked rather uncomfortable.

Still, no one could deny Siobhan's beauty. Her black hair cascaded to her waist, almost lost against her dark but elegant clothing. The woman's piercing, gray-blue eyes fastened on Myrmeen as she pulled her lips into an enigmatic smile. As she bowed her head in greeting, the heart-shaped amulet around her neck bobbed. One side of the riven heart was blood red, the other black.

Behind the lovely Siobhan, Niccolo ran his hand through his thick auburn mane and Sauveur rolled his head, allowing his silver hair to graze his shoulders. Both men were strikingly handsome.

After exchanging pleasantries, Myrmeen asked Siobhan to proceed with her request.

"I cannot," Siobhan replied. "Our lord dominante is not among us. He must have been detained."

The doors burst open, and a devastatingly handsome green-eyed man entered. His features were sharply defined, his cheeks, nose, and jaw strongly chiseled. The man's lips were sensuous and inviting, his eyes the deepest emerald Myrmeen had ever seen. He was dressed in black with gold and light blue trim. His shirt was bright red.

Myrmeen took her throne, and the delegation crowded more closely around her. Siobhan gestured at the dark man. "I would like to introduce Lord Zacharius."

The green-eyed man moved forward, took Myrmeen's hand, and gave it a tiny lick. Myrmeen was startled, until Zacharius winked and added, "People always expect that type of thing from me." He took her hand a second time, gently kissed it, then withdrew.

"Lord Zacharius—"

"Zaz, please. My name is Zaehlas Alandovos Zacharius. But then, it's been shortened over the years. Humans seem to find Zaz most appropriate. Rolls off the tongue easier."

"In this chamber, Lord Zacharius is more fitting."

"As you wish."

Myrmeen sighed. "What may I do for you?"

"You have something we want. Something that belongs to us, actually. We have come to reclaim it. Now, to tell you what we have come to Arabel to find, I must first tell you something of our race. Long ago, wars were fought among the various tribes of the cats. Natural enemies struck out against one another. Centuries of bloodshed ensued."

"By 'the cats,' you mean the cat lords. Your people."

Zacharius hesitated. "Yes. Of course."

Siobhan laughed and knelt down to scratch the ears of the jaguar at her feet. A half-dozen of the other felines meowed jealously. The jaguar yawned, then rolled its head and turned to Myrmeen. There was a startling intelligence in the creature's eyes, and the gaze was almost hypnotic. . . .

The trance was shattered when a small gray kitten broke from the pack and leaped into Myrmeen's lap, startling her.

"Ah, you'd best beware," Siobhan said with a laugh. "That's our fiercest warrior."

The kitten looked up at Myrmeen and mewled piteously. She stroked its side, and the kitten closed its eyes and curled contentedly in her lap.

Lord Zacharius said, "Satsuma, a great leader of our people, gave his life to unite the warring tribes against a common enemy. That enemy, though defeated, played one last cruel trick. Satsuma's bones were stolen by the enemy's soldiers and scattered throughout Faerun. We have cause to believe that one of these secret burial chambers rests beneath the university. Allow us to reclaim our fallen leader and finally send his soul to the rest it deserves, and you will have our gratitude for all time."

"Beneath the university?" Myrmeen asked. "Exactly where beneath the university?"

"We don't know. The whole structure will have to come down, of course."

"I see."

Lord Zacharius cocked his head. "Is that a problem?"

"I would think so. The clerics of Tymora who staff the place are rather fond of it. So are the students." Myrmeen frowned. "What's the source of your information? Who told you Satsuma's remains were here?"

"I can't tell you that," Zacharius said brightly. "What I've told you thus far is more than any human has ever been allowed to know about our race."

"I'm honored," Myrmeen said wearily. "I'm also placed in a very awkward position. It took many years to have that building erected and to make it the success it is now. I sympathize with your needs, Lord Zacharius, but your request is somewhat extreme."

Under normal circumstances, Myrmeen would have rejected Zacharius's proposal without further discussion. She could not, however, get the image of Penn Othmann's savaged body from her thoughts. It returned whenever she glanced at the jaguar lying at Siobhan's feet.

"I will need time to fully consider your request," Myrmeen said at last.

"I understand." Zacharius wiggled his fingers. The gray kitten in Myrmeen's lap leaped from her and went to him. Zacharius paused at the door, waiting until Siobhan, Niccolo, Sauveur, and the cats had all filed out. "Summon me when you've made a decision. I will not be hard to find."

With a strange, enigmatic smile, he turned and left. The doors were shut behind him.

Evon Stralana broke from his soldiers and came to Myrmeen. "What do you think?"

The noblewoman's face was set in a scowl. "If you find as much as one cat hair on the merchant's corpse, I want Lord Zacharius and his entire entourage brought in for questioning. In any case, find out everything you can about him and have your men keep a very close watch on the entire entourage. I want to know where they're staying, who they contact while they're here—everything."

"Consider it done. In the meantime, may I suggest we try to learn more about the victim?"

*   *   *   *   *

A short time later, Myrmeen stood outside Othmann's shop. The mages soon completed their work, verified that it was safe to enter, and allowed Myrmeen to follow them inside. There were no windows, so torches had to be lit.

The interior of the shop consisted of a few shelves on the walls, several glass cases, a desk with three chairs—one behind, two in front—and a small room in the back, where empty crates were piled up to hide a large black box. They approached it cautiously, since it was warded by three spells. These proved to be simple enchantments, easily undone by the skillful sorcerers. Inside, they found several bags of gold and a handful of precious stones.

The mages examined several of the artifacts around the shop and verified that each was of very high quality. The power resting within them was quite genuine. Only a dilapidated Harp of Myth Drannor brought a skeptical frown.

The first mage, a tired older man named Volney, turned to his partner. "All right, Walcott, take this down: a ring of invisibility, five vials of healing potions, two small jars of ointments to restore youth and instill longevity, and a chalice from which a man might drink and see his future. Fairly standard stuff."

Walcott seemed world-weary and definitely unimpressed by Volney's casual dismissal of the store's contents. He nodded agreeably anyway, then turned to Myrmeen. "He has amulets that will explode upon the wrongful death of the owner. Take half a city block with for revenge, too. There are items here to trap a shapeshifter in its present form, and much more. It makes no sense at all that he was killed so easily."

"What are you saying?" Myrmeen asked.

Walcott shrugged. "The man knew the streets could be dangerous at night, yet he never traveled with guards of any kind. He obviously felt safe from any mundane threat."

"That's true," Myrmeen said, recalling the testimony of several other shop owners she had questioned while waiting for the mages to complete their task. "Unless, of course, he carried some of these objects of power on him, so that if he were attacked, he'd be able to defend himself." She paused. "But when we went over his body and his clothing, we found nothing."

"Perhaps that's what the killer was after," Volney said, hoping to reclaim his faltering position of authority. "Some object Othmann carried on his person."

"If he had a weapon, why didn't he use it?" Myrmeen asked.

"He may not have had the chance," Walcott noted grimly. "Not if his murderer was a powerful mage."

Myrmeen found it very warm in the shop. She wiped away the sweat that was starting to fall into her eyes. "So you think this was a matter of theft? Then why bring Othmann to the gardens? The wards protecting this place were already undone. Why not drag him back inside and kill him here? They could have cleaned the shop out."

"If his murderer was a true master of the Art," Walcott said, "he wouldn't have been interested in most of the shop's contents. Like we said, this stuff is all pretty standard."

Volney nodded sagely. "And to a high-powered wizard the wards at the gardens would have been child's play to undo."

All three were startled by a knock at the door. Evon Stralana appeared and ushered an attractive woman into the room. Myrmeen had sent the minister of defense to fetch the owner of Elhazir's Exotica for questioning. The woman had honey-blond hair, doe eyes, and a hardness about her mouth that seemed incongruous. She was overdressed, her wardrobe overwhelmed entirely by the cheap, flashy jewelry she sold. Her dress was a poor imitation of Myrmeen's latest formal gown.

Scurrying in behind the woman was a young girl with wide, frightened eyes and a simple white dress. The child looked beyond her mistress, to Myrmeen, and her eyes widened.

"Lord Lhal," the first woman said. "I am Elhazir. This is my assistant, Andreana."

The girl bowed and opened her mouth to speak, but Elhazir cut her off. "Is there some service I may perform for you, Lord Lhal?"

Myrmeen stared at Elhazir's red, bleary eyes. The woman's heavy makeup had been applied recently, but it couldn't hide the fact that she'd been crying for hours. "Perhaps if you could answer a few questions. . . ."

"Of course."

"How did you know Penn Othmann?"

"He came by now and then to talk. Lots of the other merchants did. Business has been slow."

"You also had a financial arrangement with him."

"Yes, but it was a rare occasion when I had cause to send one of my customers to Penn."

"Did you hear or see anything suspicious last night?"

"Nothing."

"Did he seem anxious or frightened lately?"

"No, he seemed quite normal."

Myrmeen placed her hand on the shoulder of the young girl. "Did you see or hear anything?"

Andreana shrugged. "I never paid much attention."

"Yes," Elhazir snapped, "that's your problem. You never pay attention to anything, you little halfwit."

Myrmeen watched the girl's hair fall into her eyes as she looked down. It did not disguise the hurt she saw there. Turning to Elhazir, Myrmeen asked, "Would you have any objections to my men searching both your house and your business?"

"Do what you like," Elhazir said. "I'm not hiding anything."

"Of course not, but maybe you're overlooking something important. One other thing. We've heard from several parties that Othmann was involved with a red-haired woman about my age," Myrmeen lied. "Do you know anything about her?"

Elhazir was stunned. She flinched, then bit her lower lip. "No, I can't."

"He also had a wife in Suzail," Myrmeen added. "We're thinking she may be our prime suspect."

"A wife," Elhazir said flatly. "How interesting."

"If the wife found out about the mistress—or mistresses—she might have hired a mage to kill him."

"A mage? He was killed by a mage?"

"Yes. You didn't know that?"

"I didn't."

Myrmeen nodded. "I see. And about the wife?"

"He never said anything about being married."

"Thanks for your help," Myrmeen said abruptly. "Both of you are dismissed."

The woman nodded, took the arm of her assistant, and left the shop. One of Myrmeen's soldiers accompanied her. The dark-eyed ruler turned to Stralana. "Othmann and Elhazir were lovers."

"I gathered as much from your, shall we say, *creative* inquiries."

"I want you to use your best men to conduct the search of Elhazir's home and business. Go through everything."

"You're hoping to find some tangible evidence of Elhazir's relationship to Othmann? To establish her motive?"

"That's part of it," Myrmeen said. "Frankly, I wouldn't be surprised if she's a mage herself—or knows the identity of the mage who killed Othmann. But we can't arrest her without cause."

"What if my men find nothing?"

"Then have her watched night and day. She's upset enough now after that story I made up about Othmann's wife and other lovers that she might make a mistake. Let's hope she gives herself away or leads us to the one we seek."

A scream ripped through the street, causing Myrmeen, Stralana, and one of the soldiers to race out of the shop. The mages and another soldier remained behind.

"It came from there," a young flaxen-haired soldier named Kynan Tofte said as he pointed at an alley across the street. There they found an old woman crouched atop a pile of trash. She brandished a broom as if it were a sword, holding off the collection of hissing, clawing cats at her feet. The felines had trapped the woman and seemed prepared to attack.

"This does not bode well," Stralana said as the soldiers went to the woman's aid. "Does it?"

Myrmeen watched the cats scatter into the alley, then shook her head. "No, I'm afraid it doesn't."

* * * * *

For the next three days, incidents involving the feline population of Arabel abounded: Two dozen people were assaulted by their household pets the first afternoon. Ten times that number reported confrontations that night. No one was seriously injured, though many claimed to have nearly died of fright.

A marauding pack of cats, several hundred strong, pounced upon an outdoor fish market in the middle of the day and seriously depleted the merchant's supplies before they were driven off. Bakeries and dairies were vandalized. Arabel's most prominent tailor came to Myrmeen in tears, reporting that his entire warehouse of clothes had been ripped to shreds by tiny claws. In several incidents it was obvious that human hands, or hands that were human at least part of the time, had been at work. A half-dozen outdoor performances by dramatic touring companies had been interrupted, and one which relied heavily on magic to carry off its action had been stopped dead, the actors terrified of getting their faces scratched by the animals.

Like most in Cormyr, Arabel's citizens had long believed cats to be the eyes and messengers of the gods. Killing a cat was a serious offense, and many preferred to suffer the indignations heaped upon them by the felines rather than risk offending some powerful deity. Some crouched in corners and prayed for guidance as their businesses were vandalized. They begged for illumination, horrified that they had somehow offended their gods.

Others became tired of the whole strange situation and took up arms against the beasts. Several cats had been killed, a few maimed. Those who slew them were later found to be the victims of mysterious accidents; bits of fur—some matted in blood—had been found at the site of each incident. The gods had taken vengeance, the devout whispered fearfully.

On the second night, reports of disturbances had escalated to include traders who had been accosted just outside the city's walls by monstrous creatures swathed in darkness. The merchants' wares had been destroyed. Other traders complained their stock had been similarly targeted when they'd attempted to leave Arabel.

Through it all, Stralana's men kept Lord Zacharius, Siobhan, Niccolo, and Sauveur under constant surveillance. The cat lords' whereabouts could be accounted for at all times. They had been nowhere near the sites of even the most minor conflict. Nevertheless, Zacharius had not been idle. Using his credentials as a diplomat, he had successfully charged to Myrmeen and the city outrageous bar tabs, bills for fine meals, and several visits to local brothels. At the last of these he had left a note which read, "Dearest Myrmeen, I could never resist a good cathouse. Yours, Zaz."

It was commonly believed that Zacharius was responsible for the growing number of strange episodes involving the felines. He may not have committed any of the acts himself, but he was certainly behind them. Despite the incidents throughout the city, though, the people were truly beginning to like Lord Zacharius, and it had nothing to do with his roguish charm. Myrmeen examined the pattern of attacks and realized the cat lord and his people had targeted individuals who had been known to cheat their customers, to treat their neighbors badly, or those who had otherwise achieved a hearty level of dislike among the common populace.

Myrmeen wanted to lock the man up, but it wasn't until the third day of the weird siege that she had just cause. Someone secretly poisoned the entire night watch, though none fatally so. And though the unconscious men and women weren't discovered until morning, their beats did not go unkept; dozens of Zacharius's people somehow knew of the mishap and took on the task of patrolling the night. All of the cat lords were quite friendly and performed their tasks so efficiently that the substitution wasn't noticed until the new shift came on at sunrise.

Less than an hour later, Myrmeen and Evon Stralana caught up with Lord Zacharius outside a popular eatery. He was taken to the Citadel and imprisoned. Along the way, he seemed completely oblivious to the anger of his captors and his very circumstances. In the street, some people cheered him.

"I love this city," he cried. "Arabel is an amazing and friendly place. I intend to recommend it to all my people."

Myrmeen locked Lord Zacharius in the lowest levels of the palace, demanding an end to the attacks against her citizens, but Zacharius claimed he was innocent of any wrongdoings—except the business with the guardsmen, of course. That, he noted with a smirk, had been a harmless prank.

The cat lord was clear on one thing, though: his presence was most certainly an indirect, contributing factor to the local chaos. The sooner he got what he wanted and was gone, the better it would be for all involved.

After a day had passed with Lord Zacharius in custody, Myrmeen understood why he had been completely nonplussed by his incarceration. The green-eyed cat lord escaped repeatedly from an array of cells in the dungeon, but even Stralana could not explain how he was doing it. Men were stationed to watch him constantly, and mages were commissioned to prevent his jaunts. None of it had mattered. He came and went as he pleased. Regardless of precautions, the cat lord simply vanished from the prison to show up elsewhere in the city, enjoy an expensive meal, entertain a luscious young lady, then return to the palace, making a grandiose royal entrance.

* * * * *

Night had fallen, and Myrmeen Lhal sat in her throne room, brooding over the murder of Penn Othmann. Presently, the investigation was at a standstill: Stralana's inquiries into Lord Zacharius's actions since his arrival in Arabel—before and after his incarceration—had given no indication that the cat lord had been in any way affiliated with Penn Othmann. According to the records, Zacharius arrived the morning after the murder, right on schedule for his audience. And Zacharius could account for almost every moment of his time away from his cell, and he did so willingly, even to the point of garrulousness.

Myrmeen's investigation of her other suspect was faring no better. Stralana's men had uncovered no evidence at Elhazir's home or business to substantiate the suspicions of an affair between her and Othmann. And if the woman was a mage, she kept no spellbooks, no obvious components for enchantments, and no true objects of power. In fact, Elhazir had no correspondence or records to indicate that she had ever been affiliated with mages of any skill. Myrmeen, hoping that the magic-wielding murderer might make contact with Elhazir, decided to give the situation a few more days.

The door to Myrmeen's throne room suddenly burst open, and Kynan Tofte entered. The young soldier cried, "He's done it again! One minute Lord Zacharius was in his cell, content as could be, lapping at the soup we brought him, the next he was gone!"

"Search the restaurants and brothels," Myrmeen growled. "He'll turn up . . . along with a sizeable bill."

Kynan Tofte lowered his head and nodded. "Of course, milady. Please forgive me for intruding."

"No apology is necessary."

The soldier turned his gaze in the direction of the untouched plate of food sitting beside her throne. She had been thinking about the desecration of the gardens and had been too upset to eat. The soldier seemed to consider making an encouraging comment, then thought better of it. He quickly exited, leaving the doors ajar. Myrmeen flirted with the idea of calling out to him, or to one of the servants, to close the door, then she chided herself for being so lazy. Crossing the room, Myrmeen sealed the chamber shut. She felt a slight chill at her back and turned sharply at the sound of someone biting into an apple.

Lord Zacharius sat upon the throne. He had one leg sprawled over the side, one arm over the back. The handsome visitor turned his dazzling smile upon Myrmeen as he dropped the partially eaten apple onto the tray containing the rest of her meal.

"Lord Zacharius," Myrmeen said, carefully hiding her surprise. "Is it exercise period for the prisoners? If not, I assume you have a reason for being here. You might also explain *how* you got into my throne room, while you're at it."

He shrugged. "The reason for my visit is simple. I merely wanted to extend my thanks for your warm hospitality, your old-fashioned generosity. It touches my heart, it does. I'm not often treated to free bed and board." He licked his lips. "The how? That's my secret and will remain as such."

"You were locked in a dungeon, Lord Zacharius. The 'hospitality' you spoke of was imprisonment."

"I suppose, if you want to look at it that way. But as you can see, I've hardly been confined. Why don't we try to make the best out of it?"

"Your imprisonment is as much for your protection as anything. Many hold you responsible for the acts of your people. They might attempt to harm you."

"Or they might reward me for getting back at the nasty, fat slobs that cheat them. You're aware of the protesters outside the Citadel, aren't you? Even as we speak, there are—"

"I am well aware of them," Myrmeen said curtly.

"Your citizens are outraged and frightened by the treatment I've received. They chant that the gods will be quite cross. They feel all the 'incidents,' as you call them, are the results of the higher powers defending my race."

"Those people are professional zealots," Myrmeen said, "looking for any cause."

"They've found mine."

Myrmeen narrowed her eyes. "They don't know what you truly are, Lord Zacharius. I doubt they would be so supportive if they knew of your bestial side."

"Threats don't become you," he drawled. "And please, call me Zaz."

"Lord Zacharius, this is a serious matter. Your kind has the power to hypnotize, to enchant. Is that how you've managed to get out of your cell nearly every evening for the past tenday? Is that how you got in here?"

"Nothing so crude as that. I thought we might spend a quiet evening together." The cat lord uncoiled his body and rose from Myrmeen's throne. She went angrily toward him, and they met in the center of the room. "And afterward, I thought we might once again discuss my proposal."

"I refuse to give any serious consideration to your request so long as the attacks against my people persist."

"What makes you think I have anything to do with it?" he asked as he absently brushed her arm.

Myrmeen pulled away and restrained an urge to strike the man. "I slighted you. I insulted your religious beliefs and refused your request to unearth the remains of your ancestor. Zealots have often killed for less."

"Do I seem like a zealot to you?"

Myrmeen looked away from the man's hypnotic gaze. "I don't know what to make of you."

"Of course you do. Trust your instincts. Listen to what they tell you."

"At the moment, my instincts tell me that, despite your diplomatic status, you should be questioned about the murder in the gardens."

"Do you suspect me of that murder?" he asked, genuinely surprised.

Myrmeen nodded. "You or one of your people. Your gift for getting in and out of heavily secured places has certainly done little to set my concerns aside. The way the dead man was savaged certainly seems like it could have been the work of your kind."

"Naturally you've considered that the victim may have been killed in this manner to cast suspicion upon any wild beast, not just my cats. The ploy has been successful in keeping your attention from the true murderer, if you're spending so much time worrying about me."

"Anything is possible."

"I don't even know this man who was killed."

"So you say."

He grinned, his green eyes sparkling. "Myrmeen, I could never lie to you."

Anger seized the noblewoman. "You seem to think you can get what you want by being charming."

"It's always worked before."

"Understand this, Lord Zacharius: Even if I was attracted to you—which I am not—I could make love to you tonight and order your death tomorrow."

"I see," the cat lord said. "Well, with that in mind, I think the act itself would be anticlimactic. Good night."

He walked gracefully to the door. "I want the activities of your people curtailed," Myrmeen called after him.

Lord Zacharius turned back and opened his hands in a solicitous gesture. "Even if my people are responsible for the local chaos, I'm sure they're just being playful. They like it here. I don't think I'll be able to convince them to leave. If anything, I think more will come."

"That would be unfortunate."

"I don't think so. We cat lords know how to have a good time. We'll liven the place up." He shrugged. "Oh, and would you be so kind as to summon an escort for me? I seem to have forgotten the way back to my chamber. . . ."

* * * * *

Myrmeen was unable to sleep that night. She left the palace under heavy guard and was on her way to the gardens when she heard the scream. Having faced the horror of death many times in the past, the noblewoman knew the sound of a man facing his end. By the time she had passed through the maze of buildings flanking the gardens and discovered the limp, staring bodies of the guardsmen left on duty, Myrmeen knew what she would find in the maze of shrubs and flowerbeds.

A second man lay murdered in the gardens. His body had been torn to pieces. Blood was splattered everywhere, particularly in the gazebo. Myrmeen advanced on the corpse in disbelief, choking back a scream of rage. She tried to understand how this could have happened a second time.

Myrmeen was barely aware of her surroundings as her soldiers congregated around the corpse. Kynan Tofte soon uncovered the victim's head, then guided Myrmeen to the spot where it rested. She was surprised to find that she recognized the dead man's face.

It was Volney, the elder mage Evon Stralana had employed to secure and investigate Penn Othmann's shop a few days earlier. Stralana arrived and seemed momentarily stricken at the sight of the mage's corpse. In a hoarse whisper he said, "Volney and Walcott were supervising the surveillance of Elhazir."

"He may have learned something that made him dangerous to the sorcerer we've been after. Stralana, get a search going for Walcott. Either he's in danger, too, or he's in league with the murderer."

"There's something else you should know," the minister said. "Volney's last report noted that the cats have been watching Elhazir, too."

"Where is Lord Zacharius?"

"In his cell, conducting some kind of game with the guards. Something with dice. It seemed harmless enough, and the men were bored."

"Get him. I want him with us when we confront Elhazir."

Stralana broke from her and hurried to see her orders carried out. Within ten minutes, Myrmeen, Stralana, and Lord Zacharius started off in the direction of Elhazir's Exotica. A group of soldiers accompanied them, and, by the time they reached the market district, a pack of felines trailed their every move. Myrmeen noticed the jaguar and looked around for Siobhan, but the woman was nowhere to be seen.

The door to Elhazir's was open, and the warm orange glow of torchlight could be seen from within. Before anyone could react, two cats slipped inside, one with auburn fur, the other pale silver.

Myrmeen turned to her soldiers and pointed at Lord Zacharius. "Keep him out here for now."

"That may not be wise," the cat lord said.

Ignoring him, Myrmeen went inside with Stralana and found that the place was a shambles, the ornate tapestries covering the walls shredded. Racks were filled with clothing that had been torn apart. Glass cases were shattered and displays had been overturned. The floors were covered in cheap, glittering costume jewelry.

The two cats were already there when Myrmeen discovered the girl, Andreana, huddled in the corner of a private room in the back. Elhazir lay at her feet. The older woman's hair was wild, her eyes staring. Her breathing was shallow.

Andreana was in tears. The moment she looked up and saw the cats approaching, she screamed something in a language Myrmeen had never heard before. Suddenly a reddish black tongue of flame erupted from her hands, covering the distance separating her from the cats in the blink of an eye. The felines leaped out of the way as the bolt struck the wall. As Andreana rose, her fists swathed in the reddish black energy, the cats raced away from her. "Why are you here?" she sobbed at Myrmeen. "To laugh at the halfwit?"

The noblewoman stared at the child. Here was the missing mage. Elhazir didn't need to leave her shop to contact the sorcerer; she'd been at the old woman's side all along. "Andreana? Who killed Penn Othmann?"

"He was a vile man. It's good that he died. He did things. Bad things."

"To you?"

Her tears covered her face. The sleeves of her gown fell back, revealing a network of scars on her arms. "Yes. Elhazir did, too. They beat me and burned me. They wanted to keep me in line."

"Did you kill him?"

"No," she snarled. "But I wish I had."

Myrmeen looked at the frightened eyes of the abused girl before her. "You're a powerful young woman. Why did you stay here with them?"

"My family is poor. They needed the gold I sent them."

"Was that the only reason?"

"No. Elhazir told me that my mother and father would be hurt if I disobeyed her or if any harm came to her."

Myrmeen bit her lip. "What happened here tonight? Was it the cats? Did they attack you? Or was it Elhazir?"

Beside Myrmeen, Stralana attempted to take a step closer to the girl, but the young mage fixed him with her wild stare and he froze. Suddenly, a blast of cold air came from the other side of the room and everyone turned to see Lord Zacharius standing in the doorway, a black cat in his hands. The cat had intense gray-blue eyes. Around the animal's neck was an amulet Myrmeen had seen before, a heart split in two. When she had last seen it, one side was blood red, the other black. Now both halves were crimson.

The cat was Siobhan.

"Guards!" Myrmeen shouted.

Lord Zacharius shook his head. "They won't be able to respond, I'm afraid. The same magic that made the other soldiers sleep in the garden has been employed. We're quite alone in here, except for my people."

Myrmeen looked to the door and saw the solid, brutish, human forms of Niccolo and Sauveur. A dozen other cat lords crowded in behind them. Evon Stralana grabbed for his sword. Myrmeen looked at him sharply, raising one hand. Reluctantly he released the weapon.

"You killed Penn Othmann," Myrmeen said flatly.

"Not at all," Zacharius said, raising the cat slightly. "She was the one."

"Siobhan," Myrmeen said.

"Yes." Lord Zacharius looked to the girl. Softly, he said, "Hello, child."

Myrmeen watched as Andreana drew back from him.

"You have nothing to fear. You know that," Zacharius began. "I have visited you many times. I told you that we would rescue you, if you would get what we wanted. We have fulfilled our end of the bargain. Will you renege on yours?"

"My parents," Andreana sobbed.

"They're fine. Elhazir's threats were meaningless. Even if

the woman had been telling you the truth, my people would have protected your parents, even in Daggerdale. You must believe that. You've seen tonight what we can do."

Nodding tearfully, Andreana reached into her pocket and drew out the mummified remains of a tiny leg that ended in a cat's paw.

"Satsuma's remains," Evon Stralana whispered.

Myrmeen was staring at the amulet around Siobhan's neck when the words of her husband came to her: *The dark miracle of vengeance will be mine.*

"The bones of Satsuma were a ruse," she said flatly. "Nothing but a lie. This was about revenge."

"Yes," Lord Zacharius replied as he bent low and allowed the black cat in his arms to leap free. It landed with only three legs and looked briefly to the doorway.

Following the cat's gaze, Myrmeen saw the young mage, Walcott, standing between Niccolo and Sauveur. From his eyes, glittering even in the dark room, she could tell that he was one of them. At Othmann's shop, he'd tried to guide the investigation toward a murderous mage, away from the cat lords and the truth.

As Myrmeen looked away from the mage and stared at the crippled cat, she tried to make sense of what she was seeing. This cat was Siobhan. She was certain of that. But what had happened to her leg? The cat lord who'd presented herself as Siobhan at the audience . . . Myrmeen thought of the high leather boots she'd worn, her graceless movements, and finally she understood.

The cat went to the young girl and stopped before her. Andreana set the leg beside the crippled creature and drew back. The cat lord grew in size, its features widening, the hair retreating from its skin. Soon the naked, human form of Siobhan sat before them. Her left leg ended in a stump just past her hips. She reached for the cat's paw and held it to her breast as she fought to hold back her tears.

"What's happening here?" Stralana demanded.

Myrmeen took off her cloak and draped it around Siobhan's shoulders. "A dark miracle."

The beautiful cat lord regarded Myrmeen with reddened eyes and asked, "How much have you guessed?"

"Some," Myrmeen said. "It would be better if you told me."

Siobhan looked to Lord Zacharius. "Do you trust her?"

"Yes," he said.

She nodded. "Twelve years ago, I was attacked by two men. It happened in your gardens, at that gazebo. They knew somehow that I was a cat lord. They considered me less than human and treated me as such. The mage used an amulet to trap me in my human form, then he and the other man forced themselves on me.

"I came back the next day to punish them, but Othmann carried a weapon of some power in those days. He hacked my leg off while I was a cat and stabbed me a dozen times. He thought I had bled to death and dumped my body in the trash. The leg he kept as a souvenir."

Myrmeen shuddered. "You survived and sought revenge."

"Lord Zacharius helped me. I would never have found him again on my own, since both men changed their names and employed magic to alter their appearances after the murder." She grinned wickedly, and her eyes flashed. "Maybe they thought I'd only used up one life and might come back to haunt them."

Zacharius frowned at the woman, then turned back to Myrmeen. "Some time ago Othmann learned of our quest for Satsuma's remains—which is quite genuine, I assure you. He claimed to have some information we required, but refused to part with it for a reasonable price. In truth, he tried to extort us. And when the negotiation got out of hand, he threatened my envoy, using Siobhan's leg as an example of his past dealings with our kind. Word reached me, and I put the two together. You've seen the rest first-hand."

"What about Volney?" Stralana asked.

"Volney and Othmann had a violent parting several years ago," Walcott replied. "I had to search Arabel for nearly a year before I found a sorcerer who bore the scent of Siobhan's blood."

"I don't understand," Myrmeen said. "Years have passed since the assault. Her blood had been washed from his body."

Walcott cleared his throat. "From his body, yes. But not from his soul."

"Walcott can sense such things. He's one of our most powerful mages," Zacharius said. "He befriended Volney, then guided him to your employ, where we could involve him in the murder investigation. Though the arrival of the cat lords made him nervous, Volney had no idea that it was his former partner who had been slain—after all, both had changed their appearances. And if all had gone as planned, we would have framed Volney for the murder."

Stralana rubbed his chin thoughtfully. "So, what happened?"

Siobhan answered this. "I needed my paw back as much as I needed revenge. Walcott has a spell that will restore me, you see." She rubbed the grisly prize lovingly. "Anyway, Othmann died without telling us where the paw was. We hoped Volney knew. When it became clear he was ignorant, we killed him and returned to Elhazir."

"She claimed not to know," Lord Zacharius said, "but she was using the child's powers to hide some objects from your men—including the paw—which she'd stolen from Othmann's shop. She figured the paw must be worth money, since we were searching for it, then decided it was dangerous. I suppose she thought that as long as she held onto what we wanted, we wouldn't harm her. Tonight, when several of my people went through this place in search of the paw, she snapped. The fear was too much for her."

Myrmeen glanced at Siobhan's locket. "There's one thing more, isn't there? The reason why the bodies resisted all forms of divination and spirit magic?"

"Yes," Siobhan said, fingering the locket. "How could you contact their souls when they were safely locked away?"

Myrmeen looked at the brilliant red halves of the heart-shaped locket. They seemed to pulse slightly, like a living, beating heart.

Lord Zacharius knelt before Andreana. "You're free, you know. If you like, you can travel with us for a time. We'll see that you get back to your parents."

"What about the gold Elhazir was giving me? That's what interested my parents. They didn't want me."

Confusion clouded Zacharius's handsome face. "I thought you wanted to live with them again."

Andreana bit her lip. "They'll just send me somewhere else. I might have to work for someone just like Elhazir again. Maybe even worse."

"But your concern for them—"

"I didn't want them hurt. I still don't. That doesn't mean I want to go back there."

Walcott stepped forward. "I could use some help. She could apprentice to me."

Lord Zacharius raised one eyebrow. "Would that suit you?"

"If I was getting paid," she whispered. "And if no one calls me a halfwit."

"Demanding, aren't you?" Zacharius said with a smile. "Very well. Your skills as a negotiator show you are a girl of rare intelligence, Andreana."

The girl's face lit up.

Myrmeen looked at the crowd of cat lords outside the doorway, then stared into Zacharius's emerald eyes. "I may not be able to stop you from leaving here tonight, but you cannot seriously expect there to be no repercussions. The lot of you have confessed to premeditated murder. There are laws to be upheld."

"Yes," Lord Zacharius said. "There is justice and there are laws. The two are not always the same. The choice is yours, Myrmeen. You can turn us into fugitives, or you can keep what has transpired within this room a secret. We have done what should have been done a long time ago. I have no regrets."

Myrmeen looked to Stralana. He was staring into Siobhan's gray-blue eyes. "Evon?"

"If we had caught Othmann and Volney—or whatever they were calling themselves—at the time of the assault, their sentence would have been death," Stralana said. "They got what they deserved."

Siobhan nodded silently. There was gratitude in her eyes.

Stralana regarded the woman lying at Andreana's feet. "As for Elhazir," he noted coldly, "I have too often been called upon to have my men collect the bodies of children who have been beaten, then discarded by such as this woman. I have no sympathy for her, either."

"You've described my feelings exactly," Myrmeen said. "Lord Zacharius, you are free to leave, on one condition: I want you to never return to my city. Is that understood?"

"Damn," he hissed. "I was going to recommend Arabel as a vacation spot for my kind."

Despite herself, Myrmeen almost smiled.

Lord Zacharius lowered his gaze. "I am sorry for the pain this ordeal has caused you."

"So am I," Myrmeen said.

The knowledge and shared pain of Siobhan's ordeal now tainted her memory of her once-beloved gazebo. Like the blood on Haverstrom's phoenix, she knew it would never quite fade. The sanctuary it had once offered was gone forever.

*   *   *   *   *

On the walk back to the palace, after Zacharius and his people had departed, Myrmeen came upon a cat who had trapped a bird and was slowly torturing it to death. She stopped and stared at the gruesome spectacle. Evon Stralana, who was walking beside her, touched her arm.

"Are you all right?" he asked.

Myrmeen thought of the agony Siobhan had suffered at the hands of her attackers and recalled the slight glow in each half of the woman's amulet. Penn Othmann and Russka Volney had not only wounded the cat lord, they had also taken something private and extremely precious away from Myrmeen.

She felt nothing but hatred for them.

"It's strange," Myrmeen said as she watched the cat slowly tear the life from its prey, "but somehow I feel comforted by the knowledge that *all* cats like to play with their kills. . . ."

KING'S TEAR

Mark Anthony

The spirits of the three sages writhed in the flickering, poisonous green flames rising from the copper brazier. The necromancer Kelshara prowled catlike about them, here in the highest chamber of her tower that stood among the dark, jagged peaks of the southernmost Sunset Mountains.

"Please, sorceress, we do not know the answer you seek!" one of the spirits moaned.

"We beg you," pleaded another. *"Release us from this torment!"*

"Very well," Kelshara hissed. Her features were pale and flawless, her long hair as dark as polished onyx, yet she was anything but lovely. Rage was never beautiful. "And for your worthlessness, this is your reward."

She tossed a handful of dark powder onto the brazier. Brilliant sparks, red as rubies, crackled about the pale apparitions as they shrieked in agony. The magical flames flared to the ceiling, then died down in a puff of acrid smoke. The spirits were gone, the last echo of their wails ringing off the chill stone walls.

Kelshara smiled in cruel satisfaction for a moment, but the expression soon faded. She still had no solution to the mystery. From a golden box on a table she drew out two small objects. They were jewels, teardrop shaped and as clear as winter ice. King's Tears such stones were called. Legend held that they were the tears of ancient kings magically turned to stone. Legend also told that if you looked into the heart of a King's Tear, you would see an image of what the ancient lord had loved most in life. And the legends were true.

Even now she could see the visions flickering within the jewels: parchments scribed with strange glyphs and books bound with gem-encrusted covers. It was the library of King Everard Farseer she was glimpsing. Once he had ruled over a realm that stretched for leagues along the banks of the great River Chionthar. But his kingdom had crumbled to dust long centuries before folk from Cormyr crossed the Sunset Mountains and raised the shining Caravan Cities, strung like gems along the necklace of the river. But though Kelshara had gazed into the Tears for hours on end, she never saw what she sought, the book Everard had prized above all others: the *Tome of Midnight*. Within its covers lay the key to life eternal.

"Toz!" the necromancer shouted. "*Toz!*"

Kelshara heard the scrabbling of claws against stone behind her. "Mistress?" a voice croaked tremulously. She spun to see a small, malformed creature hobble into the chamber on two gnarled and twisted legs. It blinked its red, bulbous eyes, snuffling its warty, canine snout.

"Come, Toz," Kelshara said in her icy voice. "Speak the future for me. And do not dare lie, or I promise you'll lose more than just your tail this time."

"Yes, mistress." The kobold fawningly approached the table. Its features were caught up in a mask of mock-contrition, its bulging eyes cast down to the floor. A foul odor followed in its wake, and the ratty brown piece of sackcloth it wore like a tunic looked as if it was ready to rot off its scaly back.

Once the creature had been a man, a diviner of such skill that he had told the fortunes of emperors and queens. But Kelshara had wanted him for her own. She had arranged his murder. Then, with her dark powers, she wrought his reincarnation into this new, loathsome form, bound by magic to do her every bidding.

Clumsily, the kobold opened a small ivory box, drew out a deck of ornate cards wrapped in black silk, and shuffled them. "You must draw three," it instructed the necromancer in its croaking voice, and Kelshara quickly did so.

With a misshapen hand Toz turned over the first card. *The Three of Gems*. "This signifies the heart of your quest. It symbolizes great riches, but some of them are lost."

"Of course," Kelshara crooned, her violet, gold-flecked eyes glittering with understanding. "I have been a fool, Toz. The image of the *Tome* is not within the two Tears I possess, and there can only be one answer. *The Three of Gems*. There must be a third Tear. Go on."

The kobold turned the next card. *The Priest*, reversed. "This signifies the forces of your allies." Toz moved to the last card. "And this signifies the forces that will oppose you on your quest." He turned the card. *The Warrior*, also reversed.

"What do they mean?" Kelshara demanded.

Toz's pointed ears wriggled in confusion. "I am not certain, master. Somehow, a priest who is not a priest will help you gain the jewel. But a warrior who is not a warrior will stand against you."

"'A warrior who is not a warrior?'" Kelshara said mockingly. "That doesn't sound like one I need fear."

"But, mistress," the kobold protested, its snout wriggling in agitation, "these cards speak of powerful forces at work. You must—"

"Quiet!" Kelshara snapped, striking the kobold and knocking it to the hard floor. It yelped shrilly, but she paid the creature no heed. "All I have to do now is find where the third Tear is hidden," the necromancer whispered exultantly. "Then immortality will be mine."

* * * * *

Things were in a bit of an uproar at Everard Abbey, and Tyveris knew he was the cause.

He dashed up the spiral staircase, his sandals slapping hollowly against the worn stone steps. The abbess had sent for him, and one did not keep Melisende waiting. He hesitated for a few heartbeats before the paneled mahogany door that lead into her chamber, then knocked as softly on the dark wood as he could with his massive hand. The sound boomed like thunder. Tyveris winced.

"Come in," came the crisp reply from beyond.

With a deep breath Tyveris opened the door and stepped inside, though he was forced to turn sideways a bit to squeeze his broad shoulders through the portal. He was not a tall man, but his sheer size was astonishing. The thin brown homespun of his simple robe did little to conceal the thick, heavy muscles that were roped about his powerful frame, and his dusky brown skin marked him as a foreigner in these lands. Altogether, he was a rather remarkable individual for the backward Everard Abbey.

And that was a great part of the problem.

"Oh, do stop standing there filling up the doorway and come sit down," Mother Melisende said in her typically brisk tone. The abbess was a tiny woman, with bright, dark eyes and wispy white hair. She sat before a fireplace, clad in a simple but elegant robe of soft dove gray. Despite her diminutive stature, a mantle of authority seemed to rest comfortably upon her small shoulders.

"Yes, Mother Melisende." Though he made an effort to speak softly, Tyveris's deep voice rattled the glass in the windowpanes. He sat down. A cheery fire was blazing on the hearth to drive back the autumn chill. Melisende poured steaming tea into a pair of delicate porcelain cups and handed one to Tyveris. He stared at the fragile teacup worriedly, holding it with exaggerated care in his big hand. He swallowed hard.

Melisende sipped her tea, regarding Tyveris with a wise expression. "I won't keep this from you," she said after a moment's quiet. "Several of the loremasters have come to speak to me this past tenday. They have asked that I dismiss you from the abbey."

Tyveris's dark eyes widened behind his wire-rimmed spectacles. "Have I done something wrong, Mother Melisende?"

The abbess sighed. "No, Tyveris, it is nothing you have done." She smiled fleetingly. "In fact, I daresay we've never had a handyman about the abbey who was as useful as you. The chapel ceiling no longer leaks onto the pulpit, the new hinges on the gate open without a creak, and the drains in the kitchen are working properly for the first time in a century." Her smile faded, replaced by a scowl. "No, it's not what you've done that some of the loremasters don't care for. You wear a monk's robe now, but I'm afraid that doesn't change what you are in their eyes—a sell-sword, a man dedicated to violence, not knowledge."

"But they have nothing to fear from me, Mother Melisende," he boomed earnestly. "I can control myself. I swear it!"

There was a clear, delicate snap as the teacup shattered in Tyveris's hand. He stared down at the broken shards in horror. "I've ruined your cup," he said despairingly.

"Forget the teacup, Tyveris," Melisende said, taking the broken pieces from his hand and setting them aside. "It is simply a thing. Completely replaceable." She took his big hands into her tiny ones. He almost pulled away in surprise, but she gripped him tightly. "Look at these, Tyveris. What do you see?"

Unsure what she meant he looked down at his hands. They were huge, big-knuckled, the dark skin crisscrossed with even darker scars and welts. They were a fighter's hands. Hands that had taken more lives than he could count. He told her so.

"Really?" the abbess answered. "That's peculiar. For I see a pair of hands that are gentle even in their strength. I see hands that have embraced children, hands that have freely given alms to those in need, hands that have held a book for the first time as their owner learned to read in this very room. No, Tyveris, I don't believe these are a warrior's hands at all."

He pulled away from her. "But the other loremasters don't believe that, do they?"

"Some don't," Melisende answered solemnly. "A few. Loremaster Orven speaks loudest among them. I'm afraid they fear that one day you won't be able to control your temper, and that violence will result."

"Maybe they're right," Tyveris replied, his voice just slightly bitter. Why not? he thought. It had happened often enough in the past, when he had been both slave and soldier and the only thing that had mattered was to kill his foe, so that he wouldn't be killed himself.

Melisende's eyes flashed brightly with anger. "I don't expect to hear any more such nonsense from you. I don't let just anybody into my abbey, you know. You're here because I believed you belong here. That hasn't changed." She picked up her teacup again. "I'll speak with those who have been troubled by your presence. Perhaps I can allay their fears."

Tyveris's heart leapt in his chest. "You will?" he rumbled gratefully.

"Did I not say so?" Melisende snapped. The abbess didn't like having to repeat herself.

"But what about Loremaster Orven?" he asked tentatively.

"I will concern myself with him. You may go now. Attend to your work." Tyveris knew that one didn't hesitate when dismissed by the abbess. He hastily stood and bowed before hurrying from the chamber.

"And, Tyveris," Melisende called after him. "Do try to stay out of trouble."

Tyveris spent the rest of the day repairing cracks in the

abbey's outer stone wall. After he had finished the day's work he made his way to the dim, dusty library to read for a time in the quiet chamber. Outside the window the day was fading to twilight as the deep tones of a bronze bell sounded Vespers. The shadowed plains rolled southward into the far purple distance, toward a single twinkling gem on the horizon—the Caravan City of Iriaebor.

Had Tyveris been looking, the city's lights might have been a reminder of his past, of the days when Iriaebor had been his home and the sword had been his way of life. But he was focused on something else, another, more comforting past. Tyveris flipped idly through the colorfully illuminated manuscript resting on the table before him, a historical treatise concerning the founding of the Church of Oghma. He could hardly imagine a time when he couldn't read, but in truth he had only learned a few short months before.

The library was not a terribly large room, but it was filled from floor to ceiling with books, so many that Tyveris suspected it would take a pair of lifetimes just to read them all. The abbey was devoted to the god Oghma, the Binder, who was the warden of all knowledge, and its library was its greatest pride. In fact, the abbey even took its name from Everard Farseer, a king of an ancient, forgotten land whom legend told gave his life to protect a library from marauders who sought to burn the books within.

Tyveris cringed at the memory of the countless buildings he himself had set ablaze in the days when he had been driven into battle with whips at his back. How many precious books had been consumed in the flames and lost forever?

To atone for that destruction, Tyveris had spent the last decade as part of a small band of adventurers based in Iriaebor, men and women who had done their best to work against tyranny in the Caravan Cities between Waterdeep to the far west and Cormyr to the east. But even then he'd simply been a well-trained swordarm. And when the group disbanded a year ago, Tyveris found he had no purpose.

There was no one to tell him who to fight, or where or when. Alone once more, he discovered that all his good deeds had done nothing to assuage his guilty conscience. Then, in the grips of a dark despair, he came to the abbey's gates on a rainy spring day. . . .

A fierce look crossed Tyveris's face as he banished the memories. He wasn't going to let anyone force him to leave Everard Abbey. Not Loremaster Orven. Not anyone.

A place at the abbey was the one thing Tyveris knew he was still willing to fight for.

He bent his head over the tome once more, content to lose himself in its pages. Twilight dwindled outside the window, and night gathered its ebon mantle about the abbey, secure within its walls on the hill above the moonlit plains.

"Reading dusty old books hardly seems like a proper pastime for a warrior," a voice said, startling Tyveris. Yellow light flared up as a candle was touched to the wick of an oil lamp.

Tyveris spun around, dreading to see Loremaster Orven behind him. But instead he found himself gazing into the hard gray eyes of an acerbic-looking, harshly thin man. Patriarch Alamric.

Tyveris cleared his throat gruffly. "No one is a warrior within these walls, Patriarch Alamric," he rumbled.

"So the abbess is fond of saying," Alamric said in his sharp voice. "A pity."

Tyveris watched Alamric in wary confusion as the skeletal man sat at the table opposite him. He had not had many dealings with the old man since coming to the abbey. Alamric was a patriarch in the Church of Oghma, second at the abbey to only Melisende herself. Yet Tyveris had often had the disconcerting feeling that Alamric was watching him. It appeared that feeling had been justified, for the patriarch now gazed at him intently, interest sparking in his sharp gray eyes.

"Not all who worship Oghma tremble foolishly at the sight of a warrior, like our poor Loremaster Orven," Alamric went on. His voice had a hissing edge to it, like a knife drawn through silk. Tyveris looked at him dubiously.

"You doubt me, but it is true," Alamric said with a tight, thin-lipped expression that was more grimace than smile. "I am a powerful man, Tyveris. There are many in the church who obey my orders. But even so, I admire you. No, I *envy* you." His eyes glowed with a strange, fierce light. "From the time I was young I wanted more than anything to lead others, to let my wisdom and my will be their own. I dreamed of riding into glorious battles, raising my sword in the cause of righteousness." He paused and sighed deeply. "But I'm afraid the gods have mocked my pride by granting me this frail form. I've had to content myself with spiritual battles. You are lucky, Tyveris."

"No," Tyveris said, shaking his head. "No, don't envy me, Patriarch. I would give anything to change what I am." He reverently touched the open book before him. "This is something far greater than battles or swords."

Alamric snatched the book up in his bony hand and tossed it carelessly aside, a look of disdain on his severe visage. Tyveris stared at him in shock. "Knowledge is not the only thing sacred to Oghma! No, there is something even more holy, and that is *Truth*. Knowledge comes in tomes, but there's only one way to carry Truth to people, and that's by deed." A ruddy, unwholesome flush came to Alamric's cheeks. He didn't seem to be gazing at Tyveris anymore; instead his eyes were turned to the darkened window as if he saw a glorious vision there, invisible to mundane eyes.

"Unbelievers can cast books aside all too easily," Alamric went on, his voice chantlike. "But if we armed our priests, not with parchment scrolls, but with swords, nothing could stand before us in our quest to bring Truth to all the lands of Faerun!"

Tyveris felt a chill run up his spine. "What 'truth' do you mean, Patriarch?" he dared to ask.

Alamric's gaze bored hotly into Tyveris. "*The* Truth. Don't you see? People will no longer need to read books to learn what to think. *We* will think for them. *We* will tell them what they must know."

"There will be people who will resist you," Tyveris said carefully. "There always are."

Alamric waved a hand dismissively. "Not all souls can be saved, Tyveris. But that's the price we must pay for the benefit of all. Mother Melisende and those like her may not see far enough into the future to realize the great good in this, but there are those in the church who will. I shall be the one to carry the message to them." He clutched Tyveris's wrist. His fingers felt strangely warm. "But we will need holy warriors to become the bearers of the Truth. You could be one of the first."

Tyveris pulled his hand away, rubbing his wrist as if he'd been burned. "I'm sorry. I don't think I can be . . . what you want."

Alamric's exultant expression did not waver. "Very well, Tyveris. We'll let that stand as your answer—for now. But I have faith that you will soon see the light and join me. I have great faith."

After Patriarch Alamric left, Tyveris found he had no more heart for reading. He put away the book and made his way to the abbey's stable, where he kept a room in the loft. He lay in the darkness for a long time—even past midnight, by the stars outside the window—but he could not sleep. Alamric's strange words kept echoing in his head.

Finally he threw off his blanket and fumbled about in the dark until he found a stump of a candle. He lit it with a flint and a bit of tinder. A warm golden glow filled the loft.

He dug beneath his bed of hay until he reached the floorboards. One was loose, and he pulled it up to reveal a shadowed recess beneath. He drew out a long object and unwound the thick cloth that covered it. A sword gleamed in the candlelight, sharp and clean. For a time Tyveris stared at the blade, trying to see the faces of those he'd slain, to draw them forth like a magical shield against the patriarch's words. After an hour, he rewrapped the sword and put it away.

He drew another object from the hole—a small jade figurine. Once it had been meant to represent a bird, but its features had been rounded with the wear of his touch. Still, Tyveris remembered the beauty clearly. His sister Tali had carved it for him long ago.

Once he and Tali had been bold youths, always seeking trouble together. When the ships came across the sea to the jungles of Chult, he and his sister had ignored the pleading of their parents. Enticed by tales of riches and strange wonders, they signed on to become warriors in the distant lands to the north.

But they had been deceived.

The siblings had found themselves bound, not for glory, but for slavery. The ship had been a nightmare of foul darkness and disease. Tali had not survived the voyage, and Tyveris had lived only to have shackles clamped on his ankles and a sword thrust into his hand. The jade figurine was all he had left of his sister. Her bright eyes, her brave, sweet smile, were only memories now.

Not all souls can be saved.... Alamric's terrible words burned like poison in his mind. He gripped the figurine tightly in his hand. A single tear, clear as a diamond, touched his dark cheek.

"Must there always be more dying, Tali?" he whispered into the night. There was no answer but silence.

* * * * *

It was a dreary afternoon late in the waning days of autumn when the stranger came to the gates of Everard Abbey.

Tyveris was in the great hall at the time, repairing the crumbling mortar around a window to keep out the chill winds of the coming winter. He heard the crystalline chiming of harness bells and gazed outside. Through the glass he saw a figure clad in a heavy, midnight-blue traveling cloak ride into the courtyard astride a delicate black palfrey. Even as he watched, Mother Melisende and Patriarch Alamric stepped forward to greet the stranger. The mysterious rider lifted two gloved hands to push back the cowl of a heavy traveling cloak.

She was beautiful. Her hair, as dark and glossy as her steed, cascaded over the shoulders of her crimson riding gown. Her pale features were so perfect they seemed almost exotic. The woman must be a noble of some sort, Tyveris thought, and he wondered who she might be.

Rumors tended to be repeated as often as prayers in the abbey, and by Vespers Tyveris had heard numerous intriguing whispers about the strange lady. Her name was Kelshara, he learned, and she was a benefactor of the church. Some said she had been sending gold to the abbey for months and had now made the pilgrimage here.

Other rumors spoke of her desire to see the abbey's most holy relic, the Tear of Everard. The crystalline jewel, kept in a small chamber behind the chapel's nave, was in truth a tear shed by the abbey's namesake, magically turned to stone. Several centuries ago it had come into the possession of a priest of Oghma who founded the abbey to guard the Tear. Even now, pilgrims journeyed from lands afar to see the Tear and send a prayer to Oghma.

The evening chants still echoed among the candlelit vaults of the chapel when the order for a feast came down from the chamber of the abbess. In moments the abbey was bustling with activity, and Tyveris helped to ready the great hall. He and several of the brethren scattered the stone floor with fresh rushes and pulled out long trestle tables. All the while more and more of the sisters scurried in bearing candelabras pilfered from nearly every room of the abbey. Soon the hall was ablaze with light.

After this, Tyveris did his best to keep out of everyone's way. In the tenday since his conversation with Melisende, he had been making a concerted effort to do nothing that might alarm Loremaster Orven or any of the abbey's other residents. So far, it seemed, he'd been very successful.

By the time the folk of the abbey sat down in the great hall, the tables had been loaded with roasted geese, bubbling stews, platters of spiced fruit, and mountains of steaming bread. For a few fleeting moments Tyveris was in paradise—until the loremaster sitting to his left politely remarked that he was supposed to *pass* the food-laden platters rather than *hoard* them.

After all had filled their plates and a benediction had been spoken, Mother Melisende stood in her place at the head of the great hall. She introduced the stranger as Lady Kelshara and revealed that the abbey's mysterious benefactor had indeed come in pilgrimage to gaze upon Everard's Tear. Then Kelshara herself stood and spoke.

"You have given me a most gracious welcome," Kelshara said in a silk-smooth voice, "and I look forward to seeing the precious relic you so unfailingly guard." She raised her wine goblet with a smile and tilted her head forward. "May Oghma in his kindness grant us each the knowledge we seek." Tyveris stood with the others to raise his goblet in reply, but he suddenly found himself distracted. There was something strange about Kelshara's smile, something very private and inward.

In his years as a warrior, Tyveris had learned to read the smallest of expressions on the faces of his jailers and his enemies. He could tell when they were lying by the look in their eyes, or whether they were going to attack by the set of their jaw. He wasn't altogether certain what Kelshara's smile portended, but a sudden chill touched his spine.

He picked at his food absently for the remainder of the evening, watching Kelshara out of the corner of his eye. She was engaged in an animated conversation with Alamric. The patriarch's eyes were glowing hotly, and Tyveris had no doubt he was extemporizing upon his dream of transforming the Church of Oghma into a more militant order. Kelshara seemed to be paying close attention to his words, but Mother Melisende, sitting nearby, was regarding the two with a sour expression.

Tyveris noticed then that Kelshara's smile had changed slightly. There was a faintly triumphant note to it now. Yet every few minutes her attention wavered from Alamric's ravings, and her cool gaze flickered across the sea of faces filling the great hall.

She's found something she was after, but she's still looking for something else, Tyveris thought. He wasn't certain why, but he slumped down in his chair as much as his massive frame allowed. The less anybody noticed him, the better.

Finally, Mother Melisende rose to bid the abbey folk good night. She left the table quickly, but as she made her way from the hall she paused by Tyveris's seat.

"You've been working terribly hard not to be noticed these last days," she said matter-of-factly.

Tyveris grinned a bit foolishly. "I've been trying. It isn't all that easy, you know. A year ago I thought the word 'subtle' meant using a dagger instead of a battle-axe."

Mother Melisende winced slightly, then smiled, patting his broad shoulder. "Well, do keep trying. Loremaster Orven seems to have calmed a bit. In fact, I'm calling a meeting tomorrow to discuss making your position at the abbey permanent. I have reason to believe the loremasters will be agreeing with me." Her eyes snapped fire.

Tyveris's grin broadened. "Thank you, Mother Melisende."

"Thank me by not proving my judgment foolish," Melisende said smartly.

The abbess turned to leave, but Tyveris reached up and touched her arm. "You don't like her, do you?" he whispered.

Melisende hesitated for a moment, then shook her head. "No, I don't," she said softly. "But she seems to have found a friend in Alamric."

"He wants her to be the patron of his order, doesn't he? To use her gold to buy an army of warriors to spread his truth across the Heartlands."

Melisende's usually warm visage was suddenly as hard and cold as steel. "Stay away from Patriarch Alamric, Tyveris. He may need you for his schemes, but you most certainly do not need one such as him." With that, Melisende briskly departed.

Tyveris's gaze drifted to the head of the hall once again. Alamric was still babbling at Kelshara's side, but she wasn't looking at him. Instead her sharp violet gaze was directed across the vast room. The note of triumph about her smile had deepened.

She was looking directly at Tyveris.

* * * * *

After the feast, Tyveris made his way to the stables for some much-needed rest. Yet when the moon finally rose over the distant horizon, its silvery light streamed through the open window of the loft to find him still awake.

"I know they'll decide to let me stay, Tali," he whispered. "I feel it. I belong here."

He set down the worn bird of jade on the overturned crate he used for a table. Then, pushing his wire-rimmed spectacles into place on his nose, he bent back over the tome he had been reading. It was an account of an ancient war in an empire that had long ago vanished beneath the sands of Anauroch, the great desert to the north. His brow wrinkled as he concentrated on the words.

It was late when he finished the tome, but still sleep would not claim him. Troubling visions of Patriarch Alamric's army of truth bearers, financed with Kelshara's gold, flickered through his mind. For a heartbeat he saw himself leading a crusade, carrying the symbol of Oghma on a battle standard, crying out triumphant praises to his god as the unbelievers were trampled, weeping, in the blood-soaked mud beneath the hooves of his thundering black charger. There was a dark appeal to the scene, a comforting sense of power. And if Alamric's cause proved a worthy one, Tyveris knew he could be a powerful force in such a holy war. But if Alamric spoke only from his own ambition . . .

"No," Tyveris whispered fiercely. "I will not be a pawn again. Never."

He headed quickly down the ladder. If he couldn't sleep, he might as well get another book from the library. Quietly he made his way across the moonlit courtyard and slipped inside the abbey, treading down the stone corridors as stealthily as he could manage. As he passed the doors to the chapel, he paused. A flicker of movement within had caught his eye. Curious, he peered through the archway.

Alamric was inside. The patriarch stood in the chapel's nave, no doubt sending some fervent plea to Oghma. Tyveris quickly hurried away from the chapel, his heart pounding in his chest. He had no desire to listen to any more of Alamric's diatribes. He walked quickly up a stone staircase and down the long hallway leading to the library.

He was halfway down the corridor when he noticed something odd. A peculiar orange glow spilled from the crack beneath the door to Alamric's chamber. At first Tyveris thought little of it and continued on; no doubt the patriarch had left a candle burning while he was out. Yet there was something strange about the ruddy light, the way it flickered and danced. It looked almost like the light of a . . .

"Fire," Tyveris whispered, his eyes widening. An image flashed before his mind—a candle burning too low on a table strewn with parchments, flames licking hungrily at the papers, catching, and leaping high to the ceiling. He considered running downstairs to retrieve Alamric, but it might be only a matter of moments before the fire spread out of control. Instead he burst through the door into Alamric's chamber.

He halted, dumbfounded.

Tyveris noted two things about the room. The first was that there was no fire. The flickering light emanated from an object resting on a marble table—a small glass jar filled with a strange light that washed over him in dizzying waves.

The second thing he noticed was that he was not alone. The stranger, Kelshara, sat nearby in a high-backed chair lined with crushed velvet the same purple hue as her eyes. Tyveris took a startled step backward, but she seemed not to notice him. She continued to stare straight ahead, her face pale and devoid of expression. He would have thought her dead if it weren't for the steady rise and fall of her breast beneath her crimson gown.

Tyveris felt a prickling on the back of his neck. Without thinking, he dropped his hand down to his hip, but there was no sword hilt for it to grasp.

"There's enchantment at work here, sure as the night is black," he grumbled. He'd never much cared for magic, or those who worked it. Mages were treacherous creatures, the whole lot of them.

But the weird scene in the room puzzled him. Was Alamric dabbling in magic himself? Perhaps there was nothing he would not do to achieve his bloody dreams of holy conquest. Perhaps he had ensorcelled Kelshara so that she would give him the gold he needed for his schemes. Tyveris shook his head in disbelief. He had to go find Mother Melisende.

As he turned to leave, his gaze was drawn once again to the light-filled jar. Dread fascination reeled him in, forcing him to peer into the jar's center. There was something inside.

A man—or, more precisely, the ghostly image of a man—battered at the glass prison. His eyes were wide with madness, his mouth open in a silent, endless scream. The tiny ghost scrabbled at the glass with hands clenched into claws. Worst of all, Tyveris recognized the man imprisoned within the vessel. It was Alamric.

"So, you've come after all," a hard, cruel voice said behind him. "I expected you to, of course. Toz lies at times, but the cards never do."

Tyveris spun on a heel, crouching into a defensive posture. He held his big hands out before him, ready. His nostrils flared with the scent of danger on the air.

He found himself facing Patriarch Alamric.

Yet, somehow, his battle-honed senses told him that all was not as it appeared. The body might be the patriarch's, but it was not Alamric who gazed out of those gray eyes at him. No, somehow the patriarch—or at least his soul—was locked inside the glowing prison. Someone else had possessed him, and the smug, triumphant smile that curled about the patriarch's lips gave the foe's identity away.

"Kelshara," he whispered. The woman's body still sat, unmoving, in the high-backed chair, but somehow she was in control of Alamric's form.

The smile broadened. "Perceptive," the necromancer crooned through the man's lips. "However, I think you will find yourself wishing you weren't so terribly clever. Fate decreed you would stand in my way, warrior. It is my decree that you will fall."

With a suddenness that surprised Tyveris, the false patriarch drew a long curved dagger from beneath his robes and lunged forward.

Reflexes worn into Tyveris's muscles by his years as a sell-sword sparked him into motion. He spun away from the blade as he kicked out his other foot. He felt the bones of the patriarch's arm buckle and snap beneath the blow. The dagger flew from Alamric's grip. With lightning speed Tyveris reached out and snatched the knife before it fell and brought it downward in a smooth, precise stroke.

It was over in a second.

"No," Tyveris whispered in horror, staring wild-eyed at what he had done. Alamric's body slumped against him, a bloodstain blossoming on his robes like a rose unfurling its petals. Tyveris tried to pull the dagger free, but the false patriarch grabbed his arm with uncanny strength, driving the dagger in deeper.

"And so victory is mine," Kelshara hissed triumphantly through Alamric's teeth.

A flood of orange fire burst from the glass jar, searing Tyveris's vision. When his sight cleared he saw that Alamric was gazing at him in mute amazement. And this time the patriarch himself looked out through his body's dimming eyes. With a gasp and a shudder, he died. Slowly, Tyveris let the corpse slide to the growing pool of blood on the cold stone floor.

"I am grateful to you," said a chill, mocking voice. Tyveris turned to see Kelshara rise from the chair, smoothing her silken gown. "I was finished with Alamric, and you have so kindly dealt with him for me." She picked up the now empty jar from the table and slipped it into a pocket of her gown. There was a scrabbling of claws, and Tyveris watched in shock as a small, misshapen creature hopped from the sill of the chamber's open window and hobbled to Kelshara's side. It was a kobold. The creature regarded him with its bulbous red eyes.

"Here they are, Toz, just as the cards foretold," Kelshara said. "The priest who is not a priest." She waved a hand, and an intricately drawn card appeared in her fingers. It depicted a holy man. The card was turned upside down. "His was a violent heart, and violently has he died." She crumpled the card in a fist. It burst into flame as she dropped it, turning to ash before it even hit the floor.

"And the warrior who is not a warrior," the kobold croaked.

"Yes," Kelshara said, her violet eyes gleaming speculatively, "but I think there is more warrior in this one's heart than he wishes to believe. He kills with practiced ease. But then, so do I."

Too late Tyveris realized his peril. Before he could leap forward another card appeared in Kelshara's hand, this depicting an armored knight. It was also upside down. With a swift motion, she tore the card in half.

Tyveris screamed.

He had never screamed before, not in all his years of battle. He'd taken wounds that would have killed other men, borne the torture of whip and hot iron without ever giving his tormentors the satisfaction of hearing him hiss in pain. But this time he screamed, the agony ripping the sound out of him like a claw reaching down his throat to tear out his heart.

Mercifully, a numbing coldness washed over him then. He fell to the floor, his limbs frozen motionless, his heart shuddering in his chest. Kelshara bent over Alamric's body and took something from his pocket. It was a small, clear gemstone. Everard's Tear.

"I have what I came for," Kelshara purred. "Farewell, *warrior*. Do not fear, though. You won't live long enough for your brothers to mete out justice to you for this unfortunate murder."

The dark-haired necromancer turned to the open window. She spread her arms wide and called out in a strange, guttural tongue. A huge creature swooped down from the night sky to hover before the window.

In life the thing might have been a griffin, a feral but noble beast with a lion's body and an eagle's head and wings. But Kelshara's mount was a creature of death. Rotting flesh hung in tatters from its bones, and its eyes glowed with a sick, unearthly light. It let out a shriek, but the sound was muffled by the dirt filling the thing's beak. Kelshara climbed onto the nightmarish steed, the kobold clambering up after her. There was a rush of dank, charnel-house air as the creature spread its wings. It soared triumphantly into the sky, leaving Tyveris alone and utterly defeated.

Some time later, Loremaster Orven came upon the former sell-sword lying beside Alamric's already stiffening body, still clutching the bloodstained dagger in his frozen hand.

Then came the ringing of bells, shattering the night.

*　*　*　*　*

It was a chill, gray morning. The wind smelled faintly of snow. Tyveris stood before the open gates of the abbey, alone. No one had come to bid him farewell, though that was hardly surprising since everyone believed him a murderer. And he supposed they were right, though not in the way they so smugly believed.

He gathered his travel-stained cloak about his broad shoulders. He had traded in his brown homespun robe for the worn leather jerkin and breeches he had worn before coming to the abbey. His swordbelt was slung low against his hip, the flat of the blade resting comfortably against his thigh. It felt almost as if he'd never taken the weapon off. He shouldn't have even bothered trying.

The council of loremasters had not believed his tale.

"I need no magic to explain these black deeds," Loremaster Orven had pronounced angrily. "Treachery is reason enough. You plotted with Kelshara to steal the Tear and brutally killed Patriarch Alamric to avoid discovery. But once Kelshara gained the relic, she needed you no longer. You are a fool as well as a murderer, Tyveris, for she left you to suffer punishment while she herself escaped to freedom." The others had agreed. Tyveris would never be anything but a man of violence.

Only Mother Melisende's intervention saved him from a sentence of death. But the punishment finally handed down was almost as bad: he was to leave the abbey immediately.

Tyveris gazed toward the far-off horizon. The world beyond the abbey's walls seemed empty, as though it held nothing for him. But there was no use in lingering. He started through the open gateway.

The clip-clop of hooves behind him brought him up short. He turned around. What he saw made him smile, despite his dark mood.

"I thought you might prefer to ride rather than walk," Mother Melisende said in her brusque tone. Behind her followed the delicate palfrey that Kelshara had ridden into the abbey. "I daresay no one else will ride her, though it seems foolish. She's a good horse and hardly responsible for her mistress's ill manners." She patted the palfrey's glossy neck affectionately.

"Thank you," Tyveris said, taking the reins. He stood absolutely still for a time, at a loss for anything else to say.

The abbess regarded him wearily. "I know you told the truth." Her expression seemed tired, her bright eyes dull. "I'm sorry I couldn't have defended you more properly, Tyveris, but the others would have simply thought I was bewitched somehow." She sighed. "People can be so terribly blind sometimes—even seekers after truth and knowledge."

Tyveris shook his head in amazement. "I really don't think there is anyone alive who sees as well as you do, Mother Melisende."

She laughed aloud. "Why, I suppose not." Her round face grew serious then. "This is for you." She handed him a small bundle wrapped in dark cloth.

Tyveris took it gingerly. "What is it?"

"It is a holy relic, a very old one. Once it belonged to the monk who founded the abbey. It will protect you in the dark days to come. And it will guide you."

"Guide me?"

The abbess nodded gravely. "To Everard's Tear." She sighed wearily. "I have just come from Loremaster Antira's chamber, Tyveris. There she cast an augury for me, to see what the signs portend for the future." She paused ominously. "The abbey is in great peril. The Tear was the abbey's heart, and without it we have no means to ward ourselves from the forces of darkness. The evil creatures you described as Kelshara's servants would never have been able to come within these walls had she not possessed the Tear. And now that it is gone, the auguries speak clearly. Within the year, the abbey will be destroyed."

Tyveris stared at her in shock.

"Find the Tear of Everard. Prove to the others what I already know about you."

Tyveris sighed gravely. "But how can I defeat Kelshara? All my years as a warrior meant nothing against her magic."

A mysterious expression touched Melisende's face. "Yes, but you possess something else, Tyveris, something she does not."

"Aren't you going to tell me what it is?"

She considered him carefully for a moment. "I think that's something you must discover for yourself." She pressed his fingers closed on the holy relic. "Remember. This will protect you and guide the way."

Without another word she turned and walked swiftly across the courtyard, disappearing into the abbey. Once again Tyveris was alone, though not so completely as before. The cold wind tugged at the cloth in his hand, revealing the object concealed within. It was a feathered quill pen, yellowed with time and spotted with ancient ink.

* * * * *

Three days later Tyveris glimpsed the tower rising like a jagged stump of bone from the dark hills. As he studied the castle, the sun slipped into a pool of bloodred clouds and the first flakes of snow began to fall, as hard and stinging as tiny shards of glass. One last time he carefully took out the ancient quill pen Melisende had given him. As he had done a dozen times in the course of his journey, he fastened a bit of leather string about the quill's middle. Holding the other end of the string, he let the relic dangle in the air. Despite the howling wind, the quill spun evenly until its tip pointed toward the tower. Tyveris nodded grimly, then put away the relic. After only a moment's pause, he nudged his dark mount into a canter.

The face of the hill was steep and treacherous with loose rock. Tyveris left the palfrey in a sheltered hollow and continued on foot. He loosened his sword in its sheath, his muscles tensing with anticipation. Abruptly the cold wind stopped, and the air grew strangely still. It was as if Cyric, Lord of the Dead, were watching, holding his sepulchral breath, waiting to claim his due.

Finally he reached the twin gatehouses bordering the main entryway. The tower hulked above, silent and frosted in a thin layer of snow. He pushed against the iron-banded wooden door, and it swung in upon groaning hinges. Sprinting across the deserted courtyard, he came to the keep itself—a single, massive tower that seemed to scrape the clouds high in the twilight sky. An empty archway led inside.

The keep's interior was cloaked in darkness. Tyveris cursed his foolishness, for he had neither candle nor lantern. Then he noticed a faint glow. He looked about in the dimness for its source and was surprised to see it emanated from his own pocket. He pulled out the quill. The feather glimmered now with a pure, silvery light.

"Thank you, Mother Melisende," Tyveris whispered with a fierce grin. He tucked the feather into his belt. It seemed

Oghma himself would light the way.

The first thing he saw when he stepped into the entrance hall were the skeletons. The stone floor was littered with scabrous bones and blankly staring skulls. The dank reek of decay he had smelled that night in Alamric's chamber was a dozen times stronger here. He could almost feel the stench seeping into his skin. Still, Tyveris had dealt in death for most of his life. He simply blocked his nose and crossed the hall to another door. Bones cracked and crumbled to dust beneath his boots. To either side of the archway, skulls were heaped in pyramids. Tyveris paid them no heed as he moved by.

That was a mistake. Two pinpricks of crimson light flickered to life in the empty orbits of a skull sitting atop one of the piles, and the thing began to shriek. In a flash Tyveris drew his sword and struck. Shards of bone flew in all directions, and the thing's shriek abruptly ended, but the damage had been done. Skull watchers, such things were called. The enchantment that gave them life had been created long, long ago by Prince Ketheryll of the Moonshaes. It was only a small part of the dark sorcery that had created Ketheryll's nightmarish Palace of Skulls, but if Kelshara could master it, she was more powerful than Tyveris had suspected.

And worse, thanks to the skeletal guardian, she would be expecting an intruder.

Beyond the archway, the light of the feather revealed a vast circular chamber, its ceiling lost in a shadowy vault. The chamber was bare except for a spiral staircase rising against the far wall. Warily Tyveris started across the room, his boots echoing off the cold stone. He was just halfway to the staircase when he heard the noise.

It started as a faint clicking sound but grew rapidly into a deafening whir. Tyveris felt something brush against his neck, sharp and stinging. Then a hot bead of blood trickled down his back. He drew his sword and looked up, his eyes widening in shock.

Bats filled the air, hundreds of them, flitting jerkily around the chamber. They were not living things. Cobwebs stretched between the thin, yellowed bones of their wings, and their hollow eyes glowed with the same sickly crimson light that had shone in the orbits of the skull watcher. They opened their maws in silent cries, their needle-sharp teeth glimmering in the quill's enchanted light. Tyveris swore, batting one as it came close. Another sunk its fangs into his forearm. With a grimace of disgust he shook the creature off. The tiny abominations meant to tear him apart one mouthful at a time.

He let out a bellow of rage and spun wildly, swinging his sword in a deadly arc. A dozen skeleton bats burst into puffs of thick bone-dust as the blade struck them. Yet the undead vermin continued to swoop and whirl about him. Blood snaked in fine rivulets down Tyveris's face, and countless pinprick bites covered his arms and neck. With every swing, more of the creatures burst apart in a spray of delicate, desiccated bones. The air was thick with dust, choking him, but there was no pause in the steady rhythm of his swings.

Finally the chamber was quiet, save for one last skeleton bat flopping weakly on the ground. Its bones were crushed to fine powder under Tyveris's boot as he made his way toward the stairs.

I'm coming for you, Kelshara, he was tempted to shout, but there was no need. The sorceress knew. He started up the broad stone steps, keeping his sword held ready in his hand. At the top of the stairwell a corridor stretched before him, ending at a door.

Ancient-looking stone sarcophagi stood upright to either side of the corridor, facing each other in pairs. Carved into the lids of the coffins were bas-relief death masks—likenesses of the corpses sealed within. Eyes inlaid with lapis lazuli and onyx stared menacingly at the warrior. Stone mouths carved into cruel, frozen smiles mocked him. He smirked back at them and started down the corridor.

As Tyveris passed the first pair of sarcophagi he felt a stone shift beneath his foot. A click echoed from the walls as some unseen mechanism was sprung.

Fortunately, he didn't waste a heartbeat considering his action. Even as he lunged forward, gleaming blades sprang from the mouths of the two death masks to either side of him. The blades met with a ringing sound just behind his head.

His momentum carried him forward, past the next pair of sarcophagi. Expecting another set of swords to spring from the mouths of the death masks, he hunched down. The motion nearly cost him his life, for this time the blades sprang from slots hidden at knee height; Tyveris barely managed to dive over them as they clanged together.

He charged down the corridor, blades hissing through the air all around him. The deadly barrage did little more than shred Tyveris's tunic, for he had trained long and hard to deal with such traps. But as the warrior leaped over the blades erupting from the penultimate set of stone coffins, he stumbled and skidded painfully to his knees.

The abbey's dulled my skills more than I'd suspected, Tyveris thought ruefully as he waited for the last trap to spring.

The grating squeal of metal against stone rang out in the corridor, but no blades erupted from the sarcophagi. The trap, it seemed, was stuck.

Tyveris glanced at the death masks, at the swordtips jutting halfway from them. If he moved, he might just set them off. Of course if he just sat there, Kelshara would most definitely stumble across him sooner or later.

Not daring to inhale, the warrior wriggled forward on his stomach until he was past the last pair of blades. As if in answer to his murmured prayers to Oghma, they remained locked in place.

Tyveris lay in front of the closed door, catching his breath and letting his heart slow, but only for a moment. Then he hauled himself to his feet. Beyond the door he found a narrow flight of steps. He gripped his sword firmly and headed up to the tower's uppermost chamber.

"You should be dead, you know."

Kelshara stood in the room's center, her hair shimmering in the moonlight that streamed through the chamber's open window. She smiled. It was a cruel, secret expression. "When I tore the card of fate in two, it should have ripped your heart apart. It's worked on other men."

"I don't care about your sorcery," Tyveris lied. "It has no effect on me." He watched her calculating eyes drift to his sword. Despite her cool demeanor, he could see a faint flicker of anxiety race across her features. "I am here for the Tear of Everard."

"So it appears," Kelshara replied acidly. "Toz! Bring my new treasure to me."

The kobold scurried out of a darkened alcove bearing a small box of finely wrought gold. Kelshara snatched the box from the creature's gnarled hands. "You are slow, as always, Toz," she snapped. Almost casually she pointed a finger at the kobold, and a spark of crimson fire leaped forth, striking the creature in the chest and flinging it into the chamber's wall. The kobold let out a shrill shriek and cowered against the cold stones, its eyes pulsing in pain.

Kelshara ignored her servant. She opened the box and took out a gem, clear and glittering. The Tear of Everard. "All men perish," she hissed. "But I have found the secret of eternal life." She clutched the stone tightly. "You will die this night, warrior. But I shall live forever."

Tyveris lunged forward, sword before him.

Kelshara gave a small cry of surprise, taking a startled step backward, but even as Tyveris lifted his sword for a killing blow she recovered her composure. She reached out a hand toward the warrior's heart as strange, guttural words rippled like dark water from her tongue.

An invisible hand clutched Tyveris, and he found that he couldn't breathe. His blood seemed to freeze in his veins, and his vision blurred. Slowly, shivering with cold, he sank to his knees. It was as if all warmth had been drained from him. He could even see it, like a trail of sparks on the air, flowing from his body into Kelshara's own.

The necromancer laughed, her cheeks blushed with color. She was draining the essence of his life and drinking it up, making it her own.

Tyveris tried to shout, but the sound was barely a whisper. He struggled to move, but his limbs seemed to be made of lead.

Suddenly a voice hissed, "That is the last time you will ever strike me—or anyone."

Kelshara turned to gaze at the kobold in surprise, but the magical stream still flowed toward her. Tyveris found it hard to concentrate, and the room started to tilt and spin before his eyes.

From amongst the rags of its filthy tunic the kobold drew a dark, jagged-edge knife. "Once I was strong and handsome—like *him*," Toz spat, his voice oozing malice. "And then you gave me this . . . this twisted form. And the pain. For too long I've suffered the pain of serving you." The kobold's eyes flared with countless years of spite now unleashed. "But I will suffer it no more, Kelshara. I will suffer *you* no more." The kobold lifted the knife and took a menacing step toward the necromancer.

"Halt!" Kelshara cried, lifting a hand.

Toz shuddered to a stop. He grunted, trying to bring the dagger down in a deadly arc, but his hand merely trembled, frozen.

The necromancer laughed cruelly. "Foolish Toz. Do you forget the magic that binds you to obey me? Then allow me to remind you." She made a slashing motion with her hand, and Toz gurgled in pain. As though he were some fantastical marionette, the kobold moved to mirror the necromancer's motion, plunging the knife into his own chest.

The kobold howled once in agony, then slumped motionless into a growing pool of black, foul-smelling blood. Kelshara gazed at her servant with fierce satisfaction. And in that moment of distraction her attack against Tyveris wavered.

The magical force draining the warrior's life flickered and vanished. Warmth flooded back into his limbs. He felt weak, strangely hollow, but he was alive. Kelshara turned to him, a startled look on her face, realizing her spell was broken. She lifted her arms to entrap him once again, but this time he did not give her the chance.

He sprang forward, slamming the sorceress into the wall, the point of his sword resting against the hollow of her throat. "Give me the Tear!"

Hatred glittered in her eyes like poison, but finally she lowered her gaze in defeat. "Very well," she hissed. He thrust out his hand. She opened her clenched fist over his upturned palm.

Tyveris swore as he felt a sharp sting on his thumb. He shook his hand, and a small black beetle, bright with yellow blotches, fell to the floor with a plop. It scuttled away before he could smash it with his heel. Tyveris felt fury blaze hot and crimson behind his eyes. He raised his sword threateningly. "Give me the Tear!" he bellowed.

"Never!" Kelshara spat. From the folds of her robe a dagger appeared, stained with venom. She brought it down in a slashing motion, but Tyveris easily countered the blow with his own blade. She nearly managed to twist out of the way, but not quite.

The sword cut a long, sinuous gash across her arm. At the same time Tyveris felt searing fire run down his own arm. In confusion he looked down, only to find a wound that was the mirror image of the one he had inflicted upon the necromancer.

Black words of magic began to tumble from Kelshara's lips, but Tyveris attacked again before she could complete her spell. This time his blade bit deep into her shoulder. She slumped against the wall, moaning.

Tyveris swore as his own shoulder burst into brilliant pain. Blood coursed down his chest. He leaned heavily against the table, his head swimming dizzily. Kelshara watched him, her face a grimace of agony . . . and yet that same triumphant smile twisted her lips.

"Yes, warrior," she whispered. "Each wound you inflict upon me strikes you as well. Our lives are linked by the sting of the deathmirror beetle. But I am stronger now than you. Go on. Strike me again. I will survive the blow.

You will not."

Tyveris shook his head, fighting to stay upright. He knew she was right. Darkness swam dangerously at the edges of his vision. Her magic had weakened him, drained him of his strength. His muscles felt as if they'd been turned to water. He looked down at the sword in his hand, sharp and wicked, slicked with blood. For so long the blade had been his life, everything that he was. Now it had failed him. He had nothing left.

No, he told himself, that wasn't true. Remembered words echoed in his mind. *You possess something else, Tyveris, something she does not.* But what had Mother Melisende meant? Understanding washed over him, accompanied by a wellspring of fear that eddied darkly in his chest. He pushed that fear aside as best he could. He knew what he had to do.

The sword slipped from his fingers to clatter against the stone floor. He sank to his knees before Kelshara.

"The cards never lie," she purred. "You truly are no warrior." She picked up the sword in both hands. "You are nothing."

Tyveris did not look at her. Instead he clasped the ancient quill still tucked into his belt. He had heard the loremasters at the abbey calling upon the power of their god before. He knew that, sometimes, there was great magic in those prayers. Still, he was no priest. He could only hope that Oghma would hear his words anyway.

With a look of animalistic exultation, Kelshara lifted the sword. "All men die," she said coldly.

Tyveris gripped the holy relic. "I have faith that you will help me, Oghma. Grant me your protection."

As Kelshara raised the sword to strike, a blue nimbus sprang to life about the relic in Tyveris's hand. He felt a warmth touch his heart. The soft illumination enshrouded him like a cloak. It brightened, deepened. He rose to his feet, new vigor flowing through his veins. The necromancer stared at him, the fear finally clear in her violet eyes. He was stronger than she had ever imagined.

"I've won, Kelshara," he said solemnly. "Give me the Tear, and I—"

His words trailed off as the blue nimbus surrounding him flared. A thin, gossamer tendril uncoiled itself from the magical aura, reaching out for Kelshara.

"No!" the sorceress cried out, backing away, her voice trembling with revulsion. The sword dropped from her hands and clattered to the floor. "The deathmirror beetle should only link us in pain!"

She shrank back from the divine aura, step by step, but the blue glow steadily followed her. Finally she backed up against the ledge of the chamber's arched window. The tendril of holy light coiled about her like a shroud. "It's burning me!" she screamed. "Help me! Someone please help me!"

"I will help you, *mistress*," a wet, bubbling voice croaked. Toz pulled himself slowly to his feet, the knife still lodged in his chest. He grinned, his jagged teeth stained dark with blood. "I am your servant, after all."

With a cry that might have been sorrow as easily as rage, the kobold lunged at the sorceress, grasping at her with gnarled hands. Entangled in a fatal embrace, the two tumbled backward over the window's ledge.

Kelshara shrieked. "But I am going to live forev—" Her cry ended abruptly.

The necromancer's life had ended. But her magic had not.

The tendril of azure light still linked her to Tyveris, reaching him from outside the chamber's window. Even as he watched, a darkness seemed to climb up the shimmering rope like a sinewy viper as black as midnight. It was the final culmination of her spell. Death had taken Kelshara. Now it was coming for him.

The darkness snaked toward him along the tendril, closer, no more than an arm's length away. One touch, and Tyveris knew that he would die. But how could he fight death itself?

It will protect you in the dark days to come.

There was no time to think about it. Gripping the quill tightly, Tyveris thrust his fist toward the thread of darkness.

"In the name of Oghma, be gone!" His voice boomed through the chamber.

Blue light flashed, and thunder shook the tower to its very foundation. The magic was shattered. Shards of azure and onyx flew in all directions. Then came silence. Tyveris blinked. Both the dark and light tendrils were gone. The ancient quill lay in his hand, looking dull and quite mundane.

Tyveris shook his head in wonderment. His body ached terribly, but he was alive. Carefully he tucked the relic back into his belt. He turned and walked slowly from the chamber, leaving his bloodstained sword where it lay on the floor. The weapon had failed him. His faith had not.

He made his way down the stairs and into the night. The storm had ended, and the moon was out, casting its silvery light over the new layer of snow that cloaked the ground, making everything seem somehow fresh and pure.

He found Kelshara and Toz among the rocks in the desolate courtyard, their twisted bodies covered in a burial shroud of windblown snow. The Tear of Everard lay in the necromancer's outstretched palm, unblemished and perfect.

Tyveris bent down and picked up the shining jewel from Kelshara's cold grip. Neither the sorceress's dark magic nor the fall from the tower had damaged the Tear. Just more proof of Oghma's divine presence in the world, Tyveris decided, and he headed off into the night.

* * * * *

When Tyveris finally reached the abbey on a bright winter's afternoon, he found the gates open wide. It looked as if all the loremasters had gathered in the courtyard to greet him. He swung down from the pretty black palfrey, grinning foolishly at them all. The news of his battle with

Kelshara—and his recovery of the Tear—had obviously proceeded him.

"Welcome home, *Loremaster* Tyveris," Mother Melisende said, her eyes sparkling brightly. "Welcome home."

THE FAMILY BUSINESS

James Lowder

"There's a rider coming," the Shadowhawk hissed, his breath turning to steam in the chill midnight air. "You remember what I told you? You get 'alf of what we pinch from the bloke, right?"

"Yes," the young boy replied meekly. He picked at a loaf of stale bread jutting out of the small pack at his feet, then looked up at his father. With wide brown eyes, he pleaded to be released from the frightening task that loomed before him. In reply, the Shadowhawk frowned and pushed his son through the tangled hedgerow separating them from the road.

Artus Cimber tumbled through the thorny branches, recently laid bare by the first blustery days of winter. As he stood and brushed off his threadbare tunic and breeches, he looked into the darkness down the packed dirt trade road. In one direction the way ran empty and arrow-straight much farther than the boy could see, almost until it reached

the peaceful hamlet of Irath. In the other, it made a gentle
curve around a tree-lined hill before striking north toward
Waymoot. There wasn't the slightest hint of a horseman
from either direction.

How can Father tell someone's coming? Artus wondered.
I can't even see as far as I can throw a stone.

The boy glanced up, only to find the moon hidden behind
iron-tinged clouds, swollen with snow. To one side of the
trade road, past the thorny hedgerow, trees hunched like
sleeping giants on a hill. On the other, fallow fields
stretched for miles. Lights shone in the windows of a farmhouse, nestled atop a faraway ridge, but they appeared as
tiny, flickering pinpoints. Artus would have mistaken them
for fireflies, had it been summer.

"Not enough light to see anything," he whispered and
tugged at his mask. After adjusting the tattered strip of
cloth around his eyes, he squinted into the darkness once
more.

Curiosity quickly overcame the boy's fear as he tried to
puzzle out just how his father had detected a rider. He
cocked his head and listened for the telltale sounds of hoofbeats on the frozen ground. An owl hooted occasionally
from a branch high on the hillside. At the farmhouse, a dog
barked at some annoyance, yelping and whining in fits. But
those were the only sounds on that lonely stretch of road—
though the young boy's heart was pounding so hard he
wondered childishly if someone might hear it, too, if they
listened hard enough.

Artus pressed a hand to his chest, hoping to muffle the
hammering. Of course it wouldn't stop. He softly cursed his
fear, but choked on the words; if he spoiled the job by making too much noise, his father would beat him for certain.
There was nothing the Shadowhawk cared about more
than his work, and Artus was suddenly petrified at the
prospect of failing him.

Scoril Cimber was the most famous highwayman in the
kingdom of Cormyr, known as the notorious Shadowhawk.
If Scoril himself were to be believed, that fame extended

throughout the disparate countries and city-states that made up the Heartlands, but even at seven, Artus could tell when his father was stretching the truth. And though the Shadowhawk was an overly proficient liar, it could not be denied many in Cormyr respected him as a master of his craft. Dozens of men from the Thieves Guild in the capital city of Suzail petitioned him regularly for apprenticeships. Scoril would accept none of them; if his craft was to be passed down, it would be through one of his two sons.

This cold Uktar night, it was Artus's turn to take up the mantle. His elder brother, Oric, had proved himself much more adept at robbing people. He was agile and as strong as many men twice his ten years in age. Yet Oric had also demonstrated himself incurably stupid time and time again—forgetting to disarm his victims or blurting out his father's name during a robbery. Never a patient man, the Shadowhawk couldn't bear these mistakes. So it had fallen upon Artus to become an apprentice highwayman. And even though he loathed the idea, he did his best to make his father happy.

Tonight, as on most nights, he failed.

"You're as bad as Oric!" The words struck Artus at the same time as the blow landed in the small of his back. The boy fell onto his chest, his ears ringing, his heart fluttering like a trapped songbird.

The Shadowhawk snorted. "You're lucky there ain't no rider."

"No rider?" Artus repeated.

"Course not." The highwayman tossed a small pack at the boy. "It was a test and you failed. What did I tell you about standing too long in the road during a jaunt?"

"That it's dangerous," Artus replied. He sat up and slid his pack onto his shoulders, but kept his gaze carefully locked on the scuffed tips of his boots.

"And?" the Shadowhawk prompted, pulling the boy to his feet.

Artus buried one hand in his pocket. Drawing it out again, he opened his grimy fist to reveal a blue gem, which glowed softly with a magical radiance. "And always keep this tight in one hand."

"The stone'll protect you, keep you from being trampled. You remember that stiff I showed you in Suzail, the knuckler what got run over by the wagon?" The pained look on Artus's face, heightened by the weird radiance of the stone, was answer enough. The pickpocket's bloody corpse had taken up a vivid residence in his memory. "Well, you'd look just as bad if a warhorse galloped over you."

Scowling, the Shadowhawk brushed away the lone tear meandering down the boy's cheek. "Oh, you're not 'urt," he murmured. "Right?"

"No, Father," he said between sniffles.

"These jaunts are for your own good. There's always danger if you're going to be a scamp, and I've seen a lot of blokes get killed being careless." He reached down and tucked the boy's tunic into his belt. "But you've got something they didn't 'ave, right? You've got brains. That makes you better than the little brats what only earn their blunt as buzzmen, swiping 'andkerchiefs and 'ats from the swells in Suzail. You can be a scamp, like me. Maybe even a good one."

The boy nodded and looked up at his father. The hood of the Shadowhawk's black cloak hid his stern features. That massive, shapeless cape had become a trademark of sorts for the highwayman, for it concealed both his face and his form. In the steady light of the gem, though, Artus glimpsed his father's hooked nose and the strange, predatory glint in his green eyes.

He'd seen that look many times on jaunts, but the first had been two years ago, when his father had beaten a fellow scamp unconscious on the road outside Suzail. The Shadowhawk, his hood knocked back in the fight, had stood over the man in mute triumph, assured the brigand was completely in his power. Now the gaze revealed how confident the Shadowhawk was his son had no ambitions, no dreams other than those he had instilled in him.

So intent was he upon Artus that the Shadowhawk didn't

hear the oddly muffled sounds from up the road until it was too late. There was no thunder of hoofbeats, no clink and clatter of tack to warn of the approaching warhorse; the mount's magical horseshoes did their best to mask these noises. The barely audible creak of leather as reins and harness and saddle strained on the galloping destrier—this was all that alerted the highwayman to the threat at his back. He looked up just in time to see the massive white horse bearing down on him. Its rider, oblivious to the obstacle, stared intently over his shoulder.

"Tyr's eyes!" the Shadowhawk cursed and threw himself on top of Artus. At the same instant, the glowing gem in the boy's fist flashed brightly. A sphere of light welled up from the stone to surround the unfortunate pair huddled directly in the destrier's path.

The shout and the burst of magic from the gem snared the rider's attention, but not soon enough for him to do anything to avoid the pair. He wrenched the reins, but the warhorse half-jumped, half-stumbled over the highwayman and his son, its hooves rapping a loud and threatening drum roll on the arcane shield. The force of the assault knocked the magical bubble a dozen yards down the road. It rolled like a crazed billiard ball with the two robbers tumbling inside.

As soon as the danger had passed, the gem drew in the force shield, and the battered duo assessed their situation. The Shadowhawk had gained a few bruises and a throbbing headache from the tumble, Artus not even a scratch. The highwayman shook his head, the severe frown telling the boy quite bluntly this trouble was his fault and he would pay for it. The Shadowhawk probably would have meted out that rough justice, too, if the destrier and its rider weren't sprawled, unmoving, at the edge of the road opposite the hedgerow.

"I'll check him," Artus said, adjusting his near-empty pack on his shoulders. If the jaunt went well, the sack would soon be full of coins and anything of value they might be able to fence in Suzail.

JAMES LOWDER

"Yeah, awright." The Shadowhawk rubbed the welt on his arm roughly. "Give 'im a topper if 'e's twitching too much."

Artus shuddered. Robbing people at knifepoint was one thing. Bashing them on the head was another. He knew his father didn't kill people—"doing the out-and-out" the thieves at the guildhall called it—but the Shadowhawk never shied away from roughing up a swell who resisted too much or a tax collector who threatened to bring the law after him.

The moon struggled from behind the clouds, casting its wan light over the road. Fortunately, the rider looked like he was in no shape to put up a struggle. He lay face down, his arms spread to his sides, his breath wheezing from him in bursts. He'd fallen clear of his mount, which was for the best; the horse had landed in a heap. Its neck was twisted grotesquely, and blood dribbled from its nostrils and mouth. Deep, ragged gouges marred the destrier's legs— wounds it couldn't have received in the fall—but the shattered bone jutting from its foreleg was clearly a result of the collision. The boy was glad the poor beast was dead. Its rider would have had to kill it anyway.

Artus knew his father was watching him, so he steeled himself and strode confidently toward the unconscious man. As he did, he exchanged the glowing gem in his hand for his dirk. That would please the Shadowhawk, he was certain. Besides, the feel of the dagger in his palm took his mind off the white, staring eyes of the dead horse and the uncomfortable prickle of his father's gaze.

The rider was wealthy. Of that there could be little doubt. As Artus rolled him over, the moonlight danced over the silver links of an expensive chain-mail shirt. The man's cloak was new and fur lined at the collar to keep out the winter chill. His boots were tooled from the finest leather, as were his gloves and belt. Unlike the thieves, the young knight had bathed recently and his hair was neatly trimmed.

Roughly the boy pulled the man's scabbard from his belt and tossed it aside. Then he reached for the rider's tabard,

◆ 222 ◆

crumpled by the fall. Wrought of expensive Shou silk, the cloth was emblazoned with the Purple Dragon. Symbol of King Rhigaerd II and House Obarskyr, the Purple Dragon was worn by all who served in Cormyr's military. But the soldiers in Rhigaerd's employ sported white tabards. This man's was gray. And his cloak was not military issue. Artus had seen enough soldiers around Suzail to know that.

"What's the delay, Art?" the Shadowhawk growled. "So 'e's a bloody soldier?" The highwayman eyed the man's warm clothes. "Be a good boy and give me 'is gloves. My 'ands are frozen."

The boy peeled the gloves from the knight and tossed them to the Shadowhawk. "Father, I—"

"Quit stalling! You'll be sorry if 'e wakes up. I'll leave you to fight 'im, you know." The highwayman threw his own rat-nibbled gloves into the hedges and slid the new ones on. "Grab 'is jewelry, if 'e's got any, and whatever blunt 'e's got in that stuffed purse, then check 'is nag for supplies."

Quickly Artus pulled the gold ring from the man's left hand, a wedding band with delicate engraving inside. In the moonlight, the boy could read a name there: Filfaeril. The knight's lady love, it would seem. Without pause, he thrust the ring into his pocket. Once the engraving was smoothed out, it would fetch a good price in the city.

Next he cut the purse from the man's belt. It was heavy, and Artus couldn't help pausing to glance inside. Atop the mound of silver coins lay another ring—gold and encrusted with gems. It, too, bore the dragon of House Obarskyr.

Artus froze. A cold dread spread from the ring to his suddenly numb fingers, up his arms, and finally to his heart. Only one young man would carry such a signet ring. The boy looked at the knight's face. He was the right age, just a little older than the Shadowhawk. And it was said in the Thieves Guild he often rode out of the royal castle in Suzail, disguised as a wandering cavalier, a sell-sword meting out justice as part of a brave band known as the King's Men.

"Prince Azoun," Artus whispered.

The purse slipped out of his fingers, rebounding off his

leg before hitting the ground. The coins jingled musically as they scattered over the road. "The prince," Artus said, turning to his father. "We've got to—"

But something else had captured the Shadowhawk's attention. He fell to his hands and knees, head cocked curiously. "Something's coming," the highwayman said. Artus thought he heard an edge of fear in his father's voice. "It ain't on the road, though. More like . . . *under* it."

The road trembled beneath Artus. He tried to stand, but the packed earth under his feet shifted, sending him sprawling atop the unconscious prince. Frantically he reached for the gem in his pocket.

As Artus's fingers closed around the blue stone, something burst up from the dirt next to the dead horse. The boy caught a glimpse of it—shaggy hair and beard, all wild and unkempt and matted with soil. That mop seemed to be the entirety of its head and upper body, until it flexed its stubby arms and slashed the air with long black talons.

The creature plunged back into the ground then, just as another surfaced momentarily on the other side of the horse. Together the two creatures circled the unfortunate mount, a track of disturbed earth forming around the corpse. Before Artus could cry out his amazement, a hole swallowed up the entire warhorse.

"Run!" he heard his father shout, but the words seemed to come from very far away.

Brightly the gem in Artus's hand flared to life. The force wall flowing from it pushed his fingers apart, as it always did, and spread out to encircle both the boy and Prince Azoun. Artus felt the globe sink as the earth gave way, opening a wide maw for him. He looked with staring eyes at the still form of Azoun, past him to the translucent blue floor of the sphere. At any moment, the dirt beneath it would fall away and they would be swallowed up, just like the dead destrier.

Then the rumbling beneath Artus stopped. All was silent for an instant as the globe settled in the shallow sinkhole. Nearby, where the horse had been taken, clots of dirt shot from the burrow. They rained down on the road in a soft patter. On the other side of the road, the Shadowhawk crouched near the hedgerow, neither fleeing nor lifting a hand to help his son. Like Artus, he seemed frozen by fear.

"Whatever you do, boy," came a strained, quiet voice, "don't let go of that gem."

Artus nearly did just that at the unexpected words from the prince, but Azoun reached out and gently steadied the boy's trembling hand.

"W-what are they?" Artus stammered.

Reaching up to gingerly prod the bloody wound on his forehead, Prince Azoun said, "Zhentarim assassins. Magically altered dwarves, I think. Voracious little beasts called groundlings. How—Ooch." He pulled his fingers away from the gash. "How long can you keep that force shield up? I think it's blocking the groundlings' tracking sense."

"It stays up by itself, but only as long as we're in danger and the gem's touching my skin. I mean, I can't control it other than that."

"One of the groundlings must be right below us," the prince observed. "Close, too, if it's triggering the shield." He reached for his sword, but found his belt empty. "Where's my blade?"

The boy gestured to the weapon, which lay in the road, well out of reach. Then he flinched, as if he were expecting a blow for his mistake.

"It's all right," Azoun said kindly. "Just give me your dagger."

The prince took the small, rather dull knife and rolled onto his knees. The movement caused the thing in the ground beneath the force globe to stir, and the sinkhole grew deeper as the groundling blindly expanded its burrow. The sphere of magical energy sank into the earth, far enough that Artus could barely spy his father as he huddled near the hedgerow.

The boy soon regretted even that limited vista.

From the wide burrow that had swallowed the prince's horse, a coarse laughter began to echo. The hacking was soon accompanied by the sickening crack of still-warm bones breaking. Limb by limb, rib by rib, the destrier's remains flew out of the burrow. The gory missiles landed in the grass, bounced off the force shield, even buffeted the Shadowhawk. The bones had been stripped of most of their flesh by the assassins, the tack and saddle chewed almost beyond recognition.

That was more than enough to panic the highwayman. With a single glance back at his son, the Shadowhawk sprang toward the hedgerow. He fixed his cold eyes on the hillside beyond. The trees, leafless in the Uktar wind, promised safety with their high branches. If only he could reach them. . . .

As soon as the highwayman moved, three tracks of churning earth shot across the road—two from the horse's grave, another from beneath Artus and Azoun. The groundlings burrowed furiously after the Shadowhawk, like sharks in bloody waters. They converged on him just before he reached the row of thorny bushes at the road's edge. Clawed hands burst through the topsoil and closed around his ankles. Talons sharp as swords tore deep furrows in the highwayman's boots and painful scratches in the skin below.

The Shadowhawk screamed once before he disappeared into the burrow.

The force globe vanished when the groundlings went after the highwayman. Prince Azoun hit the bottom of the sinkhole with a grunt of pain, then reached out to stop the boy from running. Artus ducked the prince's awkward grab, leaped from the hole, and raced to save his father.

"They won't kill him!" Azoun shouted. "They're after me!"

Artus wasn't listening. When he reached the burrow where the Shadowhawk had vanished, he stuffed the blue gem into his pocket and grabbed a more suitable weapon— a fist-sized wedge of stone tapering to a point at one end. Kneeling before the hole, he whispered, "Father?"

His knees had barely touched the road before two squinting red eyes appeared in the blackness. Artus didn't wait to see what the groundling would do. Savagely he lashed out with the stone. The Shadowhawk had trained the boy in knife-fighting, but his years in the roughest alleys of Suzail had given him less orthodox fighting skills, too. In his hand, the stone might as well have been a warhammer, wielded by a young dwarven warrior from the halls of Earthfast.

The blow landed on the bridge of the assassin's snoutlike nose, shattering it noisily. The groundling howled and clutched at its face. Artus attacked again, this time planting the stone squarely atop the creature's shaggy head. The sound of a skull fracturing resounded in the burrow.

For an instant, Artus felt a surge of relief. Then the groundling burst from the burrow once more, crazed with pain and fury. When he saw the flash of the creature's teeth, the boy realized what a horrible mistake he'd made.

Certain of his doom, Artus braced for the attack. He didn't close his eyes or turn away; fright had locked his arms and legs. The sole thought running through his mind was how stupid he'd been for putting the magical gem in his pocket.

Like a diving falcon, a silver blade flashed out of the night and pierced the groundling's back, right between the shoulder blades. The assassin's dirty paws went limp on Artus's arms. The thing puffed out a last stinking breath and was still.

Artus stared in horrified amazement at the groundling. Short and stocky, it vaguely resembled the dwarves who sometimes passed through Suzail as itinerant sell-swords or miners or metalsmiths. Yet its features had been twisted by the Zhentarim's dark sorcery. Whatever stunted ears it had were buried in wild fur, its eyes reduced to nothing more than narrow slits. Artus had bloodied the long, fleshy snout, probably even broken it, from the awkward bend near its bridge. Even in death, though, the bristles on the snout's tip twitched spasmodically. The creature stank of rotten meat and fetid water. Sticks and decaying leaves, worms and crawling weevils, dotted its hairy flanks and the crown of its head.

"Get to the trees!" Prince Azoun shouted.

Artus, shocked out of his frightened stupor, looked up to find the prince bracing one dragonhide boot on the corpse. He was trying to wrench his sword free. The blade had gone right through the assassin, pinning it to the ground. Now it wouldn't budge.

A shriek reverberated eerily from the depths of the burrow. It was the animalistic cry of a groundling, and from the angry snarls that followed it, Artus was fairly certain the remaining pair of assassins had discovered their mistake in grabbing the Shadowhawk.

As the angry cacocophy in the burrow grew louder, the prince grasped the sword more tightly and pulled with all his strength—to no avail. He'd simply struck the beast too hard.

"Brute force causes as many difficulties as it solves," he said bitterly, repeating a maxim favored by Vangerdahast, his royal tutor. As with most of the wizard's sage advice, though, its true meaning had come to Azoun just a little too late.

When he saw Artus still standing at the edge of the burrow, staring mutely at the corpse, the prince released his grip on the trapped sword. Grabbing the boy by the arm, he bolted through the hedgerow and ran toward the hillside beyond. They stopped at the nearest tree with branches low enough and sturdy enough for them to climb.

"Go as high as you can," Azoun said as he boosted Artus onto a gnarled limb. "Then take out that gem again and hold it tight."

The boy moved tentatively into the lower branches. He wasn't afraid of heights; it was just that he'd never climbed a tree before. After all, he'd had few chances to do so in Suzail, since only noble estates and small, well-patrolled public parks held any greenery at all. And the Shadowhawk frowned upon hiding in trees during a jaunt, since a robber was just as likely to hurt himself by leaping on a victim.

"The only time a proper scamp's found in a tree is when 'e's dangling from it," was one of his favorite sayings.

To counter the fear welling inside him, Artus tried to picture himself climbing up to the second story of the ruined tavern where he had his secret library. By scaling a flight of rickety stairs and pushing through a hole in the upper floor, he would come to his treasure trove of books. He'd stolen most of them from scribes' stalls in the marketplace, but a few proclamations had come to him from the rubbish heaps outside the city walls. Scaling the tree wasn't so different from getting up to the loft, he decided, and the climb became less of a struggle.

When at last he reached a safe vantage, high in the tree, Artus looked down to find Azoun struggling along behind him. The prince's cloak snagged branches with each move he made, and his chain mail shirt hung heavily on his shoulders. Azoun settled on a thick limb below the boy. Only then did he begin to undo the elaborate clasp holding his cloak closed.

"That was a brave thing you did," the prince noted. He puffed out a breath of relief as he slid the cloak from his shoulders. "Put this around you. It'll get cold up here fast, once the fright lets go of you."

Artus took the cloak with a softly murmured thanks. "What about my fa—uh, the Shadowhawk?" he asked.

The prince paused. "The Shadowhawk, eh? At least I was waylaid by the best." Forcing a grim smile, he added, "Don't worry. The groundlings are professional assassins. They won't harm your father—the Shadowhawk, I mean. He's got my gloves, I suppose. That's why they went after him—they could pick up even that much of my scent on him as he moved. But, like I said, they won't hurt him. Their contract is for my death. To kill someone else would be against guild rules. Do you understand?"

The boy nodded, and the cloud of concern passed from his brown eyes. If the creatures were sentient enough to follow the rules of the Assassins Guild, perhaps his father could fast-talk his way free. "Will they let him go when they figure out he's not the one they want?"

"Not right away. At least not until they've got me. Right now, the groundlings—"

A scraping noise drew Azoun's attention back to the road. There, the assassin's corpse was slowly sliding into the burrow. The sword point jutting from its chest cut through the ground like a plow blade as the groundlings dragged their dead fellow deeper into the earth. Soon, the corpse and the sword were gone.

Azoun sighed. "Right now, the groundlings are building a warren, an underground camp. They must realize they have us trapped, since nothing is moving on the ground. They'll do all they can to bleed us out of weapons, food, and hope, then wait for us to come down." Scowling, he noted, "Especially food. They'll eat almost anything. I managed to escape them outside of Waymoot by dumping my rations onto the road—that and being lucky enough to have a very fast mount with enchanted horseshoes."

"I have some bread!" Artus offered brightly, gesturing to his pack. "I mean, if you can think of a way to use it against the groundlings . . ."

"Well, at least we won't starve," the prince said, trying not to be patronizing, but failing badly. "But since we don't have a horse or any way of escaping, tossing it to the assassins won't do us much good right now."

Clouds slid over the moon once more, blanketing the hillside in a more profound darkness. A cold breeze made the branches creak and sway. The boy was glad for the prince's cloak then, for his shabby clothes gave little protection from the wind. "I'm Artus," he began softly.

The words jolted Azoun out of some intense reverie. "Eh? Well, Artus, you can call me Balin."

The boy paused, then pulled the gem from his pocket. Its blue light cast strange shadows over Azoun's face. He stared at the young man for a moment, openly sizing him up. "But that's not your name," Artus said at last.

"Of course it is," Azoun began, but he saw the frown on Artus's lips, the look of distrust stealing over his eyes. He looked down at his hands, to the indentation on his finger left by his missing wedding band. His purse was gone, too. "Was it the princess's name on the wedding ring or the signet ring in my purse that gave me away?"

"Kinda both," Artus replied. He dug the gold band out of his pocket and returned it to the prince. "And the tabard, too. Not many sell-swords would wear the king's symbol like that."

Azoun looked down at the torn and grimy Purple Dragon. "My tutor always said this was rather silly, to wear the family crest on a disguise. Still, it fooled men a lot older than you."

"People don't look for the obvious. Do you want me to call you Your Holiness?"

"No," Azoun said, trying not to smile at the boy's bluntness. "We're fighting together now, and brothers-in- arms need not bow to courtly manners. Besides, you call clerics Your Holiness, not princes."

"Sorry. I never met a prince before."

"So how do you know so much about me?"

The boy fidgeted uncomfortably with the cloak's fur collar. "Well, I've read about King Rhigaerd and about you on the royal proclamations posted around Suzail. And I saw you on your wedding day, when your carriage went down the Promenade. Well, I was too far away to see you, but I saw your carriage. And then there's the stories they tell in the Thieves Guild about you—how you dress up in disguises and play like you're a knight. They say—"

"All right," Azoun said, holding up a hand to stop the torrent. It was his turn to study his unwilling companion, to size up this worldly child-robber. Most children grew up quickly in Cormyr, especially poor children from the city. But this boy was more than world-wise. He was obviously clever. Moreover, he could read, a skill confined mostly to the nobility, the priesthood, and a few wealthy merchant families. "Your father taught you to read, did he?"

Artus laughed with surprising bitterness. "He doesn't like me to read. A priest of Oghma taught me on the sly, until Father found out, that is. It didn't matter, though. By the time he told me to stop I already knew how." He gripped the gem tightly, cutting off most of the light. Still, Azoun could see the angry look in the boy's eyes as he said, "I don't want to be a scamp like him."

The prince held his hand up to the boy. "If you don't want to be a highwayman, how about giving me your mask? I could use it right about now."

For a moment Artus thought the prince was going to try to fit the dirty strip over his face, but he began to tie it over his forehead. Then the boy noticed the gash on Azoun's head was leaking blood into his brown hair, staining it dark and masking the strands of gray already taking hold there. "So what's your ambition then—a priest, perhaps? Maybe a bard? You seem to remember stories pretty well."

A smile crept across Artus's features. "I like stories a lot. I—" He cast his eyes down at the glowing gem and paused. "I know some about you. The men at the guildhall told me about the King's Men. They say you won't be a good king, you know, that you'll be wandering off to rescue people and fight dragons."

"Indeed," Azoun said flatly. "Maybe they're right. We'll find out soon enough, though, won't we?"

Artus let the cryptic comment drop, for the cold tone in the man's voice frightened him just a little. His father sounded the same way whenever he talked about a failed jaunt or a rival in the Thieves Guild who had questioned his skill. "What will we do now?" he asked after a time.

"Wait, I suppose," the prince said mournfully. "They won't attack us once the sun comes up. It hurts their eyes too much. Besides, by dawn there'll be travelers on the road again. We can muster enough people to stand against the little monsters, if they haven't given up by then and gone back to Darkhold."

An uncomfortable silence fell over Artus and Azoun after that. Both were certain there should be some way to fight, but neither came up with a plan worth suggesting. Azoun took to whittling away bark with the boy's knife, while

Artus slumped unhappily against the trunk.

Occasionally one of the groundlings would appear at the mouth of the nearest burrow. It would sniff the air, squint uselessly into the night, then call into the darkness, "Escape is not for you, Azoun." Their voices were frightful, high-pitched and screeching like hobnail boots sliding on a slate floor.

After a time, though, even this harassment stopped. Artus dared to hope that the assassins were giving up, that his father would soon crawl out of the ground a free man. But the sudden, violent collapse of a tree perilously close to their sanctuary crushed those hopes.

"They're not going to wait for us to come down," Azoun observed bitterly.

Horror-struck, they watched another tree drop into a sinkhole, then pitch forward. The night filled with groans and cracks as the oak smashed into a leafless maple and both crashed to the ground. All around the fallen trees, groundling burrow tracks cut through the earth. Every few feet, one of the assassins would breach and test the air.

Finding no trace of the prince amongst the wreckage, the groundlings set about toppling more trees. The din was terrible as the oaks and pines tumbled, tearing branches from other trees in the path of their fall, pounding the life out of anything caught beneath their impact. Birds and squirrels and other creatures took flight as their homes swayed and collapsed. Any creature larger than a rat that fled on the hillside found itself swallowed up by a groundling burrow. As the prince had noted, it seemed the voracious assassins would eat almost anything.

Finally a tree toppled close enough to swipe at Artus and Azoun with its barren limbs. The gnarled branches clutched at them like skeletal fingers, scratching a painful line across the prince's cheek and snagging the heavy cloak Artus wore. The boy felt himself falling backward. The gem in his hand threw its magical globe around him at that moment, shielding him from a branch that careered past him. Yet the globe didn't anchor Artus to his perch; neither, he knew, would it cushion his impact with the ground if he fell. Reluctantly the boy let the gem slip from his hands and tried one desperate grab for the trunk.

His cold-numbed fingers closed on air. Shouting for help, Artus plummeted.

He didn't fall far, though. Azoun, his legs wrapped tightly around a branch, grabbed for the boy as he went past. Fortunately, the prince stopped Artus's fall. Unfortunately, he did it by snagging the cloak, which fluttered behind the boy like a sparrow's broken wing.

Artus jerked to a stop. Choking, he tried to get a foothold or handhold on the tree. Any sizeable branches were well out of his reach, so all he managed to do was set himself swinging back and forth. The clasp cut into his throat, and the tree's smaller branches battered his face. When at last Artus got a firm grip on the cloak, he gasped in a ragged breath and looked down at the site of his almost-doom.

The tree had barely landed before the assassins were swarming around it. They nosed at the glowing blue gem, which lay nearby, but it held little interest for them. The groundlings were, after all, dwarves at heart. Though mutated, they shared that stout people's disdain of unfamiliar magic.

The Zhentarim agents wasted little time on the search. As soon as they were convinced the prince had not fallen with that particular oak, they set to work undermining the next. It wasn't long before shudders began to ripple up the tree holding Artus and the prince.

His face red, his arms quivering at the strain of holding his neck out of the fur-collared noose, the boy looked up at Azoun. "Let me go," he croaked.

Ignoring the plea, the prince began to reel in the cloak like a net. Artus writhed, trying to break free. "I can . . . save us," the boy cried.

Azoun grimaced. "Don't be foolish," he snapped. "You can't—"

Another shudder wracked the oak as the groundlings cut away a major root. The prince braced himself, waiting for the trembling to pass. At the same time, Artus twisted sharply, jerking the cloak from Azoun's fingers.

The boy fell, spinning violently in the air. The momentum was enough to send him toward a heavy branch. He grabbed it just long enough to slow his fall, then dropped again, rebounding off limbs closer and closer to the ground. He hit the hillside on his feet and was running before the assassins could react.

As Artus dashed away from the tree, one of the groundlings broke off from the excavation and followed. It tried to keep up with the runner, but he leaped onto the trunks of fallen oaks and scurried into the thick branches of toppled firs. With footfalls muffled by the fresh blanket of needles, he was almost imperceptible to the hunter's keen senses of hearing and touch. Artus might have eluded the creature completely, had it not been for the cloak he wore. Even tearing through the frozen earth, the groundling could smell the prince's scent.

And that was just what Artus was counting on.

A deep groan warned the boy that the tree sheltering Azoun was ready to fall. He turned back just as it started to lean. But instead of avoiding the tree, the boy ran straight toward it.

The oak fell slowly at first, and Artus could see the prince scrambling for a vantage from which he could leap clear when he got close enough to the ground. The boy wanted to shout to him, tell him not to jump just yet, but he knew the prince wouldn't be able to hear him. Even if he did, he probably wouldn't listen, just like the Shadowhawk. . . .

Those bitter thoughts kept Artus's mind off what he was doing, which was a blessing of sorts. The chance the plan would fail was great, the chance it would succeed terribly slim. Nevertheless, Artus ran right into the path of the falling oak, the assassin bearing down on him.

As the track of churning earth touched his boot heels, Artus shrugged the heavy cloak from his shoulders and dived forward. The groundling, certain its victim had fallen, burst up and grabbed the prince's cloak—just beneath the tree trunk as it hit the ground. Like a mallet wielded by a storm giant, the oak drove the unfortunate dwarf-thing back into the dirt, shattering its skull and most of its bones.

That part of the plan worked perfectly. The rest did not.

Artus rolled away from the tree's impact and landed next to the softly glowing magical gem. The boy dared for an instant to hope he'd won. Then a thick branch dropped onto his leg. Artus managed to heave the wood aside, but it left his knee throbbing. Teeth clenched in pain, he sprawled on the soft bed of pine needles and clutched the blue gem in trembling fingers.

The prince fared no better. As he leaped from the oak, he was battered by its limbs. The tree flung him toward the ground in an awkward tumble, and his mail shirt prevented him from righting himself. Azoun hit the hillside shoulder-first and slid into the furrow left in a groundling's wake. Though he landed only a horse's length from Artus, the prince might as well have been a hundred leagues away, for all the help he'd be against the last assassin.

Azoun pushed himself to his knees and dazedly looked around. The makeshift bandage had been torn from his head, and blood ran freely down his face. He spotted Artus and managed to crawl to the wounded boy. "Save yourself," he murmured, then spiraled down into unconsciousness.

Warily the remaining groundling surfaced a dozen yards from the Artus and Azoun, squinting toward them with its slitlike red eyes. "Now you are done, princeling," it screeched and tunneled into the ground.

The assassin surfaced again, near the spot where it had scented Azoun. All it found was the blue glow of the force globe, since the magic masked the prince from detection. The groundling cried out in frustration and, for the first time, a little fear. The Zhentarim sorcerers who had dispatched the assassins from the bowels of Darkhold never brooked failure. Even if it survived this encounter with the prince and his able young protector, the groundling would find itself facing endless punishment in that foul keep's dungeons, tortures like the smiling screws or the gruesome kiss of the carrion worms.

To even the groundling's limited intellect, this proved incentive enough for an original thought to emerge.

"You cannot run," the assassin shrilled in sudden realization. "I've won!"

"We can hide in the globe," Artus said as bravely as he could, though pain and fright made his voice crack pitiably. "You've lost. Sooner or later, the royal wizards will come looking for the prince. Until then, we'll be safe in here."

The last was pure bluff, but it set the groundling digging around the magical globe. Dirt and stones rained down on the shell, the clatter underscored by the assassin's unearthly wailing. Then, all at once, the creature ceased its frightening tantrum and sidled up to the globe. The creature glared at the magical bubble, the pale light nearly blinding it, and said, "They'll find a corpse here just the same. I have the one who was with you, boy." The groundling paused and licked its snout with a long black tongue. "I'll leave his bare bones around you like a picket fence if you keep my prize from me."

"But the guild rules—"

"Mean nothing if I lose the prince," the groundling snapped. "So they take away my guild badge for killing the wrong man? So what?"

Artus's shoulder's slumped. There was really no choice if the assassin threatened his father. Besides, what was Azoun to him?

"A trade, then," the boy called. "I'll hand over Prince Azoun, but you've got to bring the other man back here."

"What about the magic wall?" the groundling shrieked. "You'll take the other and hide him there with you and never give me the prince!"

"And you'll just kill me as soon as you have Azoun!" Artus snapped.

There was an uncomfortable pause as the boy and the dwarf-thing considered their rather limited options. It was Artus who finally suggested a plan. In it, there was just the slightest chance he and the Shadowhawk would survive this nightmarish ordeal—and maybe even rescue the prince, too.

"I'm a thief, so we're brothers in trade, right?" Artus began tentatively. In truth the groundling did rather remind Artus of his brother Oric. "So we should be able to make a fair bargain. If, uh, I promise to put the magic gem away and not use it until you have the prince, the trade should be easy. Is that all right with you? I mean, once you have Azoun, you've got no reason to harm us, so we can all get what we want out of this."

It took a few moments for the groundling to wrap its limited intellect around that complicated arrangement, but at last it agreed to the plan. In a flurry of gravel and dirt, the assassin disappeared into its burrow. As soon as the thing was gone, the globe vanished. Artus unslung his ragged pack and prepared Prince Azoun for the groundling's return.

The Shadowhawk was bound hand and foot when the assassin dragged him to the surface. His cloak hung in tatters on his back, and his hood lay in useless strips around his shoulders. Fear filled his wide, staring eyes. Dirt and grime clung to his hair, transformed into clinging mud by blood and sweat. A gag pulled his mouth into a frightful rictus grin.

In silence, Artus stood over the unconscious form of Prince Azoun, who now lay with his head propped up on the boy's pack. Stepping away from the nobleman, he walked slowly toward his father. He could see the surprise in the Shadowhawk's usually cold green eyes, but that didn't concern him as much as the look of reckless triumph twisting the groundling's already horrific features.

The assassin swam through the ground at the surface, paddling straight toward Azoun. It paused at the prince's side, then reached out with a single claw. Perhaps the groundling assumed Azoun would turn out to be a phantasm, despite what its keen senses reported. Whatever the reason, the assassin started when it touched the prince's warm flesh. This was even more than it had hoped for;

bringing Azoun back to Darkhold alive would quadruple the reward, perhaps even purchase a transformation back to its original dwarven form.

Carefully the creature encircled the prince's legs and started to pull him into the burrow. As Azoun slid, the bed of pine boughs and the small pack that was his pillow slid with him. The groundling didn't seem to notice the branches falling into the burrow, but it stopped dead when the sack's contents rolled onto him—a few sticks of greasepaint used for disguises, a small length of thin black cord, and the stale loaf of bread that was to have been Artus's sustenance on the long trek home. It was this last item that caught the attention of the groundling's twitching nose.

"Hey," Artus called halfheartedly, "that's mine!"

The assassin snorted and scooped the loaf into its maw. Chewing only enough to break the bread into chunks, it gulped the prize down. The groundling then turned its weak eyes back to Artus, a snide comment on the tip of its black tongue, but found the boy standing very close to the burrow's edge.

"Leave the prince alone," Artus said coldly. He planted his hands on his hips and puffed out his chest in what he assumed to be a heroic pose. "If you go now, I'll let you live."

The groundling snarled and tensed its legs to spring, but an odd feeling in its gut made it pause. It groaned and looked down at its suddenly burning stomach. Was the boy using magic? The glowing stone, perhaps? The assassin cursed itself for trusting the human child, especially since it intended to break its vow once the prince was bound securely for the trek back to Darkhold.

"Really," Artus said, "you'd be better off to give up right now. You're beaten."

That was enough for the groundling. It threw back its head and howled, then lunged at the boy.

Artus calmly curled one small hand into a fist and raised it to strike the charging monster. But the groundling never got close enough to harm the boy. The gem it had swallowed with the bread responded to the raised fist by throwing out its protective shell. The magical wall mindlessly and methodically expanded, trying to encase its new master.

The groundling clutched its swelling gut and fell face-first into the dirt. Artus limped another step closer to the creature. "I warned you," he said.

In reply, the assassin belched as defiantly as possible, then burst like an overripe melon dropped onto a cobble-stone street.

The silence that followed was quickly filled by the mundane sounds of an Uktar night—hooting owls, the distant barking of dogs, and the chill wind rustling through the trees. Artus stood still for a time, reveling in that normalcy, then set to work untying his father. The Shadowhawk said nothing—no exclamations of pride, no cries of relief, no words of gratitude. He merely rubbed his sore limbs and watched his son without comment as he pulled the prince out of the burrow, bandaged his head again, and moved him out of the road to the safety of the hedgerow. Scoril Cimber could see there was something different about the boy now, but he couldn't quite figure out what.

When he finished with Azoun, Artus turned back to the Shadowhawk, who still sat amidst the piles of earth and gaping holes covering the trade road. "Father," he said flatly, "there's a rider coming."

If the highwayman was surprised his son had heard the faraway rumble of hooves before him, he never let on.

* * * * *

The rider turned out to be the vanguard of a large patrol, scouring the countryside for the lost prince. When the soldiers paused to search the destruction, Artus threw a few stones to draw their attention to the hedgerow and the unconscious royal. Even with his sprained knee it proved simple for the boy and his father to elude the mounted and heavily armored patrol on the wooded hill. The Shadowhawk was a wanted man, after all, and capture by the king's

Purple Dragons was something he had avoided many times before.

In the days that followed, Scoril Cimber cemented his place at the cynosure of the weblike Cormyrian underworld with wild tales of his role in the rescue of Prince Azoun. Artus did nothing to counter these yarns. In fact, the boy often lent quiet support to the Shadowhawk's claim that he'd killed all three Zhentarim thugs and single-handedly protected the heir to the throne of House Obarskyr. And since the palace never commented on assassination rumors, for such things tended to upset the commoners, the Shadowhawk rose unopposed to the height of scamp notoriety.

Such fame always proved fleeting in the back alleys of Suzail, though, and other topics soon supplanted the daring rescue and the molelike killers—foremost among them the oft-repeated rumor that the withering sickness would surely claim King Rhigaerd before the year was out. Young Prince Azoun would soon be King Azoun IV. No one seemed pleased to hear this.

"Look," a grizzled thief said, just loudly enough to overwhelm the ten or so voices vying for dominance in the Thieves Guild common room. "Rhigaerd was a bully. No one's arguing with that. All I'm saying is we knew what to expect from him."

"Yeah," someone chimed in, "a quick hanging if we got caught on the road with five copper dragons we couldn't prove as our own."

The grizzled thief frowned. "But at least we knew where we stood. He was a strong king, sure, but that also meant prosperity for the nobles—and good pickings for scamps smart enough to follow guild rules and keep away from his patrols."

From his position in the center of the throng, the Shadowhawk cleared his throat. The room quieted noticeably and all eyes turned to him. "Azoun don't want to be king, right? So maybe 'e'll spend 'is time daydreaming about fighting giants and leave us be." He put his boots up on the table right in front of Artus and paused smugly. "Yeah, I think 'e'll just leave us be. After all, the bloke owes 'is life to a scamp, right?"

"But what about Vangerdahast, that tutor of his?" another thief asked. "He's a scary one, real sly and real smart. That wizard'll be running things himself if Azoun isn't going to do it proper, and he has no love of the guild."

A pickpocket with three fingers missing on one hand nodded sagely. "Wizards ain't to be trusted," he said, wiggling his remaining digits meaningfully. "It may not matter, though. I hear said that when Azoun's son died last year he changed, started to think of things more like a prince. It took the wildness out of him. Not surprising, when a babe two winters old dies so sudden. Makes you wonder what you did to offend the gods, eh?"

Someone across the room raised a mug in mock reverence. "To Azoun," he said. "May he be half the king his father was—half as good at catching thieves!"

Silent the entire morning, Artus shook his head. "Azoun will be a great king. All the assassins and thieves in Cormyr will be sorry for it, too."

"You'd better 'ope not, Art," the Shadowhawk said, surprised by the comment. "After all, you'll be the scamp to end all scamps yourself one day."

The boy turned cold brown eyes to his father, and the Shadowhawk caught a glimpse of that strange expression he'd seen on Artus's face the night of the battle, just before he'd killed the last of the assassins. "But, Father," he announced in a voice loud enough for everyone to hear, "you said I don't have to be a scamp."

"What?" the Shadowhawk bellowed. "I never—"

"Right after the fight—right after *you* killed *all three* assassins—" Artus cut in quickly, "you said I fought so badly I would never be safe robbing people. I should be a scribe, you said, or a bard."

Everyone's attention was on Artus and the Shadowhawk, and those thieves prone to jealously and envy—which was, in fact, all of them—found their spirits buoyed by a sudden hope that Scoril Cimber's yarns might now be proved untrue. The room stood frozen for a moment as the highwayman searched in vain for some way out of his son's well-laid trap. The boy had let him tell his version of the rescue, let him take all the glory and reap the guild's rewards for such notoriety. Now, it seemed, he wanted his payment.

But when Scoril looked closely at Artus, he realized there was no escape. The predatory look in his son's eyes was a familiar one, a glint as hard as the stiletto hidden in his boot and as cold as the winter chill creeping through the guildhall's cheap floorboards.

"Yeah. You be a bard," the Shadowhawk murmured at last.

He turned away from Artus's triumphant smile and gulped his ale. Even if he isn't going to be my apprentice, the highwayman thought ruefully, the boy's learned more than I ever intended to teach him.

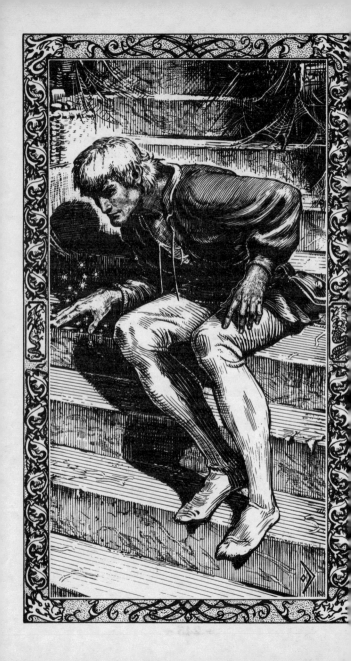

GRANDFATHER'S TOYS

Jean Rabe

The druid stood before the weathered oak door of the tower. His wheat-colored hair lay plastered against his neck, and his dark green tunic clung slickly, like a second skin, to his muscular frame. His embroidered cloak stretched to the grass behind him and tugged annoyingly at his neck as he tipped his head back and glanced upward through the soft, steady rain.

The tower's slate-gray stones merged with the dreary early evening sky, making it difficult for the druid to see the crenelated battlements. Squinting, he peered into the gloom and glimpsed a flicker of light from a window on the highest floor.

The druid dropped his gaze until his chin rested on his chest. "I haven't seen him in years," he said softly.

A rushed sequence of chitters and squeaks issued from his tunic in reply.

"Yes. It has been too long."

The druid gently tugged the lacings of his tunic, loosening the material about his neck. A moment later a weasel's shiny black nose poked out from the V-neck of the sodden garment. The creature chittered again.

"All right. I'll hurry," the druid answered, stepping forward and rapping on the tower door.

An interminable time later the door groaned inward, revealing a figure draped in a hooded cloak.

"Galvin, my friend!" The speaker brushed aside the cowl, revealing rheumy blue eyes and skin that was as pale and wrinkled as crumpled parchment. White stubble edged the man's jaw. "You must help me! She's gone missing in my tower, and I can't find her. I'm very worried."

"Can't find who?"

A weak smile played at the old man's ashen lips. "My granddaughter." The old man paused. "Please, come in. You'll catch your death in this weather." Reaching out a shaky, age-speckled hand, the man grasped the druid's sleeve and drew him into the tower. "Oh, Galvin, I was afraid Elias wouldn't find you. I wasn't sure where you were living. And this storm . . ."

"Is not so bad, Drollo," the druid offered, extracting the weasel from his tunic. "Elias here doesn't seem to like the rain much, though."

The old man gingerly took the dripping weasel from the druid and scratched the top of its head. Elias squeaked loudly and stretched so its ear could be rubbed. The weasel shot an angry glance at the druid and squealed shrilly.

Galvin nodded to the animal and closed the tower door, muffling the patter of the rain and shutting out the sweet scent of the wet earth. After the long trek in the open air, the tower smelled musty. The druid wrinkled his nose in distaste.

Little of the thick, chiseled stone that made up the structure was visible on the inside. Paintings of fancifully dressed men and women competed with meticulously embroidered tapestries depicting life along the banks of the nearby Dragon Reach. In some places the tapestries and paintings overlapped. Galvin found himself staring at a partially covered tapestry showing several men putting a large boat out into the Reach. A satyr stood at the boat's prow, one hoofed leg up on the stern, an overlarge jacket wrapped about his human torso. The druid couldn't see the entire boat. A tapestry filled with prancing unicorns draped over it.

Beneath the paintings and tapestries, piles of labeled and unlabeled crates stretched across the length of the wall and reached as high as Galvin's chest. Bundles of folded clothes, stacks of colorful clay dishes, mismatched boots, smoke-tinted jars filled with glass beads, mounds of books, carefully balanced pyramids of scroll cases, and many objects the druid couldn't identify peeked out between the crates.

Galvin continued to gape at the dust-covered collection until a hand on his shoulder brought his attention back to the old man.

"My granddaughter," Drollo began. "She's only five. I was categorizing a new shipment when she wandered off. I'm afraid I wasn't paying attention to her."

"Your grandchildren are older than I am," the druid noted. When Drollo didn't reply, Galvin found himself staring at the old man.

At one time Drollo had been tall, with square shoulders and a long stride, but the seasons had taken their toll on his frame. Now he stood stooped over, his upper back a hump and his shoulders rounded and turned toward his chest. The skin hung on his bones as if it belonged to someone larger, falling in folds like the worn, oversized robes he wore. His wispy gray hair matched the color of the spiderwebs that clung to nearly everything in the tower. Only his eyes showed a spark.

With considerable effort Drollo bent and carefully placed the weasel on one of the few sections of slate floor that was free of clutter. The creature wriggled furiously to shake the rain from its fur, then darted around the pool of water forming from Galvin's dripping clothes and slid behind a crate marked "Alguduire feathers." The old man huffed, then stretched out an arm to grasp a nearby crate. Using it for support, he righted himself.

Drollo rubbed his hands together nervously and looked about for something. At last, after gathering his thoughts, he met the druid's gaze.

"I used to play with your grandchildren," Galvin said a bit more loudly. "I used to run after them in the marketplace close to three decades ago. They're older than I by several winters."

"Did I say 'granddaughter'? Er, she's the child of one of my grandchildren, or one of my grandchildren's children," the old man said, shaking his head. "The years have sped by so quickly that I can't recall. She calls me Grandfather. That's what's important."

"And you're certain she's here?"

Drollo nodded absently. "Somewhere. I call her, but she doesn't answer. Maybe she's playing a game on me. Maybe she's hurt."

"Her mother?"

"Isaura. She's a hundred miles away," Drollo replied. "The girl's spending a few months with me. Isaura thought it would do me good to have some company. But she'll have little to do with me anymore if she learns of this."

"So you sent Elias for me." Galvin's tone was sympathetic. He could tell the old man was frightened, and the druid never remembered him being concerned about anyone—only about the junk he collected. "How long has she been missing?"

"Two days," the old man answered quickly. "Perhaps three. But not more than that, I don't think. Time runs together." Drollo stared into Galvin's emerald green eyes. "I sent Elias as soon as I noticed her gone."

"We'll find her," Galvin stated simply, hoping his tone would help lessen Drollo's worry.

The druid tugged his cloak loose and glanced about for a rack. There was a pole-shaped object behind a large crate, but it was well out of reach. Shrugging, he laid the dripping garment across a tall, narrow crate lettered "frangible." Next came the boots. They made a slurping sound as he pulled them loose and water spilled out. The puddle beneath him grew to cover half of the entryway, and the water began to seep between the crates. He pulled his tunic over his head and laid it unceremoniously on top of the cloak, leaving his wet chest glistening in the light from the oil lamp overhead.

Elias poked its head out and chittered a scolding to the druid.

"The floor will dry," the druid told him.

Barefoot and shivering in the dampness of the tower, Galvin padded past Drollo, with the weasel scampering at his heels.

The lagging, shuffling footsteps of the old man followed the druid, who started picking his way down a hallway lined with a jumble of crates. In places the boxes were piled six feet high, as tall as Galvin, and the writing on most of the labels had faded with age. Dust blanketed many of the crates, showing they had not been moved in a long time. However, some had been tampered with recently. The druid noted small, round holes where mice had chewed their way into them.

Emerging into what he remembered as the sitting room, Galvin saw more crates and clutter. Stuffing spilled out of the furniture in places, adding to the disorder on the floor. Nicks covered the wooden arms and legs of chairs that Galvin recalled from his youth as being polished and perfect. The cushions and tabletops were cluttered with papers, knickknacks, and other objects. Only one piece of furniture, a large black leather chair, stood devoid of odds and ends.

"The woman was crazy to leave a little girl here," Galvin muttered.

The shuffling behind him stopped. "Oh, it didn't look quite this bad when the girl arrived a few weeks ago," Drollo nervously defended himself. "I'd picked up a bit and, er, cast a spell to hide all the crates and cover the dust."

The druid groaned and dropped to his knees. He peered under the furniture. Amongst the filth were scraps of paper and an old, toeless slipper that was much too large for Drollo.

Elias sprinted past the druid and dove into a mass of webs. The weasel returned a few moments later, trailing a cloud of gray-white webbing that was dotted with the husks of unfortunate insects. Elias brushed up against a table leg, knocking most of the webs loose, then began squeaking at the druid.

"Yes, I know she's not under there," Galvin replied. The druid rose to discover his wet leggings were coated with grime. Futilely he tried to brush them off.

"Her name?" Galvin turned to Drollo.

The old man beamed. "Isabelle. Named after my second wife."

"And you're certain she's still inside?"

"Oh, yes. She's too small to reach the door latch or the windowsills."

"And she's been missing two days, maybe three?"

"Yes," the old man stated simply.

Galvin rubbed his chin. "When I was her age," he mused aloud, "I occupied myself for days rummaging about your tower. But after two days she should have come out for a bite to eat—if she could." At once he regretted saying that, knowing the old man would fear the worst.

"The kitchen," the druid offered quickly. "If she's all right, she has to be looking for food. We'll start searching in the kitchen."

Drollo frowned and shifted his weight back and forth on his slippered feet.

"What is it?" Galvin asked curtly.

"She might not be hungry," Drollo suggested. "I have bits of food stashed all over the tower. I'm getting old, you know, and sometimes it's hard to get around. I keep things to eat here and there, so when I get hungry I don't have to come all the way downstairs to the kitchen."

The druid sighed. "Is she prone to playing games? Is it like her to just disappear like this?"

"She likes to play," Drollo said. "Hide-and-find is her favorite game."

The druid scanned the clutter. There were dozens of hiding places for a little girl in this room alone, and there were eight floors to the tower and a deep basement that had more than two levels. "You used magic to hide this mess," Galvin began. "Did you use magic to look for her?"

A pained expression crossed Drollo's face. "Oh, Galvin, would that I had that kind of magic. I can mask things, make something look like something else, make sounds appear out of silence, or silence something noisy. My magic doesn't have any real substance to it. I'm sorry." He chewed his lower lip. "What about your magic?"

"I'm a druid," Galvin noted flatly. "I can't do that sort of magic either."

"But you talk to Elias. And I've seen you talk to plants and rocks," Drollo stammered.

"I don't see how those skills are going to help us here."

Drollo blanched. "Then what are we going to do?"

"We're going to find her the old-fashioned way, by searching for her," Galvin sighed. "You start looking over here." He indicated the section of the room blanketed in sheafs of parchment.

"I've looked there. I think I've looked everywhere," Drollo moaned. "This is my fault."

The druid pointed again, and the old man complied, shuffling toward the parchment mound. Drollo began shifting through the mass. "Isabelle!" he called. Unsurprisingly, no one answered.

An hour later the druid was certain every inch of the room had been searched. There was no sign of a little girl.

Frustrated and sneezing, Galvin strode from the room and nearly bumped into a pile of crates in the hallway. "What's in all of these?" he asked.

The old man pursed his lips. "Oh, things I've collected

through the years. I've forgotten what's in most of them You'd have to look at the labels. What room shall we try next?"

The druid continued to stare, dumbfounded, at the mounds of boxes and piles of books. If he were outdoor looking for someone, he would track them like a hunte tracks an animal. Broken branches, muddy footprints, flat tened grass, and other clues would point the way.

Perhaps, Galvin thought, I was wrong about my magic especially if I treat this collection of junk like the wilder ness.

The druid looked around, searching for disturbed patches of webbing. His eyes rested on the base of a larg crate. There, nearly hidden by the shadows, a mouse wa tugging a pale pink ribbon into a hole. Galvin knelt an began squeaking to the mouse, but the little rodent wa determined in its task and ignored the druid. Reaching for ward, Galvin snatched the ribbon and squeaked again.

The mouse shuddered with fear, wriggled its nose, an darted into the hole.

Galvin rubbed his thumb across the silk ribbon, stil shiny and new. "Isabelle's?" he asked.

The old man looked at the ribbon, then nodded slowly.

"I'm tracking her," the druid said simply. "Let's try the next floor."

Only a pathway at the center of the stairs to the uppe floors was clear of debris. An accumulation of junk reste against each banister. Galvin scanned the collection o chair legs and discarded oil lamps, pausing only when he spied a brass vase precariously poised on a step halfway up. He carefully picked his way through the hodgepodg and knelt by the vase. Elias darted under Galvin's arm and sniffed it, black, beady eyes reflecting warmly in the curved surface. The weasel chittered uneasily.

"Yes, it's unusual," the druid answered.

"What?" Drollo huffed as he climbed the stairs, a thick candle in his right hand. "You found something?"

Grasping the vase at the rim, the druid turned and sat or

the step to face the old man. "This vase," Galvin began. "It's peculiar."

Drollo arched his eyebrows. "Look at my collection later, Galvin. My granddaughter is more important than a hunk of brass."

"Don't you see?" the druid continued. "It's out of place. It's clean. There's not a spot of dirt anywhere on it."

The old man shook his head. "It's not out of place. It's new. I got that a few days ago. It was in a shipment from Callidyrr." He paused for a moment, then spoke more rapidly. "A shipment I opened in my study! Galvin, I didn't put that vase here."

"Isabelle might have," the druid surmised. Placing the vase back on the step, he stood, pivoted, and sprinted to the landing above. Elias bounded after him, pausing only to glance back at the old man, who followed.

On the landing Galvin scrutinized the piles of odds and ends, which were beginning to resemble every other cache of junk in the tower. What would possess a man to hoard so much? the druid pondered. Drollo was like the most greedy of dragons, he decided. He collected anything remotely valuable, then let it sit and gather dust.

Well, in that much Drollo differed from the dragons Galvin had chanced upon in his journeys: the great wyrms tended to keep their wealth relatively clean. And it was easy to walk around in their caves—if you were an invited guest, of course.

The druid lay down on the landing and glanced around. The weasel clung to his shoulder and continued to squeak. Its small face turned from side to side as if it were imitating Galvin.

"I'm looking at things from a child's-eye-view," the druid told Elias, pushing the weasel out of the way.

"That's smart of you," Drollo gasped, nearly out of breath from the effort of climbing. "I hadn't thought of that."

Without a word, Galvin rose and padded toward a door off the landing. It was partially blocked by a stand filled with intricately carved staves inlaid with silver and gold, but there was just enough space in the doorway for a child to squeeze through. Galvin moved the staves, though he nearly dropped the entire stand when one staff began to twinkle and twitch.

As he'd suspected, the ever-present spiderwebs had recently been disturbed around the door. Keeping an eye on the magical staff, he reached for the latch. He stopped, spying small smudges on the knob—traces of Isabelle.

"I'm not such a bad detective after all," he noted reassuringly to Drollo, then turned the handle and went inside.

The druid had to shield his eyes, for the room beyond was as bright as a sunny day. The source of the light was a glowing yellow globe dangling low, just inside the doorway. The ceiling, as cracked as the earth in a dry riverbed, was painted a warm and inviting shade of rose. The color of the walls was a darker shade of rose, though much of it was hidden behind Drollo's myriad possessions.

"Isabelle," Galvin called. "I'm a friend. I'm here with your grandfather. Please come out."

He glided farther into the room and was overwhelmed by a smell that was at once acrid and fruity—no doubt the remains of a meal lost amidst the junk.

"Isabelle?" He spied movement near the windowsill. Striding forward, the druid brushed aside a thin curtain of webs. By the window sat a small oak table, in the center of which danced an ivory mermaid, no bigger than Galvin's hand. The exquisitely carved figurine rose and fell, spinning on a carved walnut wave. And all along the dusty outer edge of the tabletop ran a smudged path of handprints.

Elias skittered up Galvin's leg and leaped onto the table. The weasel chittered excitedly.

"Isabelle was here," Galvin replied. "She tried to reach for the mermaid."

"Isabelle?" Drollo called, padding into the room.

The druid gathered up Elias and faced the old man. "She was here. Perhaps she still is. The handprints are fresh enough that they're free of dust."

The old man's eyes sparkled. "Bless you, Galvin."

The druid's cautious stare told Drollo not to get too excited.

"I knew I did the right thing by sending Elias after you. I couldn't think of anyone better for finding my Isabelle. You know, people around here consider you a hero, Galvin. And just think of the—"

"Quiet!" the druid hissed. He cocked his head from side to side.

"What's the matter?"

Galvin glared at the old man, then quickly softened his expression. "I heard something." He cocked his head again and called, "Isabelle?"

An odd scratching noise was the only reply.

Galvin's senses were more acute than most men's, but the unnatural clutter and congestion inside the tower hampered them. Out of his element, it took him more time and effort to pinpoint the source of the noise, but locate it he did. Putting Elias down, he moved warily toward a shadowy recess hidden partially by a large crate.

Skritch. Skritch. Skritch.

Galvin could tell it was the sound of metal upon stone, but as he neared the crate the noise stopped. Elias, hugging his ankles, bared its teeth and hissed.

It took all of the druid's strength to tug the crate forward, leaving just enough space for him to squeeze through and get to the recess behind. The weasel remained in front of the crate, rearing back on its hind legs and pawing at the air.

The shadows were thick behind the crate, despite the light from the magical globe. Webs tangling in his hair, Galvin wondered why a little girl would brave the mess to hide here. He never came to a conclusion; something stabbed him in the right ankle and disrupted his thoughts.

The druid cursed between gritted teeth as he tried to back away. Again pain lanced through his ankle, and Galvin discovered he couldn't budge—something was wrapped around his leg, something metallic and jagged and very strong. Bending forward as much as the small confines would allow, he groped about, trying to find his attacker.

A whiplike tendril wrapped itself painfully about the druid's left wrist. Galvin cursed again.

"Galvin?" Drollo called.

"Stay back!"

The whip tightened about Galvin's wrist. Reaching forward with his right hand, he locked his fingers about the tentacle and pulled as hard as he could. Galvin heard a snap, then fell backward, a sundered metal limb in his hand. The druid quickly righted himself and grasped the tentacle about his ankle and pried it loose.

He crawled out from behind the crate and bumped right into Drollo's slippered feet.

Scritch. Ka-thunk, ka-thunk.

The druid glanced back just in time to see the crate wobble and fall forward, toppled by a metal monstrosity. A glistening black sphere surrounded by a dozen limbs, the thing wasn't alive, yet its whiplike appendages writhed like an octopus's tentacles. Oil spurted from the spots where Galvin had yanked limbs loose. The thing still had at least a dozen more of the whiplike devices, and it twirled several maddeningly while using others to move itself along, climbing over the crate and advancing on the druid.

A loud clap sounded in the room, followed by a brilliant flash of blue-white light.

The druid shielded his eyes once more. He flailed his other arm in front of him in a sorry defense against the metal monster. But no attack came. When the glare subsided, he dropped his hand and stared at the thing.

The clockwork contraption lay unmoving, cracked nearly in two. Oil spilled out of its guts and onto the floor.

Puzzled, the druid glanced up at Drollo. The old man was leaning on a carved staff he had taken from the stand—the one that had sparked and twinkled when Galvin had first tried to move it.

"Just wanted to help," the old man offered proudly. "I

remember now why I kept this room closed up. I've a few gnomish odds and ends stored in here—that vermin catcher you tussled with and some other clockwork things like it. A few of them might be dangerous." A look of panic washed over his face as he shuffled toward the broken mechanization. "My Isabelle," he gushed. "What if the vermin catcher got my Isabelle?"

Galvin slowly got to his feet and tested his sore ankle. Looking down, he saw that it was bleeding. He cautiously flexed his left hand and felt his wrist to make sure nothing was broken. "She's not back there."

"What if she's lying there dead?" Drollo asked frantically, trying to pick his way behind the fallen crate.

The druid grabbed the old man's shoulder. "I would have smelled her blood," he stated bluntly, then stalked from the room.

Galvin waited for Drollo on the landing, then closed the door to the room and replaced the stand filled with staves. Nervously, he paced back and forth, rubbing his sore wrist. Elias scampered between his bare feet, the weasel's claws slipping on the smooth stone with every other step.

He stared at the polished marble steps and the central pathway swept clean of dust by his feet and Drollo's—and Isabelle's.

"Drollo, I've been a fool. I should have done this the moment I came into the tower."

The druid sat unceremoniously on the step just below the landing, wedging himself between a pile of books and a collection of hourglasses. He closed his eyes, slowed his breathing, and rested his arms on the landing, his fingers feeling the cool smoothness of the stone at his side.

Galvin broke into a cold sweat, the sheen on his brow nearly matching the shine on the marble beneath his fingertips. His breathing became slower still. He was calling upon skills taught to him by powerful druids—the ability to speak with stones and the very earth itself.

He felt his fingers become as stiff and unmovable as the marble, his limbs rigid like the stairway. His tongue became dry and thick. Though his mouth moved slowly, no words escaped.

A little girl, Galvin said with only his mind.

Little? the stone stairway asked. The word was drawn out, sounding like rock grating upon rock.

A person. Like me, but smaller. Galvin felt his own thought processes moving sluggishly, the words he was forming in his mind becoming simpler as his thoughts merged with the marble's. *A girl. Half my size.*

Small, the stone repeated. The word sounded exotic and even soothing coming from the stairway. *Tall to us. Always above us.* The marble droned. Stone never hurried in telling its story. *Always looking down on us. We always looking up.*

Tall to you, then, Galvin continued. *But not as tall as me.* The druid was sweating profusely now, for conversing with stone was always taxing. *Remember her?*

The grinding noise became louder inside the druid's head. The stone was thinking, mumbling to itself. *Remember many feet,* the steps groaned finally. *Feet of people smaller than you. Pebbles compared to rocks. A short while ago, many, many pebble feet.*

Many? the druid gasped.

The stone rumbled and pulled a term from Galvin's mind. *Children,* the stone replied. *Many children. Up and down. Up and down. Always running up and down us.*

Many?

Many, the stone repeated. *Feet quickly grew, became larger, like yours. Then all but two feet go away.* The stone paused, then added, *But soon more pebbles came. They got larger, too, and disappeared. Now left with only two feet again—and yours.*

The druid was confused. All but two? All but Drollo's two feet?

No, Galvin growled. *You're remembering Drollo's children and his grandchildren. That was a long time ago.*

Short time, the stone corrected.

Galvin chided himself wordlessly. Stone existed for an

interminable time. The life span of a human could seem
like mere moments to it.

Think, Galvin coaxed. *The last two pebble feet.*

Always up and down us.

Yes.

Smooth like us, the stone continued. *Always stopping to ...
to ... look at things resting on us.*

The junk, Galvin clarified, picturing the mounds of debris
stacked high against each railing.

Junk, the stone groaned. *Yes. Can't see through it. Want it
to go away.*

Galvin sighed. *I'll see what I can do,* he offered. *But first,
help me. Those pebble feet, where did they go?*

Moments ago, the stone began, choosing words from
Galvin's mind. *Pebble feet went up, up, up. Near the top, but
not the top. Did not come back down.*

So she's still in the tower, Galvin concluded, perhaps hiding on the second or third floor from the top. He was grateful he wouldn't have to search all the levels below. With
luck, it wouldn't be long now and the girl would be safely
back with Drollo.

The druid thanked the stone and began to separate his
mind from the steps, when the marble added, *A moment
later the . . . thing . . . came down and went away.*

Thing?

The stone growled, loud enough that Galvin was certain
even Drollo heard it. In the end, the stairway explained in
simple terms that it had no words for what descended
shortly after the girl climbed to the upper floors.

Is the thing here now? the druid continued.

*No. Gone like all the pebble feet. Come and go. Up and
down. Up . . .*

"Galvin? Galvin? Are you all right?" The words belonged
to Drollo, who bent next to the druid, shaking him.

Galvin slowly opened his eyes, reluctantly discovering
his connection with the steps severed. This was the longest
conversation he'd ever managed with stone, and the effort
had apparently caused him to pass out. He lifted a heavy

hand to his throbbing head. His arm felt stiff, and his pallor was tinged with gray.

"Galvin?"

"I'm all right, Drollo. Let's go upstairs. I think we'll find Isabelle there."

The old man beamed and helped Galvin to his feet. The trek up the stairs seemed a lengthy one to the druid; he paused at each landing to rest a moment. Drollo and Elias had no trouble keeping up with Galvin's sluggish pace. However, the druid had trouble keeping up with the old man's questions.

"So my steps told you she's up here?"

"Something like that," the druid answered.

"They saw her?"

"They paid more attention to her feet."

"Galvin, this is wonderful. After I have my Isabelle back, could you teach me to talk to the steps?"

"I'll think about it," the druid said flatly. Then a smile tugged at the corner of his lips. "You'll have to clean them off before they'll talk to you, though."

"I can do that."

At the sixth landing Galvin looked out a thin window. It was dark outside, and the rain had stopped. The moon, high in the sky, was poking through the clouds. Gathering his energy, he climbed to the seventh landing and faced an opened door.

"Isabelle?" the druid called softly. "Isabelle?"

No answer.

Another search then, the druid decided. The weasel chittered animatedly, wrinkled its nose, then squeaked and began running about the jumble.

"Yes, you can help us look for her," Galvin sighed.

To the druid this room looked like the rest of Drollo's tower, packed with an assortment of oddities and lined with crates containing more unused things. It was as filthy as the other rooms, but Galvin could see patches where the dirt had been wiped free by small feet. He strode forward, Drollo shuffling behind him.

The dust on many of the small crates was dotted with tiny fingerprints. Packing material lay strewn about some of the crates, and the contents—a veritable treasure trove of useless objects—covered the floor. The druid noted that the crates were all labeled in flowing Elvish script. Intrigued, he began searching the room more carefully, paying attention this time to the words on each crate.

Behind him, Galvin heard Drollo rummaging around. Elias was searching, too. The weasel's plaintive squeaks nearly drowned out the old man's rustling.

At last Galvin's eyes settled on a particularly large crate set against a wall, one that had been pried open. There was little stuffing near it, so whatever had occupied the crate had likely taken up most of the space. He ran his fingers along the rough wood and read the Elvish label.

"Oh, no," the druid whispered.

"Isabelle!" Drollo continued to call.

"Drollo," the druid began. "Do you do any trading with the sea elves in the Dragon Reach?"

"No," came a muffled reply. The old man had his head stuck into a crate. "Well, at least not anymore."

"You did at one time?"

"Yes. Quite a few years ago. I don't go down to the shore much nowadays. The sea air makes my bones ache."

The druid scowled and reread the label. "Drollo, stop looking," he said quietly. "She's not here."

"We'll go on to the next room, then."

"No. She's not in the tower."

The old man's face turned ashen, and Galvin quickly added, "But I know where she went. Don't worry. I'll go get her."

"I'm—I'm coming with you," the old man stammered.

"Not where I'm going."

With that, Galvin bounded down the stairs. Elias was fast on his heels. When the druid reached the bottom of the stairs, he glanced back and saw Drollo just starting to descend.

"Stay here," he cautioned. "I'll be back with Isabelle."

Galvin hoped he sounded confident enough, because he wasn't sure he could locate the girl. Still, he didn't want the old man to follow him. Then he would have two people to worry about.

Throwing open the tower door, he ran out into the damp night.

"Your boots," he heard Drollo call.

But the druid continued to run. Boots were the last things he'd need where he was going.

Galvin angled his path away from the tower and toward the south. In the distance he heard waves washing up on the beach. Overhead, the clouds were thinning, pushed away by a freshening breeze. By the time the druid reached the beach the moon was fully visible, shedding light on the night-black waters of the Dragon Reach.

With shrinking confidence, Galvin ventured into the surf. The cool water swirled about his ankles, then his knees. A wave came in, splashing him thoroughly and plastering his leggings to him like a second skin. He waded out farther and began to concentrate.

The druid willed his face to become more angular. His nose and mouth extended outward, and his skin became blue-gray. He hurled himself headfirst into the water as the transformation continued. His arms shortened, became thinner, then took on the appearance of flippers. His shoulders flattened, joined with the fins, and pressed close to his changing torso. His legs grew together into a muscular tail; waving rhythmically, strongly, the tail propelled the dolphin that was Galvin farther into the Dragon Reach.

The dolphin covered miles, darting in and out of sea caves that stretched across the Reach. The seascape was rocky, with spires of stone twisting upward, cloaked by patches of reedlike plants. Beyond the caves the seabed flattened, the evenness disrupted here and there by large rocks and giant clams. Colorful seaweed extended toward the surface and moved with the current. Farther into the Reach the seabed dropped off sharply—"the Cliff," the sea elves called it. The cliff's wall was a large coral reef of brilliant hues that teemed with life.

Galvin swam back and forth across the reef, quizzing jellyfish, yellowtail damselfish, and patches of seaweed. He rose to the surface only for air. A queen angelfish, disturbed from its sleep, finally provided a few clues and sent Galvin past the Reach, into the deeper, cooler water of the Sea of Fallen Stars.

Here the terrain resembled a plain, with ripples in the sand marking shifts in the current. The plants were fewer and taller and not as colorful as the ones along the reef. Galvin swam deep, hugging the sandy bottom. He noted that the fish here were schooling, perhaps out of habit or because a large predator was nearby. He scanned the sand, looking for some unusual disturbance. However, all he saw were the fading reed-fine prints of lobsters and other shellfish; the current kept tracks from staying for more than a few minutes in the sand.

The druid continued his search, swimming miles out to sea. Finally he found a set of tracks that resembled cleft hoofprints; they were not made by any sea creatures familiar to the druid. Galvin followed the quickly dissipating tracks across the ocean floor. The druid knew he was scouting over the Death Knell, a shallow point in the Sea of Fallen Stars that was dangerous to deep-hulled ships.

Sparse patches of seaweed, some of it nearly torn free from the sea floor, provided still more information.

A monster that frightens all fish, said one clump.

A thing that tears us from the ground and leaves us to die, cried another.

The druid pieced together clues and continued on, many minutes later passing over a large, rectangular bed of kelp. He thrust with his tail and dove toward the bed. The kelp was planted in rows, and there were signs each plant was being carefully tended.

It was a garden, he decided, but whose? Sea elves, perhaps, though the elvish communities resided closer to the Reach. Besides, elves needed much larger gardens to sustain their tribes.

Galvin swam slowly, keeping about a foot above the bed. There was less chance the current would wipe away the tracks here, as the kelp helped to hold the pulse of the water at bay. At the far edge of the bed he found evidence of his quarry's passing; a section of kelp uprooted and strewn about. It looked as if a big dog had been digging in a row of carrots. Several pairs of deep hoofprints showed in the sand.

A half-hour more, and the object of the druid's search came into view. The thing, which seemed hard at work destroying a flowering sea-frond bed, resembled a cross between a bat and a wolf spider. Its bulbous body was nearly three feet across at the middle, and its round head was about a foot in diameter. Silvery pincers protruded from its bottom jaw and cut through the fronds with ease. Attached to what passed for shoulders were wings, scalloped like a bat's. The contraption sat atop two stubby goat-like legs that ended in hooves; the legs were alternately balancing the bulky body and uprooting plants.

The back of the contraption—for like Drollo's gnomish vermin catcher, this thing had never truly lived—was decorated with scrawls of red and blue. Various sized circles of green and yellow were clustered beneath its wings. The hooves were painted a bright red and edged with a light green trim. It was garish. And inside, visible through its rounded glass eyes, Galvin saw the grinning face of a little girl.

Like a manta ray, the device glided over the sea fronds, then stopped to uproot a row at the end. The bulbous spider's head turned from right to left, then stopped, spotting the dolphin.

Galvin swam behind a clump of seaweed as questions danced in his head. Is Isabelle controlling the thing, or is it running away with her? How am I going to bring it to land? How do I . . .

He paused and let the sea current wash the tumultuous thoughts away. I meet it head on, he decided. Determination showing in his black dolphin eyes, the druid shot out from behind the seaweed—then stopped short.

Galvin wasn't the only one to notice the garden-wrecker. Swimming rapidly toward the sea fronds and the spider-bat was a quartet of sahuagin, gill-men of the deep. Roughly humanoid and exceedingly muscular, they had scaly green bodies, long pointed ears, and webbed hands and feet. Each hefted a trident in one hand and a weighted net in the other.

The contraption and its passenger seemed oblivious to the threat and concentrated on dislodging more plants. Its bulbous spider head only turned toward the sahuagin when a hurled trident landed in the sand next to a cloven metal hoof.

Panicked, the druid propelled himself forward and willed another transformation to take place. His skin took on a darker shade of gray and expanded outward to accommodate his growing body. The dolphin fin atop his back enlarged and became more angular. His head grew thicker and flatter, his lungs swelled with water, and his once bottle-shaped mouth stretched and filled with a double row of sharp teeth.

The shark sped toward the sahuagin, who had already reached the spider-bat. The gill-men were circling the thing, three of them jabbing at it with their tridents while the fourth retrieved his weapon from the sand. Through the water Galvin heard their odd battle chant, a singsong drone. The chant rose in volume and culminated in a whoop when one of the sahuagin was victorious in thrusting his weapon through the spider-bat's wing, pinning the construct to the sea floor. The contraption began to circle madly, like a buzzing, wounded fly.

Galvin saw the frightened face of Isabelle through the spider-bat's bulbous glass eyes. He reached the nearest sahuagin just as it slammed the butt end of its trident against the contraption's head. Wincing inwardly, the druid watched a glass eye crack. This instant of delay gave the gill-man an opening.

The sahuagin whirled on the shark, leveling the barbed

trident in Galvin's face. The druid found himself oddly transfixed by the sahuagin facing him, and the creature began moving its trident from side to side while mouthing something that was audible, yet foreign to Galvin's ears. It was a variation of a battle chant, perhaps. Whatever it was, the sound comforted Galvin's jangled nerves, and the druid felt himself growing sleepy. The sahuagin continued to drone, lulling his foe into a dreamlike state while the current nudged him away from Isabelle and the contraption.

The shark felt the water play all about its skin. It was so restful, so . . .

Kchink!

Through the water came the muffled sound of the tridents striking the metal of the construct. The noise roused the drifting shark. Forcing his tired eyes open, the druid watched the sahuagin hammer away at the spider-bat. A net had been placed over the thing's head to prevent the pincers from reaching out for them.

Kchink! Kchink! Kchink!

Galvin fought off the effects of the sahuagin's sleep spell. His mind began to clear, and he once again saw the gill-men as a threat to Isabelle. He swam forward, determined to rout the sahuagin from their grim task. As he raced through the water, the natural instincts of his adopted form took over.

This time when a gill-man began weaving his trident and droning, the shark focused his thoughts on the endangered little girl, shutting out the sounds that only moments before had seemed like a lullaby. Catching the chanting creature off guard, the shark darted under the trident and slammed his snout into the sahuagin's belly, pushing him backward into one of his fellows. The pair floated, stunned and unmoving, above the ocean floor.

The two remaining sahuagin turned their attention to the shark, which had veered away and was building up speed to come in for another attack.

Galvin felt a rush of pain as a trident jabbed deep into his side, just below a fin. Blood mingled with the seawater. He tried to ignore the pain, to press his attack; he was rewarded when he felt his teeth close about a gill-man's tough hide. Tearing like a savage animal, the shark shredded the sahuagin's armorlike scales and dug his teeth deeper into the torso. All the while he shook his head back and forth, turning the sea black with blood. The gill-man tried to extricate itself from the death grip, but it was no use.

Again pain shot through Galvin's flank, this time originating closer to his tail. Another trident jab, his mind screamed, feeling the barbs still embedded in his flesh. The shark opened his mouth, letting the dying sahuagin float to the ocean floor. In a pain-maddened frenzy, Galvin turned on the remaining gill-man, who was attempting to flee. He sped after the sahuagin, closing the distance with two swishes of his tail. Gleefully the druid rolled his eyes back, ready for another kill.

Stop! Galvin's mind screamed. The druid fought to regain control of himself, to quell the bloodlust overtaking his soul. Isabelle. Save Isabelle.

The shark slowed his pace and turned back toward the pinned contraption. Galvin continued to focus on Isabelle and the spider-bat, trying to avoid looking at the sahuagin corpses floating in his path. His thoughts were filled with self-recrimination. It wasn't uncommon for a druid to be overwhelmed by the animal instincts of a creature he imitated, but Galvin could never quite reconcile his love of life with the strange, savage things he did when he transformed—even if such violence was integral to everyday life in the forest or the sea.

Sadly the druid clamped his jaws about the trident that pinned the spider-bat to the seabed. One yank and the weapon was free. Next he worked to get the trident free of his own hide. Then he quickly tugged the net loose from the spider-bat. Peering through the cracked glass eye, he saw the frightened little girl. Water was seeping into the construct; it sloshed all the way up to Isabelle's shoulders.

Galvin locked his jaws on the spider-bat's good wing and

laboriously dragged it toward the surface. His wounds, though not serious, were painful, and he found himself thinking of the old man and Isabelle to keep himself moving. The druid's shark head broke the waves some time later, and he squinted in the face of the bright sunlight. The search for Isabelle had taken him well into the next day.

With the contraption in tow, the druid started the long swim back to shore.

Galvin resumed his human form in the shallows of the Dragon Reach, near Drollo's tower. He pulled the spider-bat a few feet up onto the sand, then lay back, ready to let exhaustion take him. His side ached from the trident wounds. Fortunately, they were more painful than life-threatening.

Just a brief rest, he thought, closing his eyes.

Clunk, clunk ka-thonk!

The sound roused Galvin and he watched the contraption's lid fall open. A blond-tressed head poked out. A sheepish, wide grin covered the girl's face.

"Hi!" Isabelle beamed between yawns. "Who're you?"

"A friend of your grandfather's," Galvin said softly, rising sluggishly to his feet and extending a hand to the soaked girl.

She grabbed it and scrambled out of the spider-bat.

"Will he be mad?" she asked quietly, pointing with a stubby finger at the contraption. "Will he be mad 'cause I broke one of his toys?"

Galvin shook his head. "No. He has plenty of others."

The walk up the beach to Drollo's tower seemed lengthy to the druid, who found himself inundated by the little girl's chatter along the way.

"Isabelle!" Drollo cried as he threw open the door. He ran out into the courtyard and lifted the girl into his arms.

"Oh, Grandfather," the girl squealed. "I've had such a wonderful time! There were water flowers and green men and a big shark! It was fun!"

Galvin frowned and pushed past the embracing pair into the entranceway, where he found his dry cloak. Throwing it on over his shoulders, he gathered up his tunic and boots and turned to see Drollo carrying the tired tot inside.

"Wherever did you find her?"

"Out beyond the Dragon Reach," the druid stated simply, pulling on his boots. He reached for his sword and strapped it about his waist.

"But, how did you know she'd be there?"

"You said you traded with the sea elves years ago," the druid began. "The Elvish writing on the big empty crate upstairs indicated it came from Mercea. That's a city a few dozen miles from here—underwater. As close as I could translate, the label described the contents as "one water spider." So I played a hunch that Isabelle, uh, borrowed your device. Knowing sea elf technology, I figured it would do its job whether she knew how to run it or not. And since Mercean water spiders are supposed to walk under the sea . . ."

"Thank Tymora your hunch was right!" Drollo chirped, setting Isabelle down on a clear section of floor and patting the top of her head. "Don't you get out of my sight, now," he instructed.

The little girl yawned and dutifully grabbed the hem of his robe.

"How can I ever repay you?" the old man asked. "I must do something. I must give you something."

The druid shook his head. He had no need for possessions, especially any of the junk cluttering up the tower. But as he turned to go, a thought occurred to the druid. Eyes twinkling, he spun around to face Drollo. "How about giving me some of your collection?"

"Yes! A splendid idea!" Drollo exclaimed. "As much as you can carry."

Galvin spent the next several hours toting an impossibly large sack up and down the tower stairs.

"What is this?" the druid asked on the top floor, pointing to a long cylindrical object aimed out the window.

"A star-watcher."

"Well, I don't need one of those. And this?" He gestured

at a half-sphere covered with beads and bits of metal.

"I don't recall."

"Fine. I'll take it."

"What about this?" Galvin asked as they descended to the next floor.

"It's called a hudabit. Imported from Zhentil Keep. I'm not sure what it does."

"Good. I want it."

The druid pawed through a collection of gnomish devices and pointed at a small box covered with gears and dials. "What's this?"

The old man shrugged, and Galvin promptly put the box in his sack.

On and on the druid went, picking up anything the old man couldn't identify. By the time he was finished, Galvin was loaded down with satchels, pouches, sacks, and packs. He strained under the weight, and Drollo had to open the front door for him.

"Thank you, Galvin. For everything," Drollo said.

"Until swords part," the druid replied formally. "And fair days to you, Isabelle."

The little girl yawned and waved, but the weasel in her hands chittered in mock offense.

"Yes, I'll come back for a visit," Galvin told the weasel. "I'll not stay away so long again."

Like an overburdened peddler, Galvin staggered away, dragging his bundles for nearly a mile. At last, he found a shady copse of trees and dropped his gifts on the ground. The druid unstrapped his sword, stretched, and fell to all fours.

He willed another transformation. This one covered him with coarse gray fur and gave him long, sharp claws.

The badger started digging a hole at the base of a massive willow tree. Hours later, when the hole was deep enough for his purposes, Galvin returned to his human form. He deposited all the junk into the hole, covered it up, and stamped the earth flat.

He carefully loosened ferns and mosses from elsewhere

in the copse and transplanted them over Drollo's buried possessions. Like a careful gardener, he arranged the plants and made it look as much as possible as if the ground had not been disturbed.

Satisfied that Drollo's toys would remain undiscovered, the druid strode south toward the Reach. He intended to have a chat with the sea elves of Mercea about selling water spiders to people who haven't the foggiest idea of how to use them.

THE CURSE OF TEGEA

Troy Denning

From the look of things, times were hard for the Inn of the High Terrace. Although the supper hour had long since arrived, the veranda was deserted. In the center of each rough-hewn table sat an overturned bread basket and an old wine bottle filled with wilted poppies. The chairs were scattered haphazardly around the patio, as if the person who had last swept the floor had seen no purpose in returning them to their rightful positions.

"It appears you haven't had many patrons of late," Adon observed.

"Let's just say that tonight the best table in the house is yours," grumbled the innkeeper, leading the way across the patio. Myron Zenas, for that was his name, was a brawny man as hairy as a bear, with steady black eyes, a huge nose lined with red veins, and a beard that hung down to his chest.

"Does your trouble have anything to do with the curse on

Tegea?" Adon asked.

Myron stopped. "It's not my fault," he snapped. "Who told you it was?"

"No one," said Corene.

Like Adon, the young woman belonged to the Church of Mystra, though she was a novice and he was a cleric of high standing. The black-handled flail hanging from her belt seemed curiously at odds with her golden-haired beauty, for she had brown doelike eyes, a button nose, and the gleaming smile of a goddess. "In fact, we've heard very little about the evil afflicting Tegea, save that you need help."

"It's best that you don't know more," the innkeeper said, an expression of relief crossing his face. He led the way to the far corner, where the veranda overlooked the entire village. "Tegea's problems aren't your concern."

"We've come a long way to offer help," Adon objected.

"Then you've wasted your journey," Myron replied. "Even if there was anything you could do—and there isn't—our village's grief is its own. The last thing we need is a pair of outsiders sticking their noses into our misery." With that, the innkeeper moved two chairs to the table and waved his guests to their seats. "I'll send your meal out."

As Myron returned to the kitchen, Corene whispered, "This is going to be harder than we thought."

"Not at all," Adon said, removing his mace from its sling so he could sit comfortably. "The people of Tegea will be happy for our help—once we've won their confidence."

"And how are you going to do that?" demanded the novice.

"I'll think of a way," Adon said. He looked out over the village he had come to rescue.

Located in the southern reaches of the Dragonjaw Mountains, Tegea seemed idyllic enough. The mountains surrounding it were covered with towering cypresses, as slender and pointed as spearheads. Closer to the village, the terraced slopes supported huge groves of strangely gnarled olive trees. The warped boughs were laden with silvery leaves that danced in the evening breeze and seemed to whisper the soft songs of pastoral life. In the town itself, the muffled clang of a goatbell occasionally echoed off a stone wall, but no other sound rose from the narrow lanes running through the labyrinth of whitewashed huts.

On the far side of the village, the local duke's dusky castle squatted upon the edge of a thousand-foot cliff. Its craggy towers were silhouetted against the distant waters of the Dragonmere Sea, where the sun was just sinking below the turquoise horizon.

Normally Adon would have been staying in the citadel instead of the local inn. As an important cleric in the Church of Mysteries, he could expect most nobles to extend their hospitality to him. However, the patriarch had been warned that the duke of Tegea disliked all priests, so he hadn't bothered to call at the castle.

Adon felt Corene's warm touch on his arm. "Here's dinner—at last," she said.

The cleric returned his attention to the veranda. A serving girl had just stepped out of the kitchen with a heavy tray in her hands. Her bountiful figure was accentuated by a tightly laced bodice and a billowing skirt just clingy enough to hint at the slender legs beneath. She had skin the color of ginger, with black hair that cascaded over her bare shoulders in silky waves. Her almond-shaped eyes were as brown as topaz and lined with kohl.

It was impossible to see the rest of her face. From her cheeks down to her collarbone, the maid's visage was hidden by an unsightly veil. Brushing against the skin of such a beautiful girl, the shroud seemed sorely out of place. It was made of coarse, black wool and suspended from a strand of rough twine.

The young woman rested the serving tray on the edge of their table. "I'm Sarafina, Myron's daughter," she said, placing a goblet of golden wine and a steaming bowl in front of Corene. "Tonight, we have plum wine and lamb stew. I hope you'll enjoy it."

As Sarafina turned to serve Adon, her eyes fell on the left

side of his face and remained fixed there. Although the patriarch was a handsome man with a patrician nose and a cleft chin, he often elicited such stares. During the Time of Troubles, when the gods had walked Faerun in the bodies of mortal avatars, his good looks had been taken from him by a zealot. Now a red scar traced a crooked path from his left eye down to his jawline. Adon self-consciously turned his face away so the young woman would not have to look upon his blemish.

After placing the patriarch's wine and stew on the table, Sarafina asked, "Is there anything else you'd like?"

Adon continued to look away and shook his head without answering. He was not angry with the girl for staring, merely ashamed of his appearance.

"Please, Your Grace," said Sarafina. "I didn't mean to hurt your feelings. If you could see beneath this veil, you'd know that I'd be the last to mock another's scars."

Adon looked back, touched by the sincerity in her voice. "I thought it unusual for a woman to wear a veil in this part of the world," he said. "Perhaps you should let me have a look at your affliction. I may be able to heal it."

"I don't think so." Sarafina wiped sudden tears from her eyes. "Many priests have tried, and each time they've only made matters worse."

"But I'm no ordinary cleric—"

"Please don't ask again," said Sarafina, still looking away. "Can I bring you anything else?"

"Some bread would be nice, if you have any," said Corene.

Sarafina nodded. "My mother has just taken a few loaves out of the oven. I'll bring you some as soon as it's cool enough to cut."

As the young woman returned to the kitchen, Adon shook his head in frustration. "Why are these people so reluctant to accept our help?"

"You can't blame the girl for being cautious," said Corene, pointing at the crooked blemish marring Adon's good looks. "Why should she think you can mend her face when you haven't bothered to heal your own?"

"Our travels together have made you too familiar," Adon snapped. "You'd do well to remember who's the novice and who's the patriarch."

The cleric's threat did not intimidate the young woman. "So why haven't you mended it?" she pressed.

"Don't you think I've tried?" Adon retorted. "I've been praying to Midnight—er, Mystra—since she became the Goddess of Magic."

"And she hasn't answered?"

"Not in this matter," Adon said, sipping the powerful wine Sarafina had placed in front of him.

"I can't believe Our Lady of Mysteries would deny such a thing to someone she once called friend, someone who fought beside her during the Time of Troubles."

"That was before she became a goddess," said Adon, then paused. "Now that she's an immortal, I suppose she must behave as one. She doesn't even like me to call her Midnight. 'That's the name of my avatar,' she says. 'The Midnight you knew exists only as a memory.' "

"She calls herself Mystra to honor the goddess of magic before her," Corene noted dogmatically.

"The reason she hasn't healed me is a bit more complicated than an occasional breach of divine etiquette," Adon murmured into his wine.

"Meaning?"

"That she's angry with me for more important things," Adon answered, looking away in embarrassment. "Her church has stopped growing in the last two years, while others continue to flourish."

"Because Mystra doesn't resort to buying worshipers with misleading dreams of wealth and power, as do the other gods," Corene objected. "You can't be blamed for that."

"Perhaps not, but that doesn't change facts," said the patriarch. "Before allowing the gods back into the planes, their overlord made it clear their status and power would depend upon the faith of the mortals who worship them.

Mystra's church is smaller than Cyric's. And that means I've allowed Our Lady's foulest enemy to outstrip her power."

"But you've always said that the Goddess of Magic is special—"

"I know what I've said, but the truth is that I'm failing," Adon replied. He turned his scar toward Corene and pointed a finger at it. "And this is the symbol of my inadequacy."

"If what you say is true, what are we doing in this forlorn place?" Corene asked. "We should be back in Arabel, converting the masses to Our Lady's cause."

Adon shook his head. "That isn't Mystra's will," he said. "In a dream, she made her wishes clear. I must lift the curse afflicting this village—whatever it is."

The novice shook her head. "The will of the gods is difficult to comprehend."

"True, but in this case I think I understand Our Lady's design," Adon said. "We cannot hope to contend with the priests of the other churches. Chauntea gives her worshipers bountiful crops. Helm protects his followers from harm. Lliira promises her devotees a lifetime of bliss. As clerics of Mystra, we have nothing to offer except a lengthy and difficult study of the mysteries of magic."

"But the rewards—"

"Are a long time in coming and difficult to grasp," Adon interrupted. "No—if I've learned one thing since becoming a patriarch in this church, it's that we won't earn worshipers for Mystra by competing with other religions. Instead, we must try something different—something like what Our Lady sent me here to do."

"To lift a curse?" Corene asked.

"That's only the beginning," Adon said. "What's most important is what happens later."

Corene looked puzzled. "Now I'm having as much trouble understanding you as I do the gods."

The cleric smiled. "That's because I haven't told you the most important part of Mystra's plan," he said. "After I emove the curse, we'll convert the villagers to the Church of Mysteries. I've selected you to administer the priory we'll build here—if we succeed."

Corene looked flattered for a moment, then an expression of understanding came over her face. "You mean stay behind?" she gasped. "We're over a hundred leagues from anything that could be called a city!"

"Relax," Adon said. "The assignment isn't permanent. I'll replace you in a few years—"

"Years!" the novice screeched. "You can't do this!"

"I've done it already," Adon said. "There's no use arguing. This is where Our Lady needs you, and this is where you'll stay."

Corene downed her wine in one swallow. "Are you doing this because I mentioned your scar?" she demanded, wiping her mouth with the sleeve of her robe.

"It has nothing to do with anything you've said during our journey, though you've certainly given me reason enough to chastise you," Adon replied. "I selected you for this task before we left Arabel. "

Corene narrowed her eyes. "Why didn't you tell me then?"

"Because I know how much you love the city," he said. "You would've complained for the whole journey, and maybe even tried to avoid it altogether."

"I might have," she agreed. "Throwing myself into the Starwater doesn't seem an unreasonable alternative."

"I'm sure there's no need to remind you of your vows," Adon said.

"I couldn't forget them if I wanted to—which, at the moment, I do," sighed Corene, though both knew she really didn't mean it.

Despite her disappointment, the novice remained as radiant as ever. His heart softened by her beauty, Adon tried to console her. "I know this assignment will be difficult for you," he said. "But it requires someone with an independent spirit. That's why I chose you."

Corene did not answer, keeping her eyes fixed on the far

edge of the veranda. Adon turned to see what had captured her attention. There, standing just inside the cafe's entrance, was a handsome newcomer. The man had striking features, with high cheekbones, a dark brow, and a roguish mop of auburn hair that hung down to his collar. His figure was trim and solid, with broad shoulders covered by a fur-lined cape and a narrow waist entwined by a cummerbund of the finest purple silk. Ignoring Adon's presence, the fellow flashed a scoundrel's smile at Corene.

The newcomer moved toward the back of the veranda. At the same moment, Sarafina stepped out of the kitchen with a covered basket. As soon as her eyes fell on the stranger, the basket slipped from her hands, spilling slices of dark bread over the floor. She backed toward the door, yelling, "Father, come quickly!"

"What's wrong?" Adon asked, rising to his feet. "Do you need help?"

The stranger paused to sneer at him. "If you know what's good for you, traveler, you'll tend to your own business."

Myron came bustling out of the kitchen and placed his brawny form between his daughter and the stranger. "Tell your master no, Broka," said the innkeeper. "The answer was no yesterday, and tomorrow it'll still be no."

"I must hear that from your daughter's lips," said Broka. He bent down and began gathering up the bread Sarafina had dropped. "Why don't you take this to your guests? I'm aware that you've a shortage of customers these days, and it wouldn't do to let these go hungry."

"We've no complaints," said Adon. He moved toward the handsome stranger, intentionally leaving his mace behind. If it became necessary to intervene on behalf of Sarafina, there were more effective ways to do it than by resorting to weapons.

Myron raised his hand. "Stay out of this," he said. "I can protect my own daughter."

Broka returned to his feet and shoved the refilled basket toward Myron. "Protect her from whom?" he asked. "I've only come to ask a question of fair Sarafina."

"Then ask and be gone," Myron said. He slammed the basket onto the table next to him.

Broka smiled wickedly at Sarafina, "Are you ready to return the love of my master?"

"No!" she yelled. "I'll never be ready—even if he turns me into a harpy!"

"Are you sure?" Broka asked. He stepped past Myron, at the same time reaching into his pocket and withdrawing a small mirror. "Have a look at yourself, and remember that all the women of Tegea share your fate."

He reached for Sarafina's veil, but Myron shoved him away. As Broka fell to the floor, the mirror flew out of his hand and shattered against a chair.

"How dare you touch me!" Broka leaped to his feet, a dagger in his hand.

As Broka stepped toward Myron, Adon smiled. The lout was providing him with a perfect opportunity to prove his power. Calling upon the magic of his goddess, the patriarch cast a spell that would make the dagger too hot to hold.

Nothing happened.

Adon stared at his hand in dumbfounded shock. Something was terribly wrong.

Broka grabbed Myron and pressed the blade to the innkeeper's throat. "Perhaps you'd remember your place if you looked more like your daughter," he hissed.

"Do something!" whispered Corene, stepping to Adon's side. Following her patriarch's lead, she had left her weapon on the table. "He'll be killed!"

Desperate to save the innkeeper, Adon attempted another spell. This time, a ray of green radiance sizzled from his fingertip, leaving a streak of white vapor in its wake. When the beam hit the blade, a high-pitched chime rang across the veranda. The knife shattered into a dozen shards.

Broka cried out in surprise, then tossed his useless hilt aside and stepped out of Myron's reach.

"Before you leave, I suggest you apologize to Sarafina and her father," Adon said.

Broka whirled around to face the cleric. "Do you know

who I am?" he demanded.

"A bullyboy who torments women and hides behind hi
dagger," said Corene. "And it's a real shame, too. Befor
you behaved so badly, I thought you rather handsome."

Broka ignored Corene's rebuke and pointed at the castl
on the far side of the village. "I'm seneschal to the lord o
that castle," he reported. "And at present, I'm conductin;
my master's business. I suggest you keep out of it—o
you'll be answering to him."

With that, he turned back to Myron. "My instruction
are to examine your daughter's face," the seneschal said
staring into the innkeeper's eyes. "If you deny me again, I'
have your whole family lashed."

"Let him, Father," said Sarafina, reaching up to undo he
veil. "It will cause me no pain to have him look."

As Myron reluctantly stepped aside, Broka smirked a
him. "If your daughter cared about the women of Tegea a
much as she does her family, she would come with me t
the castle," he said. "Then, perhaps, your customers woul
forgive you for Sarafina's stubbornness."

"She's done nothing wrong," said Adon. He grabbed th
seneschal by the arm. "After you apologize, you'll return t
your master and tell him to leave Sarafina alone."

"By whose order?" Broka scoffed.

"By the command of Adon of Mystra, patriarch of th
Servants of Mystery," volunteered Corene.

This only made the seneschal laugh. "My master recog
nizes the authority of no churches here," he said, returnin;
his attention to the innkeeper's daughter. "Now, let me se
what my lord's curse has done to your beauty."

Adon jerked Broka back, and the seneschal came aroun
swinging. No stranger to a fight, the cleric blocked th
punch easily. He countered by driving a palm into his foe'
chin, at the same time slipping a foot behind an ankle an
sweeping Broka off his feet. The seneschal slammed int
the floor with a resounding thump, his pained cry leavin;
no doubt that his impact had been a hard one.

Adon placed a knee on Broka's ribs. "Apologize."

The seneschal's only reply was to utter a colorful curse.

"Perhaps you'd be more sympathetic if you weren't so handsome," said Corene.

The novice uttered a spell and touched Broka's brow. Her magic worked perfectly.

The seneschal's face darkened to a deep shade of red, then it erupted into a rash of boils and festering sores. Screaming in alarm, he crawled away and grabbed a piece of the mirror he had dropped when Myron pushed him.

"My face!" Broka howled, staring at himself in the shard.

"You've nothing to complain about," said Corene. "It's better suited to your personality."

The seneschal rose and faced the novice. "Lord Gorgias shall hear of this!"

"That's all I ask," said Adon, moving forward. "Now go!"

The seneschal flung the shard of mirror at Adon, who ducked it easily. As Broka fled, the patriarch turned to face Myron and Sarafina.

"Why don't you tell me more about Lord Gorgias and what he's done to Sarafina and your village?" the cleric asked, certain that his display of courage had won the confidence of his hosts.

"You're a madman!" roared Myron. "I want you out of my inn—now!"

Adon scowled. "What's wrong?" he demanded. "Can't you see that Corene and I are here to help you?"

"You mean to get us killed!" snapped Myron. "You insulted the duke's man. I only hope Lord Gorgias will settle for your lives and leave my family alone."

"He won't murder anyone," said Adon.

"It's kind to offer your protection, but you can't stop the duke," said Sarafina. "In Tegea, at least, no cleric can challenge his magic."

"His spells can't be more powerful than Mystra's," said Corene. "No mortal's can."

"Mystra's not here," Myron growled, pushing Adon and his novice toward the exit. "And until you bring her back with you, you're not welcome, either." The innkeeper pushed them off the veranda, then took his daughter and went into the kitchen.

"What's going on here?" asked Corene, staring at the door through which Myron and Sarafina had disappeared.

"I don't know," said Adon, thinking more about his failed spell than Myron's ingratitude. "Did you notice that Mystra didn't respond when I asked for my first spell?"

Corene bit her lower lip and could not quite bring herself to meet Adon's gaze. "Maybe we're in an area of especially wild magic," she suggested. "Since the Time of Troubles no one's really bothered to map out all the places where the gods' fall made spells unpredictable. Tegea could be—"

"The devoted of Mystra need not refrain from casting spells in areas known for wild magic," Adon said pedantically, then faced the young woman. "You know that as well as I do. Besides, we can both guess why my first spell didn't succeed."

The novice shook her head. "There must be another explanation."

"No. What happened is a sign of Mystra's disappointment in me," he said. "If I don't discover why she's displeased with me before we leave Tegea, I fear I never will."

* * * * *

When the sun rose the next morning, it found Adon standing in the center of Tegea. Behind him, a bubbling spring spilled out of the mountainside to fill a stone basin with cold, clear water. In front of him was a small plaza enclosed by the stone walls of several two-story houses. Dozens of women wearing white blouses and colorful skirts stood in the square, their heads swaddled in black shawls and veils. In their hands, they held the empty wooden buckets they filled each morning at the water basin.

"Mystra's magic will protect you from Lord Gorgias," said Adon, one hand casually resting on the head of his mace. "All I need from you is one who'll trust me to prove it."

When none of the women stepped forward to volunteer, Corene moved into the crowd and touched the veil of a thin woman. "Come now, do you wish to wear these masks for the rest of your lives?"

"What's done is done," said the woman. "Sarafina thought she was too beautiful to marry the duke, and now we must all live with the consequences."

"This is not Sarafina's doing!" boomed Adon. "Lord Gorgias cursed your village, and it's cowardice to blame Sarafina because she won't yield to his demands."

"That's easy enough for you to say," yelled a matronly woman. "You don't live in Tegea."

A chorus of agreement answered from the crowd, then another woman said, "Even if you can help us, what happens when you leave?"

"I'll tell you what happens," said the thin woman. "Lord Gorgias punishes us for defying him."

"No, he won't," said Corene, stepping to her patriarch's side. She gave Adon a dutiful glance, then added, "I'll be staying behind to make sure that doesn't happen."

"A lot of good she'll do us," said the matronly woman, glaring at Adon. "If your idea of bravery is to leave a little girl behind to fight the duke, I want nothing to do with you."

"Inside a week, she'll be scrubbing Lord Gorgias's floors and begging for gruel," called another.

"No!" cried Adon. "With the power of Our Lady, she's strong enough to prevail over any foe—even Lord Gorgias."

From the back of the plaza, a familiar voice called, "Then let her prove it." A narrow lane opened in the crowd, and Sarafina walked forward, a pair of empty water pails in her hands. When she reached the basin, she dropped the buckets at Corene's feet, then reached up to her veil. "If you are strong enough to protect us from Lord Gorgias, then make me beautiful again."

"No, Sarafina!" shouted the matron. "If you ask strangers for help, we'll all pay the price."

"At least we still have our hands to work with," cried

another woman. "Don't make Lord Gorgias any angrier, o
he'll take those away, too."

The thin woman stepped toward Sarafina. "Haven't you
caused enough trouble already?"

"I'm suffering the same as you—probably more so, con
sidering the hardship your anger has caused my family'
inn," Sarafina replied. "But the duke is evil, and I'd rathe
die than marry him."

"There are tortures worse than death," said the thin
woman. "And your stubbornness is visiting them upon u
all."

"If you prize your appearance so highly, then you marry
him," countered Sarafina, ripping off her veil. "As for me
I'll parade my ugliness past all the men of the village before
I sell my virtue and yield to the duke."

Adon gasped at what the duke's curse had done to Sara
fina's face. From the eyes downward, her appearance wa
that of a monster. She had shriveled green skin, stretched
tight over a dozen bony lumps jutting out from her face
Her nose was hideously pointed and covered with carbun
cles, while her lips were frozen into an ugly sneer tha
revealed a mouthful of jagged, yellow teeth. From her chin
sprouted a short gray horn, which curled back toward he
throat.

All of these deformities, however, could not hide Sara
fina's inner beauty. She held her head high and met Adon'
gaze without shame, her strength and determination show
ing in her unwavering brown eyes. In a steady voice, she
asked the patriarch, "Now who's gaping?"

The cleric did not look away. "If I am staring, it's becaus
I am captivated by your spirit," he said honestly, stepping
toward her. "It's not because the duke's pitiful mask ha
engrossed me."

"All the same, the people of Tegea won't trust you
novice until she proves her power," said Sarafina, facing
Corene. "Give me back what Lord Gorgias has stolen."

Corene cast a nervous glance at her patriarch. Adon nod
ded at her. "Lift the curse," he said. "Trust in Mystra. Yo

have more than enough power."

The novice's eyes ranged over Adon's scar, then she swallowed hard. "If you think so." She laid a hand on Sarafina's deformed face, then spoke her incantation.

A yellow radiance spread outward from the novice's hand and crept across Sarafina's visage. The young woman's skin returned to its normal swarthy color, and the lumpy protrusions covering her face began to subside. The carbuncles on her nose slowly healed, and her gray horn began to soften and shrink.

An astonished murmur rustled through the crowd.

"You see?" cried Adon, facing the women. "Armed with Mystra's magic, even a novice can undo Lord Gorgias's—"

An alarmed cry from Corene cut his statement short. When Adon looked back, he saw that a gray shadow was replacing the golden luminescence of Corene's magic. As it worked its way over Sarafina's face, the young woman's newly restored beauty was replaced with the hideous mask of Lord Gorgias's curse.

When the shadow touched Corene's fingers, she screamed and pulled away. The grayness followed her hand, quickly gliding up her arm. The terrified novice plunged her hand into the water and desperately tried to scrub the thing off, but her efforts were to no avail. The shadow slipped over her shoulder and onto her face. It lingered there for an instant, then faded away as rapidly as it had appeared.

For a moment, Corene remained where she was, staring into the basin's rippling waters. Then, all at once, a horrified howl escaped her lips and she threw herself at Adon. "Forgive me!" she screeched, wrapping her arms around his chest. "It was your scar. It made me doubt Our Lady!"

Adon pried Corene away and looked at her. From her cheeks downward, her skin had become leathery and shriveled. Her button nose had tripled in size and turned red, with gaping pink nostrils larger than those of a swine. Her lips were covered with black bristles and curled back, while a fringe of silky white wool hung from her jawline.

"I understand," Adon whispered. "Don't worry. I'll set things right."

"How?" demanded the matron. "By staying here yourself?"

The patriarch shook his head. "My duties in Arabel—"

"Then I suggest you return to Arabel right away. Just leave us to our troubles," said the thin woman, moving forward. "Now stand aside so I can fill my bucket."

Corene blocked her path. "You don't understand. This failure was mine, not Mystra's."

"Our Lady of Mysteries is the patroness of magic itself," Adon explained. "No mortal's spell can withstand her power."

A deep voice boomed across the plaza. "But your goddess is not here, and I am!"

A hulking, leather-clad figure lumbered out of the lane. Although he had a hunched back and a gnarled frame, he stood half again taller than any normal man. His legs were thin and so badly bowed that he seemed to scuttle rather than walk. One gaunt arm hung so low that his knuckles dragged on the cobblestones, while the other was twisted and held to his chest at an awkward angle.

The newcomer had a face as horrible as any Adon had ever seen. It was impossibly haggard and covered with cracked, black skin. The figure's brow jutted out so far that it cast an impenetrable shadow over his eyes. His nose was as narrow as a dagger blade, his cheekbones were grotesquely misshaped, and a pair of yellow tusks curled up from beneath his lower lip.

Behind the figure stood Broka, wearing his fur-trimmed cape and purple cummerbund. His face remained covered with boils, and his swollen nose and black eyes suggested that he had suffered a harsh beating after returning to Castle Gorgias last night.

As the women began to scurry for their homes, the seneschal yelled, "Stay! The duke wishes you to see what passes here."

The crowd stopped moving instantly, leaving a wide

swath of open plaza between the gruesome figure and the patriarch. Adon stepped away from Sarafina. "Lord Gorgias?"

The duke tipped his head in acknowledgement and scuttled forward. "I've come to thank you for the change in my seneschal," he said, waving his gangling arm at Broka's ulcerating face. "He's much more interesting to look upon."

"Perhaps to you," Adon allowed.

The duke stopped a dozen steps away. "And now that I have expressed my gratitude, you and your novice must go," he said. "Had you called at my castle when you arrived, you and I might have had an interesting debate regarding the Church of Mysteries—with a few hours on the rack to help you think clearly. As it is, however, I cannot allow you to spread your lies among my villagers."

Adon shook his head. "We won't leave while your curse remains on Tegea."

"Curse! Do you think I would curse the woman I love?" demanded the duke, gesturing in Sarafina's direction. "I'm broadening her sense of beauty, so that she'll appreciate the subtle elegance of my form."

"It's not your form that repulses me!" Sarafina snapped. "I loathe what you are inside."

"And what am I—*inside*?"

"A tyrant, as cruel as you are vain," said Sarafina. "I'd rather die alone than marry you!"

A forked tongue flickered between the duke's lips. "I wonder if the other women of Tegea share your feelings?"

"No!" screamed several of the women in the square.

"Go with him now, or you'll make widows of us all," ordered the matron, stepping toward Sarafina. Others moved to back her up, but Corene quickly drew her flail and blocked the women's path.

Adon pulled a pinch of yellow brimstone from the pocket of his cloak. He uttered a silent prayer to Mystra, begging her to look favorably on the spell he was preparing to cast, then said, "Lord Gorgias will kill no one."

"Perhaps not—if you're gone by dusk," said the duke, fixing his shadowed eyes on the cleric. "But if you're still here after highsun, every man in this village will die. Mark my words."

"If you threaten others, I've no choice but to strike you down in Mystra's name!"

As the patriarch raised his arms to cast the spell, the women screamed in alarm and fled the plaza. The duke merely smiled while a fiery breach opened in the sky above his head. A pillar of flame crackled down toward his face. He watched it come, laughing wildly.

When the first tongue of flame licked his bony brow, the fiery shaft stopped descending. The blaze fizzled away, and the crimson rift abruptly closed, leaving nothing but a column of gray fumes behind. Within moments, the smoke had disappeared in the breeze. No sign of Adon's spell remained in the sky.

"He worships Cyric!" Corene gasped. "Only someone under the Lord of Strife's protection could withstand Mystra's magic—and do this to a woman's face!" She touched her fingers to her deformed cheek.

"Don't be foolish," scoffed the duke, stepping toward her and Adon. "Your pitiful gods don't interest me. The only being worthy of my adulation is me."

Corene leaped forward, swinging her flail at the duke's ribs. "For the women of Tegea!"

Lord Gorgias allowed the blow to land. It glanced off his leathery hide. Then he grasped Corene by the wrist and uttered an incantation. A soft coat of downy fur immediately sprouted all over her body. Her arms and legs suddenly curled backward against the joints, becoming gnarled, pitiful things that could not even support her weight. She collapsed to the ground, screaming in agony.

Adon wasted no time making another attack, this time drawing his mace. Calling Mystra's name, he leaped forward and swung his weapon toward Lord Gorgias's face. As though transfixed, the duke watched the flanged head arc toward his nose and the patriarch dared to hope he would strike his enemy down with a single blow.

Moving so fast that Adon saw nothing but a blur, Lord Gorgias intercepted the mace and plucked it away. He tossed it aside, then clamped a powerful hand on the patriarch's throat, lifting him off his feet.

"Enough of your foolishness," hissed the duke.

Adon glimpsed Sarafina's lithe form approaching from the side. She was using both hands to swing Corene's flail at the duke's leg. The blow glanced harmlessly off the knee.

"You ally yourself with this stranger against your future husband?" he demanded, glaring down at Sarafina.

She raised the flail and struck again. The duke hardly seemed to notice. Gorgias looked back to Adon. "How did you make Sarafina love you?"

"What she feels for me isn't love," Adon gasped. "It's gratitude for trying to help her."

The duke looked down at the girl. "Is that true?"

She glared back up at his misshaped face. "What I feel for this man is not your concern."

Lord Gorgias turned his shadowy eyes on Adon. "I would kill you now, but I fear that would only make you dearer to Sarafina's heart," he said. "I give you until highsun to show yourself for the coward you are. If you have not left my village by then, Sarafina becomes my wife whether she wishes it or not—and I'll honor my promise to kill every man in this village."

"I'll throw myself into the sea!" Sarafina threatened.

"I think not," the duke replied, glaring down at her. "I will have a woman from your house as a wife. If not you, then your mother."

With that, Lord Gorgias threw Adon into the pool. By the time the cleric had struggled back to his feet, his foe had scuttled halfway across the plaza, Broka's fawning figure trailing a step behind. Sarafina helped the patriarch out of the pool, and they went to where Corene still lay in the street. With her limbs twisted backward and her pained eyes staring straight into the sky, the novice looked more like a fur-covered crab than a young woman. Adon kneeled at her side and once again prayed to Mystra.

"Corene has not failed you," he whispered. "If you are angry, be angry with your patriarch alone! Let me undo the damage I have caused this poor woman. Let me show this village that I am your true servant!"

Adon closed his eyes, laid a hand on Corene's trembling brow, and spoke his incantation.

The novice remained in monstrous form.

Looking skyward, Adon cried, "Why, Mystra? Why did you send me here if you intended to abandon me?"

"Your goddess hasn't abandoned you," Sarafina said, covering her face with her veil. "She can't hear you."

Adon frowned. "Of course she can," he said. "She's the patroness—"

"Of magic, I know," said Sarafina. "But she still can't hear you, not as long as you're in Tegea."

"What are you saying?"

"Will you leave us in peace if I tell you?" she asked. "Lord Gorgias is quite capable of carrying out his threats, and you can't stop him. No one can."

"Mystra wouldn't have sent me here if that were true."

"If it is, will you leave?"

"I came to save Tegea, not destroy it," said Adon. "If I cannot do that, I'll go. But if I think I can stop Lord Gorgias—despite what you reveal about his power—you must promise to help me in any way I ask."

"Done," said Sarafina. She gathered her water pails and began to fill them, at the same time telling Adon the story of Lord Gorgias. "The duke has not always been so ugly—on the inside or the outside. Once, he was quite a handsome young nobleman who cared a great deal for his people."

"What happened?" Adon asked, gathering Corene's twisted form in his arms. She lay silently in the patriarch's comforting embrace.

"It was during the Time of Troubles," Sarafina said. "For the first few days, we were spared much of the wild magic and unnatural beasts caused by the gods' fall. But one day, when we went into the groves to pick olives, we found that Tegea hadn't escaped completely." She shuddered. "The trees bled when we took their olives. Then they shrieked curses at us and tried to club us with their branches. Lord Gorgias came and cast a spell to calm them, but something went wrong. He cloaked the entire mountain with black fog so thick you couldn't see a pace ahead."

Sarafina started up a narrow lane toward her father's inn, motioning for Adon to follow along. "We didn't see Lord Gorgias again until the fog had lifted."

"And when was that?"

"A month after the gods ascended to the heavens again," said Corene. "He'd become the monster you see now. Somehow, though, he'd come to believe that he was more handsome than ever. He still believes that."

"This is all very interesting, but there's nothing in what you've said that convinces me Lady Mystra is powerless to help us," Adon said, already puffing from the exertion of carrying Corene up the steep slope.

"I haven't finished," Sarafina replied. Unlike the cleric, she showed no strain at carrying her heavy burden. "After the fog lifted, Gorgias cursed the gods for harming his people and for letting magic become unstable. He cast a spell over the village to hide us from the heavens. We were safe from the gods—but they could no longer hear our pleas. It was as if Tegea had died to them." She paused and turned sad eyes to Adon. "We had a church of Chauntea here, but the priests found they could no longer commune with the Great Mother. They lost their status in Tegea, so they left. When our crops didn't suffer for their leaving, Gorgias said it was only more proof that gods held nothing for us."

"And what did it prove for you?" Adon asked softly.

"That the clerics mustn't have been very holy." She sighed mournfully, making her veil flutter. "They were only interested in being important people in the village. A few other wandering priests have been through here, but they leave when they discover they're cut off from their gods."

"But Corene cast spells to protect the village. You saw

her cover Broka's face with boils," Adon noted. "And I summoned that pillar of fire to strike down the duke."

"It's true," Sarafina admitted, "you and Corene are the only clerics who have been able to call upon your goddess for even the most minor magic, but . . ."

"Go on," Adon prompted kindly.

"Forgive me, Patriarch, but your flames did nothing to the duke." She looked down at the misshapen woman in Adon's arms. "And Lady Corene's magic couldn't save me—or save herself from a fate worse than mine."

Adon stopped walking. "You just might be right," he said softly. "The duke's spell may make it difficult for Mystra to answer our prayers, but I can't give up."

The patriarch laid Corene on the ground and tried again to dispel the magic that had turned her into such a hideous thing. This time, though, Adon prayed only for Corene to be healed, with no thoughts of his own part in bringing her to this sorry state.

The novice's body began to glow with a greenish aura and was quickly swaddled in swirling lights that obscured her from view. For several moments, Adon waited in silent anticipation. When the radiance finally died away, he saw that his spell had worked, more or less. Corene's body had returned to normal, but her face remained disfigured.

Corene returned to her feet, staring at her arms and legs as if seeing them for the first time. "You've saved me!"

"Not entirely," said Sarafina, pointing timidly to her face. "But it will make your journey easier."

"What journey?" Adon demanded. "We're staying. You've seen that I can undo the duke's magic."

"And what of her face?" countered Sarafina, reaching down to stroke the white fleece hanging off Corene's chin. "Her curse isn't so different from mine. You haven't rid her of that."

"If it's the only way I can prove to you I'm right and you should have faith in Mystra, I shall," Adon said.

A yellow glow spread from Adon's hand to engulf the novice's head. For a moment, her features seemed to soften and the hideous lumps began to recede. Then, just as Adon was certain of his victory, a gray shadow started to creep back over Corene's face.

As the lumps began to rise again, Corene backed away, breaking contact with Adon. "Stop, before it affects you too!"

Adon closed his hand and hung his head. "It won't work until Mystra can hear our prayers," he said. "The duke's curse makes his magic stronger than any I can cast while cut off from Our Lady."

"The only true faith that exists in this village is that which Lord Gorgias places in himself, and it's clear that you're not powerful enough to overcome that on your own," Sarafina said. "You must honor your promise and leave."

Adon did not answer for several moments. Finally he said, "Perhaps you're the one who will have to honor her promise, Sarafina."

The innkeeper's daughter frowned. "What do you mean?"

Adon turned to Corene. "I assume you've studied the spell of true sight recently?"

"Of course, but—"

"Good," Adon said. He looked back to Sarafina and smiled. "I hope there's a mirror in your father's inn."

* * * * *

As it turned out, Sarafina had an ideal mirror. It was just large enough to cover Adon's forearm like a small buckler, yet small enough to support with one hand.

Holding it as though it were a shield, the patriarch stood before the oaken gates of Castle Gorgias, his mace held firmly before him. At his side stood Sarafina, her veil fluttering in the warm breeze. Behind them, waiting at the edge of the cobblestone street, were Corene and Myron. The innkeeper did not approve of Adon's plan, but, at his daughter's insistence, had reluctantly agreed to go along.

Broka's pocked face appeared in the window of the gate-house. "You still have time to leave, cleric," he cried, peering at the blazing sun. "It's not quite highsun."

"I've come to challenge your ugly master for Sarafina's hand," Adon called. "If he's not too much of a coward, he might win himself a wife this day."

Broka raised a brow at Sarafina. "Is this so?"

"It is," she answered. "If Lord Gorgias wins this combat, my father will offer my hand to him."

She had barely finished speaking before the castle gates crashed open. Lord Gorgias scuttled into the street and glanced at the mirror on Adon's arm. "Do you really think that will protect you?" he snickered.

"You can't hit what you can't see," the cleric answered.

He angled the mirror so that it reflected the sun's brilliant rays into his opponent's eyes and rushed forward. Sarafina fled to her father's side.

"This will be a short combat," the duke promised, his fingers already working to cast a spell. He pointed at the patriarch, his deep voice growling his spell. When his gaze fell on the mirror's silvery surface, though, he stumbled over the syllables of his incantation.

Taking advantage of his enemy's blunder, Adon lashed out at Lord Gorgias. The blow struck him in the head, knocking him senseless. It also made the duke's spell misfire; a black beam shot into the wall of the gatehouse. Amid the clatter of broken stones and crumbling masonry, Broka's death scream rang out as the tower collapsed around him.

Adon thrust his shield toward Lord Gorgias's face. "Take a good look, hideous duke," he said. "This is your true self—inside and out!"

The duke turned away. "That's not me!" he growled, lashing out. "It's an illusion!"

Adon ducked, then moved around to keep the mirror in front of Lord Gorgias. "You're the one who has been casting illusions, but you've fooled yourself and no one else!"

Lord Gorgias snapped a foot out, catching Adon in the ribs. The cleric stumbled several steps backward before finally falling to the ground. He clutched the mirror to his chest and struggled to draw a breath.

The duke pointed in Sarafina's direction. "Tonight, you sleep in my bed!" he said, his tusks gnashing in fury.

Adon leaped to his feet and moved forward warily. "The only enchantment on this mirror is a spell of true sight," Adon said, thrusting the silvered glass toward Lord Gorgias's face. "Look!"

The duke peered into the mirror for barely an instant, then whipped his head around so that he would not have to see himself. Adon sprang forward, swinging his mace again and again. Lord Gorgias gasped in pain and a bloody welt rose each time the weapon struck, though any one blow would have killed most normal men.

The duke tried to strike back, flailing his arms and legs about blindly. He landed only glancing blows that bounced harmlessly off Adon's armor. Several times, Lord Gorgias tried to look at the patriarch, but he always glanced away when he saw his own image. Twice, he lashed out at the mirror itself, but the cleric was ready for this tactic and knocked the hand aside with a sharp blow of his mace.

Finally, Lord Gorgias dropped to his knees. "It's me!" he cried, covering his head. "I admit it. That's me."

Adon stood over the cowering duke. "It doesn't have to be," he said. His voice sounded thin and reedy, winded as he was from the fight. "You can change what you see here."

The duke raised his head and stared into the mirror. "Don't you think I've tried?" he demanded, grimacing at the image. "It's impossible!"

"No, it isn't." Adon kept the shield in front of Lord Gorgias. "You have to face this, like you're doing now. Then we can get help."

"Help?" Lord Gorgias asked. He used a filthy-clawed finger to scratch at the image in the glass. "Who can help me escape that?"

"Our Lady of Mysteries."

"No!"

The duke lashed out and plucked the mirror away, then swung his legs around and swept the cleric's feet from beneath him. "The gods are the ones who did this to me!" Lord Gorgias yelled, throwing himself on Adon.

"Not Mystra," the cleric gasped. "She wasn't even a goddess then."

Lord Gorgias smashed his bony forehead into the cleric's nose. Adon heard cartilage snapping and his cheeks exploded into pain.

"Have a look at yourself!" snickered the duke, holding the mirror over Adon's blood-smeared face.

The patriarch had no choice but to do as Lord Gorgias commanded. His nose had been broken and lay spread across his face, and both eyes were already turning black.

But it was what he did not see that astonished him. The ugly scar on the left side of his face was gone. Yet, when he reached up to touch it, he felt the same cord of rough skin that had been there since the Time of Troubles. It simply was not visible in the mirror.

"Mystra?" the cleric gasped.

Lord Gorgias brought the mirror down. Adon barely managed to throw his arm across his eyes, then his entire face exploded into agony as the glass shattered against him.

A fiery streak shot from across the street, where Corene had been watching the battle with Myron and Sarafina. A magical arrow of flame buried itself into Lord Gorgias's ribs. The shaft continued to sputter for an instant after it struck, filling the air with the acrid stench of burning flesh. The duke cried out, but didn't even glance in the direction from which the attack had come. Instead, he closed his fingers around Adon's throat and began to squeeze.

A dark curtain began to descend inside Adon's mind. He thrust a hand up, sticking his fingers into the smoking hole that Corene's fire arrow had opened. Lord Gorgias tried to pull away, but Adon hung on tight, at the same time uttering an incantation. A wave of unimaginable cold ran down his arm and directly into the wound. With a sizzle, a cloud of red steam shot from the puncture, making the duke scream in agony. He threw himself off the cleric and rolled away, clutching his stomach.

Adon stood and, after wiping the blood from his eyes, retrieved the largest mirror fragment he could find. It was about the size of his hand and shaped like a squat triangle. He walked toward Lord Gorgias cautiously, at the same time enchanting the shard with one of his most powerful spells. The duke struggled to his knees and glared at the cleric.

"Your hatred has consumed you," Adon said, holding the blood-smeared shard toward the duke. "That's what made the monster you see here, not the gods."

"But they abandoned me—and my village! *They* did this to me! *They* refused to answer my prayers!"

Lord Gorgias sprang.

Adon tossed the mirror fragment at him, at the same time speaking the command word that triggered the spell it contained. The shard struck the duke's arm and sank deep into his flesh. A silver light flashed from the wound, and Lord Gorgias's anguished voice rang off the castle walls. In the next instant, he vanished.

The mirror triangle tumbled to the ground.

When Adon picked up the shard, it felt so cold that it stung his fingers. No longer was it possible to tell that it had once been part of a mirror, for its smooth surface had become as hard as polished stone. In place of the cleric's reflection was the image of Lord Gorgias, his shadowed eyes glaring out at the world, his tusks gnashing in anger.

The patriarch studied the shard for a long time. He felt a great sense of relief and hope, but also of loss and fear. Today, he had vanquished a monster, but he had also vanquished something even more terrible—something that he'd been afraid to face for many years.

Just before Lord Gorgias had smashed the mirror against his face, Adon had seen himself without his scar. It was then that he had realized why Mystra had sent him to Tegea. The power to remove the scar always lay inside him, just as the ability to defeat the duke had been his all along—if only he turned his gaze outside himself, focused his thoughts on something other than his own petty concerns. The clerics of Chauntea who'd abandoned the village had done so because their own selfish interests had stopped them from breaking the silence the duke had imposed upon their souls. And all the spells that had failed Adon in the last few days had done so because he'd cast them, not to help others, but to prove himself a worthy servant of Mystra.

By the time he realized where he was, Adon had walked back to the center of town. Myron, Corene, and Sarafina were trailing along behind him, keeping a respectful distance from the pensive young patriarch.

Finally Myron came forward. "I didn't believe anyone could banish the duke, but you have." He paused for a moment, then pointed at Castle Gorgias. "Corene and Sarafina are already talking about making a House of Mysteries out of that."

"You'll have plenty of help," Sarafina said from beside the crowded pool in the center of the square.

"Yes, when our husbands return from the fields this evening, they'll be so glad to see us without veils that they'll have it converted before morning," said another.

Dozens of women were filing into the street, all without veils, all smiling broadly. Some had big noses and some double chins, while others were missing teeth and had cheeks as leathery as saddles. Nevertheless, Adon would not have called any of them unattractive. Too him, they were all as beautiful as Corene.

"Well, Corene," Adon said, turning to the novice, "are you looking forward to seeing Arabel again?"

"I'll be going back with you?" asked Corene, stepping to Adon's side.

"Not exactly," the cleric replied, looking down at her. Her button nose had returned to its normal size, and her pale cheeks had begun to shine with their old radiance. "I'll be staying here. I don't think the spell the duke cast to shield the village from the gods has been lifted entirely. It'll take someone of the right temperament to maintain contact with the Lady once the church is established here."

Corene kissed Adon's cheek. Then, wiping the blood from her lips, she said, "I don't know if it will work, but I could try to heal your nose and those cuts."

"Fine, but leave my scar alone," said Adon.

Sarafina, still hidden behind her veil, stepped up to Adon's side and slipped a slender arm around the patriarch's waist. "I've thought from the start that it gives your face character."

"Maybe you're right," the priest said, laughing. "But I'm not going to spend any more time worrying about it. My concern now is how to help Tegea."

Sarafina lowered her veil and smiled at him. It was the most beautiful thing Adon had ever seen.

DARK MIRROR

R. A. Salvatore

Sunrise. Birth of a new day. An awakening of the surface world, filled with the hopes and dreams of a million hearts. Filled, too, I have come painfully to know, with the hopeless labors of so many others.

There is no such event as sunrise in the dark world of my dark elven heritage, nothing in all the lightless Underdark to match the beauty of the sun inching over the rim of the eastern horizon. No day, no night, no seasons.

Surely the spirit loses something in the constant warmth and constant darkness. Surely there, in the Underdark's eternal gloom, one cannot experience the soaring hopes, unreasonable though they might be, that seem so very attainable at that magical moment when the horizon glistens silver with the arrival of the morning sun. When darkness is forever, the somber mood of twilight is soon lost, the stirring mysteries of the surface night are replaced by the factual enemies and very real dangers of the Underdark.

Forever, too, is the Underdark season. On the surface, the winter heralds a time of reflection, a time for thoughts of mortality, of those who have gone before. Yet this is only a season on the surface, and the melancholy does not settle too deep. I have watched the animals come to life in the spring, have watched the bears awaken and the fish fight their way through swift currents to their spawning grounds. I have watched the birds at aerial play, the first run of a newborn colt. . . .

Animals of the Underdark do not dance.

The cycles of the surface world are more volatile, I think. There seems no constant mood up here, neither gloomy nor exuberant. The emotional heights one can climb with the rising sun can be equally diminished as the fiery orb descends in the west. This is a better way. Let fears be given to the night, that the day be full of sun, full of hope. Let anger be calmed by the winter snows, then forgotten in the warmth of spring.

In the constant Underdark, anger broods until the taste for vengeance is sated.

This constancy also affects religion, which is so central to my dark elven kin. Priestesses rule the city of my birth, and all bow before the will of the cruel Spider Queen Lloth. The religion of the drow, though, is merely a way of practical gain, of power attained, and for all their ceremonies and rituals, my people are spiritually dead. For spirituality is a tumult of emotions, the contrast of night and day that drow elves will never know. It is a descent into despair and a climb to the highest pinnacle.

Greater the heights do seem when they follow the depths.

*   *   *   *   *

I could not have picked a better day to set out from Mithril Hall, where my dwarven friend, Bruenor Battle-hammer, was king once more. For two centuries, the dwarven homeland had been in the hands of evil gray dwarves, the duergar, and their mighty leader, the shadow dragon Shimmergloom. Now the dragon was dead, killed by Bruenor himself, and the gray dwarves had been swept away.

The snow lay deep in the mountains about the dwarven stronghold, but the deepening blue of the predawn sky was clear, the last stubborn stars burning until the very end, until night gave up its hold on the land. My timing was fortunate, for I came upon an easterly facing seat, a flat rock, windblown clear of snow, only moments before the daily event that I pray I never miss.

I cannot describe the tingle in my chest, the soaring of my heart, at that last moment before the yellow rim of Faerun's sun crests the glowing line of the horizon. I have walked the surface world for nearly two decades, but never will I grow tired of the sunrise. To me, it has become the antithesis of my troubled time in the Underdark, the symbol of my escape from the lightless world and evil ways of my kin. Even when it is ended, when the sun is fully up and climbing fast the eastern sky, I feel its warmth penetrating my ebony skin, lending me vitality I never knew in the depths of the world.

So it was this winter's day, in the southernmost spur of the Spine of the World Mountains. I had been out of Mithril Hall for only a few hours, with a hundred miles before me on my journey to Silverymoon, which must be among the most marvelous of cities in all the world. It pained me to leave Bruenor and the others with so much work yet to do in the mines. We had taken the halls earlier that same winter, cleared them of duergar scum and all the other monsters that had wandered in during the two-century absence of Clan Battlehammer. Already the smoke of dwarven furnaces rose into the air above the mountains; already the dwarven hammers rang out in the relentless pursuit of the precious mithril.

Bruenor's work had just begun, especially with the engagement of his adopted human daughter, Catti-brie, to the barbarian lad, Wulfgar. Bruenor could not have been happier, but like so many people I have come to know, the dwarf could not hold fast to that happiness above his frenzy over the many preparations the wedding precipitated, above his unrealistic craving that the wedding be the finest ceremony the northland had ever seen.

I did not point this out to Bruenor. I didn't see the purpose, though the dwarf's incredible workload did temper my desire to leave the halls.

But invitations from Alustriel, the wondrous Lady of Silverymoon, are not easily ignored, especially by a renegade drow so determined to find acceptance among peoples who fear his kind.

My pace was easy that first day out. I wanted to make the River Surbrin and put the largest mountains behind me. It was along those very riverbanks, sometime around midafternoon, that I encountered the tracks. A mixed group, perhaps a score, had passed this way, and not too long before. The largest few sets of tracks belonged to ogres. What worried me the most, though, since such creatures are not uncommon and not unexpected in the region, were the smaller bootprints. By their size and shape, I had to believe that these markings had been made by humans, and some seemed to belong to a human child. Even more disturbing, some bootprints were partially covered by monster tracks, while others partially covered monster tracks. They were all made at approximately the same time. Who, then, was the captive, and who the captor?

The trail was not hard to follow. My fears only increased when I spotted some dots of bright red along the path. I took some comfort in the equipment that I carried, though. Catti-brie had loaned me Taulmaril, the Heartseeker, for this, my first journey to Silverymoon. With that powerfully enchanted bow in hand, I continued along, confident that I could handle whatever dangers presented themselves.

I stepped carefully, keeping to the shadows as much as possible and keeping the cowl of my forest-green cloak pulled tight about my face. Still, I knew that I was gaining rapidly, that the band, holding to the riverbank, could not be more than an hour ahead of me. It was time to call upon my most trusted ally.

I took the panther figurine, my link to Guenhwyvar, from my belt pouch and placed it on the ground. My call to the cat was not loud, but it did not have to be, for Guenhwyvar surely recognized my voice. Then came the telltale gray mist, a moment later to be replaced by the black panther, six hundred pounds of fighting perfection.

"We may have some prisoners to free," I said to the cat as I showed Guenhwyvar the trampled trail. As always, Guenhwyvar's growl of understanding reassured me, and together we set off, hoping to discover the enemy before the onset of night.

The first movement came unexpectedly from across the wide expanse of the Surbrin. I went down behind a boulder, Taulmaril pulled and ready. Guenhwyvar's reaction was similarly defensive, the panther crouching behind a stone closer to the river, back legs tamping the ground excitedly. I knew that Guenhwyvar could easily make the thirty foot jump to the other bank. It would take me longer to cross, though, and I feared I could not lend the cat much support from this bank.

Some scrambling across the way showed that we, too, had been spotted, a fact confirmed a moment later when an arrow cut the air above my head. I thought of responding in kind. The archer ducked behind a rock, but I knew that, with Taulmaril, I could probably put an arrow right through that meager stone cover.

I held the shot, though, and bade Guenhwyvar to stay in place. If this was the band I had been tracking, then why had no more arrows whistled out beside the first? Why hadn't the stupid goblin-kin started their typical war-whoops?

"I am no enemy!" I called out, since my position was no secret anyway.

The reply let me ease my pull on the bowstring.

"If you're no enemy, then who might you be?"

This left me in a predicament that only a dark elf on the surface can know. Of course, I was no enemy to these men

—farmers, I presumed, who had come out in pursuit of the raiding monster band. We were unknowingly working toward the same goal, but what would these simple folk think when a drow rose up before them?

"I am Drizzt Do'Urden, a ranger and friend of King Bruenor Battlehammer of Mithril Hall!" I called. Off came my hood and out I stepped, wanting this typically tension-filled first meeting to be at an end.

"A stinking drow!" I heard one man exclaim, but another, an older man of about fifty years, told him and the others to hold their shots.

"We're hunting a band of orcs and ogres," the older man—I later learned his name to be Tharman—explained.

"Then you are on the wrong side of the river," I called back. "The tracks are here, heading along the bank. I would guess they'll lead to a trail not so far from this point. Can you get across?"

Tharman conferred with his fellows for a moment—there were five of them in all—then signaled for me to wait where I was. I had passed a frozen section of the river, dotted with many large stones, just a short distance back, and it was only a few minutes before the farmers caught up with me. They were raggedly dressed and poorly armed, simple folk and probably no match for the merciless orcs and ogres that had passed this way. Tharman was the only one of the group who had seen more than thirty winters. Two of the farmers looked as if they had not yet seen twenty, and one of these didn't even show the stubble common to the road-weary faces of the others.

"Ilmater's tears!" one of them cried in surprise as the group neared. If the sight of a dark elf was not enough to put them on their nerves, then the presence of Guenhwyvar certainly was.

The man's shouted oath startled Guenhwyvar. The panther must have thought the plea to the God of Suffering a threat of some kind, for she flattened her ears and showed her tremendous fangs.

The man nearly fainted, and a companion beside him tenatively reached for an arrow.

"Guenhwyvar is a friend," I explained. "As am I."

Tharman looked to a rugged man, half his age and carrying a hammer better suited to a smithy than a war party. The younger man promptly and savagely slapped the nervous archer's hand away from the bow. I could discern already that this brute was the leader of the group, probably the one who had bullied the others into coming into the woods in the first place.

Though my claim had apparently been accepted, the tension did not fly from the meeting, not at all. I could smell the fear, the apprehension, emanating from these men, Tharman included. I noticed the younger farmers gripping more tightly to their weapons. They would not move against me, I knew—that was one benefit of the savage reptation of my heritage. Few wanted to wage battle against dark elves. And even if I had not been an exotic drow, the farmers would not have attacked with the mighty panther crouched beside me. They knew that they were overmatched, and they knew, too, that they needed an ally, any ally, to help them in their pursuit.

Five men, farmers all, poorly armed and poorly armored. What in the Nine Hells did they expect to do against a band of twenty monsters, ogres included? Still, I had to admire their courage, and I could not discount them as foolish. I believed that the raiders had taken prisoners. If those unfortunates were these men's families, their children perhaps, then their desperation was certainly warranted, their actions admirable.

Tharman came forward, his soil-stained hand extended. I must admit that the greeting, nervous but sincerely warm, touched me. So often have I been met with taunts and bared weapons! "I have heard of you," he remarked.

"Then you have the advantage," I replied politely, grasping his wrist.

Behind him, the sturdy man narrowed his eyes angrily. I was surprised somewhat; my benign remark had apparently injured his pride. Did he think himself a renowned fighter?

Tharman introduced himself, and the tough leader immediately rushed forward to do likewise. "I am Rico," he declared, coming up to me boldly. "Rico Pengallen of the village Pengallen, fifteen miles to the south and east." The obvious pride in his voice caused Tharman to wince and set off silent alarms that this Rico might bring trouble when we had caught up with the monsters.

I had heard of Pengallen, though I had only marked it by its evening lights from a distance. According to Bruenor's maps, the village was no more than a handful of farmhouses. So much for the hopes that any organized militia would soon arrive.

"We were attacked early last night, just after sunset," Rico continued, roughly nudging the older man aside. "Orcs and ogres, as we've said. They took some prisoners. . . ."

"My wife and son," Tharman put in, his voice full of anxiety.

"My brother as well," said another.

I spent a long while considering that grim news, trying to find some consolation I could offer to the desperate men. I did not want their hopes to soar, though, not with ogres and orcs holding their loved ones and with the odds apparently so heavily weighted against us.

"We are less than an hour behind," I explained. "I had hoped to spot the group before sunset. With Guenhwyvar beside me, though, I can find them night or day."

"We're ready for a fight," Rico declared. It must have been my expression—perhaps it was unintentionally condescending—that he did not like, for he slapped his hammer across his open palm and practically bared his teeth with his ensuing snarl.

"Let us hope it will not come to a fight," I said. "I have some experience with ogres and with orcs. Neither are overly adept at setting guards."

"You mean to simply slip in and free our kin?"

Rico's barely tempered anger continued to surprise me, but when I turned to Tharman for some silent explanation, he only slipped his hands into the folds of his worn travelng cloak and looked away.

"We will do whatever we must to free the prisoners," I said.

"And to stop the monsters from returning to Pengallen," Rico added roughly.

"They can be dealt with later," I replied, trying to convince him to solve one problem at a time. A word to Bruenor would have sent scores of dwarves scouring the region, stubborn and battle-ready warriors who would not have stopped their hunting until the threat had been eliminated.

Rico turned to his four comrades, or, more accurately, he turned away from me. "Guess we're following a damned drow elf," he said.

I took no offense. Certainly I had suffered worse treatment than the blustery insults, and this desperate band, with the exception of Rico, seemed pleased enough to have found any ally, regardless of the color of my skin.

The enemy camp did not prove difficult to locate. We found it on our side of the river, as twilight settled on the land. Conveniently—or rather, stupidly—the monsters had set a blazing fire to ward off the winter night's cold.

The light of the bonfire also showed me the layout of the encampment. There were no tents, just the fire and a few scattered logs propped on stones for benches. The land was fairly flat, covered with a bed of river-polished stones and dotted by boulders and an occasional tree or bush. Pig-faced orc sentries were in place north and south of the fire, holding crude, but wicked, weapons in their dirty hands. I assumed that similar guards were posted to the west, away from the river. The prisoners, seeming not too badly injured, huddled together behind the blaze, their backs against a large stone. There were four, not three: the two boys and the farmer's wife joined by a surprisingly well-dressed goblin. At the time, I didn't question the presence of this unexpected addition. I was more concerned with simply finding a way in and a way out.

"The river," I whispered at length. "Guenhwyvar and I can get across it without being seen. We can scout the camp better from the other side."

Rico was thinking the same thing—after a fashion. "You come in from the east, across the river, and we'll hit them hard on this flank."

His scowl widened as I shook my head. This Rico just did not seem able to comprehend that I meant to get the prisoners without an all-out fight.

"I will get at them from across the river with Guenhwyvar beside me," I tried to explain. "But not until the fire had burned low."

"We should go at them while the light is bright," Rico argued. "We aren't like you, drow." He spat the word derisively. "We can't see in the dark."

"But I can," I retorted rather sharply, for Rico was beginning to bother me more than a little. "I can get in, free the prisoners, and strike at the sentries from behind, hopefully without alerting their fellows. If things go well, we will be far from here before the monsters even realize that their prisoners are gone."

Tharman and the other three men were nodding their agreement with the simple plan, but Rico remained stubborn.

"And if things do not go well?"

"Guenhwyvar and I should be able to keep the monsters confused enough so that you and your freed kin can get away. I do not believe that the monsters will even attempt to pursue you, not if they think that their prisoners were stolen by dark elves."

Again I saw Tharman and the others nodding eagerly and when Rico tried to find a new argument, the older man put a hand firmly on his burly shoulder. Rico shrugged it away, but said nothing more. I did not find much comfort in his silence, not when I looked at the hatred deeply etched on his stubbly face.

Crossing the half-frozen river proved easy enough. Guenhwyvar simply leaped across its width. I followed, picking a careful path along the ice. I did not want to depend wholly upon such a fragile bridge, though, so I chose a course to e opposite bank that offered the most prominent stones.

My new perspective on the enemy camp from across the river revealed some potential problems—more precisely, he gigantic ogres, standing twice my height. Their skin hone dull and dark in the flickering firelight, prominent arts shining darker, and their long, matted hair shone luish black. There were two at least, squatting amidst a umble of boulders to the north of the prisoners. The prisners themselves faced the river, faced me, their backs gainst the stone, and now I saw another guarding orc, siting with its back flat against the north face of the same tone. A bared sword lay across its lap. Having often witessed the brutal tactics of orcs, I figured that this guard as under orders to slip around the stone and slaughter the risoners if trouble came. That orc presented the most danger, I decided. Its throat would be the first I slit this night.

All that was left for preparation was to sit low and wait for he fire to dim, wait for the camp to grow sleepy with boreom.

Barely half an hour later, angry whispers began to drift to he from across the river—but not from the enemy camp. I ould not believe what I was hearing; Rico and the others ere arguing! Fortunately, the two orc guards nearest the en's hiding place did not react at once. I could only hope hat their ears, not nearly as keen as my own, had not icked up on the slight sound.

Another few moments slipped by, and, thankfully, the oices went silent once more. I did not relax. My instincts arned me that something drastic would soon happen, and uenhwyvar's low growl confirmed the feeling.

At that critical moment, I did not want to believe that Rico ould be so incredibly foolish, but my instincts and warrior enses overruled what my mind refused to believe. I had aulmaril off my shoulder, an arrow nocked, and searched ut again the exact route that would get me quickly across he water.

The two orcs of the southern watch began to shift nerously and converse with each other in their guttural lan-

guage. I watched them closely, but more closely I kept m
attention on the orc nearest the prisoners. I watched th
ogres as well, by far the more dangerous foes. An eigh
hundred-pound, ten-foot-tall ogre might not be easily o
quickly felled by my scimitars, though a well-aimed strik
by Taulmaril could bring one crashing down. Still, m
whole plan was predicated on getting the prisoners ou
without the ogres ever knowing—a battle with those brute
could cost me more time than I, or the prisoners, had t
spare.

Then my plan unraveled before my eyes.

One of the orcish sentries yelled something. The or
beside him put an arrow into the bushes shielding th
farmers. Predictably, the sword-wielding guard was up ii
an instant, right beside the helpless prisoners. The ogres i
the boulder tumble were stirring, but they seemed mor
curious than alarmed. I still held out some hope that the si
uation could be salvaged—until I heard Rico's cry for
charge.

There is a time in every battle when a warrior must let g
of his conscious thoughts, must let his instincts guide hi
moves, must trust in those instincts fully and not waste pre
cious time in questioning them. I had only one shot to sto
the sword-wielding orc from killing the nearest prisone
Tharman's wife. The creature's blade was up in the ai
when I let fly the arrow, its powerful enchantment trailing
silver streak as it flashed across the Surbrin.

I think I got him in the eye, but wherever the missil
actually hit, the orc's head was virtually blown apart. Th
creature flew back into the darkness, and I started acros
the river, finding what steps I could without taking m
attention from the opposite bank.

The orcs nearest the farmers fired their bows again, the
drew out weapons for close melee. And though I did no
bother to look, I knew that Rico was leading a charge. Th
three orcs to the north cried out and looked to the rive
trying to figure out what had killed their companion. Hov
vulnerable I felt out there, with only emptiness about me

noving slowly as I picked my careful way! Those fears roved valid, for the orcs spotted me almost immediately. I aw their bows come up to fire.

Perhaps the guards could not see me clearly, or perhaps heir aim was simply not as good as mine. Whatever the eason, their hasty first shots went wide. I paused in my rantic charge and returned two arrows of my own; one hit ome, its tremendous force throwing the middle orc of the hree back and to the ground. I heard an arrow whistle by ny ear, just inches away. I think Guenhwyvar, leaping past ne, took the next, for I never heard it and, by the luck of he gods, never felt it.

Guenhwyvar hit the bank ahead of me and completely hifted her momentum, sleek muscles pulling hard, bringng the panther about. I had seen Guenhwyvar execute naneuvers like this a hundred times, yet my breath, as lways, was stolen away. The cat's flight was directly westvard, but as soon as her paws touched down, without a sinle extra step forward, she cut an incredible pivot to the orth and fell upon the archers before they had another rrow out of their quivers.

To my relief, I heard the sounds of battle joined to the outh as Rico and the others clashed with the orcs. They ad stirred up this hornets' nest. At least they were going o share in the task of putting it right.

I saw the ogres get up then—four, not two—and I let oose another arrow. It got the leading brute in the chest, earing through the dirty hides the giant wore and burying tself to its silver fletchings. To my amazement and horror he smelly creature continued on for a few steps. Then it ell to its knees, stunned, but not dead. As it slid to the round, it looked about curiously, as though it had no idea vhat had stopped its charge.

I had time for one more shot before I reached the bank, nd I wanted desperately to kill another ogre. But an orc ppeared behind the prisoners, and its evil intentions were bvious as it lifted its cruel sword over the children's eads.

The orc was turned sideways to me. I shot it in the near
est shoulder, the arrow blasting right through to the oppo
site shoulder. The orc was still alive when it fell to the
ground, flopping helplessly with no use of either arm.

It seems strange to me now, but I remember that when
at last made the opposite bank, dropping the bow and draw
ing my scimitars, I was truly concerned that I might lose
Taulmaril. I even thought of the scolding Catti-brie would
give to me when I returned to Mithril Hall without her pre
cious weapon! The images were fleeting, though, a needed
diversion until battle was rejoined.

Twinkle, the blade in my right hand, flared an angry
blue,
aptly reflecting the fires within me. My other scimitar flared
bluish white light, a testament to the winter's chill, for the
blade would only glow when the air about it was very cold.

The three remaining ogres came at me in no concerted
way—whenever I battle such strong but stupid beasts I am
reminded of how powerful they would surely be if they
could find some order to overrule their natural chaos.

They had erred in their charge, for the lead ogre was too
far ahead of its companions. I came in faster than the mon
ster expected, charging low. Twinkle banged hard against
one kneecap, and my other blade dug a gash into the oppo
site thigh as I passed between the huge legs and dived into
a headlong roll. The ogre tried to stop abruptly—too
abruptly—and it skidded to a jerking halt on the smooth
polished stones.

It fell to a seated position just as I came up to my feet
behind it. One does not get many opportunities for so clean
a strike at an ogre's head, and I took full advantage, slam
ming Twinkle hard against the beast's skull, cutting one ear
almost exactly in half.

The blow didn't kill the hulking thing, but it was stunned
Before the ogre could recover, I leaped up, caught a
foothold on its shoulder, and sprang off, soaring straight for
the next brute's face. The move caught this second ogre by
complete surprise. Its formidable club was postured for a

ow defense. It couldn't possibly get the heavy weapon up in time to block.

Twinkle slashed across the side of the ogre's thick neck as my other blade bit into its cheek, tearing away the skin so that the monster's black teeth gleamed in the starlight. Neither wound was mortal, though, and I feared that I was in serious trouble when the monster wrapped its free arm around my back, pulling me in tight against its massive chest. Fortunately, my right arm was angled so that I managed to pull back Twinkle and get the scimitar's point in line. I drove in with all my strength, knowing that I needed a quick kill, for my sake and for the sake of the helpless prisoners.

The magical blade slipped through the ogre flesh, nicking off a rib that must have been as thick as a fair-sized tree trunk, and then probed deeper. I actually felt the throbbing as Twinkle found the ogre's heart, the violent pumping nearly pulling the scimitar's hilt from my grasp.

I'd needed the quick kill, and I got it. The ogre gasped once, and we tumbled together to the ground. I was away in an instant, the dying ogre taking the club hit its remaining companion had intended for me.

The battle was far from won, though. This last standing ogre crouched low, poised and ready. Even worse, both the brute I had shot with the arrow and the one whose ear I had split were not dead. Stubbornly, they were trying to rise, to get themselves back into the battle.

I took some comfort when Guenhwyvar raced past me again, right between me and my newest opponent. I thought the cat was going to finish one of the wounded ogres, but Guenhwyvar went right past the struggling monsters and leaped over the terrified, huddled prisoners. I understood why when I heard the twang of bows; the orc guards from the west had arrived. There came a thunderous roar, followed, predictably, by terrified screams.

It would take more than a few orcish arrows to slow mighty Guenhwyvar.

I noticed, too, when I glanced to the side, that the goblin

prisoner was up and running, fleeing into the night. I too
little note of the creature, having no idea then of how pr
foundly this particular goblin would affect my life.

All thoughts of cowardly goblins disappeared as th
unwounded ogre drew me back into the battle. It got in th
first swing, the first two or three, actually. I kept on th
defensive, picking my openings carefully. As I expected, th
ogre's frustration mounted with every miss. Its attack
grew more wild, more open to counters. I had hit the bru
four times, cutting painful, if not too serious, wounds in i
hide, when I noticed the ogre with the split ear starting
rise.

My opponent swung again and again, forcing me
dodge. I rushed in for a quick and furious flurry of stingi
strikes, pushing him back on the heels of his huge fee
Then I turned and rushed the groggy ogre. The beast lift
its great club pitifully, hardly having recovered the streng
to line the weapon up at all. Its swing was slow and clums
and I easily stepped back out of danger. I followed the cl
in on its follow-through, slashing wildly with both scimitar
How many lines of blood I drew on that ogre's face, I do n
know. In barely an instant, the monster's features a
seemed lost in a gory mass.

I scanned the camp as the huge corpse fell away, and w
heartened, for the ogre with the arrow in its chest ha
given up the fight, had given up everything. It lay fac
down, so very still that I knew it was dead.

That left only the one behind me, slightly wounded
knew I could beat any ogre in an even fight, knew that
would never get close to hitting me if I kept my concentr
tion absolute. Always eager to battle such vile creatures
admit an instant of regret when I turned around and foun
that the ogre had run off into the night.

The tinge of regret disappeared when I remembered th
prisoners. To my relief, the orcs in the south had bee
defeated by the five farmers, with only one of the men, th
youngest, showing any wounds at all. Rico wore a smu
expression, one I dearly wanted to pound from the boastf

nan's face.

Guenhwyvar came trotting back into the camp a moment later at an easy gait, the western area secured. The panther showed a couple of small wounds from orcish arrows, but nothing serious. Thus the fight ended, three ogres and eight orcs dead, another ogre and perhaps a half-dozen orcs fleeing into the night. A complete victory, for not a single companion had been slain.

Still, I could not help but consider that this battle needn't have happened at all. Any thoughts I held of berating Rico did not remain for long, though, not with the ensuing greetings between Tharman and his family, between another of the farmers and his lost younger brother.

"Where is Nojheim?" Rico demanded. His callous tone surprised me. If he'd lost some kin, a child or a sibling, I would have expected sorrow. But I heard no sorrow behind the man's question, only a desperate anger, as though he had been insulted.

The farmers exchanged confused glances, with all gazes finally coming to rest on me.

"Who is Nojheim?" I asked.

"A goblin," Tharman explained.

"There was a goblin among the prisoners," I told them. "He slipped out during the fight, heading northwest."

"Then we go on," Rico said without the slightest hesitation, without the slightest regard for the beleaguered prisoners. I thought his request absurd; could a single goblin be worth the pains of this man, woman, and boy who had gone through such trials?

"The night grows long," I said to him, my tone far from congenial. "Bring the fire back up and tend to your wounded. I will go after the missing goblin."

"I want him back!" Rico growled. He must have understood my confused and fast-angering expression, for he calmed suddenly and tried to explain.

"Nojheim led a group of goblins that attacked Pengallen several weeks ago," he said and glanced around at the others. "The goblin is a leader, and will likely return with allies.

We were holding him for trial when the newest raiders came."

I had no reason not to take Rico's claims at face value—except that it seemed odd to me that farmers of the small village, so often besieged by the many monsters of the wild region would go to the trouble of holding a trial for the sake of a goblin. The hesitating (or was it fearful?) expressions of those other farmers, particularly of Tharman, also gave me pause, but I dismissed their apparent reservations as fear that Nojheim would return with a sizable force behind him and lay waste to their vulnerable village.

"I am in no hurry to get to Silverymoon," I assured them. "I will capture Nojheim and return him to Pengallen on the morrow." I started off, but Rico grabbed my shoulder and turned me about to face him.

"Alive," he snarled. I did not like the sound of it. I have never held any reservations about dealing harsh justice to goblins, but Rico's cruel tone seemed to tell of a thirst for vengeance. Still, I had no reason to doubt the burly farmer, no reason to argue against the accepted code of justice of Pengallen. Guenhwyvar and I were away in a moment, tracking to the northwest, easily finding the trail of the fleeing Nojheim.

The chase took longer than I'd expected. We found the tracks of some orc stragglers crossing those of Nojheim, and I decided it to be more important to prevent the orcs from getting back to their lair, where they might find some reinforcements. We found them, just three, a short while later. Using the Heartseeker, so marvelous a bow, I finished the beasts from a distance in a matter of three quick shots.

Then Guenhwyvar and I had to backtrack, rejoin Nojheim's trail, and head off into the darkness once more. Nojheim proved to be an intelligent adversary, which was consistent with Rico's claim that he was a leader among his wretched race. The goblin doubled back constantly and climbed among the wide-spread branches of several trees, coming down far from his original trail and heading in an altered direction. Ultimately, he made for the river, the one arrier that might defeat pursuit.

It took all my training as a ranger and all the help of
Guenhwyvar's feline senses to close ground before the goblin got across to safety. I admit in all honesty that if Nojheim
had not been so weary from his ordeal at the hands of the
merciless raiders, he might have eluded us altogether.

When we at last reached the riverbank, I used my innate
ability—common to the Underdark races—to view objects
by their emanating heat, not their reflected light. I soon
spotted the warm glow of a form inching across a rock
walkway, picking his strides carefully. Not trusting the obvious limitations of infravision, where shapes are indistinct
and details revealed only as patterns of heat, I lifted Taulmaril and loosed a streaking arrow. It skipped off a stone
and hit the water just a few feet ahead of the goblin, making
him slip one leg hip-deep into the icy flow. The lightninglike
flash of silver left no doubt as to the goblin's identity. I
rushed for the stone crossing.

Guenhwyvar flew by me. I was halfway across the bridge,
running as swiftly as I dared, when I heard the panther
growl from the darkness beyond, heard the goblin cry out
in distress. "Hold, Guenhwyvar!" I called out, not wanting
the panther to tear the creature apart.

The slight, yellow-skinned Nojheim was on the ground,
pinned by huge paws, when I caught up to them. I ordered
Guenhwyvar back, and even as the panther moved away,
Nojheim rolled about and grabbed for my boot with his
long, spindly arms, his hands still showing the remnants of
torn leather bindings.

I nearly slammed him with the butt of my scimitar, but
before I could react, I found the pitiful Nojheim slobbering
kisses all over my boots.

"Please, my good master," he whined in his annoying,
high-pitched voice, so typical of goblins. "Please, oh, please!
Nojheim not run. Nojheim scared, scared of big, ugly ogres
with big clubs. Nojheim scared."

It took me a few moments to recover my wits. Then I
hoisted the goblin to his feet and ordered him to be silent.

Standing there, looking down into Nojheim's ugly, flat face and sloping forehead, his gleaming yellow eyes and squashed nose, it took all of my control to hold back my weapons. I am a ranger, a protector of the goodly races from the many evil races of Faerun, and among those evil races, I name goblins as my most hated enemy.

"Please," he repeated pitifully.

I slid my weapons away, and Nojheim's wide mouth stretched with a strained smile, showing his many small but sharp teeth.

It was nearly dawn by this time and I wanted to be off right away for Pengallen, but Nojheim was half-frozen from his stumble into the river. I could see by his crooked stance that the goblin's drenched leg had little or no feeling in it.

As I have said, I hold no love for goblins and normally offer them no mercy. If Nojheim had precipitated a raid on my own community, I would have put a second arrow in the air before he had ever lifted his leg from the river, ending the whole affair. But I was bound now by my oath to the farmers, and so I set a blazing fire, allowing the goblin to warm up his numbed limb.

Nojheim's actions when I had first caught him continued to bother me, continued to raise quandaries in my mind. I questioned him early the next morning, after I had released Guenhwyvar back to rest on the Astral Plane. The goblin would say nothing. He just took on a resigned expression and looked away from me whenever I tried to address him. So be it, I told myself. It was not my concern.

Later that afternoon, we arrived in Pengallen, a cluster of about a dozen one-story wooden houses set in the middle of a flat field cleared of the common trees and surrounded by a high picket wall. The others had come in a few hours earlier, and Rico had apparently warned the two gate guards manning the village wall of my impending approach. They did not immediately allow me entry, though they were far from inhospitable, and so I waited. Rico was there in a few moments. Apparently he had left word that he should be summoned when I arrived.

The burly man's expression had changed much from the previous night. No longer was his square jaw set in a grimace, revealing Rico's happiness at the turn of events. Even his wide-set blue eyes seemed to smile as he regarded me and my prisoner, all the lines on his ruddy face tilting upward.

"You've been generous with your aid," he said to me, looping a rope about Nojheim's neck the way some in crowded villages leash their dogs. "I know that you have business in Silverymoon, so let me give you my assurance that all is well in Pengallen once more."

I had the distinct feeling that I had just been summarily dismissed.

"Please take a meal at our inn," Rico quickly added, motioning for me to go through the now-open gate. Had my confusion been that obvious? "A meal and a drink," he added cheerfully. "Tell the barkeep, Aganis, that I will pay."

My intention had been to deliver the prisoner and head off at once, trying to get a good start on my way to Silverymoon. I was anxious to see the wondrous city on the River Rauvin, to walk freely with the blessings of the ruling lady along the marvelous curving boulevards, to visit the many museums and the unparalleled library. My instincts told me to go in for that meal, though. Something about this whole scenario wasn't quite right.

Aganis, a barrel-shaped, thick-bearded, and oft-smiling man, was indeed surprised to see the likes of a dark elf enter his establishment, a larger two-story building set in the middle of the village's back wall. The place served as inn, trading post, and a variety of other public functions. As soon as he got over his initial reaction—I suppose that terror-stricken is the only word to properly describe his expression—he became quite anxious to please me, at least, judging from the large portions he set before me, portions far larger than those of a farmer sitting not so far down the end of the bar.

I let the obvious pandering go without comment. It had been a long night and I was hungry.

"So you're Drizzit Do'Urden?" the farmer at the end of the bar asked. He was an older man with thinning gray hair and a wizened face that had seen countless days under the sun.

Aganis blanched at the question. Did he think I would take offense and tear apart his place of business?

"Drizzt," I corrected, looking to the man.

"Jak Timberline," the man said. He extended his hand, then retracted it and wiped it on his shirt before putting it back out. "I've heard of you, *Drizzt*." He took extra care to pronounce the name correctly, and I'll admit, I was flattered. "They say you're a ranger."

I accepted the shake firmly, and my smile was wide, I am sure.

"I'll tell you right here, Drizzt—" again, the extra care with the name "—I don't care what color a fellow's skin might be. I heard of you, heard good things about what you and your friends've done up in Mithril Hall."

His compliment was a bit condescending, and poor Aganis blanched again. I took no offense, though, accepting Jak's clumsiness as inexperience. The greeting was actually quite tactful, weighed against so many others I have received since I came to the surface world—so many others that took place at the end of a drawn weapon.

"It is a good thing that the dwarves have reclaimed the halls," I agreed.

"And a good thing, too, that you happened by Rico's group," Jak added.

"Tharman was a happy soul this morning," put in the nervous barkeep.

It seemed so normal to me, and you have to understand that I was used to anything but normal in my dealings with the various surface races.

"Did you get Rico back his slave?" Jak asked bluntly.

My last bite of food suddenly refused to go down my throat.

"Nojheim," Jak explained. "The goblin."

I had seen slavery in all its brutality in Menzoberranzan,

he city of my birth. Dark elves kept many slaves of many
races, working them brutally until they were no longer use-
ul, then torturing them, butchering them, breaking their
bodies as they had broken their spirits. I had always felt
slavery to be the most repulsive of acts, even when prac-
iced against the so-called unredeemable races, such as
goblins and orcs.

I nodded in answer to Jak, but my sudden grimace put
he man off. Aganis nervously cleaned the same plate several times, all the while staring at me and occasionally
putting his towel up to wipe his sweaty brow.

I finished the meal without much more conversation,
except to innocently discover which farmhouse belonged to
Rico. I wanted no answers from these two. I wanted to see
for myself what I had done.

I was outside Rico's fenced-in yard by dusk. The farmhouse was a simple structure of boards and logs, mud patted in against the cracks to keep the wind out and a roof
angled to handle the winter snows. Nojheim was going
about his chores—unshackled, I noticed—but no one else
was in sight. I did see the curtains of the single window on
this side of the farmhouse move a few times. Rico, or one of
his family, was probably keeping an eye out for the goblin.

When he was done tending to a goat tied near the house,
Nojheim considered the darkening sky and went into the
small barn, barely more than a shed, a short distance from
the house. Through the many cracks of this rough structure, I saw the light of a fire come up a moment later.

What was this all about? I could not reconcile any of it. If
Nojheim had initially come to Pengallen at the head of a
raiding force, then why was he allowed such freedom? He
could have taken a brand from that fire he had burning in
the barn and set the main house ablaze.

I decided not to get my answers from Rico—decided,
since I knew in my heart what was going on, that I would
get no honest answers from him.

Nojheim went into his pitiful slobbering as soon as I
walked into the shadows of the dimly lit barn.

"Please, oh, please," he whined in his squeaky goblin voice, his fat tongue smacking against his lips.

I pushed him away, and my anger must have been obvious, for he suddenly sat quietly across the fire from me, staring into the orange and yellow flames.

"Why did you not tell me?"

He glanced up at me curiously, his expression a clear image of resignation.

"Did you lead a raid against Pengallen?" I pressed.

He looked back to the flames, his face twisted incredulously as though that question should not even be justified with an answer. And I believed him.

"Then why?" I demanded, shifting over to grab his shoulder and force him to look me in the eye. "Why did you not tell me Rico's reason for wanting you back?"

"Tell you?" he balked. His goblin accent had suddenly flown. "A goblin tell Drizzt Do'Urden of his plight? A goblin appeal to a ranger for compassion?"

"You know my name?" By the gods, he even pronounced it correctly.

"I have heard great tales of Drizzt Do'Urden, and of Bruenor Battlehammer and the fight to reclaim Mithril Hall," he replied, and again, his command of the proper inflections of the language was astounding. "It is common talk among the farmers of the lower valleys, all of them hoping that the new dwarven king will prove generous with his abundant wealth."

I sat back from him. He just continued to stare blankly at the flames, his eyes lowered. I do not know exactly how much time passed in silence. I do not even know what I was thinking.

Nojheim was perceptive, though. He knew.

"I accept my fate," he replied to my unspoken question, though there was little conviction in his voice.

"You are no ordinary goblin."

Nojheim spat on the fire. "I do not know that I'm a goblin at all," he answered. If I had been eating at the time, I surely would have choked once more.

"I am like no goblin I've ever met," he explained with a hopeless chuckle. Always resigned, I thought, so typical of his helpless predicament. "Even my mother . . . she murdered my father and my younger sister." He snapped his fingers to mock his next point, to accentuate the sarcasm in his voice. "They deserved it, by goblin standards, for they hadn't properly shared their supper with her."

Nojheim went silent and shook his head. Physically, he was indeed a goblin, but I could tell already by the sincerity of his tone that he was far different in temperament from his wicked kin. The thought shook me more than a little. In my years as a ranger, I had never stopped to question my actions against goblins, never held back my scimitars long enough to determine if any of them might possibly be of a different demeanor than I had come to know as typical of the normally evil creatures.

"You should have told me that you were a slave," I said again.

"I'm not proud of that fact."

"Why do you sit in here?" I demanded, though I knew the answer immediately. I, too, had once been a slave, a captive of wicked mind flayers, among the most evil of the Underdark's denizens. There is no condition so crippling, no torment so profound. In my homeland, I had seen a contingent of a hundred orcs held under complete control by no more than six drow soldiers. If they had mustered a common courage, those orcs could surely have destroyed their keepers. But while courage is not the first thing to be stripped from a slave, it is certainly among the most important.

"You do not deserve this fate," I said more softly.

"What do you know of it?" Nojheim demanded.

"I know that it is wrong," I said. "I know that something should be done."

"I know that I would be hung by my neck if I tried to break free," he said bluntly. "I have never done any harm to any person or any thing. Neither do I desire to harm anyone. But, this is my lot in life."

"We are not bound by our race," I told him, finding some

conviction finally in remembering my own long trail from the dark ways of Menzoberranzan. "You said that you have heard tales of me. Are they what you might expect of a dark elf?"

"You are drow, not goblin," he said, as if that fact explained everything.

"By your own words, you are no more akin to goblins than I am to drow," I reminded him.

"Who can tell?" he replied with a shrug, a helpless gesture that pained me deeply. "Am I to tell Rico that I am not a goblin in heart and action, just a victim of merciless fate? Do you think that he would believe me? Do you think that sort of understanding is within the grasp of these simple farmer folk?"

"Are you afraid to try?" I asked him.

"Yes!" His intensity was surprising. "I'm not Rico's first slave," he said. "He's held goblins, orcs, even a bugbear once. He enjoys forcing others to do his own work, you see. Yet, how many of these other slaves did you see when you came into Rico's compound, Drizzt Do'Urden?"

He knew that I had not seen any, and I was not surprised by his explanation. I was beginning to hate this Rico Pengallen more than a little.

"Rico finished with them," Nojheim went on. "They lost their ability to survive. They lost their usefulness. Did you notice the high cross-pole beside the front gate?"

I shuddered when I pictured what use that cross-pole might have been put to.

"I'm alive, and I'll stay alive," Nojheim declared. Then, for the first time, the determined goblin allowed his guard to slip down, his sullen expression betraying his words

"You wish that the raiding ogres would have killed you," I said to him, and he offered no argument.

For some time we sat in silence, silence that weighed heavily on both of us. I knew that I could not let this injustice stand, could not turn my back on one—even a goblin—who so obviously needed help. I considered the courses open to me and came to the conclusion that to truly remedy this injustice, I must use what influence I could. Like most of the farming villages in the region, Pengallen was not an independent community. The people here were within the general protection of, and therefore, under the overseeing law of the greater cities nearby. I could appeal to Alustriel, who ruled Silverymoon, and to Bruenor Battlehammer, the nearest king and my dearest friend.

"Perhaps some day I will find the strength to stand against Rico," Nojheim said unexpectedly, pulling me from my contemplations. I remember his next words vividly. "I am not a courageous goblin. I prefer to live, though oftentimes I wonder what my life is truly worth."

My father could have said those very words. My father, Zak'nafein, too, was a slave, though a slave of a different sort. Zak'nafein lived well in Menzoberranzan, but he detested the dark elves and their evil ways. He saw no escape, though, no way out of the drow city. For lack of courage, he lived his life as a drow warrior, survived by following those same codes that were so abhorrent to him.

I tried to remind Nojheim again that I had escaped a similar fate, that I had walked out of a desperate situation. I explained that I had traveled among peoples who surely hated me and feared me for the reputation of my heritage.

"You are drow, not any goblin," he replied again, and this time I began to understand the meaning behind his words. "They will never understand that I am not evil in heart, as are other goblins. I don't even understand it!"

"But you believe it," I said firmly.

"Am I to tell them that this goblin is not an evil sort?"

"Exactly that!" I argued. It seemed reasonable enough to me. I thought that I had found the opening I needed.

Nojheim promptly closed that door, promptly taught me something about myself and about the world that I had not previously considered.

"What is the difference between us?" I pressed, hoping he would see my understanding of the truth.

"You think yourself persecuted?" the goblin asked. His yellow eyes narrowed, and I knew that he thought he was being shrewd.

"I no longer accept that definition, just as I no longer accept the persecution," I declared. My pride had suddenly got in the way of understanding what this pitiful wretch was getting at. "People will draw their own judgments, but I will no longer accept their unfair conclusions."

"You will fight those that do you wrong?" Nojheim asked.

"I will deny them, ignore them, and know in my heart that I am right in my beliefs."

Nojheim's smile revealed both an honest happiness that I had found my way, and a deeper sorrow—for himself, I came to know.

"Our situations are not the same," he insisted. I started to protest, but he stopped me with an upraised hand. "You are drow, exotic, beyond the experiences of the vast majority of people you meet."

"Almost everyone of the surface has heard horrible tales of the drow," I tried to reason.

"But they have not dealt directly with drow elves!" Nojheim replied sharply. "You are an oddity to them, strangely beautiful, even by their own standards of beauty. Your features are fine, Drizzt Do'Urden, your eyes penetrating. Even your skin, so black and lustrous, must be considered beautiful by the people of the surface world. I am a goblin, an ugly goblin, in body if not in spirit."

"If you showed them the truth of that spirit . . ."

Nojheim's laughter mocked my concern. "Showed them the truth? A truth that would make them question what they had known all of their lives? Am I to be a dark mirror of their conscience? These people, Rico included, have killed many goblins—probably rightly so," he quickly added, and that clarification explained to me everything Nojheim had been trying to get through my blind eyes.

If these farmers, many of whom had often battled goblins, and others who had kept goblins as slaves, found just one creature who did not fit into their definitions of the evil race, just one goblin who showed conscience and compassion, intellect and a spirit akin to their own, it might throw their whole existence into chaos. I, myself, felt as though I had been slapped in the face when I'd learned of Nojheim's true demeanor. Only through my own experiences with my dark elven kin, the overwhelming majority of whom well deserved their evil reputation, was I able to work through that initial turmoil and guilt.

These farmers, though, might not so easily understand Nojheim. They would surely fear him, hate him all the more.

"I am not a courageous being," Nojheim said again, and though I disagreed, I held that thought private.

"You will leave with me," I told him. "This night. We will go back to the west, to Mithril Hall."

"No!"

I looked at him, more hurt than confused.

"I'll not be hunted again," he explained, and I guessed from the faraway, pained look he gave me that he was remembering the first time Rico had chased him down.

I could not force Nojheim to comply, but I could not allow this injustice to stand. Was I to openly confront Rico? There were implications, potentially grave, to that course. I knew not what greater powers Pengallen held fealty to. If this village was sponsored by a city not known for tolerance, such as Nesme, to the south and west, then any action I took against its citizens could force trouble between that city and Mithril Hall, since I was, in effect, an emissary of Bruenor Battlehammer.

And so I left Nojheim. In the morning I secured the use of a fine horse and took the only route left open to me. I would go to Silverymoon first, I decided, since Alustriel was among the most respected rulers in all the land. Then, if need be, I would appeal to Bruenor's strong sense of justice.

I also decided then and there that if neither Alustriel nor Bruenor would act on Nojheim's behalf, I would take the matter unto myself—whatever the cost.

It took me three days of hard riding to get to Silverymoon. The greeting at the Moorgate, on the city's western side, was uncommonly polite, the guards welcoming me with all the blessings of Lady Alustriel. It was Alustriel that I needed to see, I told them, and they replied that the Lady of Silverymoon was out of the city, on business with Sundabar, to the east. She would not return for a fortnight.

I could not wait, and so I bade the guards farewell, explaining that I would return within a tenday or two. Then I set off, back the way I had come. Bruenor would have to act.

The return ride was both exhilarating and tormenting to me. The greeting at Silverymoon, so different from what I had come to expect, had given me an almost giddy hope that the wrongs of the world could be defeated. At the same time, I felt as though I had abandoned Nojheim, felt as if my desire to follow proper etiquette was a cowardly course. I should have insisted that the goblin accompany me, should have taken Nojheim from his pain and then tried to mend the situation diplomatically.

I have made mistakes in my life, as I knew I had made one here. I veered back toward Pengallen instead of traveling straight to Bruenor's court at Mithril Hall.

I found Nojheim hanging from Rico's high cross-pole.

There are events forever frozen in my memory, feelings that exude a more complete aura, a memory vivid and lasting. I remember the wind at that horrible moment. The day, thick with low clouds, was unseasonably warm, but the wind, on those occasions it had to gust, carried a chilling bite, coming down from the high mountains and carrying the sting of deep snow with it. That wind was behind me, my thick and long white hair blowing around my face, my cloak pressing tightly against my back as I sat on my mount and stared helplessly at the high cross-pole.

The gusty breeze also kept Nojheim's stiff and bloated body turning slightly, the bolt holding the hemp rope creaking in mournful, helpless, protest.

I will see him that way forever.

I had not even moved to cut the poor goblin down when Rico and several of his rugged cohorts, all armed, came out of the house to meet me—to challenge me, I believed. Beside them came Tharman, carrying no weapon, his expression forlorn.

"Damned goblin tried to kill me," Rico explained, and for a fleeting moment, I believed him, feared that I had compelled Nojheim to make a fateful error. As Rico continued, though, claiming that the goblin had attacked him in broad daylight, before a dozen witnesses, I came to realize that it was all an elaborate lie. The witnesses were no more than partners in an unjust conspiracy.

"No reason to get upset," Rico went on, and his smug smile answered all my questions about the murder. "I've killed many goblins," he quickly added, his accent changing slightly, "probably rightly so, too."

Why had Rico hedged by using the word "probably"? Then I realized that I had heard those exact words spoken before, in exactly the same manner. I'd heard Nojheim say them, and, obviously, Rico had also heard! The fears the goblin had expressed that night in the barn suddenly rang ominously true.

I wanted to draw my scimitars and leap from the horse, cut Rico down and drive away any that would stand to help this murderer.

Tharman looked at me, looked right through my intentions, and shook his head, silently reminding me that there was nothing my weapons could do that would do anybody, Nojheim included, any good.

Rico went on talking, but I no longer listened. What recourse did I have? I could not expect Alustriel, or even Bruenor, to take any action against Rico. Nojheim, by all accounts, was simply a goblin, and even if I could somehow prove differently, could convince Alustriel or Bruenor that this goblin was a peaceful sort and unjustly persecuted, they would not be able to act. Intent is the determining factor of crime, and to Rico and the people of Pengallen, Nojheim, for all my claims, remained only a goblin. No court of justice in the region, where bloody battles with goblins are still commonplace, where almost everyone has

lost at least one of his or her kin to such creatures, could
find these men guilty for hanging Nojheim, for hanging a
monster.

I had helped to perpetrate the incident. I had recaptured
Nojheim and returned him to wicked Rico—even when I
had sensed that something was amiss. And then I had
forced myself into the goblin's life once more, had spoken
dangerous thoughts to him.

Rico was still talking when I slid down from my borrowed mount, looped Taulmaril over my shoulder, and
walked off for Mithril Hall.

* * * * *

Sunset. Another day surrenders to the night as I perch
here on the side of a mountain, not so far from Mithril Hall.

The mystery of the night has begun, but does Nojheim
know now the truth of a greater mystery? I often wonder of
those who have gone before me, who have discovered what
I cannot until the time of my own death. Is Nojheim better
off now than he was as Rico's slave?

If the afterlife is one of justice, then surely he is.

I must believe this to be true, yet it still wounds me to
know that I played a role in the unusual goblin's death, both
in capturing him and in going to him later, going to him
with hopes that he could not afford to hold. I cannot forget
that I walked away from Nojheim, however well-intentioned
I might have been. I rode for Silverymoon and left him vulnerable, left him in wrongful pain.

And so I learn from my mistake.

Forever after, I will not ignore such injustice. If I chance
upon one of Nojheim's spirit and Nojheim's peril again,
then let his wicked master be wary. Let the lawful powers of
the region review my actions and exonerate me if that is
what they perceive to be the correct course. If not, . . .

It does not matter. I will follow my heart.

AFTERWORD

The (Not-So) Secret History of the Realms

Jeff Grubb

The Realms is a world crafted by many gods. I'm not talking about the everyday, common gods, the ones you usually hear about in fantasy stories. No, these beings are the secret gods, the gods that move behind the scenes, creating, crafting, and presenting the world of Toril to the world at large. They have arcane names like Greenwood, Salvatore, Niles, Denning, Lowder, and a host of others, and they wield mighty powers. They are the writers who have combined forces to create the Realms that all of you know and love today.

But who are these individuals and how did they come together under one creative roof? Where did this marvelous land come from, and where is it heading? That's the *secret* history of the Realms.

The Realms began in the fertile mind of Ed Greenwood, and predates DUNGEONS & DRAGONS® role-playing itself. As a young boy, Ed was inspired by the works of many fantasy writers, including Lord Dunsany and Fritz Leiber. Ed loved the fact that most of Leiber's high-fantasy stories shared common characters and a common world. With each new story, familiar faces and places reappeared, creating a long-standing, fully-developed, living world.

Ed's own nascent writing sought to string together his adventure stories in a similar setting. Ed reports that his first story attempt (written at the tender age of eight winters) was situated on the Sword Coast, a lost epic titled "One Comes, Unheralded, to Zirta." It was, by Ed's own description, a horrible example of the bronzed-barbarian school of writing, and both the story and Zirta itself have long-since disappeared (the latter falling into the sea). This was in 1967, long before the fantasy role-playing phenomenon began.

Ed continued to develop the Realms in pieces of short fiction, but with the introduction of the DUNGEONS & DRAGONS role-playing game, his world took the first of many giant leaps forward. As opposed to a solitary creation, his setting became the basis for a gathering of friends and associates who all put in their two cents worth and took the characters they created in directions Ed neither anticipated nor controlled. The efforts of the Company of Crazed Venturers and the Knights of Myth Drannor did much to establish the early Realms and transform it into its present incarnation.

DRAGON® magazine took the Realms to the next stage. Ed was, and is, at heart a tinkerer, a crafter who delights in making myriad clockwork creations—monsters, tomes, magical items, dungeon doors, and all manner of minutia. Ed found a ready market for these items in the pages of *DRAGON* as early as 1979. To introduce his newest creations he chose a powerful mage known to his players as the "spokesman" for the Realms. Elminster appeared publicly for the first time in 1981, and has since grown to become a readily recognizable and eminently popular fantasy figure. Another giant leap had been made.

The Realms continued along this path, existing primarily

s the setting for Ed's home campaign and appearing in articles for *DRAGON*, until 1986. By that time, the DRAGONLANCE® shared world had blossomed, an epic setting dominated by great adventures both in games and novels. The cry went up within the hallowed halls of TSR that we should ready another world for development, should the excitement toward the DRAGONLANCE world fade (something that has yet to happen). After much discussion, a lowly game designer (who shall remain the writer of this afterword) hit on the idea of contacting Ed Greenwood and finding out if there was truly a world behind all those articles. And if there was, would he be interested in letting the Realms become the basis for new stories and adventures?

Well, there was and he would. Correspondence began between Lake Geneva and Colborne, Ontario. This exchange of many, many file folders resulted in the establishment of the most familiar parts of the Realms, the true heart of the shared world.

A delightful chaos ensued, as a double handful of creative individuals all began to erect the structure that was to become the Realms. Building was not as much planned as guided, everyone intent on creating a useful and intriguing world. Like Ed back in the sixties, these collected creators were hunting for a place where they could tell stories. A lot of stories—all happening at the same time. In this way the Realms set itself apart from the tightly focused DRAGONLANCE series.

The pieces of the newborn world drifted into place as often by accident as by design. Doug Niles had a half-written novel with strong Celtic ties, so an island chain was redrawn on the Realms maps—and the Moonshaes were born. Bob Salvatore proposed a sequel to the first Moonshae novel, but later changed its setting and introduced his own heroes—including the now-popular Drizzt Do'Urden. Steeped in Realms lore and freed of creating the initial setting for the games department, Ed roamed Shadowdale in *Spellfire*, while Kate Novak and I introduced Alias and

Dragonbait to the world.

And the Forgotten Realms continued to grow. On the gaming end, a dozen individuals began to explore, define and expand the Realms. Kara-Tur appeared in the Far East. Computer games were developed, tied in with the novels, first by Jim Ward and Jane Cooper Hong, later by Jim Ward and Anne Brown. Work began on comic books, miniatures and board games.

It became time for an epic in the Realms, something that would affect the entire land, and with this epic a new generation of secret gods joined the fray. The Avatar Trilogy, released in 1989, brought to light the talents of Scott Ciencin, Jim Lowder, and Troy Denning. In the trilogy, these three literary lights were hidden by the house name "Richard Awlinson" ("Richard All-in-One"), but since that time each has emerged with his own voice in the Realms. With Avatar, the Realms made another leap, into epic, world-shaping fantasy adventure.

As an interesting sidelight, concurrent with the Avatar Trilogy, the ADVANCED DUNGEONS & DRAGONS® game moved into a second edition, which modified and improved the game system used for role-playing in the Realms. The avatars-on-the-loose plot line in the novels provided an excellent opportunity for us to explain the changes in the Realms without all the game mechanics, but this confluence was never really planned. The trilogy had evolved on its own. Yet again, fate and fortune worked to bring together diverse elements and talents in the Realms.

By now our modest shared world had become a sprawling madhouse of creative ability. It was and remains a house built by fifteen engineers, each following his or her own plans, checking with the others as need be, but pursuing an individual vision. The Realms was large and became larger still. Bob Salvatore's Drizzt gained his own series. Doug Niles discovered Maztica. Jim Lowder, Troy Denning, and another new god, David Cook, filled the lands between the East and West with the Tuigan hordes and immediately launched an invasion. Characters from the

Realms disappeared into the new dimension of Ravenloft. The tales of the Harpers, individual visions of the world by both experienced writers and newcomers, came into being. Another generation of gods appeared: Jean Rabe, Elaine Cunningham, and Mark Anthony, all adding to the luster of the Realms. New pieces drifted into place, new walls and doorways were erected, new windows looked out into new dreams, ceilings were put up and then removed again as the Realms continued to grow.

Each writer, each creative, each of these new gods brought his or her own voice to the Realms, and this collection of short stories reflects this diversity. There are stories both light-hearted and sinister within this tome. There are authors who draw strongly from history and those who strike out into unexplored and undiscovered territories. There are writers who base their works heavily on the game that has so long been an integral part of the world, and those whose seek new heights of imagination and walk new paths of wonder, quite separate from anything suggested in the Realms game releases.

It's often disorderly, but it's a glorious disorder that amazingly produces a solid, coherent world. Its product leaders and editors are more traffic cops than dictating elder gods, finding out where everyone is and trying to keep the collisions to a minimum. In 1967 young Ed Greenwood had no idea his lands would become so well-known. The handful of original writers had no idea in 1986 that the Realms would be such a monstrous success and inspire so many people to aid in shaping the world.

The Realms is a shared world in its purest sense. Yes, it all operates under the auspices of a higher set of gods (read "management"), but that influence is often muted, allowing the creators to work wonders. Within the Realms, there are still more than a dozen master craftsmen hammering away. Creating beautiful works of art. Telling stories. Having fun.

CONTRIBUTORS' NOTES

While **Mark Anthony** has paid visits to both Krynn (as co-author of *Kindred Spirits*) and the Realms (as author of *Crypt of the Shadowking*), Colorado is his usual home. Naturally he loves mountains, but he thinks that books, friends, Celtic music, and beer are pretty good, too.

Scott Ciencin lives in Florida with his wife, Denise. He writes both horror and young adult novels, but refuses to explain the relationship between the two. As Richard Awlinson, Scott penned *Shadowdale* and *Tantras*. His more recent Realms book, *The Night Parade*, sports his own name.

By designing games and writing books, **David Cook** has avoided "real jobs." His credits include the novels *Horselords*, *Into the Void*, and the upcoming Realms entry, *Soldiers of Ice*. He has a passion for giant monsters, robots, and his wife.

Elaine Cunningham recently moved to Southern California, where she raises kids and works toward an advanced degree. She enjoys music, baking, haunting bookstores, and plotting new adventures for Arilyn Moonblade and Danilo Thann, the stars of her first Realms novel, *Elfshadow*.

Troy Denning found his return to the cool forests of Faerun a refreshing interlude from his current sojourn in the deserts of Athas. There, he is working on the Prism Pentad, the first novel series in the fiery DARK SUN™ shared world. Troy's previous Realms work includes *Waterdeep* (under the name Richard Awlinson), *Dragonwall*, and *The Parched Sea*.

Though more at home in the dark confines of Ravenloft, Christie Golden was only too happy to venture back to the Realms to spin a new yarn about Jander Sunstar, the elven vampire she introduced in *Vampire of the Mists*. Christie's other novel, *Dance of the Dead*, is also set in the Dark Domains of Ravenloft.

Ed Greenwood, creator of the Forgotten Realms, is more like the wizard Elminster than he likes to admit. In addition to his many game-design credits, he's the author of the Realms novel *Spellfire* and its upcoming sequel, *Crown of Fire*. He lives in Canada with his lady Jenny and far too many books.

Jeff Grubb knows of what he speaks when it comes to the Realms, having served for many years as architect, co-conspirator, and traffic cop for the shared world. In addition, he has created numerous game products and is the co-author of the Finder's Stone Trilogy with his wife Kate Novak.

Editor and author James Lowder has written two Realms novels—*Crusade* and *The Ring of Winter*—and he's happy to have found a way to include characters from both in his short story for this volume. Jim is now working on *Prince of Lies*, which features Cyric, God of Strife and Tyranny—no relation, despite what some other Realms authors claim.

Douglas Niles penned the first FORGOTTEN REALMS novel, the best-selling *Darkwalker on Moonshae*. He's gone on to complete the Moonshae, Maztica, and Druidhome trilogies set in the Realms, as well as several DRAGONLANCE® novels and short stories.

Former news-hound **Jean Rabe** now works for TSR coordinating the RPGA, an international association o role-playing game enthusiasts. She also edits the *POLYHEDRON®* Newszine, the network's official publica tion, and writes and edits role-playing accessories. Her firs novel was *Red Magic*, set in the domain of the very evil Rec Wizards of Thay.

R. A. Salvatore was coaxed into contributing to thi anthology by the prospect of writing a story from the per spective of his most popular creation, Drizzt Do'Urden. The famous drow has appeared in many Realms books, includ ing the Icewind Dale Trilogy, the Dark Elf Trilogy, and the hardcover best-seller, *The Legacy*. Bob is now hard at work finishing up the Cleric Quintet, also set in the Realms.

FANTASY ADVENTURE

The hero of the
FORGOTTEN REALMS® Dark Elf Trilogy
returns in TSR's first hardcover volume
by *New York Times* bestselling author
R. A. Salvatore!

The
Legacy

Life is good for Drizzt Do'Urden, better than it ever
has been for the beleaguered dark elf. His dearest
friend, the dwarf Bruenor, has reclaimed his throne,
and Wulfgar and Catti-brie are to be wed in the
spring. Even the halfling Regis has returned. All the
friends are united in the safety and prosperity of
Mithril Hall. But Drizzt did not achieve this state of
peace without leaving powerful enemies in his wake,
one of whom has vowed to take vengeance.

FORGOTTEN REALMS®

FANTASY ADVENTURE

THE LONG-AWAITED SEQUEL TO THE MOONSHAE TRILOGY

Druidhome Trilogy

Douglas Niles

Prophet of Moonshae　　　　　　Book One

Danger stalks the island of Moonshae, where the people have forsaken their goddess, the Earthmother. Only the faith and courage of the daughter of the High King brings hope to the endangered land.

The Coral Kingdom　　　　　　Book Two

King Kendrick is held prisoner in the undersea city of the sahuagin. His daughter must secure help from the elves of Evermeet to save him during a confrontation in the dark depths of the Sea of Moonshae.

The Druid Queen　　　　　　Book Three

Threatened by an evil he cannot see, Tristan Kendrick rules the Four Kingdoms while a sinister presence lurks within his own family. At stake is the fate of the Moonshae Islands and the unity of the Ffolk.